The
Damsel
and the
Dragon

SEVEN OF STARS

Also by Mae McKinnon

DAWN OF THE WINDS
(credited as M. Aei)
Seven of Stars

WOLF'S BANE
(credited as M. Aei)
Seven of Stars

ACADEMIA DRACONIA
Seven of Stars

The
Damsel
and the
Dragon

SEVEN OF STARS

Mae McKinnon

DRAGONQUILL PUBLISHING

The Damsel and the Dragon
A DragonQuill book

Cover art and logo by Juliane Völker
nightpark-art.de

Edited by Ashley Lachance
scribecat.ca

Illustrations by Elizabeth-Rose Best
Dot-doll.deviantart.com

Printed by Amazon, City of Luxembourgh, Luxembourgh 2017

ISBN 978-91-983535-6-3
A CIP catalogue record for this book is available from the National Library of Sweden

DragonQuill Publishing
www.dragonquillpublishing.com

Chapters

MORE PRECIOUS THAN SILVER
MORE PRICELESS THAN GOLD
FAR BEYOND THE GREATEST JEWEL
IS THE VALUE THAT YOU HOLD

TALONS OF FATE

Her breaths came in laboured huffs. Strained lungs fought against the air, the oxygen burning its way through her small constricted wind-pipe.

She couldn't see. Shrubs whipped against her legs. Low-hanging branches slapped her in the face. Everything was aching. Hurting.

Where was she? Did it matter?

Away. She had to get away. Linandra tried running faster. Faster than she'd ever run before.

It was getting dark. She could barely tell where her feet landed. The canopy above blocked everything now. It was a whole different world in here, in the deep forest.

There was no one to help her. Not in here. The only thing in here was more danger. More darkness. Never-ending darkness.

Maybe the forest would have been quite welcoming during the day? With bright colours and singing little birdies? She didn't know. It was day no more. That was all that mattered. That, and why she was running.

Distracted by her thoughts, the young girl fell, rolling over a jumble of roots hidden in the undergrowth. Shots of pain ran up her spine as the world hit her from every direction at once.

Up. She had to get up. Don't think, just run. Linandra fought back against the tears. The forest snagged her shirt, tearing it as she struggled to get back on her feet. Her lungs were burning. Every bit of her body was battered and bruised. It ached, complaining at every step she ran, every breath she took.

How long had she been running for? It felt like hours. It probably wasn't.

She wouldn't have lasted that long.

What a way to die, she thought. Chased down like a rabid beast. Bastards!

The autumn thicket bit and snapped at her as she passed. Vicious snappers lurking in the protective shadows of large oaks nipped at her body as it tumbled past, barely aware of what it was doing.

Ducking under a low-hanging branch, her legs screaming in protest, Linandra kept barrelling forward. By now, she was hardly in charge of her own body any more. It was going on automatic, being fed on a steady stream of fear and adrenaline, forcing it to keep going long past when she should have fallen over.

Every step she ran forwards brought her closer to what was behind. No matter what, they were faster than she was.

Linandra tripped over a protruding rock. 'Damn it!' she cried out, heart beating so fast it was trying to punch through her chest.

With a grunt, she forced herself up. Swallowing, trying to get her arms and legs back under control, the fear and the sounds behind her egged her on.

The hunters couldn't *see* her. But they could hear her and they could smell her. And so they tracked her, one great leaping bound after another.

Something could see her though. From the bluff, running perpendicularly to her path, far above, two voluminous eyes followed the movements of the tiny human, as she picked her way through the thickets below.

Most people who lived on the lands bordering the forest didn't come this deep into these woods. There simply wasn't anything for them here, and of those that entered anyway, few left again. There was the odd hunter—yes—but they always ensured that they were well out of the forest before twilight.

This one appeared to be of the human persuasion. It seemed very small. It was hurrying, too, how curious. When was the last time anyone not of the forest had been running this fast in here? Picking up their feet and charging through the forest as if the messengers of the abyss itself were coming around the bend behind them.

Admittedly, they usually *did* try to run. But in the opposite direction. This was something new.

The large eyes turned eastward. Small, sharp ears flicked, picking up the baying of hounds. All that noise was annoying. It was making it very hard to sleep in peace. Why did humans and their ilk persist in making such a racket when they hunted?

You will have to do better than that, *human*, the owner of the eyes thought to themselves.

Not that Linandra would have been able to hear even if the words had been spoken out loud, not from this distance. Human ears weren't that good. The pack of canines, their voices booming through the trees, hot on her heels, now they would have heard. Even as absorbed in the chase as they were, they would have taken notice.

They might have been better off if they *had* heard. For all their bone crushing jaws, armoured hides and spikes that could take out your eyes if the fangs hadn't already torn your throat apart, there were things in this forest that would barely even have noticed their presence. Back home, they were used to being the ones that everyone ran *from*. In here, there were things that were bigger, nastier and far more well-endowed in the fangs department. They just hadn't encountered them—yet.

Had they been wolves, Linandra would have been less worried. A scattered moorland forest had far tastier pickings than her scrawny self. This increasingly dense and deep wood certainly had more appetizing prey. But these beasties, they weren't interested in eating her. It was not hunger or fear or desperation that drove them. It was the people that came behind them.

No, best to keep on running. Run until your heart gave out. Until your feet bled and your bones broke.

Branches clad in red and yellow slapped her face, tearing at her delicate soft skin with their rough bark, as she headed deeper into the woods.

She didn't know where she was going.

Bashing and bouncing from one misbegotten trunk to another her body slammed itself with even more bruises than it already had. It was getting hard to focus. Her field of vision seemed to be shrinking.

The forest floor snapped at her feet, tripping her up again and again until her progress was nothing but a series of stumbles.

She could barely feel their bites. She could barely feel anything. The only thing now were those white-hot words driving her on. Urging her to stay up. To stay alive. To keep going. 'Run,' the dread whispered. 'Run. Run! RUN!'

Racing ahead without seeing where you were going had its drawbacks. The biggest one was that you missed things, possibly quite important things. Like where your feet were going and your body followed.

And so the ground dropped away beneath her. The trees had ended. Actually, the ground was still there. It was just now of a more up-and-down persuasion than before. Mostly, it went down. Linandra teetered on the edge of the hogback ridge. She reached out for a branch, a tree, a rock. Anything to stop what was about to happen.

Her fingertips brushed against rough bark as her balance lost its battle with gravity. Wet leaves slipped through her hands as she desperately tried to hold on.

'No. No. Nooooooo!' she cried out. And in a shower of dirt and stones, Linandra tumbled over the side.

Every stone and rock, every stump, battered and bruised her as she rolled past. From every side, things hit her as she desperately tried to right herself, to slow down. A shin smashing against a rock was followed by a yelp of pain erupting from her parched throat. Her fingers clawed at the miniature avalanche, but it was no use. Whatever she grabbed at was moving just as much as she was.

A few thunderous heartbeats later and she was unceremoniously dumped on the bottom of the ridge, skidding along just a little further on sharp pellets of rock and earth. The remainder of the landslide continued for a few more moments, bouncing and leaping around her until it, too, came to be still.

With a groan, Linandra pushed herself up. Expelling air like a furnace's bellows, she tried to see where she was. The world was spinning fast and the blood draining from her brain did little to help. Every time she tried to get back on her feet, everything around her started to whirl as if she'd been a stone in a sling. Having little choice but to lie down, her ears strained to hear the sounds of her pursuers. Swallowing hard, she tried to force herself to calm down.

Where was she? It had all happened so fast, she'd had no chance to take in where she was going. So, if she'd ended up at the bottom of something, the bottom of what exactly?

Shutting her eyes for a moment, willing things to settle, Linandra lay on her back. She'd ended up sideways it seemed. Her hands involuntarily knotted into tight balls, dragging through the dirt and moss. It felt coarse and chilly against her skin.

'Gross…' she murmured.

Linandra squinted hard. There was a blueness just above her, the kind of blue that wasn't blue, but for which there was no other name, that you got just before the sun started to set.

It was cool and damp where she was. Not even during the day did this place get much sunlight, despite the very sparse trees dotting the area.

'What is this place?' Linandra asked herself and rolled over, managing to push herself onto her knees.

The ridge on the left didn't look too steep. Maybe she could climb back up?

She stuck a foot and a hand into the vertical mound of earth trying to get some purchase. She scrabbled ineffectually a couple of times, but the ridge was so soft it yielded to the smallest pressure. 'Good luck getting up that,' Linandra shook her head. If she was a mad squirrel bunny-hopping, maybe. And even then it'd be a close call. It was a miracle that all the trees lining the ridge didn't fall over themselves.

Actually, some of them *had* fallen; the shorter ones scraping their crowns against the steep crag, lodging themselves firmly about halfway down. A couple of older ones, including a dry-looking pine, spanned between the ridge and the crag opposite like an impromptu bridge. One you'd have to be desperate to use as you would, as likely as not, end up at the bottom in a shower of splinters.

Taking a deep breath, Linandra almost called out for help. Her hands, having more sense than she did right now, slapped themselves over her mouth before she managed to get a sound out: all that escaped was a muffled whimper. She sniffled a couple of times, dragging a dirty sleeve over her wet eyes.

'Forget it, Lin, you're never gonna get up that,' she said, trying to fight the muscles in her stomach creating a Gordian knot all over again.

Looking up, one side seemed to be made up of dirt too soft to climb, while the other was of craggy rock and mosses and too steep. Besides, it protruded outwards just a little, so she'd have ended up trying to climb something upside down.

The glum shadows already covered the small space located at what might as well have been the bottom of the world. Nightfall, was approaching quickly.

Turning around, there were only two ways she could go: forwards or backwards. They looked the same. There was the barest space to move between the ridge and the stone. If she'd been older, she probably would have been stuck.

Pushing on, Linandra picked the direction away from those following her. She could still hear them, though down here the sounds echoed strangely, reverberating yet mute.

She wanted to run. Everything told her to run. But there wasn't much space to move down here and she was too exhausted. She settled for a kind of nervous skip, her hands groping at the rock to keep it from hitting her when the path turned and she didn't follow fast enough.

All she wanted to do was to curl up somewhere safe and cry. But if she stopped, they'd catch her. No one was coming for her—no one knew where she was. Unfortunately, it was unlikely that this state of affairs stretched to include what else there might be in this forest or those that hunted her.

Finding her way mostly by touch now, trying to avoid the fungus that squished under her fingers, Lin inched forwards as the trail narrowed until it spat her out into a treeless, dead-looking gorge.

Lin stumbled, trying to find her footing in this new place. It seemed to rise up all around her, though the highest walls were too far to make out as more than an undefined blur in the distance. There were plenty of closer ones though, except some of those weren't actually walls at all. They were more like *things*. Very big *things*.

This wasn't a gorge at all. It looked like a mine … a stone mine … a—what did they call them again? A quarry! Yes, that was it. If you could even imagine anyone actually carting away the largest of the blocks it must have been mined by giants. Those things were huge.

Great cubes hewn from the exposed vein of some sort of whiteish grey were scattered all around. Big ones. Small ones. Somewhere-in-between ones. Mostly they were square. Some carefully chipped, others rough and barely wrestled from Mother Earth herself.

Several looked like they'd been resting on something when the place was abandoned. Why else had they tipped over like dice standing on a corner, with said corner having dug meters and meters into the ground?

Maybe they'd been made that way? You couldn't push one bit of rock into other rocks, could you? They'd shatter, surely?

Lin stomped a small foot on the ground. It was rock she was standing on, all right. Beneath the layer of grit and dirt and moss, the world was as solid as ever. So, how was she going to get out of here?

It was hard to see anything beyond the nearest set of blocks. As she moved through them, there'd be a couple of huge ones blocking everything out, except some smaller cubes that she could clamber over and a few medium-sized oblongs that just lay there, nestled up against the big ones, as if they'd all fallen out from a giant wheelbarrow in the sky.

Some threatened to fall over as she passed, had it not been for all the vines and moss growing on them, suggesting that they'd been threatening to do so for a long time. Others had once been stacked neatly and really had fallen, creating jumbles of cubes or what had once been cubes before grit loving field mice had begun to nibble at their corners.

Lin peered into one that had cracked, splitting the block down the middle. It didn't look any more interesting on the inside.

She'd been to the mines with her father. Once. They'd gone to pick up her uncle's … something. It hadn't been that long ago, but all she could remember was the smells … and the noise. It hadn't been a big mine. It had barely been a hole in the ground.

It hadn't been anything like this. This place was … different. It was also very abandoned, even Lin could tell that.

It wasn't just that it looked like an oversized junkyard for a hundred-foot stonemason who'd been asleep for a thousand years.

It wasn't because of the fungus, gross as it was, that was growing here and there; the same squishy ones that had been on the crag, except these were bigger and considerably less squishy Lin discovered, more like old leather soles. They were still yucky.

It wasn't even the drip, drip, drip, coming from, always, just beyond sight. It was more of a feeling, as if she really, really shouldn't be here. The kind you get when you walk into a house that's supposed to be empty; one where you're just ever-so-slightly frightened of the people that had lived there and, when you wake up the cat by stepping on it, it terrifies you ten times as much as it should have. She'd done that once. Back then it had only been the old abandoned barn down by the river, the one where the miller used to work, and her ears still burned with the memory of her father's punishment. Here there wasn't a cat. There wasn't any reason, any obvious reason, to be afraid. But she was.

Reaching somewhere a little bit more open, Lin tried to get her bearings. She'd tried to stay close to the outer wall but there had been so many twists and turns and paths you had to double back on that it looked more as if she'd been carefully herded towards the centre.

Looking up, the part of the cliff wall that she could see had had great chunks of squareness chopped out of it—as though a giant had reached out and just scooped up the stone as a human would have mashed potatoes.

Guess that's where they got the stone from, she thought. She still couldn't see a way out of there in the enclosing darkness. Vines and sparse bushes did crawl down from the forest above, but they didn't reach anywhere near the terraced layers that she could have hoped to climb up on.

When the builders—no, the miners—had abandoned this place, the wind and the rain had taken over, breaking it apart further, trying to give it a more natural appearance. Rainwater had collected in places and what could have looked like a miniature lake—if it hadn't been for the odd shapes sticking out of it—had formed in the central depression.

The whole place smelled damp and dry and that should have been impossible. There was a tinge to the air she couldn't quite place too. No, it wasn't the least bit inviting in her mind, not even as somewhere to hide.

High above, there were rustling in the undergrowth. Five dark shapes darted along the edge of the mine. *They* were looking for a way down.

Lin's heart began to throb wildly once more. How could she have forgotten? Hiding? Yes, hiding would be good. Where? Where could she possibly hide in here, where there was nothing but stone and steep walls you'd need wings to ascend?

Try as she might, she couldn't see a way out. Maybe if she climbed one of the blocks? One of the smaller ones? No, anything small enough for her to climb on top of, the hounds would surely just leap up on, far better than she could. Lin stretched, toes outwards, but it was no use. She couldn't reach the edge of anything tall enough to protect her.

There was a noise, some way away. Lin tensed, eyes wide. Was there something living in here, in this friendless capital of the world? Something, she gulped, worse than the hounds?

Linandra let go of a series of expletives that would have made her mother thrash her, had she been here to hear them. She did so quietly though. The hounds had good ears.

'Where's the bloody way out?' she wailed.

Wait? What if they caught her in here? No. Lin shook her head. That didn't even bear thinking about. She gulped some more of the strangely tainted air, trying to calm herself. Was it just her imagination or was the smell stronger now?

Looking around, there was nothing here but stone, tall and imposing and cut so vertical that they seemed to be little more than huge edifices of smooth walls.

'Well, I'm not climbing that,' she breathed for the second time.

Think. Think. Think. There's got to be a way out. If they could get in, then you can get out. There. You just need to find it. Wait. If they run down and you run up? Okay, bad idea. Scratch that. Think of something else.

The gravel crunched underneath her feet. It echoed unpleasantly. Harsh and sinister sounds when you were all alone. Except she wasn't alone. The sighthounds would be here any moment how. She could hear their voices calling to each other.

Something chirruped angrily at her feet. As she looked down, too frozen to even jump in fright, a small lizard scurried out of the way: She'd nearly stepped on it.

Lin's eyes remained fixed on the tiny creature as it scampered across the bare face of a rock and disappeared into a submerged crack at its feet.

The lake. She'd run to the lake. They'd lose her scent over the water, wouldn't they? It wasn't as if she was wearing much, she could manage to swim out to one of the blocks. Some of them didn't stick up much over the surface. She should be able to scramble on top of one easily. She had to. There wasn't anywhere else to go.

The water felt like ice as she splashed into it. Despite that, Lin raced out into the lake as far as she could, legs pumping. Then she threw herself forward, swimming awkwardly, kicking her heels.

Hurry. Hurry, her fear cried out. They'll soon be here. They'll find me. Move, body. Yes. That's the way. Up on that rock there. The one only half-way out of the water. Now. Lie down flat and don't move. They can't smell us over the water—I hope, her inner voice added, sounding worried. What was she going to do it that was just hearsay?

Just when she thought they weren't coming, that they'd run around the mine unable to find her, the sighthounds appeared at the edge of the lake.

Lin's stomach turned yet again into a twisted knot. They were here.

There were five of them. Five heaps of muscle and fangs and natural armour. They looked like sleek moving boulders on legs from here. They weren't, she knew that. Grey, they looked permanently dusty and, lying still or, even better, curled up, a sighthound could be mistaken for a very large, very dull-spiked hedgehog—if said hedgehog had armour plating and jaws that could snap the thickest bone she'd ever seen in half without even trying. Most animals, and certainly most people, stayed well away from even one of them, to say nothing about a whole pack. And that was just the wild ones.

They were pacing at the water's edge, all five of them. She could hear them from here, growling and snarling and sniffing. One of them bounded out a couple of steps into the lake, until it reached its knees. It snarled at the water, as if it had somehow offended it.

The other four seemed reluctant to follow. But then Lin heard the splashes as they, too, plunged into the lake, she squashed her eyes tight and whimpered. Expecting to be pounced upon at any moment, when the water erupted, her heart skipped a beat and, at the hands of fear and exhaustion, she passed out.

Quite some distance away, one of the hunters reined in his horse with force. 'Hold up, what was that?'

'You heard it too then?' the second hunter, struggling to control his somewhat larger mount, asked. He cast his eyes across the shadows of the forest. They'd grown long since they'd entered. Who knew what else was out there?

'What d'you think it was?'

'Not sure. Sounded like a waterspout.'

'Can't have been. There aren't any even remotely near here.'

'Well, something made that noise and it sure wasn't the hounds,' the second hunter snapped irritably.

Beneath them, the horses stomped. Throwing their heads about, they fidgeted, ears pinned. It felt like they were ready to bolt at any second.

'Something's out there. I can feel it.'

'More interesting prey than some useless child perhaps?' the first hunter bared his teeth in anticipation.

'Curse this thicket,' his brother replied. 'We'll never be able to run anything down at the pace we are going.'

'Onwards nag. Forwards!' the first hunter kicked at the beast's sides, but now it just danced sideways, eyes slowly turning to white. Their mounts weren't nearly as keen as the men that rode them to move forwards.

Then the whole forest shook. The top of the trees swayed as a reverberating noise, like drawn-out thunder, swept over them.

The sound came again: but now it seemed far more alive. This time they recognised it for what it was; a deafening roar.

'Was that a bear?'

'I ... I don't think so, my lord,' the third rider tried to shrink back, making himself as small a target as possible. There were things in these woods. You heard stories. Even from a distance that had sounded big. Really big. And angry.

Trying to control the terrified horses, the three riders clutched their weapons just a little bit harder. They hadn't come here to hunt something of that size. If they had, they would have brought other weapons, more men. Maybe they shouldn't even have come here at all.

'If the hounds didn't finish her, that will,' the first hunter called out, his ears still ringing.

'And the hounds?' his brother, a tall man with red hair, shouted back. He wasn't keen on being caught out here, but he wanted his beasts back. Good sighthounds were hard to train, he'd hate to lose them. What they lacked in brains they more than made up for in fierceness.

'Buy new ones,' the elder brother fired back. He whirled his horse around and the panicking animal practically bolted for home with the two others close behind.

Back at the quarry, the three sighthounds that were still alive scrambled for purchase on the incline that was the way in, and out, of the pit. Had they ears, they would have been pinned, their tails tucked in.

They ran with no thought of where they were going, except away. Far away. For all their bloodlust, today they ran, whining and whimpering as they did so.

Behind them, the black dragon flicked its head, tossing the mangled body of one of their pack against the walls of the mine. Coming back down on all fours in an earth-shaking movement, it sent an ear-splitting roar after his fleeing assailants.

Folding its wings back, the dragon grunted and tried to pick its teeth with a claw far too big to do the job.

Those things tasted awful. He ran a tongue over fangs and lips. Had he ever tasted anything so bad? Well, there was *that* time… He shook his head. Next time, he would simply have to remember not to bite the creatures.

Heaven forbid that he'd actually *eat* one of them. Indigestion would most likely be the least of his problems. He shuddered at the thought.

Attempting to turn around in the midst of all the cubes, the dragon looked, for a moment, an amusing sight. He then moved down to the waters of the lake, taking several gulps of the cool, refreshing liquid. That helped to wash away the taste— at least a little.

The dragon of midnight sniffed around where Lin had fallen. It wasn't likely that the hounds, or their masters, would return, but, just in case … yes, just in case. Small humans were, after all, such frail creatures. So were not so small ones, for that matter. And this one was cold and wet and, if he was any judge, not about to regain consciousness for several hours.

With the water level of the lake having retreated considerably, the ground around Lin's rock was now bare, if somewhat soaked, gravel and dirt inter-mingled. Watching her for a few minutes, the dragon's eyes narrowed ever so slightly. A warm hiss sprung up from what clothing there remained as it dried. Then, taking a final look around, the dragon curled up, in a massive circle, around the small body.

He'd only meant for today to be a quick outing to stretch his wings. It looked like he was going to be late getting home, again.

"Never underestimate the power of a wizard,
especially if you've just annoyed him."

Any spellcaster to any tax-collector, anywhere

THE TWO TOWERS

Nearly a decade later, Lin again cursed at the lack of light as she brushed aside another set of leafy summer branches. You'd think that with four moons, at least one of them would bother to show itself. Clouds were not the intrepid wanderer's friend when he or she wanted to see where they were going. Nor was dense woodland for that matter.

Even after all these years, forests still weren't something she felt all that comfortable with. Too many memories ... too many unpleasant memories.

By this point, having made her own way in the world ever since accidentally overhearing her parents arranging her betrothal and deciding she wanted nothing to do with it, she had, unfortunately, seen enough woodland over the last few years to last a lifetime.

Having finally huffed and puffed herself all the way to the crest of the tree-covered knoll, it was a welcome relief to see that the wood was thinning out. In fact, it did more than just thin out—a little further on and the vegetation stopped trying to take your head off. Instead, the grass that replaced it was almost tall enough to disappear in.

Lin sniffed the air, catching the changing scent of the landscape. It was heavy on grasses and apples and hay ... and pie and toast.

Wait. Pie and toast?

'That can't be right,' Lin mumbled and took another sniff. 'Nope, definitely food. Got to be someone living around here then. That's nice.'

Trudging on a little farther, following her nose this time, Lin eventually got enough trees out of the way to see clearly. As for *what* she was seeing, now that was an entirely different matter.

In the distance—the very far distance—she could make out warm specks of light, like miniscule fireflies, if fireflies had the patience to stand still.

'Windows.' She scrutinized the buildings. 'Several floors of them and no shutters. Must be rich, a place like that. They'll definitely have something better than mushrooms and berries,' Lin muttered. As if in agreement, a low rumble resonated from her stomach.

Spurred on by hunger, Lin didn't pay much attention, at the time, to the sparkling blue lights hovering and dancing high above the far end of what she figured was an ordinary mansion. Everyone knew that rich folk were a little strange. Her papa had always said so. And so had everyone else in the village.

'Did you hear that?' a voice called out from behind the arched glass-window.

'Hear what?' came the sleepy reply.

'That! It was a noise, just a moment ago.'

'It's the middle of the night,' the second voice complained. 'You're from the big city, aren't you? You're in the countryside now, mate. What we've got, outside of our borders, are miles and miles and miles of … nothingness. Plenty of wild animals and other things going bump in the night. What we don't have here are apple-carts, street-cleaners, jugglers and coaches of all sorts rattling over the cobblestones right outside your window.'

'It wasn't like that,' the first speaker sounded insulted. 'It was really weird. A sort of pitched … I don't know … something.'

'Mate. You see weird stuff every day … and you're worried about some noise in the dark?'

'But—'

'Oh, give it a rest, will you! I'm trying to sleep here. It's probably just Pickles, 'gain.'

'Alright, alright,' the first voice backed away from the window.

He'd stuck his head out of it earlier. Now he closed the two green-glazed panels behind him.

Lin dared not breathe for another full thirty seconds as she pressed herself against the wall beneath the window.

Her teeth were clenched tightly when she eventually moved from her spot.

Thank goodness it was dark out here. What would she have done if they'd looked down?

That was too close. She needed to be more careful. Hobbling another few steps until the row of windows immediately above her came to an end. There, she let herself sink to the ground.

Damn, her foot hurt. Just what had she stepped on? Linandra pulled the offending body part towards her.

By now it was dirty, scratched and generally in need of some serious care. It would appear, this was one downside of no longer having any shoes. She'd lost those a while back after a fight with some very persistent mud. Definitely unpleasant walking around like that, shoeless. The world was a messy place, she'd discovered that early on. And if you thought streets were bad, wait until you started wandering around in the great outdoors.

It meant you stepped on all the things your feet just weren't meant to. So far, her feet had had encounters with things she didn't even want to think about.

Right now, it meant that when you stepped on something unpleasant, you had nothing to protect you from it. In the case of her foot, it had been the humongous remains of a rosebush that shouldn't have been laying around like some random rubbish on the ground as she'd snuck through the hedge.

No wonder it hurt like hell, Linandra thought. She winced as she touched it gingerly. Boy was that sore. Wonder how deep it goes?

Not that she'd ever had "dainty" feet, like some of her sisters, but they sure weren't used to this kind of treatment.

Either way, she'd have to find something to treat it with or it'd get worse. Maybe she could snag new shoes while she was at it? One thing was certain, she couldn't keep going like this.

It had been a close call, back up in the hills. Lin didn't think she'd have such luck a second time. The universe didn't play that kind of game, not in her experience. Nor did it play fair.

She hadn't actually expected to stumble across something like this all the way out here. The place was huge. Sprawling even. There was the odd tower poking up, like a straight stairway into the heavens while the rest of the house alternated between one and four floors from what she'd seen so far.

Admittedly, all she had to go on at the moment was counting where there were lights in the windows and that she'd just come in via some sort of garden. Those windows shone like beacons in the night. That's what had attracted her to this place. Around here, they were the only things that did.

A few hours ago, she'd thought she'd seen a faint blue glow hovering over one of the buildings. But when it was gone as she looked back, Lin had dismissed it as her imagination.

If this place was so big, there'd be all sorts of things to find if she stayed out of sight. Places like these always had storages and "stuff" laying around, didn't they? Probably had more than they needed too. It wouldn't hurt if she liberated some, right? It'd be like that re-distribution of wealth that that young guy had prattled on and on about a few villages back and that was a good thing, yes?

First things first though. She needed somewhere to lay low during the day. No, wait, reverse that. First, she needed to find something to help with her foot, *then* she could look for somewhere to hide.

There had been some sort of big barn back a-ways. That probably had something she could use. If she was really lucky it'd also have something to eat.

What the heck was this place anyway? It felt odd.

* * *

Eventually, morning light drifting in through some cracks had woken Lin up early. It hadn't been easy trying to find anything in the barn, in the dark, so she'd eventually curled up in a pile of straw.

'Stop poking me you useless vegetable,' Lin brushed some of it out of the way. It had been better than sleeping on the ground, but now they itched … and the ends were still sharp enough to be felt.

Her parents would undoubtedly have told her off for calling the straw a vegetable, but she figured that anyone that would call flowers a weed—just because you couldn't eat them—didn't have a say in the matter.

'So, what do we have here then?' Lin asked of the world in general.

Stretching, a sharp sting shot up through her leg. Her foot was feeling its morning dues. She slapped it a couple of times. It still tingled unpleasantly.

'Looks like a barn,' Lin mused while taking a look around. 'But where's all the animals?

Not seeing any evidence of any living inhabitants, she smiled. Okay, so, no animals. Some sort of extra-large storage shed then? That was even better.

At first, she kept a tense ear out for anyone approaching, but it didn't seem like anyone ever came here. From time to time, she'd press her right eye against a crack to see if anyone was about, but aside from catching sight of some vague figures in the distance, there wasn't much happening. Looked like the barn sat quite secluded compared to the main buildings she'd been sneaking past last night.

It did provide ample materials though. Now that the suns were up, she'd even found a couple of shelves with food while exploring the building. It all stood in the open, even the apples. And they weren't gnawed on, at all. She'd felt a slight tingle as she'd reached out for it. Probably guilt, Lin figured.

'Who just leaves stuff like this lying about? Do they actually expect it to still be there when they get back?'

To Lin, that didn't make any sense. Back at home, you never left food like that. It'd be gone or half-eaten the next time you saw it.

She shrugged. Her stomach was complaining too loudly for her to worry about the implications right now. Whatever they'd be, better to face them full than half-crazy with hunger.

And so, she made herself a little nest, up in the hayloft, deciding that any further excursions would have to wait until nightfall and her foot had time to heal a little.

A few days later and Linandra felt a whole lot better, and so did her foot. She began ranging further and further from her little sanctuary, surprised at the amount of people she *didn't* see.

That wasn't anything compared to the surprise she had when, late one day, as she was snoozing, waiting for the cover of darkness, she heard a pair of voices getting closer and closer until the side-door of the barn began rattling.

Lin pressed herself against the straw, trying to see without being seen. 'What are they doing?' she wondered. The people were poking their long noses into all sorts of dark nooks and crannies, completely ignoring any of the tools, tack or other random things Lin hadn't been able to identify. She shifted her weight a touch to see better.

'Did you hear that?'

'No.'

'Shush, not so loud. Wait for it.'

'What're your ears picking up this time? A mouse taking a leak?'

Lin froze. Had they heard her? She hadn't made any noise. Swallowing, her panic gland was yelling louder and louder. True, the second voice did sound exasperated, as if it wasn't the first time his companion had done this. But that was no reason not to worry.

'Shh ... There! Did you hear that one?'

'Come on, Aelin. Can't you just get it into your head! I don't have your super hearing, remember?'

'Oh, sorry,' Aelin sounded sheepish. 'I forgot. It was a kind of thunk,' she added in a hushed voice. The young woman threw a wary glance around them.

'They say this place is haunted you know,' her companion supplied helpfully. He cast his own eyes around, keen to spot anything out of the ordinary. Sadly, the place looked as usual as it had the last time he'd snuck in here. How exciting—not.

'There're no such thing as ghosts, Ronald,' Aelin stated.

'You mean mages like us aren't supposed to believe in them,' Ronald corrected.

'Mages in training.'

'Whatever.'

'Always analyze, cogitate and conclude. That's the mantra, isn't it? Doesn't matter if we believe in them or not, if they're real.'

'If there're monsters and demons and vengeful spirits, then why not ghosts? What was that?' Ronald jumped when something much louder hit them, something he too could hear.

'What was that?'

'I don't know ... something?' Aelin tried to see through every shadow in the barn. 'I think it came from outside.'

'I think I want to leave. We're not supposed to be in here you know,' Ronald said, his earlier bravado melting through the floor ... or at least through the strewn straw.

'Oh, alright then,' Aelin gave in. She wasn't too fond of being here either if she had to be honest about it. The barn was strictly off limits. 'Let's just find the blasted fungusmold and get back, okay!'

'I like that idea,' Ronald sounded relieved.

Not long after that the voices stopped being muffled and just disappeared altogether, Lin heard the bar on the door being slid in place from the outside.

This wasn't normal territory for anyone, least of all those still training, but on rare occasions one or two would stop by anyway. Somehow, places that were supposed to be out of bounds became all the more attractive. She should know that herself. None of them stayed very long though. There was something about the place…

Back up in the loft, in a far corner, Linandra breathed out and finally dared to move again. It was quite comfortable up here, all things considered. Just not when she was making a violin's impression of tension.

'That was close. Phew,' Lin said and forced herself to relax a bit. Rubbing cheeks that had grown pale compared to their normal healthy self, she relaxed a little.

By pressing the straw outwards from the two walls, she'd managed to create a little bit of home. It wasn't much space, but it was enough for her.

Lin had spread out a couple of the blankets that she'd "acquired," draping them so that they covered not only the floor but parts of the walls of straw as well. That made her feel a bit better; it was homelier. Her mother would have had a fainting spell, she imagined, given that the patterns on the blankets clashed horribly.

Since she'd come here other things had started drifting in. A satchel, here. Some candles, there. A plate. You know, everyday stuff.

By the wall there was a small lamp with a glass dome and a candle in it. She lit it with shaking hands. The light was welcome in here. Even if the barn walls themselves weren't exactly tight-fitted, what light filtered through them was blocked out by the straw or the blankets. She'd learnt that she needed to keep a steady supply of candles. That wasn't easy.

Several of the things were courtesy of the barn, or stable or whatever it actually was, itself. If it was a stable it wasn't holding much in terms of creatures needing to bed down for the night, though it did contain a few stalls at the far end. In essence, it was four walls with a roof and an attached loft tucked away among the rafters and some general bric-a-brac of architectural disposition.

The lower half of the building was made of stone; all different sizes and locked in place with a sort of white paste as far as Linandra could tell. The upper half was entirely made of wood. The enormous barn doors were, as well. They almost covered the entirety of one of the structure's short ends. It was probably easier to think of them as a movable wall really.

Lin wasn't sure what they kept in here—if anything. There were no familiar scents outside of the straw, wood and stone. What food there was didn't smell, not until your nose was right next to where it was piled. To be truthful, there wasn't much in terms of smells outside of those at all, just a tint in the air of something that had long since departed, one that she didn't quite recognize.

Since no one ever came here, not really, Lin had had it all to herself, so far. In other words, it was the perfect hiding place.

Actually, there was *one* more thing.

In one corner, on the opposite side of the doors and nestled between the few stalls—if that was indeed what they really were—there was a small room built entirely out of stone, from top to bottom.

It wasn't your ordinary rock either. It was like one giant block for each wall—or so she assumed, she couldn't actually see the back one. There was a door, but while it looked a little shabby, some of the timber definitely being past their prime, it wouldn't budge no matter how much she'd rattled it. If it had a lock was anyone's guess, she hadn't found one of those either.

Lin had, eventually, dismissed it as some sort of tackroom used by some extremely protective, or possibly paranoid, owner. It remained locked no matter what you did and she'd never seen anyone enter it.

Mind you, she didn't spend all her time holed up here watching the thing so, technically, someone *might* be using it. It just didn't seem very likely to her; unless they were really good at coming and going without leaving a single trace behind.

Maybe they were invisible? Flying, invisible little people? Gathering for centennial celebrations and dancing the night away in the pale moon light?

Nah, that sounded ridiculous … even in this place.

The truth, as she was about to find out, was much less mundane.

* * *

It began with a rumble.

Lin sat up straight, moving from being fully asleep to fully awake in so little time that it barely even had the right to call itself time to begin with. Her slumber had been fitful. This was worse.

Little did she know, but the noise had grown steadily louder within the last few hours, which went some way towards explaining her lousy sleep.

'What the hell?' she exclaimed.

The world shook again. Actually, physically wobbling, the barn was overrun with the acoustic onslaught. One part just replaced another … the noise screaming at her from walls shivering, as if in fear.

'What the—oh my—that was right over my head,' she ducked instinctively at a particularly loud boom.

Then, in less time than it took to draw a breath, there was another one. Linandra jumped again. This time she thought she'd been prepared, but it really was just that deafening. It just didn't stop. And then there was the light. Her little hideaway was flickering between light and shadow.

Pressing her eye against a crack in the wall, Linandra shot back only a moment later. Rubbing at her eyes until the little dots stopped dancing in front of them, she tried to stop her heart racing.

'Holy Mama!'

When Lin returned to her link to the outside world, again she thought she was prepared for what followed. But when the next bout of lightning struck, it was like being hit over the head with a hammer: a very large, very angry hammer.

'What the hell is going on out there?' Lin swore. Fumbling with her light, without having something to see by, she was completely lost.

'This doesn't sound like any thunderstorm I've ever known,' she muttered darkly.

For a moment, she debated climbing down out of the hayloft to take a proper peek at the spectacle. The barn shuddering in the wind persuaded her not to.

From the sounds alone you could be forgiven for thinking that the whole sky was, after eons of service, giving up and caving in.

Good thing she slept in these clothes, she thought. That kept her warm. It also meant that right now she didn't have to blunder around for them trying to get dressed because she still hadn't managed to find the lamp or something to light it with.

Maybe that was for the best. She needed more tinder anyway. Better to save what she still had for more important things. Also, it saved her from setting fire to something every time she jerked at the noise, which would probably have very quickly turned into everything.

The last thing she wanted right now was trying to escape from this place in the middle of a fire.

It was scary, climbing down the ladder like that. It was the easiest way to get from the loft to the ground, but it sure wasn't something you shimmied up and down just like that, not in the dark. Not for her.

It was a good thing that she'd done it plenty of times before or she'd have fallen off when something practically exploded right outside the walls.

In an instant, it was as if the whole place had been caught in the centre of a wild tornado. Lin lost her footing. Managing to hold on with just one hand, she forced herself to stay what passed for calm right now. Her heart was pounding in her ears. But not even that could drown out the storm.

Clinging to the bars, the young woman, breathed heavily. Now she wished she hadn't decided to watch, after all. Staying in the loft and burrowing under something soft was so much more appealing than this. Stupid idea really.

What she really wanted right now was to be back in her bed at her last attempt at holding down a job. Even more, she wanted to be back in her *own* bed. The one she'd always had, growing up.

It had been hard and narrow and there hadn't been much in terms of bed-clothes, but they had been there. Right now, even that sounded appealing. Being back home, going about what you did every day. Was that really so bad?

Lin's thoughts strayed, as if trying to find anything else to think about but the current situation, while edging another step closer to the ground. Her knuckles turned white where she gripped the bars.

A shivering foot swung down, searching for the next rung in the dark.

What had she been thinking, switching that dead certainty of her future for this? That every day would be the same? That she'd know what she'd be doing ten, even twenty, years from now?

And what had she exchanged it for? All this? She hadn't even found a place for herself yet. Not after her last position went down the drain, quite literally.

A tumbled drop down to the ground and a loud 'ouff' when she misjudged the last bar on the ladder and she couldn't fall any further. Once there, Lin knew that the path between her and the barn doors was devoid of obstacles and those had, inside of them, a much smaller normal door that she could go through without all the hassle of towing open the big ones.

That's what she normally used when sneaking out.

Tonight, she never got the chance.

Accompanied by a whole series of rumbles and forks of blazing light zig-zagging through the air those large barn doors flew open. As if forced aside by the sheer power of the wind, they greeted the storm beyond in its unbridled fury.

Linandra became transfixed to the ground. Her vividly green eyes, thrown open as wide as the doors, stared almost without seeing. Her mouth fell open, gaping like a fish out of water. The gale tore at her long hair, whipping it all around her, but she didn't notice.

The next bolt of lightning caught her off-guard and as she peered out into what was left of the night, the night looked right back.

'Oh, mother of all that is,' Lin whimpered, while the rest of her mind went blank.

The lightning strike had just lit up what was in front of her. She'd been happier if it hadn't.

It was big. No, big didn't even come close. It was huge. Humongous. A veritable mountain of flesh and armoured plating. The rainwater wasn't just trickling off its skin, it was cascading down from its body in torrents and lightning reflected off the powerful flanks every time the sky sizzled and frayed.

If it hadn't been for the illumination of the thunderbolts, she never would have seen it. From tip to tail it gleamed with a deep, inky, black. It was as if the night had coalesced from smooth velvet into rocky crags. If crags could move with a purpose.

Had it been moving away, Lin would have followed its progress, even been impressed by the sheer, raw, power it exuded. But it was getting *closer* and every part of her mind that hadn't already shut down, was screaming with primal urges to run away—if only she hadn't been frozen in intimidation.

While the storm continued to rage around them it was being pushed into the background for Lin. The rain kept streaming in through the opening in the barn, hitting her in the face, but she no longer saw that either.

The body before her gleamed, slick with rainwater. The muscles bulged even as it stood still, as if had been caught in motion, readying a leap into the sky.

Immense wings, still partly extended, blackened out parts of the heavens, drowning her world in shadow, like an eclipse to the suns.

The head, this close up, seemed elongated with noble, if craggy, features as they reached the crest, and it was crowned with a whole array of short horns and spikes carrying on down the neck.

But that wasn't where her attention was. It was the eyes. Luminous orbs in the dark. Yellow and red with fire, they filled her world. Looking into them you could, almost, believe you could see beyond them, into a world twirling and spinning and, without any doubt whatsoever, looking right back at her.

For a brief moment, the two of them stood there, motionless, in the rain and the wind. Then, lowering its head, the dragon approached the gaping hole in the barn.

Held by the same almost hypnotic gaze as the mouse caught out by a viper and, foraging for food, becoming food itself, Lin couldn't move. Her breath came in short, jagged bursts.

The jaws, slightly parted, were only meters away when Lin finally managed to break away. She scuttled backwards.

To her horror the dragon pursued, even if it had to crouch down to fit through the doors. But it didn't pounce. Surely it saw her? It couldn't be ignoring her, could it?

Its steps light, each one still made the nearby ground shiver every time one of those clawed feet hit the ground. And what claws they were … more like an armful of talons. Or should that be a foot-full of talons? Four whole sets of them.

Creeping forwards, moving with a grace and dignity that belied the cramped location, the midnight dragon entered the barn. And as it wrapped its tail around its feet, the doors slammed shut behind it.

She was trapped. Trapped, with a huge, toothy beast only meters away. Why, oh why weren't any alarms sounding? They must have them in this place, surely? No one wanted a rampaging dragon dropping in unannounced. Dragons raided places like this, didn't they?

A calmer mind might have asked itself that if a dragon raiding party *had* arrived, then why was it curling up like a cat that had just returned home from a three-day excursion, in a wooden, very flammable structure, rather than roaring and gnashing its teeth at everything in sight.

By now, body parts should have been raining from the sky, screaming and wailing coming from the people still alive.

That's what dragons did. Everyone she knew said so. That was why all those knights in all those stories had always needed to go off protecting the kingdoms from them.

Dragons were beasts: huge, hulking brutes that breathed fire and trampled everything in their wake.

This one, however, was making itself comfortable in the middle of the open planned structure. The tail was, slowly, draping itself around the series of support pillars that held up the loft. Its tip scraped against the bottom wood, creating furrows where the soft material was no match for the hard scales.

Guess that explained those marks she'd seen earlier, Lin figured, in between the madness. What an odd thought to have pop into your mind at a time like this, Lin chided herself.

By now, the dragon had nestled its head on top of its front paws. It didn't seem like it was planning on going anywhere, anytime soon.

The problem—and since she was still alive it was a somewhat smaller problem than, say, five minutes ago—was that the dragon was looking right at her. It was a calm gaze, filled more with amusement than cunning. But it *was* looking right at her.

Lin's chest heaved, tension running through her veins like spectral fire, and about as welcome.

Right. Calm down. It's not looking at you. It can't possibly see right through the pillar I'm standing behind, can it?

After several moments, Lin wasn't sure how many, she dared move again. An eye carefully snuck around the support pillar, sneaking a peek.

Nope, it was still watching the very same spot. Maybe dragons didn't need to see you? Maybe they could smell you? That made sense. Those nostrils were huge. In and out they breathed. In and out.

Lin ransacked her mind for everything and anything that she remembered about dragons. Sadly, apart from some overbearing advice from her childhood, that dragons liked to eat little girls who ventured out too far from home, stealing their innocent lives in one big gulp, there wasn't much information in there.

She'd heard that there were dragons, far away and long ago, that would collect hoards of treasures. Maybe it was here hunting for prizes? Big gold discs or statues it could drag back to its lair and sleep on? Precious jewels that'd shine in the torchlight of an approaching hero?

Wait. It was looking for *that* in a barn? That sounded absurd, even to her. It wasn't as if there was anything in here to eat either. Well, besides her.

Risking a second look, Linandra wished she hadn't. Every time she did, she just got more and more nervous. The dragon was still looking in exactly the same spot. Its large eyes were fixed on where she'd disappeared. The jaws weren't parted, not even a little, but the breath from the nostrils was like the sound of bellows on the furnace but without the heat. That could probably change in an instant.

Was it asleep? Could dragons sleep with their eyes open? Lin had never heard of anything like that, but they had to catch all those thieves and knights somehow. If they were asleep and couldn't see a thing they'd end up on the losing side quickly enough, right?

Did it look like a firebreather? Maybe it'd toast her quickly? What were you supposed to look for, anyway? Was it the shape of the snout? Maybe the structures around the throat could channel liquid flame?

Why did it look like it was waiting?

There passed both one and two hours, but the most exciting thing to happen, was the storm that continued to rage outside.

Forcing down the fear left in her stomach (though it had subsided substantially), Linandra tried to make herself move. It was only on the third attempt that her body responded and, even then, her foot edged sideways only a little. Slowly, she crept around the pillar.

Taking herself by a virtual hook, Lin pushed herself forwards. But not too much, the pillar was still safely against her back. She was still pressed against it. It wasn't like it could possibly protect her if that beast tried something, but still, she wanted it there. The safety it brought might be nothing more than an illusion, but it was welcome.

'Greetings, Little One,' the dragon rumbled.

The deep voice caught her off-guard. Dragons couldn't speak, could they? At least, she'd never heard of any that could. Not a single one of all those stories from her childhood had dragons that did more than grunt or roar or spew fire.

Dragons were supposed to be able to do all sorts of things: Fly. Breathe fire. Raze a whole town to the ground with a flap of their wings. But speaking was something new. It was also rather unnerving.

Lin mumbled something unintelligible under her breath.

'Why have you come to my home, Little Mouse?' the midnight dragon asked.

'Ehhhr? I'm sorry my lord dragon,' Lin stuttered, not sure what she was expected to say. 'I didn't know this was anyone's home. I thought it was a mere barn.'

The dragon raised his head off his paws, looking down that long elegant snout at her. Just as she thought he might snap forwards and wolf her down in a single bite, she heard a loud kind of thrumming. It was as if he was … laughing.

'A barn,' he chuckled deeply. 'How very peculiar.'

'If it would please you, kind sir,' Lin fell into her best "be nice to guests" manners. She'd never been good at it, but having several tons of armoured teeth and muscle looking your way could work wonders for your manners, even if he was, now that she had stopped staring at his teeth, very impressive looking. Lin wasn't sure she'd have called him handsome, well, maybe in a rugged sort of way, but he *did* have quite the presence.

'If I could take my leave now?' she asked, hoping to make a quick escape.

When the dragon didn't immediately reply, Linandra was reluctant to continue. Instead, she just stood there trying to look as meek and unthreatening as possible—a feat which she was particularly well designed for at the moment. Maybe it wouldn't want to eat someone with so little meat on them?

There was a set of talons right up close to her, to the left. They looked, she thought, remarkably well cared for. So, he/she/it didn't spend much time scrabbling around on the ground and rocks, scratching things up. Did that mean he was an important dragon?

She felt she was getting a little cheated, since he didn't have a single proper horn on him, not the type you saw in paintings, long and white and curvy and sharp. His upper head, from the eyebrows and onwards seemed covered in a sort of ever larger set of protrusions. They looked a bit like if the hackles on a dog had been raised, enlarged and covered in scales. Like a crown, but not a crown. It actually suited him. No, it. It was definitely an it.

Linandra shook her head. She was not admiring this *thing*. No.

'Excuse me,' Lin finally ventured when it became apparent that the next move was hers, after all. 'But don't dragons live in caves?' she asked. 'That's what I've always heard ... eh, sir.'

'My house,' the dragon chortled again, seemingly bemused by her reaction. 'You believe this *barn* is my house? Ohhoho...'

'You mean it isn't?'

'A little cramped if it was, would you not say so?' he motioned with his head to encompass their surroundings.

'Tell me, Little One. Where would you go on a night such as this?' the dragon asked.

Lin drew back in alarm. He, no, *it*, had just reminded her of just why she'd woken up. It certainly hadn't been because she'd heard dragons.

'I—'

'No, child. I shall not run a little mouse out of such a dry and comfortable foxhole on a night like this, though be glad there is no fox to chase you.'

Linandra shuddered. She was relieved, but she hated him thinking she was bothered by the idea.

Not that she would have had much of a choice if he'd wanted her to go. There were few other places she knew of nearby that were convenient to hide in, especially not long term. She'd be good and soaked by the time she got there, either way. Maybe she'd be fried and well-toasted too. Even if the dragon wouldn't turn her into kindling, that didn't mean that the lightning gods shared such forgiving sentiments.

'Tell me, Little Mouse. Why have you come to my house? Many come here seeking that which they do not already possess. From the far corners of the known world they travel here. Some never leave.'

Was that a threat? Lin couldn't tell. 'I ... I'm sorry noble sir,' she stuttered. 'I ... I don't want any money. I just want somewhere to rest. Please, sir dragon, I didn't mean any harm.'

'You have been living here then for some time,' the dragon with scales like ink, said. This was more of a statement than a question, but Linandra felt compelled to answer it anyway.

'Yes, sir,' she nodded.

'You have been clothed in the cloth of my house then,' the dragon said and ran his large perceptive eyes over her. 'You have eaten of the food from my table.'

'Yes, sir. Sorry about that, sir.'

'And you have taken from my house those things which were not yours to take.'

'Yes ... yes I have.'

Lin tried not to tremble. She didn't know why but somewhere deep inside she just knew she couldn't lie to him. She felt compelled to speak the truth, no matter how much trouble it would get her into.

'We will have to see to that,' he rumbled at her.

'I'm ... I'm sorry, Master Dragon.'

'Mhm. Master Dragon. Well, that is a start I suppose.'

'Yes, of course, Master Dragon. Anything you say,' Lin said. Maybe if she could stall him long enough, she could run away later?

'Then it is settled,' the noble head nodded thoughtfully, almost hitting the ceiling in the process. 'You too, I shall find a place for.'

'Wha-what?' Linandra barely got the words out of her mouth. What was going on here?

Did she really want that? To become some scullery maid for the rest of her life? Or maybe something else? Suppose even households of dragons needed someone to do all those things they couldn't do, or reach, themselves. Strange, she'd never seen any evidence of any dragons here, not until now. Just a lot of rather peculiar folk. *Very* peculiar in some cases.

Was that really better than what she'd been doing for the last few months? Wasn't that the kind of future she'd run away from in the first place?

Before then, when younger, she'd so boldly announced she was going to find her fortune with the Couriers. Her parents had been fiercely opposed to the idea. Wasn't their life good enough for the likes of her? To say nothing of the fact that little girls didn't do that sort of thing, even when they grew old enough.

Sure, she'd always been a bit of a tomboy. She'd probably had more scraped knees and dirty fingers than all of her sisters together. But going on adventures was surely a step too far, her parents had thought. She was their daughter. Only *strange* people "joined up," as they'd told her empathically

The Couriers was something that most people held in awe. It certainly wasn't for the likes of her, people said. Her last employers had even laughed coarsely at the idea when she'd accidentally let it slip.

'You'll be back in a week,' the proprietor of the inn had snorted at her before slamming the door in her face.

'Now. If you will excuse me, I shall have to change before we continue this conversation,' the dragon rumbled Linandra out of her memories. 'And try not to run away, Little Mouse. I have many eyes and it is quite the unpleasant night out there for the likes of you.'

Somehow that idea didn't make her feel the least bit better. It made him sound like a giant spider, tentacles everywhere. Or was that river squid? At least only two of those were set in his head, under deep and knobbly ridges. They were eyes that were filled to the brim with life, no argument there.

Wait. Change? What did he mean, change? Dragons changed? Changed into what exactly? It wasn't as if he was wearing clothes.

Lin expected him to rise, at the very least. But despite his words, the black dragon remained perfectly still. A regal, towering mass, unmoved by anything less than an absolute cataclysm, for just a moment, that was how he seemed to her.

Instead, the doors to the room that had previously been so closed, and locked, swung open, as if pushed aside by invisible hands.

Whirling around, her beautiful almond-shaped eyes grew almost round in astonishment. She was plenty nervous as it was and suddenly being surrounded by things that moved, as if of their own accord, did little to improve that.

And now, from within the stone chamber, was spilling out a gentle blue nimbus. As flecks of white, like tiny pinprick stars, grew inside the glow, this erupted a steady stream of "something." They looked like bunches of sheets tumbling over and over, no, wait, sorry … were those clothes?

In an erratic formation, what became more and more discernible as garments floated out of that room. The nimbus moved with them. They began circling the dragon slowly, then faster and faster they went until the whole thing was just a whirlwind of light spinning so fast she had to look away when her stomach heaved.

Even if it hadn't been for the dragon's warning, she wouldn't have run away now, so transfixed was she by the sight that played out before her, to say nothing about being so dizzy she could barely remain upright.

Except when the light faded away, there was no more dragon.

Where the mighty beast had been now stood a tall, black haired man in a collection of robes and other garments. He finished "getting dressed" by pulling out his long silky tresses from beneath the cloth.

Well, they looked silky to her, but he winced as the unbrushed mass snagged on his collar.

'Always the same. I really should consider adding an hære element to that spell,' he said philosophically.

Reaching up, he pulled out the ornate comb sitting at the back of his head and began brushing it, wincing every time he came upon a vicious snarl. Linandra, too astonished to blink, just stared openly.

What the hell just happened? Lin wasn't sure what was more unexpected, having a big salivating beast turn into a man right before her eyes or having an elegantly and richly dressed man stand in the middle of a barn, with straw on the ground, brushing his hair.

Her astonishment didn't fail to be noticed.

'This will, of course, remain purely between us,' the man's still deep voice intoned the words carefully before tasting each one.

Actually, he sounded exactly the same as before, just with a less metallic tinge and not nearly as loud. That was … odd, Lin thought. In her experience, big things boomed and small things squeaked. This one was doing neither.

She had no doubt, at all, as to what he meant, though. Lin swallowed hard and shivered. She had no desire to end up as someone's lunch. She was willing to fight a lot of things if she had to, but you definitely had to draw the line at fighting dragons, even small ones. Only someone completely insane or possibly suicidal would fight one of the big dragons and taking on one that could do magic on top of that? No, they could find someone else for that!

Seemingly unconcerned by her lack of response, the man brushed off some imaginary dust from his shoulders and shook out his sleeves.

'I do believe that the storm has subsided,' he announced calmly. 'Do tell, Little Mouse … Have you ever seen your new home during the light hours of the day? Or have you hidden from the sun like the bird of myth from whence it takes its name?'

He watched her but didn't wait for her to finish deciding to answer or not. 'Then, let us go out and greet the new day, Little One, because I do believe that dawn is finally upon us,' he said.

The self-assured and somewhat imposing man turned and strode confidently towards the doors. To her surprise, rather than opening them with a flick of his fingers, he just used the handle.

It was the small door, a size much more convenient for a human than a beast, and she was further astonished when he surreptitiously scanned the environs. She wasn't sure what he was looking for but, apparently, he didn't find it as he gave a satisfied nod before looking over his shoulder to her.

'Come then, Little One. One day even an amaranthine has to come to the ground for the first time.'

'Huh?' Lin said.

Watching as he motioned with his hand for her to follow, after biting her lip, Linandra did. Whoever he was, he was right. She'd never dared to poke around the place as long as the suns were up. Far too easy to be seen that way and, despite her worries about the future, she was curious.

'Then let me introduce you to your new home, Little Mouse,' he said, a smile tugging at the corners of his mouth where she couldn't see it.

Linandra hesitatingly stepped through the door, nearly tripping over the section that remained attached to the larger one. She held up a hand to shield her eyes from the bright light.

'Dawn comes late here. The mountains nearby do lend a great deal of shade to our mornings during this season,' the strange man offered as a way of explanation.

He couldn't help but feel amused by her reactions. Somehow they seemed so innocent. Most of those that arrived here usually had some idea of what to expect, maybe even had some experience to draw on. Often, they would learn that they were wrong, that they didn't, in fact, know everything there was to know, but then that was part of their appearance here in the first place.

'Welcome, Little Mouse,' he said with an electrifying sweep of his arm, 'to the Twin Towers of Retmia.'

If Linandra had heard that last bit it was only on the periphery. Right now her ears were overruled by her primary sense: sight.

She'd always suspected the place was big, but she hadn't expected it to be this big.

There was still more than a trace of wind in the air and storm-bossed clouds, now a mere shadow of themselves, raced across the sky, as if eager to join up for their next concert elsewhere.

The scattered trees added a musical accompaniment to what opened up before her. Whatever she had imagined, it hadn't been this.

Framed by the mountains in the far distance, set in the golden playful light of first dawn and nestled within lush green grounds, and fields and orchards, lay what might have once been a mansion that subsequent owners had kept adding their own twists and turns to over the centuries.

Mostly constructed out of a slightly reddish-ochre looking sandstone it sprawled ... *everywhere*.

Rarely reaching above the three main floors, Lin could see that there were the occasional windows dotted in what had to be the attic as well. Those were small and lowly arched. The windows on the main building were tall, some reaching from floor to ceiling, spruced and with iron frames. Some she could see, even from this distance, sparkled in colour.

There were arches, miniature towers and strange add-ons sprinkled all over it. Balustrades bordered some of the roofs, leaving others looking naked, despite a number of spikes or spires stretching towards the sky.

There were several smaller outbuildings and sheds dotting the grounds between the barn and the main house. Not all of them looked terribly functional to her and some looked plain weird.

Most of them, she had no idea what they were supposed to be for. With some, like the almost round, but yet not, globe of glistening glass and wrought iron, which was stuck on to the middle of the back wall, Lin could at least hazard a guess. It looked like a conservatory. She'd heard of those, even if this was her first time seeing one.

But what drew most of her attention were the two towers that rose just where she'd seen the strange nimbus-like lights when she'd initially scouted the area.

One seemed to be made out of corners. The other was round. Where one went straight up, the other kept getting interrupted by bulbous protrusions that she couldn't imagine were of any use whatsoever. They were both covered by a round slanting roof and adorned with spires. The towers climbed way above the rest of the place, casting long thin shadows as the sun rose.

'Those, those glow,' Lin finally managed to squeak, pointing at the right-hand tower spire that now loomed almost directly above them. 'I've seen them.'

'External discharges for superfluous disharmonic ethereal energy,' her benefactor agreed.

'Eh?'

'Lightning rods for magic.'

'Magic?'

'Yes, Little Mouse. If you wish to use the common denomination under which the practice is known in these lands: magic. Allow me to introduce myself. I am Kaheiron,' he made a small bow. 'Archmagus of the Twin Towers.'

Lin was too overcome at this point to hear him properly.

Magic? Lin's eyes kept going between the outer walls of the mansion and this strange man, not sure what she thought of either.

It wasn't just him? This whole place was magic? That explained a lot. She'd always felt like she was getting turned around in the strangest of places when out "exploring," going in somewhere and coming out somewhere else and then discovering that the same way back led elsewhere else yet again. She'd just thought she'd gotten lost a lot in the dark. Just what had she gotten herself into?

TO BE OR NOT TO BE

Seth tucked his arms behind his head, resting comfortably on his back. It felt peaceful up here, just him and the stars. Somewhere in the night there was the hooting of an owl.

'Make that, *mostly* peaceful,' he chuckled.

He shifted a bit. The gently sloping roof was comfortable enough, but the plates that made up the repellent surface wasn't enjoying his presence. The last thing he wanted to do was to slide off. It was a long way down to the ground. He'd break a whole lot more than just a few bones if he went that way.

It was worth it though. It was one of the most restful places he'd found here: the rooftops. It helped that not many others came up here.

The young man drew some of the moist night air into his lungs. Yes, it was good to get away from the life below sometimes.

'Enjoying yourself?' someone asked, interrupting his contemplations.

'Yes, I rather think I am,' Seth replied, a small grin appearing on his face. 'It's different than I imagined it would be.'

'How wonderful,' the new voice dripped with sarcasm. 'While you are, of course, more than welcome to stay, as always, kindly do not abuse my hospitality,' the presence behind him said before disappearing off the roof even more suddenly than it had appeared.

Seth rolled his eyes. 'That man really needs to learn the meaning of the word "relax,"' he murmured.

'I heard that,' drifted back from the darkness beyond.

'I'm sure you did,' the young man couldn't help but smirk. 'But, since you're not my mother, I think I'll live.'

If he had been, Seth was pretty sure that the conversation would have played out very differently, not to mention louder, just like it had done back then…

'This is unacceptable!' the piercing voice had rung out among the outcroppings and crags of the rocky mountain years and years ago.

Up here, most of the inclines were devoid of such dampening coverings as trees, grass or even moss. Nor were they high enough that everything was covered in snow. The call ended up echoing back and forth far longer than it had a right to, Setharrion felt. It was like being scolded not once, not twice, but again and again, and by a whole host rather than just one person. It didn't improve on his day at all.

When it eventually faded away, Setharrion stopped wincing. It was bad enough to have heard it the first time. It wasn't quite torture to be assaulted with it, but it did more than merely grate on your ears.

Guess it did save his mother from having to repeat herself, he thought. Heaven forbid her having to do that.

Too bad it also announced this little argument for the rest of the world to hear. Her voice did carry, a lot. She wasn't going to be happy about that, when she stopped being livid enough to notice. Unless she was doing it on purpose? Heck, that'd probably end up being *his* fault, just like always.

Not that there were many others up here, not in the immediate vicinity. This close to his mother's residence only the most select members of the clan were allowed to approach and none of them lived here. They were the lucky ones, Setharrion thought.

But the sound of her voice carried for quite some distance when she was getting all that worked up, and the remainder of their people weren't that far way … unfortunately. While none of them were particularly keen on being all that close, the majority didn't wish to be seen to be "setting themselves apart" either, he knew that. If they did, it usually ended in trouble.

Besides, apart from a few who wouldn't be able to tell if a giant was snoring right next to them, most of the clan had the kind of ears that could probably hear what the field mouse was thinking … let alone doing, had they been bothered with such small, unimportant, rodents. It certainly was hard enough to gain any kind of privacy without going to some extensive troubles to do so. And if his mother found out, that would have led to even more trouble.

'—and you will certainly stop leaving on your little adventures,' the imposing lady before him declared firmly, rolling the word as if it was a bitter tasting berry bush. 'It is highly unbecoming.'

What? Wait? Setharrion's shoulders sagged. He'd not been paying attention to his mother's voice as she'd kept droning on and on about things he didn't care about. What was she saying?

No! His precious alone time, the only time when he didn't have to bother with what everyone else was thinking. He could see it vanishing before his very eyes, like a galleass shrouded in mist disappearing on the sea.

Those escapes from the clan had been growing increasingly rare as it was, lately, as his mother had chosen to "gift" him with even more responsibilities. Since those duties were something that Setharrion wasn't exactly keen on shouldering, her increased generosity was getting on his nerves. He knew he needed to take on a more active role in the clan, that he was expected to do so. It was just that he didn't want to.

Those few short breaks were all that kept him going. She had no call to be so cross with him. All he wanted was enough time to feel that he was himself and not some buffed-up trophy paraded around for all to see. He hadn't done anything wrong. He hadn't, actually, even gone very far, now that he thought about it. So why did she have to act so upset?

As usual, what he wanted, no one ever seemed to care about. It was all about her, her, her—disguised under a thin veil of "what's best for you." It set his teeth on edge.

Anyone else in the clan would have jumped at the opportunity, he knew that. And he would have been more than happy to give it to them, but apparently that wasn't done either.

It wasn't the only thing that had led to this moment, to be honest, but it had played its part. Maybe he should have gone even further away? So far away as to never be pestered and ridiculed like this again. Was that even possible?

'You!' the great queen thundered, drawing her head even higher and puffing out her chest, 'are not listening.'

His mother's sharp tones bit into his ears almost as effectively as if her teeth had done so. It jerked him away from his musings. The owner of the words that were lashing over him in scolding wasn't some mere second-rate female, small and demure. When Hui'syqussedin drew herself erect, she towered above most without even trying. With her footing on a ledge so much further up, he felt even smaller than usual.

'You should act as benefits your station,' Hui'syqussedin instructed him. 'Not flitter away chasing … chasing …' she tried to think of an example that wouldn't spoil her tongue, '*butterflies*, like some common miscreant. You need to consider who you are at all times.'

'Poo on my station,' Setharrion huffed under his breath as he tried to tune out the rest of her speech. He'd heard this one before.

'What did you say?' his mother's words came as a low growl, her throat vibrating threateningly.

Had Setharrion possessed hackles they would have risen at this point. As it was, parts of the membranes on his body kept undulating, uneven ripples running through them like minute shockwaves of light as the shadows from the suns interrupted the reflections. He backed down, a little.

He hated arguments like these. Around here, the only one he ever had them with was his mother. The rest of the clan might not accord him quite the same respect as they did her, but it was close enough. They still made him knot up inside for hours, if not days, afterwards.

It did have advantages. It made for less physical intimidation from the members of the clan or visitors. That was good. On the downside, it also meant his relationship with the various members of the clan couldn't exactly be considered normal. Not the "everyone is your pal and buddy" kind of normal, anyway. He would have liked that.

So far it seemed to benefit everyone else a whole lot more than it did him. It wasn't that he was averse to being responsible. He *liked* looking out for others. It was just that, well, that ... oh, he didn't know how to put it into words. Seth just wished that things could be different. With his mother's attitude, he doubted that it ever would be, and he said so.

'Don't talk like that to me,' the queen snarled back at him, her snout suddenly mere inches from his as she leaped down onto the lower ledge.

Setharrion backed up, tucking in his wings tightly. Still, he wasn't going to give up that easily.

'It's only for a few weeks. That's like, no time at all,' he insisted.

'Weeks? I know you. You'd be gone for years! Years! This is an important time for our people. I trust you understand that you cannot possibly earn your place by gallivanting around the countryside? Associating with, with ... *creatures*!' she nearly spat out that last word as if it burned her to speak it.

'No, the clan must know that you are a capable leader or they will not follow you.'

'They follow *you*, mother,' Setharrion sighed. 'Not me.'

'Enough! I will hear no more of this. Of all my children, you are by far the highest in rank. It is unfortunate that you are also the most insolent.'

'But mother...'

'And the celebrations? How would you prepare for those if you were not here? No, I will not allow you to bring shame on me by failing in your duties.'

'No, mother,' Setharrion sighed.

'Gain enough in status and even older rulers will look to you when seeking a mate. It is the perfect way to expand our influence without having to expand our borders.'

'Yes, mother.'

'Will your preparations be enough? Do you need the elders to instruct you further? I hear that Ragnheidur considers you to be quite talented. An uncut diamond, I believe he calls you. Do you know your lines?'

'By heart, mother,' Setharrion answered in the same monotone voice he used when he knew trying to reason with her was no longer an option.

He always came to her with so much decisiveness in his heart. Somehow, he never left feeling the same. Where in it all did he lose all that? He wasn't sure. How many times had it been now? How many times had he left having accomplished nothing but agreeing to do exactly what he had come to avoid in the first place?

He'd lost count: that was how many there were.

'I've taken the lead in the celebrations for the past two hundred years, remember?' Setharrion muttered rebelliously.

'That is irrelevant. You are still such a child. You have much to learn.'

'I *am* learning mother. And whatever you think, if you like it or not, no matter how distant they are, we aren't alone in this world. We're not even alone in these parts of the mountains.'

'Insolent child!' Hui'syqussedin snarled. 'You think they matter? They are nothing. Do the birds ask the worm for permission before feeding? They have learnt to respect us as you clearly have not. They will not enter our territory and we will not degrade ourselves by entering theirs.'

'Their cultures are not like ours, mother. Each generation passes so quickly. In the blink of an eye whole parts of their societies change.'

'Does the sun notice the passing of the ant?'

'Should we not seek to learn more of them?' Setharrion persisted in his attempts to make her see. 'Should we not try to understand what drives them, so that we can avoid any future confrontations?'

He felt that was a valid political strategy, but the large female bared her fangs at him, puffing herself out until she seemed almost twice her normal size.

'We do not care for them. We do not live side by side with such feeble creatures. They come here, they come only to greet death. This is what they know. This is what they need to know.'

'But, mother,' Setharrion whined imploringly.

'No. We are not interested in such useless species.'

'There are some, young ones of low rank, that seek out adventures in the lands of these "lesser creatures." Some even who take up work there,' Setharrion said.

If he had thought that such words would mollify her, he couldn't have been more wrong.

'Traitors!' she roared. 'Renegades and insects! Scum of our forebears!'

A great expulsion of flame blasted forth from just before her lips. It shot up into the air, lighting, like a beacon, and entire section of rock and stone.

She aimed it downwards, blasting away a whole set of boulders right next to where he stood. They were little able to stand the sudden onslaught. Several of them melted, so intense was the heat in which they were bathed.

As the rock surface bubbled unhappily, Setharrion shifted his right wing even closer to his body. The heat might not bother him, much, but molten rock scarred and dried out the membranes on your wings. It was also a pain to clean off until it had caked completely, like the scab on an old wound.

He had no desire to spend any time looking like a mud monster from the pits of the earth, no matter how good a camouflage it would otherwise have been for his brilliant silver skinscales.

'No one from our clan would lend themselves to such a demeaning task. If they had, I would have heard of it.'

Hui'syqussedin peered at him, eyes narrowed into slits, the pupils dancing with red and orange. 'You speak in jest, child. You seek to trick me.'

'No one from our clan has gone,' Setharrion hurried to agree. 'But I have heard that some of the lowland clans...'

'Bah,' his mother interrupted him. 'So, it is nothing more than talk,' Hui'syqussedin huffed, as if offended by the very thought.

'Listen carefully, my son,' the lady relaxed visibly and bent forward, as if ready to impart some of the great secrets of the ages. 'Do not take heed of such talk. Those from the lowland clans seek to appear more than what they are. They are low in ranking and their members even more so. Many centuries have passed since there was any queen worthy of note among them, worthy of us to converse with or capable enough to ask for our allegiance and being awarded accordingly.'

'Since they have so little they "invent" ways in which they can appear interesting to those they wish to impress. You, my son, are most certainly a visitor they would wish to impress. So, take no heed of such foolish talk. No one worthy of his wings would lend themselves to such folly.'

Apparently satisfied that the matter had been settled, she reached out with an affectionate caress, claws and all.

Setharrion did not return it. His mother might now be mollified, now that she had bent the words to mean what she wanted them to mean, but he wasn't. She always did that, he thought. She could take even the most simplistic and innocent of sentences and twist and turn it until she had wrung it into such a shape that it said something completely opposite to what it had started life as.

What had he expected? That she'd understand? That she'd welcome the proposition with open arms? Hui'syqussedin ruled the largest clan in these mountains and her further influence stretched far beyond the immediate territory that she governed personally, and govern she did.

There wasn't a dragon here that would not yield to her. Not even a dragon from the nearby clans, even those that lived so far away that they'd only visit once in a lifetime, would challenge her or her decisions. The rule of any queen was absolute—as set in place as the path of the suns and about as flexible.

Only another queen would dare argue in earnest and then only if they were of matching rank.

He wondered what would happen if she was ever to meet someone that outranked her? That'd be a terrible blow to her self-esteem, but, she would probably find a way to twist it to her advantage, Setharrion sighed. She usually did.

His mother might not actually *be* a High Queen: that legendary figure steeped in mystery, but Setharrion felt that she certainly acted like she expected that one day the clouds would part and some ray of light would bathe upon her already golden skinscales and bestow upon her the status of the absolute ruler of the draconic world.

If they did, she'd become completely intolerable, Setharrion thought darkly. As far as he was concerned she was bad enough already.

Thankfully, it wasn't likely that the High Queen was anything more than just a legend. There certainly wasn't a dragon alive today that could remember a time when one had existed, either in their lifetime or the lifetimes of their mothers' or their mother's mother.

'Then I will take my leave,' he bowed his head in submission, his mind elsewhere.

The silver dragon turned and in one smooth motion his large wings snapped open. He launched himself into the sky. That wasn't hard. From here all you needed to do was essentially step off the ledge.

Hui'syqussedin watched him go for a little longer, then returned to what other business she had to settle today. There was always a retainer on call, ready to relay her orders, news and pleads alike. Few in the clan ever approached the queen directly. Not only was that out of protocol, but, with Hui'syqussedin, it also reduced the chance that she would hear you out to absolutely zero.

The thought rose unbidden from deep within him as he rode the winds. While open rebellion was not really an option, she had forgotten to actually forbid him to go himself. Well, as long as he made absolutely sure she didn't find out, he might really get away with it. The excitement bubbled inside his chest like a flock of fluttering starlings. Best to keep a tight rein on his tongue for a while, or he'd give himself away.

Good thing he hadn't told her "everything" he'd been up to, either. For a moment there, it had seemed like she knew, but he had no doubt that she would not have let that go (or him for that matter) if she had. His mother might even have, horrid thought, decided to deal with the matter personally. Setharrion shuddered mid-flight, losing altitude for a moment.

With little effort, he made his way to one of his minor hideouts, one which he knew both his mother as well as the remainder of the clan knew of. Maybe that meant it wasn't actually a hideout at all, but it was very visible and curling up there in the sun, said, as clearly as if it had been stamped into the mountain by giants, that he wanted to be left alone.

Nibbling dreamily at an itching wing tip while mulling things over, Setharrion tried to figure out what to do. He'd have some peace for a while, even if he couldn't actually *do* anything here. Other dragons might be a little more likely to approach him than his mother, true. But, as being the only others with such a metallic sheen aside from the queens, silvers held their place second to none, regardless of whom they were born to.

In fact, a high enough ranking silver could *almost* trump a very low-ranking queen in terms of authority, if she wasn't old enough, or experienced enough, to stand her ground. They were, however, even more rare, so he'd never heard of something like that actually happening. And the queen would have her whole clan to back her up.

Maybe it wasn't even true. It was just his luck that his mother also happened to be a queen. Why couldn't she just have been an ordinary dragoness? He'd probably have ended up drowning in lessons on manners and duties anyway, but at least it wouldn't have come from family.

One day, when his best friend (or the closest equivalent in these parts) had commented on how lucky he, Setharrion, was, with the queen taking such a personal hand in his upbringing (unlike his siblings, whom she carefully manoeuvred from afar), Setharrion had lost it. The ensuing roar had almost brought down half a mountainside.

Okay, it had been a very small mountain and a lot of what came down was loose rock and gravel, but still.

'She just wants to groom me so that she can mate me to some queen somewhere,' Setharrion had muttered. 'Someone whose clan would bring more status and influence to the clan my mother's already got.'

His friend had looked at him, confusion written all over, from nose to tail. Wasn't that a good thing, the other had asked?

No, it wasn't, Setharrion had insisted. And he hadn't cared for being reminded of that for ages afterwards, with the rest of the clan having kept their distance even more rigorously than usual. His "friend" had never broached the subject again.

No, best to lay low for a while. Setharrion was certain his mother would keep an eye on him until she believed he would no longer go off and do something that was, in her eyes, foolish.

It felt like anything that was remotely fun was always foolish, or worse, disgraceful, in his mother's eyes.

He snuggled up on the warm ledge. At least he still had time to enjoy the way the suns warmed his skinscales. An afternoon snooze was never wrong.

Tucking his nose in under a wing, Setharrion drifted off ... dreaming of happier days.

It had taken several weeks before Setharrion dared to even try and sneak away again. This time though, it wasn't the distance he was interested in. No, what he needed was somewhere he could be absolutely certain was private. If Hui'syqussedin had become vexed over learning that he'd taken an interest in the "lesser creatures"—as she referred to them as—she would undoubtedly have become livid, absolutely and completely hop raving mad, had she learned exactly how close an interest it had become.

Safe in his new hideout, Seth experimented. What strange creatures they were, these bipedals, he thought. He flexed some muscles and watched his fingers move.

How many times had he tried this? It didn't matter. He doubted he'd ever get used to it. Balancing on merely two legs all the time was tricky, but it could be done. It was when he tried to actually move, especially quickly, that things started to go wrong. The moment he stopped concentrating, he'd end up with his face full of dust.

Losing a whole set of appendages was disturbing. He kept thinking part of him was missing and, worse, the way he was used to controlling his body didn't work entirely the way it had always done.

It seriously messed up your balance, especially when you wanted to turn. It wasn't like he had a lot of reasons to go running on the ground under normal circumstances. A dragon that was in a hurry would do everything they could to get into the air and, barring being trapped in some underground cave system, there would rarely be a reason to run on all fours.

Besides, every time he changed into this form, there was a moment, sometimes a very long moment, of disorientation. It caused blood to rush to his head or maybe it was away from it? Either way, he'd end up with this twisted knot in his guts; the world would go unfocused, as if trying to see and hear everything both as a dragon and as a human at the same time; and he'd fall over, again, head spinning.

The bewilderment had faded with every occasion, so far, so he hoped that one day it would be gone completely. Somehow, he doubted it. There was, after all, still one tiny little part of him that balked when stepping up to a high crag or a steep ravine. And *he* knew how to fly.

It wasn't that he was afraid of heights. He loved heights. There was no better feeling than drifting among the clouds, seeing the world from above. It was just that sometimes… He'd never mentioned that to anyone. That wasn't the draconic way.

Seth picked himself up, brushing off bits of grass and dust. Involuntarily his hand jerked back.

'Ouch,' he yelled, looking down at it.

Great, something else that had stuck in him. With nails that were barely of any use—stupid tiny things—he tried prying the even tinier remain of a prickly shrub out of his finger.

This skin certainly had its drawbacks. For starters, it was about as useful for protection as a snowflake in a lavastorm. Okay, maybe it wasn't *quite* that bad but…

Seth yowled. Jumping up and down on one foot, *another* thorn was sticking out of the other.

'Stupid, ridiculous, half-baked body,' Seth swore at it. How was he supposed to get used to this? Actually, in a way, becoming accustomed to it was a scary thought. If he did, that'd mean that he'd be as familiar with this body as he was with his own. Freaky.

Guess this was *also* his body. How confusing was that? Seth winced. It wasn't well known, even among the draconic population, that some—a tiny few—dragons had the ability to shift form. And of those, even a tinier amount ever bothered.

The memory of his first attempt made a trickle of ice flow down his spine. It had been a frightening experience and he hadn't stayed in that other shape for long enough to know if he'd even gotten it right (including whether there were more or less than the required number of arms and legs and heads). The switch back had been almost instinctive, as if he'd been repulsed by something that made his insides twitch at the very memory.

No, he'd never get used to it, but, by now, he'd done it enough times that he didn't need to think about it too much. He could even do it while moving, badly, but still. Doing it while flying, well, he'd only tried that once. Seth wished he'd dismissed that idea as insane *before* making the attempt.

Humanoids, while they had their uses, weren't very well equipped in the membrane department … being not much more wind-resistant than your average rock and a rock was probably what he'd resembled on his way down. At least he'd had the foresight to do it over a lake. Inquisitive he might be, but it was a rare thing to feel such fear and he had no wish to experience it again.

It took quite the amount of concentration and effort to pull off such a smooth change of shape and while he had plenty of strength to spare in that department, he saw no reason to waste it so frivolously.

* * *

'Mind your concentration,' Ragnheidur had always told him.

Setharrion had always wondered if the old, practically ancient, dragon had suspected back then when he'd first come to study under him, that this young-ster wasn't quite like the others?

The reason for carting him off to learn the ways of power earlier than most was clear enough. It had been evident from the day he hatched that the young dragon would require more specialized attention than most. As he grew, it had also become obvious that he had far more power than was good for him. Certainly more power than sense and, on top of that, his control over that power was even less than most young dragons.

It had been a constant source of trouble for him at the time, and not only with his mother and siblings. Although, Setharrion had to admit, it had prob-ably been even more trouble for those around him.

All dragons had a small degree of magic inherent in their very essence, he knew that. It was a remnant, a tiny fragment, of those great beings from the beginning of time from which the dragons originated, or so it was said. What-ever its origin, it was the primary reason they were able to take to the sky, or wear such armour as they did, when the common laws of nature stated that they should be able to do neither.

'Mind your breath. If you cannot control your breathing, you cannot stay focused. If you cannot stay focused, you cannot control your energies. That is where your power comes from, young one,' his instructor would say.

'Remember, a dragon does not *breathe* fire: he channels his essence, what some beings call arcane energy, to create fire. You can make it into a ball, small or large. Allow it to hover or blast forth, circle you or engulf you. What you can call forth is limited only by your imagination and your ability to ma-nipulate that energy.'

For the majority of dragons, their limit was themselves. The energy they drew on came from within. It was instinctive. They didn't have to concentrate on flying to actually fly, for instance.

'No, no, no, not like that!' Ragnheidur would scold him time and again. 'The further away you aim, the less power there will be behind it. Try to re-member that the energy is tied to you, keep it close and it will sunder mountains. Direct it into the distance and it'll be nothing more than an aurora.'

Distance mattered. The stronger you were, the further afield your abilities would be effective. That had seemed self-evident, even to the young Setharrion.

He'd also learnt quickly that it didn't matter if his power was channelled into fire, ice, earth or any other substance; his personal affinity was for that raw ethereal energy itself rather than any of the elements. That was, for him, the easiest to work with. He could literally feel it around him. Other than that, the second easiest was fire. For a dragon at this latitude, it usually was.

His attempt at casting ice usually shattered and melted in no time and things like earth or moving things around without touching them was out of the question: he just couldn't do it. For once, it hadn't been because he hadn't tried. With Ragnheidur as your teacher you tried … if for no other reason than because the old dragon was grumpy and you'd end up working twice as hard the next day if you offended him by not taking your studies seriously.

'Feel it within you, around you. Let it be a part of you that flows with it— a never-ending stream of life, of energy. It connects us all: every living creature with the world around you. Extend your consciousness to every part of yourself and just breathe.'

Setharrion hadn't been big on the whole mystical side to his training, not even as a youngster. He had picked up enough of the important bits, in his mind, but that was it. The rest went in one ear and promptly out the other.

Apparently overexerting your use of this whole energy "thingy" could cause all manner of problems, but he'd always found that he got very sleepy and physically tired long before that became a threat.

It might be more impressive to blast forth fire and roast something alive, but it was ten times easier to just swat it with a paw and be done with it, as far as he was concerned. Ragnheidur hadn't agreed with using it like that at all, period.

'Watch and learn, young one,' had been another bit of wisdom the older dragon had shared with him. He'd said that a lot.

That one had actually been something that the unruly youngster had taken to heart. At first, it was because it was fun—at times—and later, well, because it was still fun, though in a different way.

So, he'd watched and he'd learnt and what he'd learnt most of all was that his mother had an extremely narrow point of view. At least, that's what it seemed like to him.

To her, everything that wasn't draconic occupied not just a lesser place but was cast from existence altogether, almost everything anyway. A few were tolerated as long as they kept their distance; like the elves, who were allowed passage over her territory (not that they usually passed this way, they knew where they weren't welcome), but, even then, a scout would be watching them from the sky, so far away that not even the fabled eyes of the elves could spot them.

She had special scouts for that. She had special "someones" for nearly everything. Setharrion doubted that there was a single "useless" member of the entire clan. If there had been, she would probably have cast them out. They all had a role to fulfil, should they be called upon: all except him. He was just supposed to exist.

🜲　🜲　🜲

Now, Seth watched the matching appendage draw a small circle in the soft earth as he twitched another set of muscles. How peculiar it felt not to have wings, even now. All the muscles in his back felt like they were in the wrong place. Still, practice had helped.

Looking further down, he saw the pale pink feet he couldn't seem to escape. Were they really so strange compared to his own? Mind you, in the department of claws and talons, these flat little things were of no practical use whatsoever. Why did they even have them?

At first, he'd thought that he'd let them grow so that they'd help him get a better grip, not understanding why people broke them on purpose. A dragon didn't like his or her talons breaking. Aside from feeling sort of skewered, it also made your grip less effective. But *these* things … if you let them grow they started gnawing their way through your expensively purchased footwear. And if you still didn't do anything about it, they'd go really long and start to impede your ability to walk. How strange was that?

Actually, there were a lot of things about this form that seemed to have no active purpose at all.

For a dragon, this was a difficult concept to come to terms with. Everything, from the smallest scale to the tip of the tail, every muscle, every horn, served some purpose. Sometimes, you didn't realize what that purpose was until you lost it, but it was there.

Seth knew some dragons that had broken off a horn or lost a sail and boy were they grumpy about it, ever complaining about how it messed up the wind stream when they were flying. Mind you, he wasn't sure how much of that was down to the aesthetic preferences of the dragons in question.

Along those lines, his still remembered his first introduction to a hairbrush. Almost as fascinating as the ones he'd had since coming here. Of course, the Towers was full of interesting, and possibly not entirely sane, people—so that made it really easy.

It was one thing to watch others from afar going about their daily lives and trying to work out why they did what they did and a whole different thing trying to do the same right in the middle of them. What kind of infernal creature went about with fur that it couldn't groom on its own?

And he still couldn't reach all over himself, either. When he tried scratching that itchy part on his back, he just ended up going round-and-round like some silly-looking puppy stumbling over his own feet and taking a very inelegant dive into the dust. Very undignified, he felt.

Not that Seth was big on this whole "dignified" style anyway, but what a limiting difference compared to the flexible elegance of a long, curved neck. This one couldn't even look behind without having to turn the whole body. How *did* they cope?

Yes, those early days had been filled with enough trouble to make anyone have second thoughts, but he'd persevered and, while there were still times when he found it annoying, now, it had also made him appreciate his natural form so much more. He pitied those that did not share it.

🐉 🐉 🐉

The memories came flooding back: Seth had been rummaging around in the small strongbox he'd acquired, pulling out a few objects and setting them aside, before finding what he'd been looking for. And after some careful, or in the case of the trousers, slightly unbalanced, attention, he had managed to get himself dressed.

He did up the soft leather belt another hole. That felt better. By now, this didn't feel as strange as it had done the first time. It still itched, but he felt okay in it. He hoped he looked okay too. Humanoids had turned out to spend a whole lot more attention to their clothes than he'd expected. Maybe he should get himself a mirror?

Seth nodded to himself and, making sure no one saw him, slipped out of his hideout and started walking.

At least the footwear, as uncomfortable as it was, kept any more thorns out of the soles of his feet. He hated the thought of what would happen if he ended up falling into a nest of thistles or brambles. How did anyone stop worrying about what might happen to them next long enough to actually have a life when everything around you were likely to cause you harm? It didn't really help that most of it didn't mean to.

It had taken a few tries, but once he'd grasped the general idea of clothes as both protection and something to keep you warm *and* signify your status and allegiances in one go, Seth had been able to move beyond the basics.

Indeed, he'd already made some important discoveries. For one thing, armour, which, if you were humanoid, was supposed to make you feel the opposite of vulnerable, did everything but, for him.

He shuddered at the memory. It had been an otherwise fine day and the dragon had slugged what seemed like a well-equipped looking male ruffian beyond the village where he'd been lurking. Back then, his main method to gain something had been to steal it. Even if, as a young dragon, he still had a lot of growing to do, compared to something only mere meters tall and not even half of that wide, he was a giant. Lying in wait for the odd bandit had proven easy.

Unfortunately, most people who actually did *have* armour, didn't randomly leave it drying on a washing line, so he hadn't had a chance to try on any before then.

Having tried on the rest of the clothing, Seth had ended up leaving the thick leather armour and the chainmail. They had turned out to be cramped and, when he'd eventually managed to do it up, it smelled even worse than it felt. It also made him rustle when he walked, making stalking nearly impossible.

A dragon might look like several tons of meat shaking the earth as they went past (and yes, sometimes, to impress the impressionable, that's what you did) but, by nature, they were stealthy, preferring to ambush their prey rather than chasing it down by brute strength.

And if he hadn't liked the leathery type, he certainly hadn't cared for the metallic option.

At that time, he hadn't just left the armour, he'd left the horse the male had been riding, too. It had been all fur and beady eyes and had towered above him. Though, truth be told, maybe it was more the horse leaving him. Approaching it had left him with a ripped hole in his shirt and he'd gotten the impression he was being left off lightly.

He had taken the man's purse though. That had sped up his progress. Most of those he'd relieved, so far, had either been a) not present at the time or b) not carrying any. All right, there was c) too, which was before he'd figured out what those tiny clinking things were.

Setharrion had been very surprised when he'd learned what most people in these parts thought a dragon was: big fiery things that ate princesses and apparently slept on hoards of gold and precious stones.

He wasn't sure if princesses tasted better than, say, caribou or elk, but he was absolutely certain that anyone wanting to curl up and go to sleep on, or in, a mass of cold, noisy metal that moved about all the time, needed to have their brains examined.

Money, those shiny (when buffed up a bit) things apparently didn't have a distinct owner. So far, he hadn't come across any that would hiss and spit as you made them yours or turn into small blue birds and fly off. No, these things drifted from person to person, seemingly without rhyme or reason.

It had taken some time before he understood the concept. By then, he'd also decided that having lots of it was good—as long as he didn't have to sleep on it. It also meant he could alternate between outfits depending on where he was and what he wanted to achieve. So, as he'd moved from village to hamlet to towns he'd tried out various ways of presenting himself.

Today, he was shopping around for something that would help him blend in, at a comfortable level, as he prepared to move his base of operations to yet another location. He'd heard of the Temple City of Amorix and was now curious enough to want to visit.

But first he needed to spruce himself up a bit. That's why he'd come to this market town, after all.

So, for a while he'd ambled amongst the stalls in the square. They were bright and fluttery, but, while he did find several things that agreed with his stomach, none of them carried any clothing to his liking.

'Looks like I'm going to have to spend a bit more than I planned to,' Seth mused as he headed in amongst the streets where the more discerning salesmen traded their wares.

The entry-bells jingled one after another as he continued his search. He really hoped that he'd find something ready-made. The tailors offered a much greater variety, of course, but he still wasn't entirely comfortable having to spend the amount of time needed for something to be fitted properly.

In the end, he ended up in a small shop, drawn in by the eclectic display of adornments in the window. As it turned out, the owner, a short lithe male who couldn't possibly be entirely human, Seth thought, was more than happy to show the young man the rest of his wares—once there had been a few minutes of careful negotiation, of introductions and pleasantries to demonstrate that he could, in fact, pay for them.

Seth did insist on trying on the clothes in private though.

'I don't understand,' he mumbled as he struggled into the shirt in the small space beyond the door. 'Why does changing one's markings affect the actions of others? You're still the same inside, are you not? If someone breaks a claw or loses a horn, they're still the same, so what's so different with this?'

Proper arms, in this case a delicate but complicated set of silky strands interwoven and mixed, still presented themselves with drawbacks and it took several tries until the cream coloured tunic was firmly laced up.

Seth liked it. It was so soft to the touch, almost like water, and it felt soothing against his skin. Most cloth he'd been wearing so far had been rough and chafed against this supersensitive outer layer of his. Sadly, going around wearing nothing at all wasn't a good idea: If nothing else, it gave you chills. He didn't like being cold, he'd discovered. It wasn't a sensation a dragon was overly familiar with.

'Hmm, not sure what this does?' Seth said. 'I wonder what happens if I tug at this?' He experimentally pulled at one of the laced cords that seemed to abound on this tunic.

That turned out to be less than a good idea, as the lacing around his throat tightened up.

'Ack, awwwk, gack!' he spluttered as he tore at the string. 'Too tight … too … tight.'

'Everything all right in there, young Sir?'

'Fine, fine,' Seth hurried to reassure the man. The last thing he wanted was company. 'They really should warn people about these,' he mumbled to himself as he was able to breathe again.

By the time he wandered back out on the street, he both looked and felt like a different person.

'So, this is why they spend so much time and effort on these things. I'm beginning to understand, mmm … too bad he didn't have anything in terms of footwear,' Seth said looking down at his feet.

Whatever else you could say, even *he* could tell that his shoes no longer matched the rest of him—and not just because they'd been walking all the way into town.

'Kind of him to give me the directions to a reliable footwaremaker,' Seth said to himself. 'Maybe I can find something actually comfortable. If this is how real clothes are supposed to feel, I believe my feet will enjoy the same difference?'

Patting the elegantly cut outer coat, no, what had the man called it? Doublet? Yes, that was it. It had a nice pattern of cream on a dark green base with shoulders jutting out just a touch. The arms didn't cover his hands either, but allowed the free-flowing lace at the end of the sleeves of his shirt to rustle, quietly, as he walked.

Yes. Definitely a good buy. Guess it had been worth what he'd paid for it after all. He really needed to see about getting a better source of income. Waylaying bandits simply wasn't suitable for a steady supply, though it was to his advantage that they liked showing themselves after dark. Not their fault he could see far better at night than they could.

It wasn't far to walk; a good thing, too, since he seemed to be attracting a bit too much attention for Seth's taste. It was, therefore, a very thankful young man that slipped through the doors to the cobbler the old man had recommended.

Was he getting his hopes up? Maybe. So far, he'd found that anything that was comfortable to wear was hopeless to walk in outside of the house. Shuffling along dusty road in some household slippers just wasn't his style – if he could be said to have a style.

Unlike the last place, there were a lot more people here: a lot more going on. Seth hesitated behind the closed door. With the large windows (they even had windows in the door, how strange was that?), he could easily see outside. There was no reason to be so nervous.

Why couldn't he feel as daring and world-defying as, going by the reception he was getting, he looked?

'Try these on then,' the cobbler eventually suggested, holding out a sturdy pair of leathers.

Despite the man's politeness, Seth couldn't help but feel he wasn't entirely welcome. That was, they were happy to have him pay for their goods, they just weren't happy he had to be there to do so.

Apparently, here, people arranged to be measured as well, just as at the tailors. Only here it was just their feet. Did this entire society work like this? He could see, beyond a curtain, a room full of shelves stuffed with curious pale things that looked like feet but weren't.

They didn't have as much to choose from as he'd hoped either. He could see rows upon rows of finished footwear of every kind imaginable, but they all turned out to belong to someone else already. Their new owners simply hadn't come to collect them yet.

He was having to make do with the items he figured were made for display. They had to be, the shop itself had lots of them after all, posing interestingly on pedestals and such. A temple of feet, that's what it reminded him of.

They were, in fact, merely such goods that had never been picked up. They were the only things in the entire shop that he, or anyone else, could buy outright. Most people didn't. Those that were in the market for ready-mades purchased theirs elsewhere.

Maybe it hadn't been such a good tip after all, Seth thought as he looked down on the pair that the man had brought him.

How peculiar they looked. All hard below and such a weird shape on top. They were a similar style to his clothes, but they didn't look comfortable at all, not with those big buckles on.

Seth made a clumsy effort to put them on, ended up losing his balance and grabbing on to the wall for support. 'Woah!'

'Easy there now, young fellow. You might make someone think you'd never worn a pair of shoes before,' the cobbler guffawed at his own joke and helped Seth back onto his feet.

'Uncomfortable, are they? Hmm … perhaps a pair without a heel would be better?'

'Yes,' Seth agreed.

'Just a moment then.'

Years of studying from a distance and it turned out that these people didn't cover their feet out of some strange devotion to an even stranger deity, as had always been his only way of understanding such a custom. Turned out they did it because stepping on things when you didn't was damn painful, that was why. His sole still smarted from earlier.

At least the main language was proving less of a hassle. Thank goodness for the sharp senses of a dragon. He'd been able to pick up a lot of that from a distance. He'd still missed just as much though, giving him the impression that these creatures really stumble aimlessly through life, flailing helplessly, half-blind and nearly deaf.

'And don't even get me started on the smells,' Seth wrinkled his nose. The sharp scent of leatherworks was the least bothersome thing that his nostrils had run into today.

Eventually, he departed the shop with something that didn't pinch his toes quite as much as the old ones. True, they were more boots than shoes, but with all the walking he was having to do maybe that wasn't a bad thing. They were a lot more useful for him than some ornamentals, even if they did clash with everything else.

'Try not to fall asleep up there,' the disembodied voice instructed Seth back in the here and now. 'You look half-asleep already. The roof is a long way up from the ground and your body is not constructed for such a fall.'

Seth waved away any worry on the matter. He was sure it couldn't be nearly as bad as that and promptly went back to snoozing.

A DRAGONLING'S CRY

ven through the stout oak doors you heard the excited voices screaming at each other. That was quite the feat considering just how thick they were
—the doors, not the people, though some might argue over that.

The doors did fit in with the décor of the place, especially since the wall,
which the wood was blocking, would merely have been referred to as "a gaping hole" if it hadn't been there.

Gnarly, dark and smelling slightly like some optimistic soul had tried to
put polish on it, it didn't offer much in terms of contrast to the structure of the
rest of the surroundings. The difference between it and the stones was mostly
in that it was brown and the stones were a muddled grey. Well, that and you
didn't run the risk of splinters if you tried running your hand over them,
checking for dust.

Lin sniffed the air instead. It smelled old. Old and just a tiny bit neglected,
as if whoever lived up here only considered the corridor to be something that
got you places.

If it hadn't been for the tapestries that brought some colour to the place
and the small, slightly curved table that stood a little further back, it could
almost have passed for dreary. The silver candlesticks on the table where the
only reason you could see anything at all in here, being the only source of
light apart from what crept out from beneath the door.

It wasn't bleak, but it didn't suggest it was the centre of everything that
happened at the Towers, either.

She shuddered as another round of noise assaulted her ears through the door. Thankfully, despite its less than opulent appearance, it wasn't covered in moss, nor did it have anything as crass as slimy things dripping or trying to crawl over your feet, which you might have expected if it had been located in a cellar somewhere.

It had still been enough for her to ask the other girl to go fetch someone. You heard about what these wizards got up to in their chambers; there was no way she was going in there on their own.

Here, the floor had been carefully swept and the brass handle on the door polished until it gleamed. It had probably been done by the same enthusiastic individual who had had a go at the door. It certainly hadn't been Lin, despite the fact she was clutching a broom very tightly.

Something on the other side of the door yelped in pain. Lin shuddered, casting about for anything else to take her mind of things: a rug or two wouldn't have hurt the place, she thought. The stone floor felt cold even through the soles of her shoes. But despite these efforts towards conformity, it felt far from familiar.

This was largely caused by the shouting thundering against anyone that might have been eavesdropping outside, like her.

At least, one of voices was raving and doing plenty of cursing along the way. You'd have been forgiven to think that the screamer had discovered a whole new range of notes previously unheard of among humans and their kindred.

The second wasn't so much a voice as a cacophony of screeches, growls and a peculiarly high-pitched howl.

'That doesn't sound very happy,' Lin shivered. She hoped nothing was going to blow up in there. There was always so much to clean up when that happened.

She'd been trying to decide for the last ten minutes if she dared go inside or not. But if it took much longer, she'd be late for the next thing on her schedule.

Accompanying it all was the sound of furniture being overturned and paper and fabric being ripped apart. And footsteps ... only those didn't come from within the room.

Turning around at their sound, Lin saw the Archmagus approach. What was he doing here? Surely the Archmage was the last person to respond to something as simple as this, wasn't he? He had to be here because of something else then.

'Try not to worry,' Kaheiron gave Lin a comforting pat on the shoulder.

'Yes, sir,' Lin replied. She didn't feel terribly reassured by this but better him than her going through that door, that was for sure.

'Best you head on back, Little One. I'll deal with this,' Kaheiron said.

Thankful for those words, Lin left as quickly as possible. Some of the things the different mages, sorcerers, wizards and all the other strange folk around this place, got up to on their own was nothing she wanted to stick her nose into. She liked her nose too much for that.

Kaheiron cleared his throat noisily before he unlatched the door and stepped inside. Not that it mattered. One party wouldn't have heard him and the other was far too agitated to care, but it made him feel better about it.

The sight that greeted his eyes was pretty much what he'd expected; the chamber was a mess.

Books had been thrown everywhere. Loose pages flapped about every time something new happened. The large oak chest over by the window was still there, though he noticed that it had received another batch of scratches as had the shutters on the window, the glass itself broken and shattered in several places.

Things, strange and wondrous things, lay in pieces. Some, like the lights, had shattered completely, the energy that sustained their glow lost. No wonder it was so dark in here, Kaheiron thought. Thankfully, his eyes weren't as hampered by that as they might have been.

It was a tell-tale sign of another ill-fated round in Joran's current struggle. Actually, judging from the rest of the place, it was looking more like things had escalated into a small war.

Good thing that this was a study chamber and not sleeping quarters. The stars alone knew what the creature would have made with some soft eider bolsters and feather pillows. Short work, most likely.

'What has been taking place here?' Kaheiron asked in a tone that suggested someone had better answer him quickly or things were liable to get even worse.

He hadn't thought it'd be this bad already. The place couldn't have been more thoroughly smashed if it had been hit by a small, localized, hurricane. Among its victims had been the gilt mirror, usually standing over two meters tall. That was now laying on the floor having scattered its silent glass content all over the red and black Istan (of the non-flying variety).

That must have been what he'd heard hitting the floor, when he'd visited the enchanter working on the floor below.

That wasn't what he was worried about though. Not when he'd heard why all the commotion was happening.

There was an almightily clang and, firing off another set of curses, Joran straightened up and mopped his brow on a long but torn sleeve.

'That kind of language is quite unnecessary,' Kaheiron spoke sternly, a small furrow developing between his eyes.

'It's this blasted curse,' Joran retorted. He gave the cage behind him a small shake, causing its inhabitant to break out into another chain of chattering insults.

'Loud little devil, isn't he?'

'Perhaps you would be better served by another familiar?' Kaheiron suggested.

'After being lucky enough to stumble across this guy? No way! Who knew the apple orchard could hold such treasures,' Joran laughed. 'No, without that broken wing I'd never have been able to catch him. Quick little blighter too.'

Joran shook his head. 'I'm going to tame him, you just wait and see, Archmagus,' he said.

'You appear to have little success so far,' Kaheiron nodded towards the cage where the small creature hissed at them.

'Never fear, Archmagus, I'll tame him. How many mages have a dragonling as a familiar? They're hard to come by. Never understood why you don't have one yourself, Kaheiron. You of anyone would be able to get hold of one, I'm certain.'

'I would not wish to trade in Swallowtail,' the Archmagus picked up a pale white pad and turned it over a couple of times. 'Not even for a dragonling, especially not an unwilling one. You know full well that the relationship between a mage and his familiar is borne of trust and cooperation, not of coercion.'

His voice carried more than a hint of admonishment, but if Joran had heard it he was doing a good job of pretending he hadn't. 'I'll tame him. You mark my words,' he insisted.

'That remains to be seen,' Kaheiron replied. 'The reason I was on my way to see you was on an entirely different matter, however. I meant to speak to you regarding the golshae disturbances reported recently. I was hoping that you would consider taking up a place on The Committee.'

'Hmm,' Joran said, stroking his fluffy brown beard and doing his best in appearing to give the matter some serious thought.

The Archmagus rarely gave orders outright and a perfect stranger might easily be led to believe that he wasn't giving orders at all. Not so. And every resident at the Twin Towers knew that all too well.

What he did was to give you a chance to come up with a good argument for why his solution wasn't the best one. He might decide that you should be doing it anyway, but at least you got to try.

In turn, it might be *called* a committee … and it might sound like he was being offered a cushy job with good pay and very little work, but Joran had been here too long to believe that.

Most here were familiar with the idea of committees, there were enough of them around. They sometimes thought that the people the Archmagus chose for this particular one were a little different than the others but, what it really meant—on a generic sort of "everyone knows" kind of level, no one was really sure of. Not really, really sure. Joran was above that. He had a pretty good idea of what they actually did, not just what they were said to do. He'd been on it before.

And if they were putting one together to "deal" with an issue that meant nothing less than a proper battle-kit. There had been stories coming down off that mountain for some time. Guess there had finally been enough complaints for the Archmagus to begin treating the matter as a potential threat and not just a mere nuisance.

Joran wasn't fond of the idea of hiking out into the forest and meeting whatever was causing the trouble. But a full kit? That might be useful for *other* things… Maybe he should consider it?

In a way, it was kind of flattering, being asked personally by the Archmagus himself. On the other hand, did he really want to lend himself to being led into a potential battle by someone who could easily have been mistaken for being under fifty years old?

The general, uneducated, public, which in Joran's mind consisted of pretty much everyone other than himself, had a very conservative view of what a mage or wizard should look like, to say nothing about an archmage.

The very title conjured up an image of long grey hair and beard; bushy eyebrows over near-sighted eyes peering at you from beneath a set of half-moon spectacles; and, of course, robes adorned with stars and other occult symbols embroidered with silver thread on dark blue velvet.

Whatever you could say about Kaheiron, he certainly didn't fit that description.

'Do I have your interest?' Kaheiron asked again.

And there he went again, Joran ground his teeth. That infuriating habit of always being calm and polite all the time. Damnit, couldn't anything ever upset that man? Joran wished he'd get to see him distraught or dismayed, even just a tiny bit, just once.

'Perhaps I could think about it?' Joran asked.

'The Committee leaves tomorrow morning at dawn. Let me know by then. And Joran: If I hear even as much of a whisper of you mistreating this creature again,' Kaheiron looked him in the eyes, 'you will regret it.' He gave the other man an acknowledging nod and strode out of the room, as imposing as always.

Cursed man, Joran fumed. Why, of all people at the Twin Towers, did he have to be the one that was asked?

So, the Archmagus had asked others (obviously, or it would have been a very solitary committee indeed) but that wasn't the point. Couldn't he see that he, Joran, was busy?

Once again Joran asked himself how someone like Kaheiron had been able to become the Archmagus of a prestigious place as this. With his long smooth black hair that fell all the way to the lower part of his back and not a single proper wrinkle on his face, except around his eyes (and those only really showed when he laughed), he seemed ridiculously far the image conjured up in people's mind when thinking of the archmages of yore.

But he was the Archmagus nonetheless, and no matter how much Joran might resent him in terms of appearance, he certainly wasn't going to volunteer to get involved in any scuffles with the fellow.

He'd seen with his own eyes what that man was capable of. Only a fool would challenge him without backup. Actually, there were probably plenty of people who would, they just wouldn't be doing it for every long or very successfully.

Joran scoffed. Well, he wasn't that kind of fool. He wasn't going to do anything until he knew things weren't going to turn sour on him.

* * *

Istarrian shook his head once the Archmagus had finished informing him about what Joran was trying to do. He'd already done so several times during the story itself.

'He'll never succeed that way,' Kaheiron's aide said ruefully. 'Not with a dragonling.'

'It's doubtful that he would have more success with the methods he is employing with a dragon,' the Archmagus replied.

'Or any other creature,' Istarrian agreed. 'Well, you know Joran—' he said, tugging at his grey beard thoughtfully. Try as he might he could think of no way, outside a direct order, to make Joran turn his interest elsewhere. Dragonlings were rare creatures, even in the wild.

'Yes, I do know Joran,' Kaheiron said. 'Unfortunately, it would appear that the dragonling does as well, judging from how much difficulties the man in question is having.'

Istarrian couldn't help but chortle. 'It is amusing in a sad kind of way,' he said. 'The great Joran and he can't even get a simple animal to obey him. He would be the laughing stock from here to the markets of the Sandlands if this ever got out.'

'Mhm, It would not bode well for those whose tongue slipped, either. Joran is not a forgiving man,' Kaheiron agreed.

'True. I do wonder how Shatterwail put up with him for all those years?'

Kaheiron turned a raised eyebrow or two in the direction of his aid. The old man looked so saintly when he said that. You had to look at his eyes to get the whole story.

'I do feel sorry for the creature. I suppose that even Joran will, eventually, give up?' Istarrian said.

'Admit defeat?' Kaheiron's lips narrowed slightly. 'If he does not, I will have to make other arrangements. I will not have any familiar, or other being, abused while I am responsible.'

'Of course, Archmagus,' Istarrian made a small bow. 'Still, a dragonling like that. That is a rare chance. I can understand his desperation. Shatterwail was an exceptional partner and Joran wants to increase the status it brought him even more.'

'If by the end of this week he has not succeeded, he will have to find one elsewhere,' Kaheiron stated firmly.

'Of course,' Istarrian hurried to agree.

Istarrian knew his Archmagus. Once Kaheiron had made a decision it was not a path he would change the course of without good reason.

Istarrian might look like the archetypal archmage himself; with snowy grey hair (untangled) and great grey eyebrows (bushy), and alongside the robes he wore, which in many people's eyes were very bookish and magical looking, his manners were more as you would have expected of an archmage: dignified and a little absentminded. And plenty of visitors did, indeed, mistake him for one. An error that Kaheiron himself had encouraged more than once.

He'd been the Archmagus' right hand for a long time and the position as the head of the Towers was one he did not covet—he preferred less difficult complications to pass his table.

'Now, is there anything else on my desk that needs attention?' Kaheiron asked.

'Yes, if I may direct you to clause B of this contract that they sent you from the merchant's guild,' Istarrian responded.

The two of them continued to peruse the document for some time. The re-negotiations for the Twin Towers was going slowly. The guild didn't believe that the mages would turn them into frogs at the slightest provocation, but they didn't want to openly oppose them either. After all, they could be wrong.

That's what you get for becoming an academic, Kaheiron sighed. No one said it was going to be easy.

* * *

The next few weeks, Lin spent trying to learn *not* to get lost every time someone asked for something from more than a few doors away. Not to mention discovering all those small important details everyone assumes everyone else knows, so forgets to tell them: like not picking up sparkling scraps from the floor of a wizard's study without first putting on some thick leather gloves.

They also seemed to have neglected to mention the whole business about familiars and just how protective some of them were of their masters' and mistresses' studies. Then there were the playful ones. Just the other day she'd tried petting the cutest little floppy eared furball and it had turned into a lizard, right there in her hands. Made her jump several feet, it had. Even as it wriggled across the floor, she could have sworn it was chortling too.

'Thank goodness not everyone has them,' Lin had exclaimed more than once, though her actual words might have been slightly different. 'Blabbering magicians. Hadn't anyone told them that goldfish aren't supposed to bite when you accidentally drop their bowl while cleaning it? They're supposed to flop around pathetically making little gasp-gasp noises. Gods, that thing had teeth on it like a sack full of saws.'

'Perhaps next time, you shouldn't drop it, dear,' had been the calm comment from Mrs. Sarrrrinth, when Lin complained about it.

Now, there was someone that had been a bit of a surprise. Lin had never met another species before, and she kept staring at the tabby lady's tail whenever they met. It seemed almost to have a life of its own, but the fluffy appendage never seemed to knock anything over or be in the way. Lin always had to repress the urge to reach out and snuggle it. Of course, she stared at the ears of whatever elf she stumbled upon as well.

The old tavern where she'd last worked had seen its share of "others," as her papa would call them, usually with a sneer. Painted, short, pointy-eared, tusked—she thought she'd seen them all. Why not cat-like ones too? There were probably folk wandering about all scaly-like, what did she know?

While she didn't exactly find the Towers all that inspirational (unlike so many of its other visitors); it was warm, dry and had more food perks than you knew what to do with. Even if it did feel like she fell over her feet because of some crazy coot's latest improvement to reality at least once a day. It was taking a while, but things were settling down, her temper notwithstanding.

Not everyone at the Towers was as lucky.

* * *

'This is taking this too far Joran,' Kaheiron's voice trembled as he locked the other man in his sights, anger dancing in his eyes.

The atmosphere in the chamber already toed the border of viciousness and the cold voice of the Archmagus only turned things down even further.

'You can't do this!' Joran protested violently.

The fuzzy brown wizard struggled against the two men who'd latched on to his arms. Despite his oaths, he didn't manage to break free and eventually settled down to fume quietly.

'I'd stay real still if I were you,' one of his guards growled.

Joran's eyes narrowed into thin slits. It turned the world into nothing but a sliver. Good, that meant he didn't have to watch *that* man go on and on about something ... *again*. Didn't he ever shut up?

Unfortunately, while he could easily arrange to no longer see the Archmagus, preventing himself from hearing him was another matter entirely. Blast. He hadn't prepared any spells for this. If he'd known he was going to get interrupted...

'Look at the creature,' Kaheiron implored the other, trying, in vain, to appeal to the man's better sense.

Behind his beard Joran grimaced as his two guards increased their grip on him. 'It's just a stupid animal,' Joran snorted contemptuously.

'Release him,' Kaheiron ordered the two burlier wizards. 'He will not attempt to do anything foolish, now. Will you, Joran?' It was more of a statement than a question.

The two younger wizards gave their captive a last squeeze, then let the smaller man go.

Joran straightened himself up. His clear contempt of the whole situation was radiating from every move as he pulled some of his clothing back in place. He'd walk out on them all, he would. They just didn't have any concept whatsoever of the idea of progress or the sacrifices that needed to be made to achieve it.

'LOOK at it!" Kaheiron's voice boomed in the small stone chamber. 'Look at what you have done!'

Reluctantly, Joran turned towards where the dragonling lay in a small heap. 'Bah,' he huffed.

Kaheiron's fingers flexed involuntary, almost like claws being drawn over a sand board. How could one man be so blind?

The dragonling was surrounded by broken pieces of stoneware, shattered jars and what might have been a chair once in its life. Further out, what furniture there was in the chamber had been strewn across the floor like if it had been hit by a miniature tornado which had subsequently left through the barred window.

A fair amount of those now broken bits and pieces had struck the small creature. There were numerous cuts on its body. Large bruising was appearing along the spine and thighs.

Blood oozed slowly from its mouth, which had lost several teeth, leaving only gaping holes in their wake. Two legs that looked like they'd been gnawed on by some large rodent, were limp while a third was twitching uncontrollably.

Wing-membranes torn, they resembled more the tattered sails on a long-lost ghost ship than anything that would keep you airborne. They'd lift no one now. One wing even looked like it had been broken completely, almost crushed underneath something large and heavy that had subsequently rolled away.

The tip of the tail remained limp. Even one of the sturdy horns that crowned the small skull were now nothing but an uneven sharp stump.

The dragonling wheezed at each laboured breath as sharp pain stung it again and again and a low whine gurgled forth from its damaged throat.

'LOOK AT IT!'

'I can tame him. I know I can. Look, I've already gotten him to stop attacking me,' Joran insisted.

At this, the Archmagus drew himself to his full height. His eyes crackled with lightning in their fury. 'If you ever come as much as a hundred miles of this creature again, I shall take it upon myself to *personally* arrange for you to never have the chance to harm anyone else EVER again,' Kaheiron said icily.

'It's just a stupid animal,' Joran shouted back. 'You're going to put some silly beast above one of the best the Towers have?'

'If you believe that your abilities marks you as one of the best of the Twin Towers, Joran, then you are sadly mistaken. I do believe that your time here has drawn to a close. It would appear that many of the things we wish to teach are beyond your ability to comprehend. Your presence is no longer required,' the Archmagus stated, taking great effort to not rip the other man to shreds.

'You can't do that,' Joran spat.

'You have exactly one hour to pack your bags and leave. And leave you will, on the dot, I assure you of that, ready or not. These gentlemen will see to it that you don't run afoul of anything *unexpected* while you are busy packing.'

Kaheiron motioned towards the two who had been restricting Joran's movements earlier. They'd been holding on to his arms, but it wasn't so much their physical prowess that had been restraining him.

Muttering something unsavoury between his teeth, Joran spat, like a llama. It would have struck the Archmagus right in the face if it hadn't frozen in place inches away from his nose.

With a flick of his wrist, Kaheiron sent it splashing against a nearby wall.

'You can't do this to me. You can't!' Joran wailed. 'Who d'you think you are? Just some second-rate sorcerer who couldn't make the grade? Unhand me you low-lying scum. Unhand me I tell you!'

But Joran raged against his captors in vain. With the household ease of having done something a thousand times over, the Archmagus had effectively locked him down with little more than a wave of his hands. The man was still hurtling abuse as the two assistants dragged him from the room.

Although, by now, they'd had time for some improvements on their holds and Joran was being towed behind them like a small reluctant rowboat behind an oceangoing catamaran, if said dinghy had been firmly tied down with coils of swirling lights. Every time he swore at them, the coils tightened just a little bit more.

Shame they hadn't taken the time to gag him while they were at it, Kaheiron thought. He felt like he needed to go wash his ears just to get rid of the filth that had built up.

'Do you intend to strip him of his opportunities elsewhere as well, my lord?' Istarrian asked, busily noting down the result of the event in the tome he kept for the daily running of his office. It hung lazily at around eye height, its pages crackling with bits of golden flecks and lines of text appearing as the old man traced the letters in the air with his fingers.

'A small note to the more prominent figures should be enough, only to let them know that, should they wish to hire him, he no longer has any ties to the Towers and they might want to keep an eye on him.'

'As you wish, my lord.'

Pushing aside his robes, the Archmagus now knelt at the side of the injured dragonling. Reaching out, one finger gently touched it on the head.

Had it been Joran, he'd have lost the whole digit, at the very least; the dragonling wasn't dead, not yet. But now the creature merely continued to concentrate on its breathing. Misty eyes blinked at the much larger male.

'I'm sorry, my friend,' Kaheiron stroked the head gently. 'As a mage, I have no one under my tutelage who can use magic to heal such a being as you. Nor can I make this attempt. Among the powers that I possess, the ability to heal beyond mere soothings is not among them. But I will see to it that you are well looked after. Your injuries will have to heal the conventional way I'm afraid, but we have some excellent people looking after our faunatarium and perhaps your recovery could be encouraged to speed up even if it cannot be cured in a moment.'

A weak whimper came from the small throat.

'So, so,' the Archmagus spoke soothingly. He scooped up the small being, careful not to cause it further injury. Cradling the wounded dragonling in his arms Kaheiron stood up.

'We'll have you back on your feet, forgive me, wings, in no time. Please, don't let it cause you any concern,' Kaheiron said.

'Hmm … I dare say we should be grateful that Joran didn't blast a hole in this side of the mansion,' Istarrian regarded the completely thrashed chamber in which they were standing with a somewhat put-on expression.

'That too, old friend, that too,' the Archmagus agreed. 'See to this. I will take this Little One to be looked at.'

'Of course, my lord,' Istarrian inclined his head.

Kaheiron cradled the small creature gently as his long steps carried them through the mansion to where the resident animals on the estate were kept when they needed some extra looking after, especially the pets and familiars that were easier to accommodate outside of a stable.

Not once did the dragonling raise his head to investigate their journey.

Joran on the other hand did not leave quietly, quite the contrary. He did more than just throw a few dangerous glares around as, wondering what the noise was all about, curious heads appeared.

He brushed them aside, friends and enemies alike. The staff that didn't manage to get out of the way quickly enough he simply bowled over like a wrecking crew.

'Never was a good man that. Not in his heart,' Mrs. Sarrrrinth nodded to herself as the mage stomped through the hallway and out the main doors. 'You don't worry about a thing now, dearie. It'll all be alright. You'll see.'

Her young charge wasn't inclined to agree. She'd run into the scowling mage before. He wasn't the type she'd trust with anyone, from little furry animals and upwards.

'Attracts all kinds, magic does,' Sarrrrinth mused while picking up a brush. 'Species, colour, gender, none of that matters. The only thing that sets one apart from the other is how powerful they are. Why, I don't think you can even tell them apart by their titles … except for sorceresses, for some reason. So, no fretting, child.'

Usually Mrs Sarrrrinth's words would have been comforting, but Joran's behaviour wasn't actually what was bothering Lin at the moment.

She might have known. Wasn't it typical? Of course, it was. Who else would they call upon? It wasn't like there were a million members of staff in this place. No, not at all… It had to be her they asked to clean up *his* mess.

Lin sighed. It wasn't that she was completely averse to helping out, but did they have to always pick the most inconvenient times to call? Sure, she was earning her keep here, but that didn't mean she wanted to jump every time some dim-witted mage needed their study cleaned up after they'd gone and used too much crystalline incense in their latest experimental set up for a new spell or some other crazy thing pasted their walls, furniture and self with pink slime or...

Compared to that, she positively glowed when, sometime later, it turned out she'd be sent to the faunatarium instead of some wizard's closet.

What she lacked in her dealings with people, she might not make up for in dealing with animals, but she was a lot more willing to put some effort into it. Sure, she didn't get it right all the time, but she *did* try and the staff at the faunatarium didn't mind so much that she wasn't always the most polite of people.

After all, some of the younger people at the Towers came here too, both the children of the staff and those attending here for other reasons. They liked the animals.

The best access from the more liveable areas of the mansion she'd found came via a long arcade that bordered one of the many small gardens that Lin kept stumbling over. Whoever built this place seemed to have had an inexplicable desire to pop tiny, ornamental gardens around unexpected corners. Either that, or they moved them about when no one was looking.

'Or maybe they're all the same ones,' Lin mused. 'What do I know?'

That probably didn't account for the ones indoors though, she admitted. Those looked like an outdoor space, right in the middle of a section of external walls, only someone had built a pointy glass roof over it. When you stepped into one of those, the whole world suddenly turned purple or green or even sparkly, like a rainbow made of a thousand different jewels.

Unlike those, which seemed to serve no other purpose than being pretty to look at, Lin thought, the faunatarium itself was like a small maze of indoor and outdoor space sitting right within one of the outer walls of the Twin Towers, around the back.

It was, most of the time, a docile environment with small bouts of excitement in between. It smelled comforting and earthy and reminded her of home, but in a good way.

Sometimes, she even stayed on after whatever they'd needed her for had been dealt with. It was the best place in the house, if anyone had cared to ask her, to bring a plate or a jar of freshly baked cookies from the kitchen and just relax.

The reason you had to bring a jar, and not just stuff a couple of chocolate chips in your pocket, was that much of the faunatarium was free-range—for anything smaller than, say, a deer.

The faunatarium *did* have a small stove and oven, but that was mainly for making medicines or treats for the animals in its care. Mind you, some of those latter ones could be pretty tasty, you just had to watch yourself; you could just as easily end up with something that tasted like overripe seaweed mixed in jelly oil as something yummy.

Okay, so you shouldn't really munch away on someone else's treats, but when they came hot from the oven, after blowing on them once or twice, who could really be expected to resist?

'No, I suppose not,' the head mender chuckled while pushing the last plate aside when Lin said so. The small, rectangular treats slid off and into a large earthen bowl.

'Want me to take these to the stable?' Lin asked, eyeing the bowl.

'I think I'll pass on that,' the man replied, hiding a grin. 'They're all supposed to stay long enough to make some of our residents feel a bit better about themselves.'

'Then, could I take some for *them*? Pleeeease?'

'Hmm … I suppose I can't see anything overly wrong in that. Just don't eat all of them yourself, okay?'

'Right,' Lin jumped off the chair where she'd been peeling some sort of tuber with lots of brown protrusions. 'Be back in a jiffy.'

'Hey, I meant after you were finished,' Senrel called after her disappearing back. 'Who's going to finish the tubers? Get back here when you're done, d'you hear?'

* * *

Back out in the world, Joran continued through the woods with only one goal in mind.

A branch slapped him right in the face and without regret it dumped last night's entire collection of wet, though clean, water droplets and a few soggy leaves down the insides of his robes.

Joran barely flinched. It hadn't been the first to do that. He hadn't really noticed those either, any more than he could feel several angry red welts that crisscrossed his face. He'd never been meant to slug through the underbelly of nature, but right now, he barely even realized what his feet were doing.

Joran swore viciously, batting an errant butterfly out of the way. Wings broken, it tumbled to the mossy ground, where something small darted forwards from the shadows of a log and pounced on it, mandible's crunching.

The enraged mage stomped on.

* * *

When Lin still hadn't returned, Senrel decided to see what she was up to. Hopefully the girl hadn't eaten all the treats. They might taste nice, most of them, to a human palate, but they all contained medicinal herbs despite their ordinary appearance. It wouldn't be good for someone to have too many of them. The last thing he needed was Sarrrrinth, the old dear, having a go at his ear because he'd let something happen to one of her charges. He liked the old kitty. He also liked his ears in one piece.

So, picking up the next batch of treatments for the afternoon's drop-in session, he headed out.

Knowing his way around, it didn't take long to find his errant helper. She was crouched at the edge of a long table which usually held a series of "things." Right now, it only held one: a medium-sized cage.

'Poor little thing,' Lin was crooning softly at it.

The sight of the creature in the cage seemed to upset her for some reason. It wasn't just that it was the first cage she'd seen in use in the faunatarium; none of those here were forced into something like that and the door locked behind them if it could be helped. There were plenty that had their own places and little hideaways where they felt safe and could curl up in peace and recuperate, but most of them weren't locked in—not unless you counted the faunatarium itself. Some of the bigger ones did stay in large stalls to keep them from wandering about, but that was hardly the same—was it?

But this one. The bars around it clanged if you touched them, but the creature inside didn't even raise its head. It merely lay there, regardless of what went on in the rest of the room. It was just the eyes, black as night and liquid as oil, watching her every move as she poured the food into a small slot and placed it back with a click, that even told her it was alive.

'Don't feel too sorry for him,' Senrel said. 'He's attacked three people so far. That's why I had to bring out one of the cages. You have no idea of what a job that was. It's been ages since we had to use one. Couldn't even find them, so in the end had to ask around if anyone had a spare. Whatever you do, don't stick your fingers between the bars. Not unless you're prepared to lose one or two.'

'Oh,' Lin exclaimed and quickly clasped her hands behind her back.

'Now, if you're quite done with that batch, you can go help the others muck out the stalls. They're already late.'

'Right,' Lin answered unenthusiastically.

Looked like that was what she got for forgetting about those idiotic tubers. Meh, she shrugged to herself and headed out from the inner rooms of the faunatarium to the outer walls, where the stalls were, right next to a big door that led out of the Towers.

In the doorway, as she left, Lin cast a glance over her shoulder. 'Poor mite,' she murmured. 'If someone tried locking me up in a cage, I'd attack them too. Like that stupid mage hadn't done enough.'

* * *

Linandra didn't get to spend enough of the next few weeks in the faunatarium, as far as she was concerned. It had always been one of her favourite places at the Twin Towers or, at least, the best place that wasn't solitary and left her to her own devices. People were nice enough, even if some that passed for "people" here probably would have looked more than a little out of place in the village back home. But having some time to yourself when you weren't exhausted was good too.

Of course, now she had another reason to linger just a little longer over her chores in here. She couldn't help but feel bad for the small dragonling even after seeing him nearly taking a set of fingers from a careless helper.

'Horrid blighter, isn't he?' the helper had muttered loudly, mopping at the dropping blood.

Lin wasn't about to argue that she'd be happy to lose a finger or two helping the creature out, but surely, once he'd healed up, they'd let him out of that cage? Right?

Turned out things weren't quite that simple.

'It's horrible,' Lin exclaimed loudly at the news. 'Anyone who would do something like that should be skewered.'

'My, you're almost as vicious as that dragonling,' Senrel pretended to be alarmed. 'Don't worry, Lin. The Archmagus has seen to that it won't happen again. Very soft with animals, our arcane master. Now, hand me those linen-wraps over there. I need to change the dressings on these legs.'

Lin went hunting for them. They were on the top shelf of one of the cupboards at the far end of the room. She'd picked things up from here before and ignoring the bottles and small containers, some lids sealed with lead, she reached up for the soft rolled-up strips of cloth.

A surprised yelp caused her to startle and one of her hands knocked over the whole pile she'd been reaching for. Dodging the small white avalanche, Lin tried to keep as many as possible from falling on the floor.

'Damn!' Senrel jerked back.

Leaving most of the bandages on a nearby table, Linandra hurried over with a small number in her hands. She came back in time to see droplets of blood fall from the head mender's hand.

'I have to go put some salve on this,' Senrel said. 'Don't know if these fangs are poisonous or not. See to it this thing doesn't escape while I'm gone, will you!'

Lin approached the table where the dragonling was tucked up in a set of blankets. Looked like he was out of the cage, at last. Guess that made sense, Lin thought. There was no way the master mender would be able to change something like that with it still behind bars.

She hadn't been here when they'd brought him in: Had he looked like this then too? She'd seen the destruction in the mage Joran's study. It didn't take a wild imagination to make up your own mind about what had happened.

Remembering Senrel's advice from before, she carefully put her hands behind her back. Maybe it wouldn't try to bite if it didn't feel threatened? It couldn't wriggle loose, could it?

The small body below struggled against the cloth that kept it secure, biting and gnawing and ripping where it could. It was quite clearly feeling better and a whole lot more energetic.

Why hadn't Senrel sedated it? Now that she saw him up close, he looked a little dangerous, gnawing and biting like that. Then Senrel wouldn't have had to get bitten like that. Did that mean that calming herbs didn't work on dragonlings?

Without hands to hold it down, the tiny dragon soon released itself from its wrapped-around cotton prison.

It moved a little clumsily. The cast on the wing and the tightly wound bandages were hampering what movement was left over from the original injuries.

Flopping over, it turned in circles before getting the hang of balancing itself in its new state. A small angry squeak erupted as it banged against a crate at the edge of the table. It lost its balance and nearly tumbled off.

'Easy there,' Lin cried out before she could stop herself.

Having been reluctant to move before, she now rushed forward, hands stretched out, all thoughts of losing any fingers forgotten.

Linandra managed to steady the thing before it toppled over completely. The dragonling gave off an indignant squeal. Unhappy about getting its new-found freedom restricted, no doubt, she thought. Or would have thought had she'd been able to think clearly. The dragonling bared its small fangs at her and hissed.

'Oh shush,' Lin admonished it. 'Stop that,' she told it more firmly when it snapped at her as she tried to keep it from going over the edge again; it was so unsteady on its feet.

Some part of her was screaming at her, telling her to just drop the thing and run, that caring for others was one thing but putting yourself in harm's way while doing so was not an option.

That voice kept telling her that this didn't matter. It was just a stupid animal and she was going to get into trouble. If the thing didn't try to rip her head off, like it had evidently attempted to do with others (and probably would have managed if it had felt better and been a bit bigger), then they'd give her another one of those lectures about doing what she was told. They were good at those.

Normally, Lin didn't pay much attention, but sometimes, here, the results of that little trait of hers could mean more than just getting your pay docked.

For instance, she'd spent nearly a week with the fuzzy brown ears of a bear sticking out of her head (which looked doubly ridiculous since her own hair was straight and black) after ignoring someone's advice on how to clean up after one of the magicians had had a small accident among his bubbling experiments.

At the moment, the two of them, dragonling and human, were having a staring contest. Lin was too worried to look away, though her eyes were watering.

She figured it was probably a good thing she hadn't mentioned to Senrel that she'd been poking treats through the bars. They'd probably told her she ought to have learnt to keep her nose out of other people's business by now. That happened far too often, in her mind.

'Nice dragon,' Linandra said nervously. Maybe she shouldn't have been doing that. Now she was trying to subdue an annoyed dragonling that probably wouldn't mind having her throat out. What had she been thinking? What was she thinking now?

The small creature squawked at her, trying to puff out his chest.

Lin lost it. 'Oh, give it a rest,' she snapped. 'Rawr, rawr, to you too. No one here is the least bit impressed, you know. Now, stay still. You're gonna hurt yourself the way you're carrying on.'

As this a tiny mouth enveloped a whole knuckle, jaws and all.

She should have jerked back. She should have startled. Heck, she should have screamed in pain. If she had, she probably would have lost a hand. Well, a bit of a hand.

But all Lin did was just stand there.

After a moment, there wasn't any pain, she realized. That was odd. Those tiny fangs had looked sharp. Linandra was certain that having your skin and flesh penetrated by those tiny needles wasn't the least bit comfortable.

Should it feel like this? That is, not at all? Lin wondered. 'Are you done with your big monster routine now?' she asked instead.

The dragonling withdrew, just a little.

There wasn't any blood. Looked like the thing hadn't actually fully bitten her. Well, that was something to be thankful for at least.

Not that it looked the least apologetic for having tried, more like it was making a show of that she was too insignificant to bother with.

Linandra couldn't help but shake her head at the whole thing. What a stubborn little thing this dragonling was. Guess it wasn't the kind that asked for help. It was difficult enough to get it to accept it as it was.

By the time Senrel returned, he found the two of them quiet but sharing the space by the table without fighting.

Not sure why, or how, but the head mender soon discovered that this new-found minimal level of tolerance wasn't extended to all, far from it. He almost received a second sharp pain in his *other* hand as thanks for the trouble of doing what he'd tried to do the *first* time it had bit him; changing the dressing.

'Here,' Senrel handed the young woman the thinly stripped cloth. 'See if the little blighter'll let *you* do this.'

Lin accepted the tiny bandages with a puzzled look. 'You want *me* to put this on that baby dragon?' Lin asked. 'I … I don't know how to use this.'

'Dragonling. Not baby dragon. Fully grown, I expect he is,' Senrel nodded towards the creature. 'No lords or ladies down here, little lady, everyone does their share,' he told her brusquely. 'I'll tell you what. I'll tell you what to do and you do it. Just keep that little demon away from me,' the head mender said.

A look at his face told Lin that he didn't really mean that last, not too seriously, at least.

LEARNING CURVE

Lin knocked the tin box against the coarse stone wall, the last stubborn remainders of ash finally giving up and dropping out of it.

She was careful not to breathe it in and, once it was empty, rinsed it out with water from the water-butt and then doused the ground where it had all fallen liberally with the same. She did so far away from the roses and herbs of the kitchen garden, which was a good thing, as they'd have otherwise soon withered away and died.

Why were these wizards always so messy? Lin didn't know. It didn't matter if their hair was black or brown or green or silver, they were all the same: they always caused more work for her. It didn't matter if they were young or old either, the only difference was the *type* of trouble they caused.

Making her way back to Mrs. Sarrrrinth and the other staff on duty today, Lin dodged—quite expertly it had to be said—between wizards, apprentices and guests. They always seemed to have guests of some sort, and very strange guests they often were too.

'Wonder what they do when they're not here?' Lin mused, partly annoyed, as she ducked through the nearest door to avoid being run over by a group of gangly young mages. 'They sure sound like they're having a good time, don't they?' she muttered.

'They probably are,' came a voice from behind.

Lin whipped around, box in hand.

'Hey. Careful with that. I don't want a concussion on top of all my other problems,' the young man evaded the swinging metal tin by nearly half a meter.

Problems? What problems could *he* possibly have, Lin fumed inside. Just look at him: all silk and velvet with threads that glittered like gold in the sunlight streaming in from the window. He didn't look like he had a care in the world, with that pale skin (and not having the excuse of being elven either, judging by the ears) and playfully tousled, moonlight hair.

Biting back a sharp reply, Lin didn't answer and instead dashed back out of the door as quick as she could. It didn't do to insult the guests, even when she *did* rather want to hit them over the head.

Great. Now even the guests were getting on her nerves.

Why did they always have to meddle? It wasn't even as if they were any good at it, in her eyes. They just made things up and, from time to time, things didn't go quite according to their well thought out and researched equations - whatever an equation was - according to some of the other staff.

Another time, she'd had to put up with the compulsion of clicking her knees every time someone said the word "please" where she could hear them. That had been after she'd walked right into a room as the enchanter inside was practising combination incantations—a sure-fire hit for any party.

It had certainly hit her all right and she hadn't been the least bit happy about it either, especially since they weren't nearly as good at removing that little compulsion as they had been applying it. In the end, it had just been "…let it wear off naturally." How ridiculous was that?

'Bloody hocus pocus men,' Lin snapped at the world in large.

* * *

No, while Lin was quite convinced that no one at the Towers could possibly have as much trouble as she did, that might not have been the most accurate of observations. The truth was that there were just as many problems abounding at the Twin Towers as there were anywhere else where large numbers of people—and species—gathered. And people went about trying to deal with them in much the same fashion: ignoring them.

While most people saw the study of magic, and mages in particular, as stuffy old fossils, someone had clearly forgotten to inform the mages themselves of this. Over the centuries they had *diversified*. A modern arcane practitioner for a modern age, they said.

And here, to the Towers, the powerful and rich (perhaps not surprisingly often the same thing) would send younger sons, daughters and sometimes even themselves, when all other options had been exhausted. Sometimes it'd be to learn to control powers that were causing trouble for the family. Sometimes it would be because having any user of magic in said family could be quite prestigious, not to mention convenient, depending on what type of magic they showed affinity for, assuming it was a *controlled* magic.

They didn't always come just to study either. Some came in via the backdoor, drifting in here and there as the days went past. Some seemed to come and go, as perennial as the grass. She'd seen and met one or two already since she'd come here.

Those were the ones that couldn't pay their way by normal means. The Twin Towers were, after all, not a school. It just happened that such a large gathering of people able to utilize so many different styles of magic was a good place to learn more about magic.

All in all, it was the source of quite a bit of turbulence, socially, and Lin wasn't the only one who had trouble adjusting to the place.

'If you're going to remain here, you will need to learn a few things. Beginning with that you are not the only one here practicing what these people refer to as magic.'

'I know that already,' Seth made a face. 'I couldn't fail to notice, really.'

'While I do not expect you to understand their ways, at the very least, you could name a few?'

'Fine,' Seth rolled over on his stomach. After popping another sweet in his mouth, he thought for a moment.

'Let's see,' he started counting off on his fingers, 'there's wizards and magicians, sorcerers and sorceresses,' here he smiled fondly. '...and ... oh, I don't know. What does it matter anyway, everyone just ends up calling them "mages" anyway.'

'Yes,' the other man frowned. '*They* do. But mages are quite different. 'There are, of course, many, many more. Wizards channel and store power in their staffs. Magicians are more fond of—'

'—Please, please, no more. My brain's about to explode,' Seth interrupted. 'I've got enough to contend with, don't you think? Without having to learn all this stuff. I've been doing pretty good on my own up 'till now, wouldn't you say?'

'That does not mean you should become complacent,' his companion insisted. 'Didn't you tell me earlier how difficult you found it at first?'

Seth winced. Oh yes, he'd almost forgotten about that. It had been an interesting time, hadn't it? It had also been rather long ago.

🐲 🐲 🐲

It hadn't been easy, trying to keep two lives completely separate; and they slowly becoming two whole lives. The more he learned and immersed himself in the cultures, interactions and everything else that came in such abundance to what his mother termed "lesser species," the more disillusioned he became when he returned "home."

That day, on that most important of days, he had felt it more than ever.

Every dragon in the clan, and a few visiting dignitaries, had gathered there that day, at the base of the central core. While it couldn't be said that dragons stretched as far as the eye could see, far from it—and certainly not by a draconic eye—there were a lot of them and most dragons were perfectly capable of taking up quite a lot of space, not just through sheer physiology but in terms of presence, as well.

It *felt* crowded, that was it. He should have been used to it; after all, most towns had a far greater population density on an average day than the dragonlands had when everyone came together. But here, and now, the only thing it was making him was uncomfortable.

Setharrion arched his neck as he walked down the line that had formed, trying to concentrate on the task at hand. Every eye followed his progress down the way of the procession. He had to time his steps to the rhythm of theirs, even as they did no more. Every time a foot fell upon the ground, the world shook under their combined weight.

Every twitch to his tail, the way he might scrape the ground with a passing claw; from every motion he made to how the sun reflected of his nearly metallic, shining scales; everything was being watched. For this moment, the attention of the entire clan was upon him and him alone. And Setharrion found that he did not like it one single bit.

The other dragons drew back as Setharrion approached. Respectfully, they lowered their shoulders and proud necks as he passed, widening the passage as he progressed.

Getting through a crowd, any crowd, wasn't hard, not for him. If they were dragons, they moved aside out of respect. Other creatures merely vacated the spot for more predatory reasons. No one liked getting chomped first thing in the morning, for instance, or squashed merely because the rambler wasn't paying attention to where he's putting his feet.

Grabbing anything by tooth and jaw and holding it down until it stopped struggling wasn't on today's agenda though. If it had been, a few of the other dragons might have been in trouble. Setharrion already felt like gnashing his teeth at it all and bit down hard to keep from making any peculiar faces. This was no time to slip up and actually be himself.

Head held high and proud, Setharrion shuddered inside as he walked towards the central feature they were all gathered around, or, more accurately, before. There wasn't a single dragon gracing the ledges beyond, not today.

They called it "The Gateway." It was an officious sounding name for something that was just bits of rock, Setharrion thought. *Mostly* bits of rock, anyway. There might have been some chalk in there as well. No matter how hard he tried, he just couldn't think of millions of crushed little dead "things" as "rock" even if rock was, probably, pretty dead to start with.

Here, nature had chipped it out, slowly eroding away the softer stone around a stronger central core until she had left behind an arch stretching imposingly above them. Veined with a wavelike pattern of red and ochre, it stood out against the more greyish colours of the rest of the place.

Wait a minute. Wasn't chalk supposed to be white? Also, wasn't it pretty soft? It crushed easily. Maybe he'd been thinking about something else.

It was still big though. Even if you stacked several dragons on top of each other, you'd still be able to send them walking through it. A little wobbly on their feet perhaps—a stack of dragons was bound to be heavy—but they'd fit. A sole dragon, even one of his size, had no trouble.

If anything, it made you feel small. Maybe it was supposed to? You didn't feel small when looking at a mountain. The mountain was just there. It was something that just was.

But this, it was, somehow, something more than something that just was. Setharrion nearly winced at that thought. He knew what he meant, it just never came out properly.

The path beyond The Gateway wound its way up the side of the mountain, growing thinner and thinner as he climbed ever upwards.

The Gateway to what exactly? No matter who Setharrion had asked over the years, not two dragons had ever agreed. Eventually, he had just stopped with the questions. Not just about the Gateway but about a lot of other, more interesting things, too. Far too often the answer had been any out of a variety of "we don't know," dressed up in pretty words and languid expressions.

There was also the "such matters do not concern us. Remember, we are dragons". That was, if anything, even more unhelpful. Setharrion wondered if all dragon clans were as backward striving as his?

Actually, he'd eventually realized that they didn't actively aim to move backwards. It was just that they were content with remaining absolutely still, in every way and, with the world around them heading off into the future, they ended up becoming a remnant of the past.

Maybe there were clans out there that were at the forefront of invention. Who explored, not just the physical world around them and the creatures that inhabited it, but the ones you couldn't touch too. Maybe there were even dragons that had flown to the moons?

Setharrion sighed. That last part was pretty unlikely, but he could dream, couldn't he? About being so wild and free that you could go anywhere? Be anything?

All he was, was stuck on this stupid incline with several thousand feet left to go. He shook himself angrily, trying to dislodge the thoughts. The only thing that came loose were some of the rocks he was trying to climb over. Typical.

This path grew steeper as he ascended, he knew that of old. He hated climbing for no reason. No, wait, he hated climbing, period. What was wrong with using his wings? They worked. That's what they did the rest of the time. So why did today have to be so bloody inconsiderate? Traditions, bah.

Setharrion grumbled to himself now that he was no longer surrounded by scores of fellow dragons. They could see him well enough before he passed around onto the other side, but they probably couldn't hear him. Not well enough to eavesdrop on the mutterings and grumblings that accompanied him, at least.

Today of all days, he would be the only one making this climb. Would be the sole occupant of the mountain. That's what decorum dictated, and it was considered an honour to be chosen.

True, the first time it *had* made him feel special. He'd carried himself graciously and with dignity all the way to the top, thinking of every movement his body made. Wanting everything to be just perfect. Wanting his mother to be proud of him.

The whole thing had lost its golden sheen after the first couple of decades and, by now, he'd lost track of how many years he'd actually made this ludicrous journey. Before his elevation, a different dragon would be chosen every year and it had been coveted by many—young and old alike.

But no, since he'd been old enough to be chosen, Setharrion had been the only one. Every year, it was the same. Every time, he was the one. Even just a couple of years break would help, he groaned. But no. Apparently that was not done.

Curse these blasted scales of his, the silver dragon snarled, arching backwards to nibble at a particularly itching shoulder. Why did it always have to be him that had to do this, alone?

Of course, these last few years, he wasn't alone, not on the mountain anyway. Technically, he never was. Whatever tradition said, these days he wasn't the only one up here even if he *wasn't* counting the myriad of insects, small furry things and larger feathery ones that lived here. Not that there were a lot of them. It took a special kind of determination to make a life for yourself in these mountains, especially around the peaks.

But there was one here who never left, not anymore. About half way up the mountain peak, there was a cave. It was quite a large cave as caves go, more like a cavern really, and it was suitably cared for. He'd visited often, before, when he'd been younger.

Today, its single inhabitant had quite the reputation. Actually, he'd always had a reputation, but these days it was mostly for being disagreeable.

'Good Morning, youngster. Is it that time again, is it?'

A muzzle, scales faded and bleached by time, poked out of the cavern's mouth as Setharrion approached.

'Venerable One,' Setharrion tipped his head to his former teacher.

'Got schtuck with doing the duty again eh, humm? You're a fine one for tradition, boy,' the old dragon smacked his lips as if attempting to capture the next thought before it escaped.

'As you said, it is my duty, oh Ancient One.'

'Bah... Codswallop. Trinkeltrouts all over again,' Ragnheidur muttered.

The faded blue head nearly struck Setharrion when the oldster jerked it around as something streaked past them, huffing repeatedly to himself.

Setharrion looked up, wildly. What was that? Was it dangerous? He felt worried and ashamed for not having paid attention to his surroundings.

Mumbling about the ways of the people these days, the old dragon retreated deeper into his lair. For a while the only thing Setharrion could hear were grumbles and the sounds of things falling over as the not-very-agile oldster chased something around his home.

'Should I, err ... help?' he called into the mouth of the cave.

'No, no. No need, youngster,' came from within, soon followed by a snarlier 'Out. Out. Fly schouth for the winter you schtupid bird. Schooo wingflap!'

Setharrion, who'd been edging his head into the cave drew back in alarm as something small and feathery dashed past him at eye level. As he turned around again, after having watched it disappear, he nearly jumped out of his skin as he found himself snout to snout with Ragnheidur.

'Ah ... please don't do that,' Setharrion asked shakily, trying to back the remaining half of himself out of the cave mouth.

'Losing our senses, are we?'

'I don't know. Who is?' Setharrion looked confused. What was he on about now? Ragnheidur had been difficult enough to follow a few centuries ago. Now, half the time Setharrion wondered if it was him being deliberately obtuse or if his age was really getting to him.

'What? Who?'

'What you were talking about ... someone losing their sense,' the young silver tried steer the conversation onto something he might actually understand.

'Brains. All these young ones. Addled, thatsch what they are. Doescht even know what he's talking about,' Ragnheidur shook his head sadly and pulled back. 'Mark my words lad … hmpphf,' his voice called back and, a moment later, the dragon was back again—this time nearly hitting Setharrion in the chest by sticking his head and shoulders out of the wide gap.

'You really shouldn't be up here during the ceremony,' Setharrion tried suggesting meekly.

'Pfft,' Ragnheidur huffed. 'You listen to me, boy. There's only one … hmm … constant in the universe … and that's, hmm … change. The Queen doesn't like that things hmm … change. But everything does, learn that before it's hmmm … too late.'

The old dragon disappeared back into his home with a jolt, making the silver dragon almost jump out of his skin for the second time.

'I'll … I'll do that,' Setharrion called after him. He didn't get a reply.

Resuming his lonesome trek up the mountain, Setharrion decided that this had one good thing going for it. It was one of the few times he actually managed to be alone right in the middle of the clan.

Of course, he had to be shouldering the burden of their traditions instead. Somehow that didn't seem like much of a trade-off. But you couldn't have it all … apparently.

'Ha,' Setharrion snorted. 'Like any of them wanted to try and make the old codger move if he didn't want to.'

He rather liked the old dragon. Ragnheidur had probably been impressive enough, physically, in his youth, duo-wings and all. But age had taken its toll and, if ganged up on by several of the clan insisting he'd follow traditions, he'd have little choice but to conform.

Mind you, that was from a pure "this amount of meat and muscle equals this amount of power" perspective. You'd be in trouble if you were a strident believer in that up here.

It certainly wasn't the old one's fangs (which weren't much to brag about these days) that made them keep their distance. His sails—which had once been iridescent—had gone nearly transparent and had a tendency to droop, weren't impressing anyone either since he didn't do much flying anymore. And it definitely wasn't because of the slow and careful way he moved, because his bones made him ache in cold weather.

If anything, all those things would have marked him as easy prey, anywhere else.

Setharrion knew it wasn't his winning personality either, because he didn't have one. That is, he had lots of personality. It was on the "winning" side he was coming up short. He also smelled of earth and damp and like he hadn't gotten out of his cave in a long time (which he hadn't).

But that was hardly why even the Queen avoided dealing with him if she could. Not that she couldn't order him around, it was just easier to leave him alone.

So, maybe, if given a direct order to come out and join the remainder of the clan for the Sundancer ceremony, he would, of course, have done so. He would have come, no arguments, no grumbles. She was, after all, the Queen.

But Setharrion had no doubt that the next day there would also be no help. That things would start to not happen; the kinds of things that you never noticed while they were always there. The kind where, when you realized that they'd stopped working, it was already too late to start them up again, because no one remembered how to.

Questions would go unanswered. Teachings wouldn't be passed on to the young. And those were just the things where they'd know who and what was responsible. While Ragnheidur might not be actively involved in very many things, or directly teach any of the youngsters, anymore, he was the one all those that did do those things turned to when they couldn't manage. And what about all the little things that ran because they, well, did? The ones no one else had taken over because the Queen hadn't realized that someone needed to.

Besides, Ragnheidur wasn't just old, he had also been Setharrion's instructor in magic; often despairing over the exuberant way the young dragon expressed himself.

'You're supposed to lift the boulder, not crush it into rookery.'
  'What's rookery?'

'Never you mind! Just concentrate on your actions.'
'I'm trying,' *the stripling Setharrion protested.*
'Try harder!'

Actually, he'd been *everyone's* instructor. Even the Queen herself once upon a time, when she'd been young, had taken her lessons at the old one's knees. Though, in her case, it had been in a class of one.

Maybe that's why they all left him alone, Setharrion mused. He was like Oaneirkh; great to have around when you really needed him, but the rest of the time he was just an inconvenient reminder of your own inadequacies.

The Queen didn't much care to be reminded of those. She wasn't about to acknowledge she had them and looking them right in the eye and seeing them looking back at you, well, that could unsettle anyone.

Setharrion didn't care much for it either, he had to admit, but at least he knew he had them. He could at least admit to himself that he wasn't perfect … all the time. His mother, on the other hand, no, he doubted the thought had even entered her mind.

There were plenty of things he still couldn't do. When being trained, as a cub, there had been a lot more.

'Will I be able to do that one day?' the young Setharrion had asked, awestruck, while he was staring into a sky where his then instructor had made lights dance across the heavens in blue and pink and green in a gentle rain.

He had caught a sparkling green one on his snout. It had made him sneeze, sending the small light fizzing into the air again before it twinkled out.

'This is nothing,' the old dragon had confided in him. 'Lost, so many things have been lost with the years,' he'd sighed then and looked older than his young protégé had ever seen him.

'Then I can be the greatest dragon there ever was?' Setharrion had breathed, his eyes still enthralled by the display.

It felt almost close enough to touch, again. He reached out a front claw, stretching his hindquarters as far as they would go before losing his balance and ending up in a small heap further down the hill. The young dragon eventually managed to point his snout in the right direction from within the tangled mess of long, sanguine limbs. His eyes were fixed on the illumination display.

Ragnheidur had laughed at the sight before helping him up.

'Oh, you're strong alright, boy. Strong but lacking. Undirected. Unrefined. *Uninhibited*,' he'd huffed at that last.

'Oh,' the young dragon had said and shuffled back up the hill disappointedly.

'And even if you weren't,' his teacher had continued as he, too, returned to watching the stars, having chosen to ignore that last little outburst. 'You need to grow a bit before you have a chance to take *that* title. That's one even you'd need to work for. You can't merely be born to it. Can't have everything served up before you, gutted, cleaned and cooked.'

'I can make pretty glows on the water,' Setharrion demonstrated, toppling over again as he tried to see the lights climbing up over his own nostrils.

Ragnheidur thrummed with amusement.

'Venerable Teacher?'

'Yes, my boy?'

'Can I be the greatest dragonmage that ever lived?'

'Oh, *everyone* has a chance at that. But few are called and even fewer are chosen, as they say. You just concentrate on your studies.'

'Who *is* the greatest dragonmage that ever lived then?' Setharrion had asked.

'Oooh, I don't know about that,' the old dragon had drawn closer and lowered his voice conspiratorially. 'There are many from our past whose deeds are no longer visible to us. But there is one that I taught, long ago, back before you were even an egg, that might just have been one.'

'Yes?' Setharrion had said. Shiny-eyed, the young silver's tail tip had shaken in excitement.

'He was a *mighty* dragon. So in tune with the arcane forces that he could create viable storms; cloak himself in darkness and shadow and wind and then slip through it all like a passing thought. Who could call upon the earth beneath us ... the air above us. Already, when a stripling, he would make the lights dance like you have never seen, the entire sky aglow from horizon to horizon with waving bands of blue and green and purple. Why, he blew a hole in among the crags in my very first lesson.'

'Wow,' the smaller dragon hadn't realized he'd been holding his breath. 'There aren't any big holes here, are there?' Setharrion had looked about, trying to find something new in the scenery he'd been surrounded by all his young life.

'This lake below us wasn't always a lake, my boy.'

'Wow. So, can I see him? Can I? Where is he now? Who is it, Ancient One? I didn't know we had people like that in the clan. Wow. Can I go talk to him? Can I? Can I?'

Setharrion had bounced about excitedly at the idea. His older self felt a little embarrassed over the juvenile exuberance he'd so often displayed back then.

'You can certainly try,' Ragnheidur had agreed. 'Sadly, I do not believe that you will have much luck.'

'Why not?' Setharrion had pouted at the news, sliding to a stop on his rump. Finally still, he watched his teacher intently, hanging on to every word.

'No one has seen him for a long, long time now. One day, he told me that he'd decided to go on a journey. Said he wanted to learn more about magic. To know more about the world, he said. He always was one to gaze up at the stars. The other striplings used to tease him. Called him Stargazer. That was *before* they learnt of his powers. They didn't tease him much after that. Not if they didn't want their snouts burnt. Creative, too, as I recall.'

'Oh,' the little dragon had hung his head for but a moment. 'But if I get really good, then I could go on a journey too? I could find him? A dragon's home is with his people. That's what mother always says.'

Yes, she always had used to say that. Who was he kidding, she was *still* saying that, at every opportunity if someone showed signs of wishing to be elsewhere. There was only one place for a dragon and that was to be there, here. That was why he was having to be so careful when sneaking away. Her spies had keen eyes.

Setharrion clenched his teeth at the last bit. He'd see about that. One day...

Trying to shake those feelings of being stuck in the tar-pit of the past and concentrate on the task at hand; he set about climbing the rest of the way. There wasn't an actual path this far up. Here it was claw against rock, heave up and scrabble for purchase, kind of travelling.

'It'd be so much easier if I could just fly up here,' Setharrion grumbled.

What had been that other dragon's name? Had Ragnheidur ever mentioned it? Okran? Ranoth? Oaneirkh? That last sounded vaguely familiar.

Wonder what had happened to him? He never had come back to the clan, Setharrion knew that. He was sure he'd have heard about it if he had. Someone like that doesn't just shuffle in alongside the cat when the door's opened for the night.

Setharrion couldn't imagine someone so strong and cunning could possibly be killed. He wanted to believe he was still out there, chasing his dreams. Maybe he'd even found it and was living happily ever after somewhere out there. Setharrion just wished he was doing the same.

Ragnheidur was right. Things sure changed with time.

Setharrion wasn't sure that he always liked the changes that time had been so generous in delivering his way. Sometimes they just felt wrong and not just because they kept insisting at putting him at odds with everything else.

So, lost in thought, he continued upwards. Soon, all his thoughts needed to be concentrated on the here and now. The last bit he'd need to battle not only the rock itself but what surrounded it. And up here, that was only one thing: the wind. It howled around him like a strong gale at sea and was just as treacherous. There was nothing whatsoever to buffer it: no shield, no wall or mountain. A fierce gust could come at any moment.

Most of the time that wouldn't have mattered. He was a dragon after all. He'd combated worse winds in his days. The wind was a dragon's friend, allowing him to soar high and free.

But that was up in the air. Up here there was precious little purchase, leaving him dangerously unstable and he was supposed to stay put. He bent forward into a crouch as a particularly fierce one rushed past, clearly in a hurry to be elsewhere.

'See, not even the wind wants to hang around here for too long,' Setharrion muttered between clenched teeth.

His talons dug furrows into the rock as his body strained against the stream. It made his sails snap to-and-fro like mad until it passed. He lowered his head further, pressing tightly against the uneven rock. Setharrion tucked his wings against his body. He knew he'd be blown away if they were forced open in the wrong direction up here. Not to mention, if really unlucky, he'd sprain something.

Some would use the fingers on their wings to help them climb. Apparently, that made it easier to keep their balance. This was more important for wyverns, big and small, who only had their hind legs to worry about, but even those who, like Setharrion, were quadrupeds, made good use of them. Not that he'd know, since he didn't have any. Since Setharrion had never liked the look of them, he'd always been pleased about that.

Right now, he was having second thoughts. This was the fiercest wind he'd ever felt up here. Maybe they actually did come in handy, he thought, tucking in everything that could be tucked in, to become less of a target for the element of nature that normally sustained him.

Too bad it wasn't like painting some designs on some random rock, using mud that'd wash right out. If you added some, if that could even be done, you probably couldn't just say you weren't pleased and ask for them to be removed again. If anything, that was bound to be painful, right? Having bits chopped off generally were.

He dug his claws in, waiting for the wind to die down.

Smaller bits of the mountain top, already loose, came tumbling down under the onslaught. Some hit him in the face, a couple landing in his nostrils. He closed his eyes to avoid getting any in there as well.

Then, with a last heave, he snorted loudly and hauled himself up one more time.

Finally—he was here.

The wind jostled him again but now, with all four limbs gripping tightly as he turned into it, it had no choice but to yield. He wasn't some mere stripling anymore, after all.

Wrapping his long, sinuous tail around the peak of the mountain helped him stabilize.

Above him still, was the artefact that had been tethered on the very summit with what looked like the chains for a set of warships' anchors. Technically, it wasn't actually on the summit, more like floating above it—hence the need for the chains.

None of the dragons could remember it being placed there. It was one of those things that, even to them, was one of the constants of the world. Still, having a huge rectangular block of stone, its surface both rough and smooth at the same time, hovering above your head was slightly unsettling, even if he was used to it.

Looking around, the chains themselves disappeared into the mountain. Whatever they'd been anchored to was somewhere below.

You could tell that time had passed since it was placed here, though. While the block itself appeared untouched, there was considerably more space between it and the actual mountain below than there had been in ages past.

'Wonder how far down those chains go?' Setharrion wondered. Each of them was almost the size of a thick tree trunk and they would grind against the rock below as the stone above strove for freedom.

Why anyone in their right mind would want to make such a huge block of stone fly was beyond him. Why they'd bothered to tie it down when they'd obviously must have gone through so much effort to get rid of it, didn't make any more sense. Or, for that matter, why they'd anchored it to a mountain in what many others would consider the absolutely nowhere. Maybe it had actually been inside the mountain and that was why more and more chain came out every century?

Whatever its original purpose, the dragons now used it for their Sundancer celebration because of the way it reflected and enhanced light.

But it wasn't time for that yet and Setharrion instead looked out across the world now spreading out below him.

Watching from here, you could be forgiven for assuming that this was, indeed, the centre of the world.

It certainly was the centre of *his* world, even if that world had been expanding quite a bit lately. Even if the mountain didn't, as the story went, send its roots right through to where the elements still lived—to those dragons that had, in ages past, returned to the closest environment they could find to their fiery origin; becoming beings that couldn't just *use* fire but who had mastered it to such a degree they had *become* fire, no, the very spirit of fire.

Molten and fluid, yet ethereal, they lived their lives in the central core of the world, playing in what would have been lethal to any other creature, only rising towards the surface to mate, causing the earth above them to tremble and shatter before sinking back into the depths once again.

The world up here was very different. More open and not nearly as hot. But perhaps, Setharrion wondered, that closed-in space under the earth might seem open and cool to those that lived there. Maybe they, too, had mountains and valleys, solid rock instead of glaciers, precious crystals growing like petals instead of flowers and streams of fire and flame.

He preferred *this* view though. For nearly as far as he could see, and a dragon's eyes were prized for their sight, there were mountains. Small mountains. Big mountains. Enormous grandfathers of time, old and cold enough that their summits were covered with snow and ice even in the height of summer. Small mountainettes, scarcely more than grown-up hills. And in between them, harsh valleys and canyons cutting into the earth below.

These were the heartlands: the centre for the greater dragon clans. To them, it was heaven. Too many other races, the heartlands would have seemed inhospitable, but to the dragons it was pleasant and solitary. Most of all, there was plenty of space for everyone. Even those who lived in the central clans didn't like being too crowded. A dragon needed their personal space.

But there was, beyond the lower lands, on the horizon, a tantalizing flatness. Setharrion narrowed his eyes, trying to see further. On a good day, yes, beyond even that, hinted at by the merest trace of glitter in the sunlight at sunrise, lay the ocean.

He'd never seen it, the sea that was. Setharrion couldn't even say he'd read about it. Dragons didn't, as a rule, read.

It had been a wonderful discovery: reading. Once he'd gotten the hang of it, it had completely put him under its spell, seduced him into a world he hadn't even known existed. It had, in every sense of the word, opened up new worlds to him, one of frazzling pages, tightly wound scrolls and leather-bound tomes smelling faintly of the past.

How could a species so inferior, so fragile, have come up with such a marvel? He didn't know.

It was so, so free. To be able, at any time he wanted it, to find information, any knowledge. To make new discoveries every time he turned a page. To be swept away as he devoured word after word, drowning in their roaring speech.

There seemed to be no end to it. No matter how much he gorged himself, there was always room for more.

And the best of all: he didn't have to remember it all. If he wanted the same answer to his question, he just needed to go back to the same book, the same page, and there it would be. Easy.

Of course, *learning* how to read had been a pain. He still only knew one language too, but time would solve that. Time was, after all, on his side.

Wouldn't it be great if they could all adopt that approach? No more memorizing history. The past. The present. The names of all those who had come before them. Everyone and everything under the sun that their kind had ever considered important. All young dragons had to learn this.

He'd hated it.

No, reading was so much easier than memorizing everything, and, in this place, it meant *everything*. The dragons were a purely oral society. Their history, their legends, their truths … every stupid, useless thing. Setharrion growled at the very idea.

The dragons, he knew, tended to look down on the "lesser creatures," but there were so much they could learn from them if they'd only wanted to, he thought. The problem was that they *didn't* want to.

Their society had existed as it was for thousands upon thousands of years. At least if you wanted to believe the history that his mother was emphasizing. Personally, Setharrion had his doubts.

Dragons were often old-fashioned, they'd kind of needed to be. They lived a long time. If they changed every time that so many of the cultures that surrounded them did, they'd be living their entire lives in a kind of travelling seesaw, going round-and-round and up-and-down all over again without actually seeming to get anywhere. Pointless really.

It had begun back in the day when beings only even remotely considered dragons had coalesced from the plasma of the dark universe, spun out of the same material that had created the stars around them but spread thin, so thin they would have been almost invisible to the eye, had there been anything evolved that would have been able to see them.

They hadn't had any concept of "writing things down" back then and, while the draconic species had diverged a lot since then, that one thing had never changed: they were still big on oral tradition.

Maybe it was just that no one had gotten around to making dragon-sized tomes? It'd be hard to hold the quill though, he had to admit.

No, it probably wouldn't have helped at all. The dragons didn't read because they didn't have the chance to. They didn't read because they felt they had no need to. Even if they had been interested, a book that size would not only have been enormous but it would have had to be hardwearing too, all those claws and talons weren't exactly designed to turn delicate pages of paper.

No, he'd keep his little discovery to himself—for the time being.

Now, back to business. Setharrion shook himself. Scanning the sky, the light was becoming just about right. He needed to hit midday. Thankfully, as it was the middle of summer the sun was supposed to be right above them.

Sometimes, you could get hints of the other suns too, but usually their light didn't penetrate this far, much. When he thought about it, that was rather odd, but he was sure that there had to be a good reason for it.

As the sun moved above them, the light first reflected off the block above him before making it glow gently. It wasn't hot and it certainly wasn't going to be seen very far. It always needed a bit of extra help.

Setharrion tried to concentrate, drawing up the energy immediately around him, and sent forth a stream of fire. It engulfed the block from below. The resonance was immediate and a pillar of flame and light shot straight up into the sky.

⌂　⌂　⌂

Back in the here and now, Seth returned his attention to what he felt was the droning voice coming from above…

'While I agree with you in principle, Seth,' it said, 'yes, there are many humanoid Practitioners of the Arcane Arts who, as you say "merely point at something, concentrate, and hope like blazers it's going to work." But I really don't think referring to the learned residents of the Towers as "spellslingers" is suitable.'

'Bah!'

FRIENDS COME IN ALL SHAPES...

The wooden stick covered in caramel-coloured stickiness waved tantalizingly back and forth.

'No? Don't want this?' Lin tried to tempt the small creature down from the top of the cupboard. 'It's good. Really ... it is. I saved it from dinner last night.'

Okay, so technically it hadn't been *her* dinner she'd saved it from, but it seemed the chefs here always made more food than necessary. She wondered if they'd found that some sort of disaster occurred if they were to run out? Maybe the wizards rebelled and took over the kitchens or something?

Besides, if their skills at cooking food resembled many of the setting-up-of-spells she'd been a witness to, it was no wonder the kitchen staff made sure it never happened.

Actually, it was probably more likely that a lot of them simply got so engrossed in their work that they forgot to turn up for dinner ... or lunch ... or breakfast. Some spellslingers really weren't good at keeping time, in some cases showing up hours later and wondering why there was no one else there, not to mention where the food was.

Once the kitchen staff had had their share of whatever was left over, the rest was portioned out to whatever people happened to be working nearby at the time.

It was never at the same hours, so it was pointless to try and hang around and wait, hoping to pick up something extra tasty, like chocolate mousse. One thing was sure though, you certainly didn't starve when you worked here. Even what was available for her normal meals was more than some people back home saw in a week.

'Look,' Lin took a bite and chewed energetically. 'Yummy.'

Should she really be eating this, though? Lin pinched her hip. Wasn't it curvier than it had been? She'd definitely put on some weight compared to when she first arrived. Of course, considering how thin she'd been, maybe that wasn't a bad thing.

She carefully poked the chewed end at her small friend. The dragonling ignored it. It was ignoring her too for that matter.

That hadn't always been the case. When Linandra had first started taking an interest (despite that she should have been working), it had hissed at her. Sometimes, it'd even try to bite her, despite being in a cage at the time, if she got too close while she was cleaning. It still did that when anyone else got too close.

'I don't understand it,' Senrel had marvelled when he'd caught her out. 'Why aren't you getting the same reaction as the rest of us?'

He should have been telling her off for not doing the job she was there for, but he could save that for later. Just having someone who could look after the tiny creature without getting mauled in the process, especially now that it had mostly healed up, was worth getting someone else to tidy up a bit more instead.

'Is it sheer persistence on her part?' he mumbled to himself as he watched the young woman.

He hadn't thought of it when she first came in to dust, so he hadn't mentioned that the dragonling was liable to charge anyone who came too close even from inside the cage. Since there hadn't been any screaming and running away, at the time, he'd just assumed that she'd learnt to stay away from the cage.

Senrel had hated having to keep a creature locked up like that, but its personality hadn't made for a friendly co-existence with the rest of the staff or the other animals here. He did think about bringing it to the attention of Istarrian, the Archmagus' governing hand. If things went too far, the poor thing would suffer—as if it hadn't done enough of that already.

No one else tried to get close to it these days. Probably because it still tried to claw their eyes out, even Senrel, who'd been feeding him ever since he came here; a responsibility he'd since allowed Linandra to take over. It was both less messy and much quieter that way.

Most of the time the dragonling had just laid there: a sole, singular and sad ball of legs, wings and body all curled up in the middle of the cage. It *still* did a whole lot of snoozing. It was just that, instead of being stuck in a cage, it had taken up residence high up on top of the medicine cupboard.

On the downside, it meant a lot of people were unwilling to go in to this room these days. They felt uncomfortable, they said, like if the small sharp eyes of the dragonling stared right through them, just biding its time before it attacked.

There was another reason: small, black, white and yellow and a master of begging treats—especially sandwiches had a habit of disappearing—whenever they were near.

Lin tossed a bit of smoked jerky up onto the top of the cupboard only to find a cold nose trying to burrow into her waist pocket.

'No. Bad Pickles,' she said, pushing him away. 'You've already had all yours.'

'Why don't you just release it?' Lin asked Senrel, pointing at the top of the cupboard.

'You see, Grumpy here is used to humans now. We can't release him back into the wild. To him humans mean food. He'd jump on the first traveller or settlers he'd find. Easier than catching field mice and such.'

'So? They'd just shoo him away, wouldn't they?' Lin said.

As if he'd ever go after them in the first place, Linandra had resisted pointing that out in that sharp voice of hers that appeared at times like these.

'The poachers would get him first. They'd pounce on him like a demon-cat on a rat.'

'Really? Doesn't look like he likes humans all that much to me,' Linandra said and nodded towards the dragonling's homemade nest. Senrel had just placed some water beside it, safe in the knowledge that the little beastie was busy ignoring Lin down below.

'They're not safe.'

'Hmm,' Lin murmured, she still couldn't understand why they didn't just let him go.

The poachers, right? But this dragonling probably liked humans even less than any others of his kind. Heck, he'd probably attack them instead. That probably wasn't any better actually. Guess this wasn't as easy to solve as she'd thought.

It was the same problem really, in the end. If they released him somewhere where there weren't any people it shouldn't be an issue though, should it?

'Why didn't you let him go the first time you got him here?' Lin suddenly asked.

'We didn't find him. Joran did. Joran then wanted him as a familiar you see,' Senrel eventually explained after looking uncomfortable.

'I know all the mages here have one, but couldn't he just get another one?'

'Word is Joran didn't want anyone to think that a tiny, little beastie bested him. Here, want this sandwich?' Senrel offered her a cucumber selection.

'No,' Lin declined the offer. 'Would that be so bad?'

'Are you kidding?' Senrel scoffed. 'The only thing bigger than that man's talent is supposedly his ego.'

'He isn't nice. But what's that got to do with anything?' Lin frowned.

'Okay, look at it like this. Familiars are a kind of "sign" of what type of mage you are, sort of, if you believe in that stuff. What kind of creature you want to or are able to tame is supposed to be a reflection of your soul or something like that, anyway,' Senrel explained.

'So, some are more valued than others?'

'The more money you've got, the rarer a beastie you can get your hands on, yes. Of course, they're just like any other animal then, takes more than that to make a familiar.'

'I still don't get it.'

'Look at it like this,' Senrel tried to dial down his explanation a further notch. 'There are all sorts of magic users in this world, you know that, don't you?'

'Yeah.'

'Okay, good. Some use tools—rings and staffs and the like—to store selected spells or just as a, well, bucket into which they've poured extra power, which they can then pull out as needed. Others also use familiars. It's kind of a way to get more magic. Actually, lots of magic users use familiars, but almost all mages keep at least one.'

'Oh.'

'So, a familiar that can channel more power is better than one that can't. And the better you are, the better beastie you can buy, see, the more people will come asking you to help them and pay you more money.'

'Sounds fishy.'

'Business,' Senrel corrected. 'Not fishes. Even wizards, sorceresses and the like need to eat. Apparently, all that hocus pocus isn't good for eating, or there'd be roast swan legs and pork dumplings popping up left, right and centre whenever one got hungry.'

'Unless they were already rich,' Lin pointed out.

'There are better reasons to do things than money,' Senrel said.

Lin stuck out her tongue at him.

'But, seriously. A dragonling is a rare creature in its own right. Think there's someone over in the capital who's got one, but this is the only one in the Towers. Most of those that are caught get skinned for their pelts. Very fancied by some highborns, dragonling skin is.'

'That's disgusting.'

Senrel shrugged. 'You wear dead cow, don't you?'

'That's different.'

'How? Just because they're not cute and fluffy?'

Lin threw the mug at him.

It was lucky she missed. Empty, it rattled against the bench before dropping onto the stone floor below. The noise caused the dragonling to open an eye, peer at the crazy two-legged creatures and decide he was better off not getting involved.

Skinned and worn as an ornament? She couldn't bear the thought. What if that happened to this little creature? Would she know? How horrid.

'Don't worry. I won't let them do that to you,' she crooned up at it where it had curled up.

One of the dragonling's ears twitched.

As the days progressed, things looked up, Lin decided.

The chores at the Towers weren't onerous, leaving her with plenty of spare time to do something she actually enjoyed. Okay, so dusting and generally helping out was needed, that didn't mean she enjoyed it, not like that. It wasn't quite the same thing as having time for yourself.

Of course, working alongside others also meant you had a lot more opportunity for trouble, especially if they could be convinced to take part in said mischief. But some time alone to plan and test your ideas rather than running headlong into them was something to cherish. If nothing else, it might mean the difference between a laugh and getting caught doing something you really shouldn't have been doing in the first place.

There seemed to be less of that these days though as Linandra found herself spending more and more time in the faunatarium generally helping out or, more often, as company for the small vicious beast that now haunted the premises.

Then, one day when she came in, hands clutched around a bag of treats she'd weaselled out of one of the cook's helpers, the place was empty.

Not empty-empty. Everything was there: humans, supplies, animals. Only the cage was gone. And the dragonling.

The cage that, every day, she'd have to coax the small dragonling back into as she left. The cage that she'd open wide the moment she walked through the door, putting down whatever she might be holding at the time. It took a while, but Senrel eventually decided that it was pointless to argue and that as long as everyone was content to leave the thing alone and the dragonling was perfectly happy to ignore the comings-and-goings of the humans around it.

But he'd still kept the cage in full view. Perhaps as a reminder that it could be used again should the dragonling cause any trouble? Perhaps just as a backup in case it did just that.

So, where was it?

Lin looked around. It was too big to hide in this room. Even if they'd pulled some cloth over it, it'd still stand out. But there was no sign of it.

But that wasn't what was bothering her. She could do without the cage.

By now, a small head should have appeared over by the large supply closet. Maybe some inquisitive noises would have been heard.

If she'd brought treats, there'd usually be an insistent tugging at a trouser leg or, if he chose to land on her shoulder, sometimes a lock of her hair, as the small creature called for attention.

Now, there was nothing.

She bent over, checking under the bench. Nope. Not there either.

'Grumpy? Where are you? Heeere boy...'

If they were going to move him, they'd have told her, wouldn't they? They would have, surely? They wouldn't just take him? Who could have done so anyway? He was a minute menace. He'd hardly have gone quietly.

What if it was that horrible man? What was his name again? Jorna? Joran? Had he broken in here? Had he taken the dragonling away?

He was supposed to have been banished. Had he come back? No, he couldn't have. No one could be that stupid, surely? To risk the rage of the Archmagus was no light matter. It was not the choice of a sane man.

But what if he wasn't sane? What if he had it in for the creature? Maybe he blamed it? Thought it was the reason for being so unceremoniously thrown out of the Towers? He'd be right about that, in a way. It was his own fault really, but what if he held some sort of grudge? He seemed to be the type to hold on to old ills and wrongdoings ... to slowly simmer them until some new concoction of maliciousness had been distilled from it.

But this place didn't look the victim of any such disturbance. So then, where was he?

'You get your snout out here this very minute, do you hear?' Lin felt the bile rise in her throat. Her intestines were looping themselves into a knot. No, they couldn't do this. They just couldn't. That creature had been the one truly good thing about this place and now it was gone.

* * *

'I told you not to underestimate me,' Joran said, his face cold, hard and without any trace of mirth.

His hands were bathed in the shadowy light of the cluster of crystals he'd found earlier.

What had seemed so inconspicuous when delivered to him in a thick, padded box had taken on a whole new vibe. The small piece he'd been carrying hadn't only served to fuel his experiments. It had, eventually, drawn him here.

He kept his hand in place even after the tingling sensation turned from a pleasant buzz into something more sinister. Now it was as if it was bombarding him with a thousand tiny needles; enough to prick your skin, sending tiny shocks through his body.

There was something in the setup that jarred his teeth. It wasn't any more than a feeling now. It was, nonetheless, enough to know that the crystal set had been left undisturbed while he'd been gone.

And still it wasn't enough. This couldn't be all there was to it. Something was missing. But what?

Joran looked around the cave.

It seemed the same as every time he'd come here before. It was, mostly, dark and now that the rain had stopped, tiny trickles of water slipped past and fell off the rock, tumbling over the mouth of the cave and making echoing splats on the already wet ground below.

If only he could use this to strengthen his bond with the ethereal energies. That'd show them.

He tapped the dark rock experimentally. Wait, that didn't feel like stone. It should be stone. The crystals didn't grow in soil, any fool knew that.

Digging his fingers into the dirt he ripped out a clod. Peeling away, it revealed a tiny hint of sparkle. Could it be? Yes. It was. More … More! The crystals he'd been using had just been a peripheral cluster. The main one, the main one was below.

He had to … go below. Yes. Stronger. Below.

Joran tossed the clod aside and staggered off with purpose.

These cave systems had been here since ancient times. Surely, he wasn't the only one making use of the unnaturally high background radiative glow that emanated from deep below the caves?

He hadn't dared explore the very deepest passages. But now, now he could use those that would feed off that energy and those that it attracted here, from the lowest earthworm and all the way to the top of the food chain: him.

Yes. Joran twisted his hands this way, then that. To him, the flecks of light dancing across his skin were more than just pretty. They were the key. The key to what he wasn't exactly certain of, but he knew that on the other side lay everything he ever wanted.

But first... Yes, first, he'd pay back that old fool for all that he'd done. How dare he? Exiling someone of his talents? The man simply didn't have any appreciation.

Well, he'd show him. All he needed to do now was to find the right way.

* * *

Lin shuffled in under the sorcerer's arm as he pulled the door shut behind her. He shook his head: that girl had been going through the last few weeks in a daze.

'Whatever do they do with the youngsters these days? One bad day and poof, all their resilience just flies out the window—along with a great deal of other things,' the sprightly oldster said.

Better to do his own dusting, he thought. That it would literally be the same as not doing it at all didn't even enter his mind.

'There's spells that are very efficient for cleaning you know,' he said to no one in particular. 'Now, if I could only remember where I put them? Hmm ... under the stack of tomes on the treaties maybe?'

The man continued to mumble while carefully lifting up a hefty volume and finding a slim green booklet underneath.

'Why, you rascal. I've been looking for you for years. I thought I'd lost you. Hmm...'

The old sorcerer picked it up and started leafing through the pages. 'Yes, yes ... this is just what I needed. This'll settle the argument with that old dotard next door. Yes ... if I could only test out one or two of the simpler incantations maybe I could...'

The voice trailed away as the sorcerer disappeared further into his study, for the moment completely forgetting her presence.

Not that Linandra had actually been hearing him. Her ears had accepted that there was a voice. It even suggested that, since it looked like the old codger wasn't going to do any cleaning himself, she should get to it or she'd be the one in trouble.

'Rundelswollp's such a rickety old coot,' Lin muttered. 'Even Mrs. Sarrrrinth says so.' Admittedly not when she thought he could hear her. He was, after all, still a wizard. Or was that sorcerer? Lin's brow furrowed. Maybe it was something else entirely?

Despite those misgivings, Lin didn't pay it much attention. There were still things left to do today. Things didn't seem to go as quickly as they used to. She woke up and then, the next thing she knew, it was dark again already.

What happened to that time in between? There had to be something? Not that it mattered, it was just a sort of grey mess, like a lightly insubstantial reality that didn't let her focus. It had been like that for a while now.

Linandra shook her head. She really needed to get herself out of this gloom and doom stage. Nothing good ever came of it and there'd be even more work waiting for her once she got over it.

It somehow just didn't seem worth the effort right now. What did it matter anyway? Nothing ever changed. Not much. Was this really everything there was? Everything there was ever going to be? There had to be more to life than this, didn't there?

Her thoughts kept her in a haze even when she'd later made it up the stairs, knocking on the sturdy oak door at the top.

There wasn't any reply, which was kind of a relief. She hadn't really wanted to see anyone right now, especially not Kaheiron. He'd probably scold her for being foolish ... or something.

Lin pushed open the heavy door. She had to put her entire shoulder against it and shove, but open it did, a little.

'I'm sure this shouldn't be this hard,' Lin strained against the door. There had to be something on the other side. 'Oh, that's just great. More to clean up,' she muttered upon seeing the fallen stacks of thick leather volumes.

'No wonder I couldn't get in. Some of these must weigh a ton.'

A week ago, even being allowed in the Archmagus' study would have seemed like such a measure of trust, even if the reason was the feather duster in her hand. But now she barely even looked at what she was walking on.

Flick. Flick. Flick. The duster went back and forth, back and forth it went. Casual, disinterested and horribly inefficient it scuttled over the décor in the chamber like an unusually soft mouse after a three-day binge on cottage cheese. If it caught *any* dirt, it was only as a passing acquaintance, nothing more.

Working like that, it probably moved the dust around a whole lot more than dust was used to—giving it a vacation and time to take in the sights so that it could tell its friends about all the far away and exotic locations it had visited; like that place over by the oil lamp. You didn't get a high rent place like that on your first day. No, for something like that, you wouldn't believe the queues. It could take years.

One thing was for sure, that duster didn't do much cleaning these days. The only one grateful for that, however, was the dust.

'Who cares anyway?' Linandra muttered as she swished the thing with a vengeance. 'It's the same bloody thing everywhere, anyway.'

Despite her angry approach, for a little while, until the dust settled back into their new homes, the place looked cleaner. True, the rugs did absorb most of it, which was fine, as long as you didn't step on them.

'It's not like anything's gonna change,' Lin grumbled. 'It could be worse, I suppose. I mean, I could be stuck somewhere with no escape. Like back home.' Lin shuddered. What a horrid thought that was.

Now, all she needed was to be mistaken for someone's long lost sister, get zapped by some magical spell and get confined to a bottle for a thousand years and she'd be all set.

'Yeah, right. Like that was ever gonna to happen. Thank goodness. What a fate,' she'd had enough of the few years she'd been breathing the air of this world already. Being stuck here for a few thousand more was not her idea of a good time.

'I'll just get my bearings in this place. Then I can go and find my own fate,' Lin said, hitting a second shelf with absentminded strokes.

It was when whacking her way, a little too enthusiastically, through a shelf of books obscured by a series of greyish ornaments (this place had far too many ornaments) too high for her see what she was doing properly, that it happened.

Something sneezed.

'What was that?' Lin jumped back.

She looked about. What if something was there? This was an archmage's study after all. Anything could be hiding in here, right?

Had something just moved? Where was it? Was that a shadow? Lin whirled around warily, spinning in a worried circle.

She gripped the duster tighter. It might not be much of a weapon but— Maybe she should get something else?

Casting around for that something else, her eyes fell on something long and shiny that was supporting a set of tall flowers in a corner. She snatched it up. Brandishing it a couple of times, she went back to looking for the mysterious sneezing beast.

She'd kick its butt, that's what she'd do. Whatever it was, she wasn't afraid of it. No, not her.

Closing her mouth to keep her teeth from chattering, Lin peered through the chamber. 'So, come on out Mister Monster,' she said. 'I know you're there. I warn you. I'm armed.'

Lin hoped she sounded more courageous than she felt. Who knew what kind of things might be hiding in a place like this?

There could be cats with the bodies of mice. Large drooping goblets that swallowed you whole when you tried to drink from them. Demons. Ferocious beasts, slobbering all over the carpet, ready to devour you.

Sounded lovely when you put it like that.

Had that been a metallic sound? Maybe it was a machine from hell, all bent on devouring her on its way to becoming alive? Okay, she really needed to pull the reins in on her imagination.

For a few minutes things stayed quiet. Then, just as Linandra had managed to convince herself it had all *been* her imagination … there was another sneeze.

Okay, Lin, hold your ground. That little noise didn't sound too bad. More like a gerbil with a cold.

Something popped a head around a large urn a few shelves above her and Lin suddenly broke out in a fit of giggles.

'Greetings, oh ferocious one,' she said. To imagine she'd been scared of that!

'Such a mighty beast you are, oh vicious pillager of kingdoms,' Linandra slapped her thighs, unable to hold in the mirth.

From one of the high shelves, a small silvery head peered down at her. It sniffed in the floating dust again, rattling off another sneeze.

'You bad, bad boy!' Lin scolded the creature good-naturedly. 'You shouldn't do that you know.'

The dragonling cocked its head to one side. It blinked as Lin waved a finger at it, following her movements with a curious kind of fascination.

'You know how worried I was about you? I looked *everywhere*! I thought maybe that stupid mage—what was his name again? Jaron? Joran? Whatever, I thought he'd snuck in and carried you off or something. And now I find you *here*, making yourself at home like some fat book ornament.'

At the mention of that name, the dragonling let out a loud hiss.

'Sorry, sorry … shouldn't have brought that up. My bad. But, seriously, does the Archmagus know you're in here? You could be in real trouble if he finds you here and you're not supposed to be. I mean, he's a nice guy and all that, but I'm sure he wouldn't be too keen on small uninvited disasters just appearing in his rooms. Get down from there!'

The dragonling took a leap to the side, landing on a protruding pedestal that was more likely to hold a small statue than a small, curious, creature. It wrapped its tail around the thin support.

'No, I really mean it. Get down from there … this very minute. D'you hear?'

Linandra tried wheedling. She tried threats. She tried tempting the thing with a bit of cured meat she'd managed to dig out of a pocket. That was supposed to have been *her* snack. Oh well, it went to a good cause.

But no amount of coaxing could get the miniature draconic brat to abandon its pedestal.

While it watched her every move, seemingly with great interest, it took little note of her attempts to make it move.

Finally, Lin gave up. With plenty of glances back, she took an extra-long time going about her chores in the chambers that made up the Archmagus' private study. She didn't know what Kaheiron might do if he found her clawing friend … or found *her* dawdling.

He seemed friendly enough for a guy like that. But men with lots of power were probably used to being obeyed without fuss. They were probably used to their staff doing their jobs too.

They certainly wouldn't be used to cheeky maids … even if Kaheiron didn't quite fit the image she'd always held either of magicians *or* of people with power.

In fact, if you didn't know who he was, and he wasn't wearing anything particularly ostentatious—which was most of the time—it'd be easy to believe he was just another man in the tavern, albeit one that was fond of robes rather than leather britches and knew equally the meaning of soap and shaving.

But the point was, he wasn't anything like those wizards from the stories she'd always loved and been just a little afraid of. He wasn't anything like the kings or lords or knights, either. Lin didn't know what it was about him. It was like a kind of quiet power. Sleeping.

And if it were ever to fully awaken…

Besides, he wasn't someone she wanted to get on the bad side off even if that *hadn't* been the case. She might spend the next couple of years as a scudgemunking or worse.

There were more horrible ways of getting through your future than chasing a few specks of dust about or picking up a few stray items here and there. An ordinary maid would certainly not have the kind of days she enjoyed here. If there was anything Lin was certain of, it was that.

In this place, *nothing* was what it seemed. Or *anyone* for that matter.

How would she explain this? If anything happened that was. 'I'm sorry I took so long to dust your books, sir. Your pet was watching me?'

No, way too lame.

'Excuse me, but d'you know you have a dragon in your library?' Great hopping monkeys, who'd say something like that? Never mind, who'd listen to someone saying something like that and still believe that they were sane? Mind you, in this place, was there really any way to tell the difference?

It'd be likely to get her friend into more trouble even if she got away with it. Which she probably wouldn't.

Eventually, Lin was no longer able to stall for time. After some final attempts at trying to get her friend to abandon his lookout post, she gave in. Reluctantly, she left.

At least he wasn't in a cage anymore. That had to be good, right?

Maybe the Archmagus did know the creature was there. Maybe he liked Kaheiron all the better than he had Joran. Okay, so that wasn't hard, but the sudden change was a bit unexpected. He'd always seemed to hate other humans … or those resembling them.

No matter how busy she tried to keep herself over the next few days, Lin wasn't able to get the predicament involving her four-legged friend out of her head. The thoughts kept coming back again and again no matter how many times she pushed them away. As a result, she spent more time absorbed in her own worries than she did doing what she was supposed to.

In the kitchen, while helping out in the scullery, she'd ended up putting flour in the scouring pot instead of soap. The soap had ended up in the rice the sub-cook was boiling. She'd even tried to absentmindedly pick up a hot pan straight from the oven with her bare hands. Only the quick thinking of the cook had saved her from getting her hands severely burnt.

'I think we've had all the help we can survive today,' the sub-cook growled while quite pointedly shooing her out of the kitchen.

Back in more familiar territory things didn't exactly improve. Lin wasn't sure if the boiling point was reached before or after she dumped a whole bucket of dust over the newly-washed floor instead of polish. It did earn her the second major scolding of the day and the third one wasn't far behind as, bringing back the supplies to clean up the mess she'd caused, she tripped over the edge of a rug and caused two pedestals, a suit of armour and a small statuette of a lion to come crashing down.

It wasn't like she'd done it on purpose, but those who ended up nearly getting crushed beneath the objects making their bid for freedom, sure didn't see it that way. The two young apprentices ended up chasing her out of the building and were halfway across the yard before they gave up.

'Suppose I should be grateful they were so angry they completely forgot to resort to magic,' Lin mused as she, lost for breath, ducked behind a wooden column. 'Either that, or they were just lousy magicians in-training.'

'Seriously girl. I don't know what's wrong with you today. You're all claws and no whiskers,' the slightly rotund speckled Sarrrrinth shook her head as she helped the three girls to clean up. She'd pointedly waited until Lin had gathered herself together enough to return to the scene.

Now Lin sorted through the scattered armour, broken pottery and odd assortment of weaponry that littered the floor, in a pensive mood. Her two companions occasionally threw her dark looks. They'd been looking forward to an afternoon off, and now here they were, all thanks to her.

'Sorry, Mrs. Sarrrrinth. I didn't mean to, honest,' Lin apologized profusely.

'Never mind, kitten, some days are just like that. Why, I remember once when my Ralph came home and walked straight into the bath, clothes and all. Hadn't even realized he was in the house he had.'

Sarrrrinth picked out some clean aprons to replace the soiled ones. 'Now, just use these for now and we'll put the others in the wash. Shush now, I won't hear a word about it.'

'Thank you, Mrrwsus. Sarrrrinth,' Lin and the two other girls chorused.

'Oh, shoo with you. I'll finish this off myself. You three get yourselves cleaned up before this old kitty changes her mind.'

The dark cream tabby twisted her whiskers as her three young "assistants of the day" disappeared around a corner, quick as they could. These young ones, these days…

Still, sometimes you got more done *without* having them under your feet. Had her own kittens been like that? It was so long ago and it still felt like yesteryear that they'd gone off, seeking new lives for themselves. As was good and proper, of course, but she did miss having them around the house.

Having the occasional rowdy apprentice carousing through her garden wasn't quite the same, but, at least, those she had the pleasure of swatting with her broom.

They usually never did it more than once. They learned quickly. It was amazing what a set of claws in the right place could do to change someone's mind.

Sarrrrinth chuckled. Maybe it was her years coming back the wrong way around, but things seemed to move so fast these days. One occasion replaced the last. One Archmagus, another.

True, this last one had been with the Towers for quite some time now. Long enough for her to learn his ways. Would she have to get used to another one? She hoped not. She was too set in her ways by now to want her daily routines upended.

That wasn't saying some routines couldn't do with replacing. A narrow frown rippled through her fur. Like that crick in her leg that came exactly four minutes after she'd started clearing out, what was his name now? Rundelswollp's cabinets.

It happened every time, just like clockwork. Oh, but to be able to rush around just like the youths of the day. She'd get ten times as much done and with enough time left to take a snooze on the balcony over on the west end, the one that got such a lovely bit of sunlight just after lunch. It did you good basking in that. Made you feel like you'd had ten hours of sleep after only ten minutes.

It was too troublesome to climb all the way up there these days. Still, Sarrrrinth was beginning to suspect that it wasn't her age that was showing when it came to Rundelswollp's cabinets. Why, that rascal had probably put a spell on it to keep her from going through it.

Sarrrrinth made a few gruffing noises. Well, they'd see about *that*. What one sorcerer could make, another one could undo. She cracked her knuckles. She'd have to let herself into the library. If there was some easy solution, she wouldn't have to bother the Archmagus with such trivial details. Wasn't that what old friends were for?

While Sarrrrinth got to grips with theoretical spellwork and how to detect them, by the end of that week, Lin had left quite the trail behind her throughout the Towers.

It was a good thing that Linandra's newly discovered, no re-discovered, penchant for trouble didn't extend to the Archmagus' own study. It didn't really have to though, the dragonling caused enough trouble for the both of them. If anything, she had to be the responsible one and the previously forlorn room saw a serious increase in the amount of cleaning it received on a daily basis.

Through begging, no small amount of chicanery and just a soupçon of intimidation, Lin managed to rearrange her work schedule, such as it was. She could only hope Kaheiron himself didn't notice.

Now she came to these chambers almost every single day. It was a fortunate thing for her that the Archmagus seemed to spend so much time away from his study or he'd probably have wondered why his non-existent (by now) dust was getting so much extra attention.

Not that she actually *did* much. There were only so many times you could buff up a cup or chase away the dust mites from under the table before people started asking questions such as 'Why is my table now thin enough to make origami out of?'

Every day, she tried to make the dragonling see reason, if such a thing was even possible. Every day, she tried to tempt him into leaving.

It wasn't so much that she thought leaving the study would be a good thing for him. She missed having someone around she could talk to. Someone who didn't react to what she might say if she misspoke or went a little crazy should she insult someone she shouldn't have; telling her off every five minutes and then spending the next ten stapling up examples of how good and well everyone else was doing.

Her family had been good at that, all of them. But the absolute master had been her mother.

The worst thing was, Lin had started catching herself echoing that very voice. When challenged and unable to retreat, it was the last line of defence. After that, there was nothing but an all-out attack.

Linandra didn't care for that one bit. She hated having to keep herself under control all the time.

'I'm not gonna turn into my mother. I'm absolutely *not* going to become anything like her,' Lin shivered.

No, the dragonling usually didn't give her those lectures.

That wasn't saying that he didn't scold her, quite the contrary. Especially when he wasn't getting the rest of whatever treat she was portioning out to him fast enough for his liking.

He disagreed with her on plenty of matters. Like, for instance, the matter of being dunked in soapy water and scrubbed. Normally, the dragonling was a very clean little creature, but some of the ointments from his treatment took on quite a nasty odour after a few days.

The idea that someone else should decide when and where he got a hot bath had not been to his liking and the resultant mess had taken out a huge chunk of Lin's afternoon.

Thankfully, perhaps, her friend was treating her coaxing with a much less fierce opposition. He simply ignored her, at least, when she didn't have food. And as long as she wasn't trying to lay some sort of breadcrumb trail out through the door.

Who wanted to eat stale old breadcrumbs anyway? He wasn't a duck.

It was when it didn't even work with his favourite: freshly baked frog pastries, that Lin finally gave up on the idea of trying to get him to come away with her.

'You're just one big bag of trouble, you are,' she chided him gently as she tried to pry open a particularly stubborn fruit.

'Just like this, stupid, frigging thing. Ahhh ... I give up,' Lin let the hard fruit roll to the side. 'Never listens, just like you really. Haven't I told you to stop chewing on the candles?' she said, staring hard at the dragonling, who didn't even bother trying to look guilty.

'Drop that! D'you have any idea how many of those I've had to replace since you took up residence in these chambers? Do you? They're gonna start asking questions soon. Besides, I'm sure they can't be good for you. It's not like you're suffering from wax deficiency or something.'

The dragonling stoically ignored her and spat out a stump that had gotten lodged between its teeth.

'You don't eat them, so why do you have to keep on chewing on them? Stop that I said,' Lin pulled the next one away from him. 'It's not like you're teething, you know. You've *got* all your teeth. Sharp, little devils they are too. I ought to know.'

The dragonling showed her his full complement of pearly jawriders and promptly disappeared around the side of the large oak desk she was leaning against.

A moment later, a screeching noise came around the same way he'd left.

'Yes, yes. I'm *terrified* of you. I told you, stop that. Don't munch candles. Don't swipe things under the rug and stop trying to move the urns around. Seriously...'

Lin shook her head at the dragonling's antics. 'At least you're not messing up MY room,' she said. 'Guess that's something. Now, if your Royal Troublemakerness doesn't mind, I'm going to go make friends with my pillow instead of you.'

It was a good thing she didn't have to trundle off to the barn anymore, Lin thought as she made her way back to her own quarters. The corridors were lit, if a bit sparingly, and you weren't likely to get gobbled up by some passing creature looking for a midnight snack either.

Of course, she mused as she dodged a wizard in blue-striped pyjamas pelting down the hall as if his life depended on it, chasing down a nightcap having sprouted wings, the trek out to her "old" room, had been nice and quiet.

'Well, at least this is warmer and dryer,' Lin said to no one in particular as she eventually pulled the covers over her head. 'And more comfy too.'

A GENTLEMAN IN THE MAKING?

'Right. Get the ball. Get it,' Lin dangled the small spiky seed capsule on a piece of string, making it jump at every pull.

The dragonling swatted at it with a paw. He danced around it, tail in the air. His neck swivelled from side to side, following its every move.

His legs tensed.

He jumped.

Lin yanked the string back.

Whoops. Too slow. The sudden weight tore it right out of her hand. Both dragonling, string and fruit ended up in a small tangled mess on the floor. The creature set off an indignant squeal and then tried to right himself again.

'I see you two are getting along well,' someone said from behind them.

The voice made her jump into the air like a startled child caught with their mouth full of mother's best Sunday cheese.

Drat. She'd been completely absorbed in the mix of string and dragonling. She hadn't heard anyone come in. She should have been more aware. Should have taken more care.

'Archmagus? I—I...' Lin stumbled back onto her feet.

A heartfelt laugh exploded from the Archmagus' lips at her expression. 'Easy there, Little One,' Kaheiron reached out and steadied her. 'My apologies. I didn't mean to startle you.'

'No, sir, of course... I mean ...'

'You should see yourself. Believe that you are going to be "tied up" long?' Kaheiron laughed and nodded towards the bundle of string and dragonling on his floor.

Linandra still wasn't sure exactly what foot to stand on with the Archmagus. On one hand, she spoke respectfully, most of the time. But when she messed up, or plain didn't care he, never seemed interested in punishing her for it ... much.

Still, neither felt quite right to her. It was as though she was constantly missing the point. And a point here or there could be everything that was needed to tip the scales of whatever game life had taken to play with her since she'd left home. Or even before then.

'Well, just look at you,' Kaheiron knelt by the side of the dragonling. 'All tangled up. Now, let me help.'

He spoke steadily and firmly and, as he reached out and teased the bits of string loose from where it had wrapped itself around small necks, legs and other bits, the biggest surprise was that the dragonling didn't try to bite him.

'That's ... just ... amazing,' Lin gasped. 'He's always tried to chew off the hand of anyone who tried to touch him at the faunatarium.'

Free again, the dragonling shook his whole body to make sure there was nothing left of what had trapped him, snapping a couple of times at an itch in his side. Satisfied that he wasn't going back into entanglement, he cast about for something more fun and decided to jump up onto one of the stone tables where he proceeded to curl up, watching the two two-legs intently.

Lin withdrew slightly, satisfied to hover in the background. For every movement she made, she edged towards the door inch by inch.

'I have to confess to being somewhat surprised,' Kaheiron said as he poured some water into a glass bowl for the dragonling to drink. 'Usually he takes to no one.'

'Please, sir. Is he *your* familiar now?' Lin asked hesitatingly.

'What? No. No, nothing like that,' Kaheiron dismissed the idea with a wave of his hand. 'A mage usually doesn't have more than one familiar at a time. A wizard, two. Enchanters shun material creatures for those of the outer ethereal planes and warlocks generally don't look to them at all. What a Kech does is anyone's guess—we don't exactly invite them to stay. There are many more practitioners of the arcane arts in this world. We have only a small selection of them here at the Towers.'

Great. Thanks for the history lesson, old man, but that didn't answer my question, and did it have to be so longwinded? Lin tried not to pout.

'Senny, that is Master Senrel, says that these "dragonlings" are very popular ... with furriers.'

Kaheiron winced. This was an expression rarely seen upon the Archmagus' visage in public. In private, however, it was far from unknown. In fact, he was a whole lot more emotional in private, period.

'We try to discourage it. But aside from posting guards everywhere that these little fellows live, that is just not a viable option. It would end up attracting even more of the kind of attention that we are precisely trying to avoid.'

'Why would anyone do that?'

'You will find, Linandra, that in this world, there is *at least* one person somewhere willing to do that "something" that other folk will not. And if that someone is endued with power and wealth then an idea or an infatuation can spread very easily and very fast.'

'It's not fair.'

'Most things in life aren't,' the Archmagus agreed. 'Still, it's nice seeing the two of you getting along so well. He doesn't seem to have made many friends here and he adamantly refuses to leave.'

At that last, he threw the dragonling an only half-mocking dirty look. The dragonling ignored him. He was far too intent with trying to get the lid off an earthen jar at the other end of the desk. So far, the jar was winning.

'I would be happy to be rid of him,' Kaheiron confessed. 'If only for a while. I've had to put a spell on all storage containers in here. He insists on poking his snout into anything. Don't even get me started on when he and Pickles decide to team up,' the Archmagus sighed, sinking into a large but comfortable-looking chair.

The high-backed ornate wooden backrest might be more suited for a castle, but Lin doubted that any of them would be as forgiving to sit on. Who'd ever heard of *soft* wood?

'So, he's not a familiar then?' she asked.

A small chuckle escaped Kaheiron's otherwise collected image. 'Indeed, he is not,' he said. 'I suppose you could think of him as a pet. A very unruly pet.'

Behind Lin, the dragonling showed his teeth.

'You'll have to train him, of course.'

'What? What do *I* have to do with it?'

'You can hardly be considered to be looking after him if you can't have him obey you, at least a little. I'm not allowing the two of you to band together and run rampant on the premises. I know you both far too well. One walking disaster at a time is more than enough.'

The Archmagus looked over his shoulder to the dragonling that had now curled up into a small tight ball with his tail over his snout several times around.

'Why?' Lin objected. 'What's wrong with the way he is?'

'We require all animals at the Towers to be suitably trained. This is true whether they are familiars or pets or even wild. The Towers' own are, of course, handled separately, but for those who need an extra hand with familiars or pets, there are group sessions running at regular intervals. I'll make arrangements for you to join them. I'm afraid I really can't let this little fellow run around without learning some manners and he seems to like you.'

If the Archmagus had expected this piece of news to be greeted with any enthusiasm, he could hardly have been more mistaken.

'I imagine that it will take a great deal of work,' Kaheiron added ruefully when he caught the look on the young woman's face.

'Great,' Lin rolled her eyes.

For a moment, Kaheiron wondered if this was actually a very wise course of action. Just what had he started? By the looks of things, it was hard to tell who'd need more training, Linandra or the dragonling.

'I don't think he'd obey me,' Lin muttered mutinously.

'Oh, I think he will,' Kaheiron chuckled.

Lin still didn't look particularly happy about it by the time she was ready to leave. She'd wanted a buddy, not a bunch of extra responsibilities.

'Keep in mind,' Kaheiron called after her as she walked out, duster and dragonling in tow, 'that a master is responsible for all the actions of his or her pet or familiar.'

'Wonderful,' Lin grumped. And just as she was getting used to how things worked around here. Well, she had asked not to be alone anymore, that was true. And she had lamented the monotony her days had gained when the drag-onling was lost. This just wasn't what she'd had in mind.

And what were the regulars going to think? It wasn't like she was an established part of the place after all—not like that. To say nothing about her not enjoying the thought of facing one of those classes where young mages and other people paraded around their perfectly behaved pets.

* * *

'I do wish you'd stop that. I'm sure that good boys don't swing around tree branches like pirouetting monkeys.'

Seth landed lightly on his bare feet.

'You know, you can be a stuffy old bore when you want to be,' he said. 'Lighten up a bit, won't you?'

'I really do wish you'd stop treating this like an expedition into the unknown put together merely for your own amusement. There are other factors at play here, so stop playing around.'

'Didn't you just contradict yourself?' Seth laughed at the older dragon's expression.

'You know full well what I mean. And do desist from changing the subject. Will you or will you not take this matter seriously?'

'Oh, very well,' Seth settled down. Yawning, he stretched himself to his full extent. 'And I'm not "playing around".'

'You better not be or I will be seriously disappointed with you. You've made some remarkable progress on your own. I shall look forward to seeing you continue to do so in more social settings.'

'It better not involve me picking up strange smelly packages again,' Seth eyed his mentor suspiciously. 'I had to bathe *three times* just to get the stench out, last time.'

It was Kaheiron's turn to let out a hearty guffaw. 'If you hadn't left it out in the sun while going fishing for lunch, then the concoction inside wouldn't have heated up and begun to ferment,' he said.

Seth tried not to pout. Maybe it was time for a change? Another one.

🐲 🐲 🐲

'And good riddance too,' Seth had said to his reflection, years and years ago. Odd how they seemed to matter so much more now than before?

His shop window self hadn't replied back, but it didn't disagree with him either. How nice of it, he thought. Of course, it was a *nice* reflection: anyone could see that. It had taken him several years to make enough preparations and to learn the "lay of the land," as the people around here called it, but he'd finally done it. He'd finally taken the step to move into the outer world *permanently*, well, for the time being.

Maybe he'd tire of it. Maybe he wouldn't. Who could tell?

'Is this the appearance of someone who has become bored with life?' he asked.

His image looked back at him. His hair was as unruly as ever, he thought. If he forgot to brush it, it ended up looking like someone had dumped a mop on his head, steel-grey colour and all. Currently, it was poking out from underneath a jauntily placed green velvet hat. Seth wasn't sure about the green *or* the hat. Maybe hats weren't his thing, after all.

The rest of him was much more appealing, he thought, even if he still looked a bit boyish around the face. Of course, he was dressed for the occasion, in something splendid and rich-looking, even if he had no idea what it actually was. It was enough that it lent him passage into the places he wished to enter and that it kept people from mistaking him for someone even younger than he was.

'Right. Best be off, you, or you'll miss *all* the fun,' the reflection seemed to say, a mischievous twinkle in its grey eyes.

'Time doesn't move *that* fast,' Seth replied.

'What do you know of time?' his reflexion taunted him. 'How long have you kept a house in this city? A year? A decade? A semi centennial? And only now do you attend yourself? What of the other places you've claimed?'

'A dragon's way is not the same as others,' Seth insisted.

The mirror image said nothing in return, just stayed still and blank like always.

'And I *do* know what a year is,' he muttered as he walked out the door. 'It's a measurement for a very short amount of time.'

Strolling down the rest of the street, he enjoyed watching the people as he went by.

He couldn't really say what fascinated him so much about other species. Maybe it was simply that their lives weren't his? And as an added bonus, their troubles weren't his either.

It certainly wasn't because their lives were often so very, very short indeed, if they weren't near the top of the food chain. But he couldn't help finding them intriguing all the same.

Everything, from the way they changed with the seasons (well, some of them did, either by alternating their outer layers of clothing or by growing thicker fur) to how different the interactions between the individuals could be: small, social, lonely and everything in between and not just for the individuals, either.

Of course, for some peoples he didn't have access to a whole lot of information, but he could still extrapolate, build theories and come to conclusions. How many of those conclusions were actually right? Seth didn't know. He hadn't found a way to actually verify things yet. All he had was his own company. It'd be easier if there were others, peers, that he could discuss things with but so far anyone like that had failed to appear.

Until a certain point, the creatures at the lower end of the great circle of life were simpler to study. The fact that the "societies" (if they had any) evolved so quickly meant he could follow successive generations very swiftly, and any questions he had might be answered much sooner than if studying something that led their lives on par with the aging of a dragon such as himself.

The trouble with them was that what made them so easy to examine also meant that when he studied them at a more individual level, it felt like if he took his eyes off them for even a minute they'd have vanished into thin air.

There were few things more frustrating than having taken an interest in what, say, subject A was doing and how things were going to work out now that subject B was no longer interested in them, than going away for lunch and, upon your return, finding that not only did subject A and B seem nowhere to be found, but there was a big fat toad C there instead.

There were plenty of scratch marks around his old home relating to his frustration by now. Even his best friend—hah, some friend—had given him some very queer looks when Setharrion had first attempted to interest him too in this new hobby of his. His mother had thought him crazy to be interested in the first place. Guess he'd been lucky that she'd ended up misunderstanding the reason for said interest.

What would they have done if they'd known the whole story? Seth had spent a lot of time thinking about that. It wasn't a comforting thought, so he'd kept it to himself.

Now, he wasn't as worried. It was highly unlikely that he'd find one of them wandering down the street. And even if they had, they had no way of recognizing him, not like this.

Seth scratched at an itch on his left hand. 'So, what should I do today?' he asked of the air when stomach twisted a little. 'Hmm, maybe I start with finding some food. Honestly, this body seems to be constantly hungry. Another inconvenience.'

No doubt his so-called friend, and anyone that sad excuse for a dragon had told, had believed that he'd studied these creatures from as far away as possible, using the excellent vision that so many dragons were blessed with, to see without being seen.

They had a point, no matter whatever else you could say about it, several tons of flying teeth and muscle had a tendency to gather attention whether it wanted to or not.

So he hadn't. It could be quite upsetting to disturb your studies by scattering them for miles in the case of some of the more volatile and speedy ones. It had wreaked havoc with his plans at times.

If they'd know just how close he was now? 'No, best not to go there,' Seth shuddered.

After changing his form, being able to creep up, to get really close, had turned out to have its drawbacks too. He'd discovered that quickly. No one liked having pointy barbed things imbedded in your soles. As a dragon, he'd hardly ever had to pay attention to where he put his feet. Not beyond the "will this cliff hold me or am I going to sink too deep in this mud,' anyway.

For some time, his whole self had seemed little more than a walking disaster waiting to happen. Learning how to cope had been an interesting experience. He might even have had second thoughts about the whole thing if he'd known all that from the beginning.

Because it meant he spent a lot of time worrying about such insignificant things as sharp objects (what dragon was bothered by something as ridiculous as knives?) or things with more teeth than himself (few dragons did that either. There were creatures out there that even a lone dragon didn't care to face off with. They just didn't *worry* about them. Sensible dragons settled inland, far away from where such beings staked their territory).

No, his early escapades had hardly been the equivalent of taking an evening stroll along a river by a market town or perambulating down the main avenue of a major city; where the streets were bordered by trees and fountains played in the gardens.

Once he'd reached those, he'd grown to like those visits, and, by now, he'd learnt to put up with the frailties of his new form. That didn't mean he had to like it. Naturally, he took every precaution, but you never knew when the unexpected would strike.

Besides, this wasn't a mere market town. It wasn't anything as grand as the cities he'd thought of either; well, maybe it'd be more accurate to say it didn't have the same sort of glittering, airy, quality to it. It was sizeable enough though, and it certainly didn't lack in immense buildings either.

'Oh, excuse me, young man. Wasn't watching where I was going,' a man, wearing, what to Seth looked like a towel, draped over his body, said before hurrying off on sandaled feet.

Seth nodded as he passed. You saw quite a few people like that here, of all ages and species. It meant they were heading to one of the large bathhouses.

There hadn't always been bathing houses, almost everything in the city's higher reaches had once been temples or structures attending the temples, and it showed. All of them had been converted within, but the bathing houses remained almost entirely as they had once been inside and outside.

Not that he was sure of *what* they'd been. Some sort of ritual pools maybe? He'd visited them often enough. They were pleasant, especially if you could afford a private pool rather than a public one. Sure, they were smaller—a lot smaller—and usually housed in rooms all to themselves, but Seth liked his privacy at times like that. Society was something you visited: it wasn't something you invited into your house.

Unlike the bath houses, which tended to be calm, quiet places with curious echoes, out here, the streets bustled with life. There was no other way he could describe it.

True, they didn't bustle quite as much up here as down in the market district, where, since it was in the middle of summer, many of the traders had moved both some of their stock as well as a suitable member of the family to keep an eye on it, out, to line the street outside of the shops themselves.

Those streets didn't have the fortune of having a surface of bricks laid out in decorative patterns. They weren't even cobbled. While a little soggy in winter, after the odd rain shower, the ochre dust turned a touch muddy, right now the place was filled with colours of every kind; from the marquees used as sunshades to the hastily erected roofs of cloth, vibrant shades impacted on your eyes from every direction. And that wasn't even counting the wimples and flags and myriad of other decorations and bunting that proudly declared this to be Founder's Day: a day that, if you'd been further north, would have been the solstice celebrations.

The mixture of people who inhabited the quite sizable town, or minor city (depending on how you looked at it), of Amorix had found a time of year that they *all* celebrated (if all a bit differently), stuck a convenient label on it, and had just taken things from there. Over the years, the different traditions marked by individuals or groups had sort of melted together until none that now lived here could remember what the original customs had been.

Seth didn't care about any of that. *He* came here for the sweets. The city veritably exploded with them at this time of the year. If he wasn't careful, he'd end up spending a whole lot more than he should, but he didn't really care about that, either. It was worth it, he thought.

'I'll have that one,' the elegantly dressed young man pointed at a plain white bun. 'Two of the stuffed rolls, a score of the chocolate mints and some of those toffees.'

'Very good, sir. Which toffee would the young gentleman like?'

'Hmm,' Seth peered closer at them. 'Those ones, with the blue petals. What are those?'

'Oh, those are River Roses. That's a candied blue rose petal on top. They taste quite different. Would you like to try one?' the stallholder asked.

'Yes,' Seth replied. Chewing thoughtfully for a moment, he then asked for the entire plate.

The old lady who was serving him chuckled at the way his eyes had lit up. Her two younger helpers satisfied themselves with tittering and giggling behind their hands.

Seth didn't quite understand what they found so amusing, but he smiled at them, which just set them off again. He left the stall having arranged for his purchases to be delivered to his house (well, one of them anyway), feeling like he was missing the joke.

'There's still so much left to learn,' he mused.

It was the first time he'd been out on the streets during the celebration. Usually, he just stayed indoors and had the servants bring him anything he wanted. He swallowed reflexively at that thought. It was the one time in the year when he actually shuddered at the idea of what would be waiting for him when he eventually returned "home."

Trying to shake off the gloomy feeling, Seth looked around him.

He knew that the day hadn't remained a purely decorative holiday mix for long. The rulers had quickly appropriated it for themselves.

As such, wimples of the sun or moon, some with four rays, others with six and yet others with squiggly lines going in all sorts of directions, mixed with those adorned by stars, an axe of wheat or other, older, symbols that were generally only seen when people were trying to be nostalgic and traditional at the same time and didn't quite remember why.

Most prominent among them all were those that proclaimed this to be Founder's Day: a blue double tail stamped with a stylistic, garishly red, twisted twin boar. This was the mark of "The House," as the king and his family were referred to out here, far from their centre of power.

Sometimes, people said it reverentially, sometimes there was a snarky touch to the tone, but they all knew of whom they were speaking. It had been sneaked into much smaller versions as well.

Symbols that were popular among customers, selling well as earrings or medallions usually weren't very popular in wimples. They preferred, often, more generic items.

There was one other though, that, while not signifying a ruling house, here or anywhere else, wasn't going to be mistaken for an old symbol dusted off for a new era. Strangers from distant lands—very distant even, it had developed quite the reputation over the years—might even know of it, but if you lived anywhere within these borders you made it your business to know it.

That was because you were much more likely to encounter an irate mage, upset that he'd just stepped into the snare that you'd meant for that wily fox whose pelt you were after, out in the wilds here, than you were a tax collector. This was also generally considered more troublesome for you, as the government official *wasn't* likely to turn you into a small red vegetable or make you grow six extra legs.

There might be *more* tax collectors, but mages and the other arcane users were generally more seasoned travellers and they didn't always feel the need to use the roads provided. As unpleasant as getting on the wrong side of one of the king's men could be, at least they were restricted to mundane means of ensuring that you learnt just how upset they were. Even a novice user of magic was inclined to get … creative under such circumstances.

No, no one here would mistake the two pointy towers crowned by the sliver of a moon as new as day for anything other than what it was: the symbol of the "nearby" collection of "magical hocus pocus fellows"—as some less generous members of society called them—though rarely out loud and *never* within hearing range of said fellows.

While not the Twin Towers weren't actively involved in politics, the local and not-so-local powerhouses had, eventually, learnt to leave the place alone.

Aside from that they would have needed to round up a fair amount of highly skilled arcane users themselves (which wasn't as easy as it sounded, as most wizards and their ilk didn't like sharing geography with each other, and often settled far apart) there was another drawback.

Most of the time, you didn't need high-end mages, but when you did, you needed them fast, and having, just the other month, tried to swat them out like flies, might turn out to not having been such a good idea, after all. Not that some hadn't tried.

They also tended to live longer than the average ploughman and could hold a grudge like no other. It was a terrible thing to still be paying for what your great-grandfather might have done to the specialist you were now trying to elicit the ear of, especially when you'd never even met the man.

As someone had said in passing when Seth had carefully queried about it:

'Sonny... *anyone* taking on that bunch of nutjobs has to be either crazy or *crazier*. They blow things up even when they're *not* supposed to.'

'Surely they can't be *that* powerful?' Seth, sounding rather dubious, had asked. He was accustomed to "draconic" magic. Surely, such meagre lived species couldn't hope to have learnt to wield such forces?

'I think the Archmagus *alone* would do,' a fellow bather had chuckled heartedly.

'*I* heard one of the lords at the king's court sent someone over years ago to talk to them about the land the king "owns" up there. Spent three days as a newt, that negotiator did,' someone else joined in.

'I heard it was a groundhog.'

'No, no. What you need to worry about are the familiars,' a wizened male had interrupted. 'Gouge your eyes out they will. Well, some of them would,' he muttered mutinously.

'So would a carrioncrawler.'

'And *they* wouldn't need a command either.'

'Wouldn't accept one. Could you imagine? One of those things, trained? Who'd want one?'

As the people got into a discussion over whether they liked it one way or another, Seth had wondered if he should pay the place a visit after all.

Well, since then, he had. It hadn't been quite what he'd expected.

'You know, I've been meaning to ask you for a while. *Can* anyone here really turn someone into an animal?'

'It is not an easy task, but yes, I do believe several should be able to do so with greater or lesser success. Why do you ask?'

'Oh, just something I overheard, once.'

'Well, it is not something I intend to teach you,' Kaheiron said. 'You would, without doubt, get creative.'

PECULIAR PRIORITIES

They were back in the apple orchard, she and the dragonling. Why did they so often seem to drift here these days? Maybe it was because so few others did? It was, mostly, nice and quiet and devoid of company.

You heard stories about what happened to anyone caught lifting apples they weren't supposed to. Some tried anyway, of course. Hence the stories, Lin figured. But she had no interest in scrumping. Apples weren't her favourite anyway, even if they *did* grow on trees.

Anyway, if anyone was going to be doing that—scrumping that was—it'd be her four-legged friend. If there *was* something protecting the orchard, and she'd never seen anything, it obviously didn't have any orders regarding small obnoxious lizards with wings.

After Lin's chores—which had grown remarkably light since her new-found friend had decided to bestow his company on her—had ended for the day, you often found them retreating here for some peace and quiet. Everyone had heard the stories and mostly they stayed out of the orchard if they could help it.

Actually, it wasn't so much since she'd ended up chained to the small creature that her chores, such as they were, had grown steadily less abundant. It was more since he'd decided that *he* should be getting the attention that she normally had to reserve for pots and pans.

Whatever a small dragonling was, it certainly wasn't welcome company for people trying to get on with some serious work. And with him being under the Archmagus' protection, any desire to squash him that the staff might have—and he'd given them reason to have plenty—was, well, squashed. So, they shooed her and the dragonling away.

Not that Lin minded terribly. It wasn't like she went out of her way to throw her energy at others, but she did feel it should have been her choice not to, not theirs.

True, dusting was probably the only thing she did fairly regularly these days. It wasn't as if the dust was afraid of the small inquisitive thing and ran away screaming should it decide to, unannounced, launch itself upon it, or try to burrow into your hair or pocket, after all.

The maids were resolutely refusing to go anywhere near her these days, as long as the dragonling was around. But the local spellcasters were a little more tolerant. Besides, most of the time it became a staring contest between their familiar and the dragonling, with some rustling and hissing to add a bit of colour to the occasion.

'Guess they see enough trouble on their own. One small dragon isn't going to add much,' Lin had mused.

She'd also kept helping out at the faunatarium. That didn't count as work. That was something she enjoyed. He had growled about that too, of course. But this time he'd been overruled. There was no way a tiny winged lizard was going to stop her.

Not that he'd given in quietly.

'Don't be so selfish,' Lin had told him sharply while examining an abrasion on the leg of a piebald draft.

He'd sulked for days after that. She kept calling him Grumpy and that suited him perfectly.

Lately though, he'd taken to do no more than just fly up to a high shelf or beam and emit a kind of low-level grudging sound until it was time to leave. It was a bit like the opposite of a cat's gentle purr bestowed upon those around it when it was anything but content. It went straight into your bones.

Lin thought he was being silly.

While not exactly being the "faithful mutt bringing his master's slippers" she'd always wanted (rather than the torn-eared rags that had been around the family farm), he had begun to leave little things out for her—like that time she'd found her best scarf below the bed rather than in the cupboard where it belonged, or the dead mouse in her sockdrawer.

Or maybe she was reading too much into it. It could just be him telling her she wasn't paying enough attention to him. That'd be just like the little darling too, she thought.

'Greedy little menace, aren't you?' Lin said, a fond smile tugging at the corners of her lips.

Turning her eyes upwards when something dropped on her head, she frowned at her companion. 'You're not liking me much today, are you?' Lin asked of the small flapping being while picking up the brown pit and tossing it from hand to hand.

The dragonling cocked his head at her as he made himself comfortable among the branches.

'Aren't you supposed to be the one keeping *me* company? If you're not gonna bother, maybe you should go chase a mouse or something? That'd keep you busy, but probably not out of mischief.'

The curious behaviour didn't end there, either. While he usually stayed quite close by, he still didn't seem too keen on physical contact. 'Strange little bugger, aren't you,' Lin had said so often she felt she was wearing out her vocal chords.

She downed a handful of nuts and, sure as rain follows a forecast of sunshine, there was an indignant squeal from above.

'Well, I'm not getting up. If you want some, you're the one that's gonna have to move your little legs.'

The dragonling, realizing that he wasn't going to get any nuts unless he dislodged himself from the branch where he'd finally managed to get all nice and snug, snorted at the idea.

'This is why this place is sooo good,' Lin stretched, fighting back a yawn. 'No one ever comes here. What I could do with is a nice, long nap.'

Make that *almost* never comes here, her mind added all on its own, insisting that people probably came here all the time, when there were apples and cherries and peaches or any of the other strange fruit that grew on the trees and bushes here.

She could just see the conversation. 'We have a lovely cherry tree. Would you like to see it?' 'Oh why, yes, very much, where is it?' 'In the apple-orchard.'

Oh yes, that threw people a loop, alright.

She remembered the first time she'd been sent to collect some berries. The one place she hadn't looked had been the orchard. Who'd ever heard of people growing berries in an apple orchard? Couldn't they just have called it a fruit garden or something? Made you wonder what else might be lurking about if you poked your nose into the wrong place.

At the moment, the branches of the particular tree she was sitting under were bare of anything, including the obligatory green leaves. There might be one or two, but that was it. What was with that? It was in the middle of summer. Shouldn't it be full of both leaves *and* fruit? Even if they were late fruits there should at least be leaves, right? There certainly were enough leaves on the other trees, well, most of them.

'Who ever heard of something stupid like that? Apples grow *every* year, they don't just skip one.'

Apparently, these did. Perennials, that's what Mrs. Sarrrrinth had called them. Linandra understood the concept easily enough. What she had trouble with was applying it to apples.

'Who wants stupid trees not having fruit every year? Maybe I've got them confused. Was it re-annuals she said?' Linandra frowned. That would have made more sense. Getting more than one crop per year was something her father sure wouldn't have said no to.

Deciding that was enough thinking, she took a bite out of her lunch instead, ripping off a large chunk with her teeth. The small brown loaf was soft against her gullet. The ham on it, mixed with the salad, was making it more dinner than lunch, had this been anywhere else she'd worked. One thing for sure, you didn't go hungry in this place. If anything, you were fed too much, if such a thing was possible.

On top of that, the bread was fresh, baked just this morning. She often wandered past the kitchen windows and the aromas that drifted out of them were enough to make any mouth water.

'Wizards,' she snorted. 'Probably some idiot getting his spell wrong made all this.'

Most people had a lot of respect (or fear) of those who used magic in any of its forms. Lin should know, she'd been one of them.

But since coming here she'd seen the *other* side of magic. Not the one where mountains blew up or whole armies were wiped from the plains on which they fought with a single word. But the one where the spells erupted and needed to be chased down by a whole horde of mages in bunny slippers before they could escape the grounds; where cauldrons bubbled over because the fire had been left on too long, just melt or, occasionally, burn up because the spell ran out and they returned to being a wicker-basket, all because the attending sorcerer had become distracted by something more interesting.

And those were some of the more mundane events—not because they didn't cause trouble, but because they happened so often.

There were mages who, while perfectly able to create towering infernos of fire, who called upon the spirits of the ether and had them obey, to nevertheless also be quite incapable of tying their own shoelaces. Good thing most of them didn't wear any then, Lin thought.

True, she wouldn't want to make either sort angry, but it was difficult to be afraid, really properly afraid, of anyone once you'd seen them running down the hall—nightshirt flapping; one foot in a red slipper and the other in a pointy silver shoe; half a braided beard and a slightly smoking eyebrow— chasing their nightcap which had suddenly sprouted wings and decided it didn't want to be drunk at all, glucking all the way down the corridor and out the door.

Respect their powers, sure, she did that. She didn't want to spend the rest of her life as some sort of rodent, after all. But fear them? No, not the way she used to. Not a chance.

There were those you should keep away from though. Not everyone here held themselves to the same standards as Kaheiron seemed to, especially not if you crossed them.

Technically, the Twin Towers didn't differ between how someone achieved their connection with the energy that was the source of their abilities. It was probably one of the few places in the world where wizards and mages, sorcerers and enchanters and goodness knew what else, all came together under one roof and *without* killing each other in the process.

That was one of the things that made the place such a powerhouse and not just in the arcane realm either. Whatever type of magic you'd try and wield against them, there was bound to be someone within those walls who had studied it, if only as a past-time, and knew more about it than you did.

No, you'd have to be insane to attack a place like this with extraordinary means, never mind with ones like swords and cutlasses.

It was a good thing it wasn't located anywhere near the coast or there might have been some very unfortunate plunderers coming along once in a while. Everyone knew that the seas brought strange.

There were, however, a much higher concentration of mages than there was of any other type of wielder of the arcane arts. Also, because of their familiarity with each other and a fair bit of crossing over between the different fields, there was a tendency to call anyone and everyone a mage, pure and simple, never mind what actual magic they practiced, as long as it wasn't something dark and dripping. That confused the blazers out of anyone visiting.

'Maybe it's meant to,' Lin frowned.

True, some things weren't allowed to be actively practiced, but you'd still be bound to find at least one book on the subject. The Towers had quite an extensive library especially considering that most of the actual population in the kingdom didn't know how to read.

'Overrated, reading. Bad for you. You can catch all sorts of things from those books you can. Never know where they've been, see.'

That had been her father's attitude towards the whole idea that some squiggly lines actually needed to be bothered with.

Linandra huffed. So far, she hadn't seen any reason to question that. She'd done all right for herself, hadn't she? True, here, that dismissiveness of the written word had earned her few friends.

They were *keen* on reading here. And if they weren't busy with that, they were scribbling away at something of their own. She wondered just how many half-burned, scrunched up, bits of parchment she'd had cleaned up by now?

Linandra didn't care much, but the ones where the dragonling had gotten to them first tended to be soggy. The little beast chewed on them. He gnawed on a lot of things now that she thought about it.

But the people? Those coming here to further their arcane studies she thought of as pompous fools.

'What's this obsession with reading that they've all got? It can't really do them all that much good. Can it?' Lin complained to the only one who'd listen, the dragonling.

Her little tirade was, however, today, interrupted.

Someone else was in the orchard. She could hear them trudging around a bit further away, going back and forth as if they were looking for something. Or someone.

Lin shaded her eyes. 'Company, Grumpy,' she said. She closed her eyes and pretended she hadn't noticed them. That usually worked. Unfortunately, it looked like they'd heard her and were now making a beeline right for her.

Why? It wasn't like she was meant to be somewhere else. And she had as much right to be here as the rest of the inhabitants, that she was sure of. As long as she didn't nab any apples or other things on the way out, that was.

Snuggling back into the bark, she pretended to snooze. It was her favourite tree after all. It had a comfortable spot just where her back bent inwards.

She could feel the change in the light as the shadow fell over her. Drat. Couldn't they just go away?

A loud 'ahem' forced her eyes open. Or, at least, the small expulsion of air that followed it, did.

'The Archmagus has instructed me to bring you to him,' the old man said.

Linandra would have preferred to ignore him, but that rarely worked out well. She sighed. Much easier to just find out what he wanted. Kaheiron was, despite that she rather liked him, not someone she'd want to test the boundaries of … too much.

'What d'you want?' she asked grouchily.

'I believe I have already informed you of as much.'

'Why do I need to go? There's a whole horde of folks at his command. He can ask someone else, easily,' Lin said, capturing the end of a piece of straw and biting into it. Yeach … sour.

Istarrian took a deep, calming breath. He was used to the antics of mature wizards. The trials of youth had long since faded into mere memory.

'The Archmagus has asked you and your companion—personally—to join him,' Istarrian's tone suggested that she should consider this quite the honour.

Pfft … what did he know? 'Oh, all right,' Lin waved the arguments away, 'alright, I'll go see what he wants.'

Istarrian, mission accomplished, turned and headed out of the orchard. It took a little while until he noticed that there were two missing from the party he was supposed to be leading. Turned out the people he'd come to fetch hadn't moved.

Linandra feigned surprise when he challenged her. 'You meant, like right now?' she blinked at him.

Istarrian didn't say anything this time. Some people could apparently get under your skin without even trying. He simply waited, hoping that his sheer refusal to leave until she came along would be enough incentive.

Trying to get the dragonling to do anything he asked, he'd already learned, was completely futile. It was content with completely ignoring his existence unless he tried to pick it up.

Yes, technically he could *make* her come. There were all sorts of means for that. He might be old, but he wasn't ready to retire from the world of magic just yet. There were one or two spells in him still. But Istarrian suspected that the Archmagus might, on this occasion, disagree with the matter being handled that way.

Eventually managing to cajole Linandra into following, they'd reached the office in question only after several bits of lawn had been traversed and stairs had been climbed. The apple orchard lay off to the side of the Tower's main building, beyond more well-manicured stretches of grass and more decorative vegetation.

Peculiar, Lin thought. She'd figured that they'd be going to the chambers she'd met the dragonling in. That place was, while studious, also private and it showed.

This place wasn't anything like that. She tried not to make a spectacle of it, as if this was somewhere she walked into every day. But she still tried to see everything out of the corners of her eyes.

This wasn't the office, either. That was kept to greet visiting dignitaries or potential clients alike. The rest of the time it was kept closed. It was only opened when someone particularly important was visiting, someone that the Archmagus wanted to impress. That was the one where everything was clean and looking the epitome of efficiency with more than a touch of grandeur.

So, this must be where he actually worked, Lin mused. Guess he didn't want to play around with strange and dangerous stuff right where he lived? Even she could see the sense in that.

Besides, she, of anyone, should know that those little excursions into the unknown often ended up causing quite a bad smell. It was the smoke and incense, she'd decided. It always gave her a headache. You probably didn't want that right next to where you slept.

Here, there were bookshelves lining nearly every wall. They weren't normally what she'd put down as "her thing," but she had to admit these ones looked impressive, all gnarly wood and carved shelves, friezes of animals running, deer and wolves and other more fantastical beasts leaping and frolicking from shelf to shelf.

The books, which fought for place here, alongside scrolls of varying sizes, seemed different from the ones in his study. It took a moment before she could put a finger on what it was. They looked … used. Yes, that was it. Well thumbed, often stained, and, by the looks of it, even scorched.

Guess staying this close to anything liable to blow up had its drawbacks.

There were several long narrow tables along the walls. Not a single large comfy chair was in sight. The only stool was a rickety old thing that had seen better days two centuries ago. Sitting on that might be outright hazardous to your health, if going by the slight tint of green. Was that mould? No, it couldn't be. Mrs. Sarrrrinth wouldn't have stood for it.

The old mirrors that brightened up the study and made it seem larger than it was were completely missing from here. It felt closed in and just a little stuffy.

The only thing to reflect the light from the candles, lit despite the time of day, were some metallic urns at the far end of the first room. Lin was staring right at one with a large crack running zigzag right through it.

Random scrolls lay about, as if they'd been absentmindedly picked up and brought along until their carrier had realized he had no idea why he was holding them.

Looking down at the stone floor, Linandra wished she was wearing thicker soles. The place was completely devoid of rugs and the flagstones were like ice. Not very slippery, perhaps, but the chill was spreading all the way up her legs.

Yikes, Linandra thought. All it's missing is the armour in the corner and it'd be just like a place for some weird lord with too much time on his hand.

'Welcome, said the dragon to the knight,' she said and shuddered. 'Grumpy, get down from there at once!' Lin cried out as the dragonling, which had been sniffing around the bottom of the bookcase, launched himself onto a higher shelf.

Ignoring her, the dragonling instead stared intently at a contraption rolled into a corner of the room. Above a set of bronze wheels, a large ball of energy crackled, shooting off small bits of magic.

Suddenly she realized that, that was where most of the light came from.

'Ah, there you are, Linandra. Very good of you to come so promptly,' Kaheiron said, narrowly managing to keep the sarcasm out of it. 'Istarrian, I do believe that one of the lords from Amorix is arriving in the morning. Could you have a suitable arrangement set up for the "Office?"'

'Of course, Archmagus,' Istarrian made a small bow.

'Get off me … Shoo!' Lin tried to fend off another new arrival who'd tottered in from the next room. This one was neither humanoid, nor the dragonling, who was content with chattering at it from his shelf.

'Don't know what I'd do without him,' the Archmagus confessed as Istarrian departed. Then he noticed the commotion happening under his nose. 'Oh, don't mind him, Little One. He's not going to bite. Just shoo him to the side if he bothers you.'

Linandra prodded the offending creature gently. It didn't seem to help. If anything, it made it even more insistent. Now it was trying to put its feathered and furry blue head into her side-pocket.

'Shoo … Get lost will you!'

At this, from up on one of the shelves, there came a small snigger.

'Fat lot of help you are,' Lin shot the dragonling a fiery glance.

Kaheiron offered her the plate he'd been holding, as if just remembering what was in his hands. It was stacked with small oval bits of pastry.

'Hold this for a moment, will you?'

'Err … right.' Lin tried to balance the bit of ceramic with its towering load, while avoiding stepping on anything or anyone.

Kaheiron knotted his eyebrows, making them look far bushier than they were. 'Swallowtail, leave the young lady alone,' he commanded.

The withdrawal of the weird beastie was quite the relief to Linandra. She moved away a bit further, just in case it'd change its mind.

'I'd say he's harmless, but their bites are poisonous. Not to fear … he knows not to bite a friend,' Kaheiron added when he saw her whitening expression. 'Do watch out for the spikes.'

'Why? Are they poisonous too?'

'No. But the barbs will break off under your skin. They are more a nuisance than dangerous, but they can cause a bit of a rash if not removed.'

'Wonderful. And that's what you keep as a pet is it?' Lin asked, narrowly avoiding a sneer.

'Swallowtail is a familiar, not a pet. Like most of his kind, he has no fondness for open spaces or people, so he usually stays here. By the way, do try one of the rolls, if you'd like,' Kaheiron said off-handedly, while continuing his search for whatever it was he'd put down.

Suddenly, he snatched up a tightly wound scroll. 'Ah, there it is. I was just wondering where I'd put that. You know, one day they really will have to come up with some search spell that actually works. Every time we try, all that ends up happening is that the room gets demolished. Yes?'

This last was directed at Linandra who was coughing, trying to get the taste of the cakeroll out of her nose and mouth. It'd be nice if it could get out of her memory as well.

'Oh dear. Not that bad surely?'

The Archmagus took one look at her expression and promptly changed the subject. 'I do believe that it is high time that we begin giving you a bit more to do around here,' he said instead.

'What?' Linandra drew herself up. Wasn't it enough what she was doing already? Cleaning and dusting and generally helping out? Okay, so right now she wasn't actually doing much of either, but still.

'You have far too much time on your hands, Little One. It is time we put that time to good use. Especially after what happened the other day,' he added thoughtfully.

Oh, that... Lin had tried to forget about it. So far, she hadn't had much success.

'Now. Not even the best teacher in the world would be able to instil in their student a connection to the ethereal energies, the life force of the universe, who does not already possess it. And I'm afraid that you do not show any such connection at all.'

Oh good. That was a relief. That left her out of it then. Lin felt better already.

Kaheiron was beginning to sound like himself again too. She couldn't say for sure why it bothered her when the Archmagus went all "ordinary folks," but it did.

The rest of the time she might only understand half of the words that were coming out of that mouth, but it felt more right that way ... more ... comforting. As if there was a big world out there and she didn't need to worry about being a part of it.

'However, there are those things that lie within the ability of any sentient, and reasonably intelligent, being to fathom. I think we will start with having you learn to read.'

'Oh yuck,' Lin screwed up her face in protest. Anything but that. What sane person cared about reading: it was for weaklings.

Wait. Where did that come from? It seemed so familiar. As if spoken by a voice from long ago that she could only barely hear but no longer identify. Oh yes, that had always been her father's opinion. Lin had never realized how many of those that had rubbed off on her. Double-yuck.

'Now, now, I already know what you are about to say but I,' and he stressed the word, 'believe it is something that will benefit you greatly in the future.'

'When do I start, sir,' Lin asked, dejected. Not that she was falling back on the old maid routine. It might have been more venomous than usual, but ever since the Archmagus "gave" her the dragonling to look after, she'd been seeing him from time to time and—considering that it was usually while trying to explain away the latest antics of the creature—the fact her head was still attached (not to mention she still hadn't spent any time as a root vegetable for being insolent), she'd kind of come to regard him as a somewhat strange uncle.

A *very* strange uncle. Twice removed.

That didn't mean he couldn't still make her jump when she thought she'd done something bad.

'Why not now?' Kaheiron said.

Oh great… Just what she wanted to do on such a nice day as today. Stay inside and bury herself in some rubbish piece of paper that'd probably make her sneeze from all the dust it had been gathering.

'Oh, bother.'

'Mind your language, young lady.'

'Yes, Archmagus,' Lin replied, still not managing to achieve the "demure" expression, despite practice.

Linandra thought she'd get away with not having to do any writing at the very least, but apparently that, too, was on the agenda. In turn, the dragonling ended up torn between sulking over not getting as much attention as he'd like and a desire to change this.

'Stop helping, Grumpy. You just got ink all over my dress, you menace!' Lin said only a quarter of an hour later.

Weeks trickled by, lessons and work soon intermingling until she could hardly tell them apart by the time her head hit the pillows for the night.

It was things like this that made her have second thoughts about staying at the Towers. Sure, it was convenient, but her idea of getting on with life wasn't trying to cram half the world and its brother into her brain. If anything, it wasn't nearly large enough, she thought.

There weren't any classes for these sorts of things. Almost all of those who came here to study were already well-versed in these basics since years back. Those that weren't, showed up too infrequently for anything official to be organized.

But, as it turned out, on top of her new schedule involving reading and writing, Lin also found herself up to her neck in the type of things that she'd normally refer to as "silly" and occasionally as "rubbish."

And all this about trying to learn to walk "properly?" What was up with that? Didn't everyone know that already? It wasn't as if she was crawling on all fours now, was it? What did they think she was, some sort of cavewoman who could only communicate in grunts?

There was an extensive and ridiculous amount of time devoted to dining, too. Sure, she'd always known that things were different than they'd be at home. But seriously, what was wrong with using a spoon when everything just kept falling off the fork?

And who cared about what stupid order things went in, anyway? Just one knife for the lot, that's what they needed. They should stop making such a ruddy fuss about it. As far as Lin was concerned, if it was on the plate, it was food and if it was food it should be in her mouth.

Despite her misgivings on that, she still got annoyed when the dragonling took advantage of her distraction, snatched something off her plate and made a run for it.

To top it all off, once she no longer stumbled through the basics—which took its sweet time, even if you counted weeks on your fingers and had more than two hands—there came even more "lessons" to learn. What use did she have for elocution? Now that was really going overboard. Kaheiron had some nerve to make her suffer through those. They were horrid … absolutely monstrous.

Hours of practicing trying to form her mouth into shaping words that it clearly wasn't designed for was a pain. More than a pain actually. More like the punishment served on you after having fallen ten flights of stairs and landing in the royal river uninvited, unwelcome, and causing a mighty splash, almost drowning the ferryman.

Annoying as it was, in a place where the majority of those present spoke, if not two then even more, languages, fluently (especially those dabbling in foreign arts), being considered as not even being able to master her own made her feel ridiculous. Everyone understood her already, didn't they?

'Why? Why? Why? Why?' Lin finally barked out in rapid succession at Kaheiron.

'Why?' the Archmagus blinked, uncomprehendingly, at her. 'Why does the universe appear to move when there's nothing outside it for it to move within? Why do quadrupeds only ever have four legs? Why does ice burn?'

'Oh, you know what I mean! You know, all THIS,' Lin flailed her arms about, trying to encompass "everything." 'I don't need to know all this strange stuff. Why should I?' she muttered rebelliously.

Kaheiron regarded her quietly for a moment. In fact, he stayed quiet for so long, Lin started feeling a little uncomfortable with how she'd yelled at him—again.

'Why don't you visit the demonstration this afternoon,' he had suggested. 'It's in the main courtyard I believe. I think you might find it instructive.'

After that, Lin had slunk off back to her room for a good sulk, not sticking as much as a nose outside her door until the afternoon came around whether she wanted it to or not.

Kaheiron had been right about one thing, she admitted, several hours later. After sitting in on a demonstration of offensive combat in the courtyard, she'd challenge anyone, including her father, to call the mages here *weak*. Lin still felt a bit faint from that experience. She'd nearly gotten her hair singed and she'd been well and out of the way and that had been *with* the protective wards they'd set up.

The wards had shattered under an intense blow of blue and green light, knocking the opponent backwards and sending a fair few of the audience scurrying for cover. And that had just been a *friendly* bout. She'd hate to see what they'd do in an actual battle.

True, most of them would be in trouble if they had to rely on picking up a sword and swinging it around for defence. Though some of the younger ones (that is, those that hadn't yet turned into ancient fossils and looking the part to boot, in her eyes) fancied both swordplay and wrestling and all sorts of physical combat more because it gave them a chance to show off than because of any practical value.

Faced with a few professional foes and soldiers, she bet they'd have a whole lot of trouble if they couldn't rely on their magic as a backup.

That was fine. As long as they didn't expect *her* to take it up as well. That'd be too much, really. Even so, Linandra could understand why it was a good thing to have a grounding in such things. If something went wrong, there could be times when, for some strange reason, magic wasn't an option, maybe it wouldn't even be available. And what would the mages do then? Knock someone over the head with their staffs? Ha. That'd be a sight.

Not that everyone here actually wanted to make magic their life—that was something else she learnt as she went along to all these things. It had taken quite a while before that little idea had sunk in though.

Why someone would devote such an amount of time to something like this, and then not actually do anything with it, was beyond her understanding.

Okay, so *some* were here just to get their manifested powers under control. For instance, she'd heard of one youngster who'd kept turning members of their household into purple gerbils. When you were changed into a small rodent by your lord and master, especially when it was by accident, even the most tolerant people would start objecting, to say nothing about his or her family.

Linandra had discovered that most of those who "messed around with magic" as she put it, were also a little … well … eccentric no matter what their age was. She could kind of understand why some families would consider them a source of embarrassment, not to mention random trouble. And they didn't exactly get *less* eccentric with age either. Maybe they felt they needed to get in some good practice as soon as possible to be able to compete with the rest of the nutjobs?

Anyone here for those reasons tended to be in their twenties or below. If you saw anyone older than that around, they'd most likely have travelled here because of the Towers' reputation, seeking to further themselves in their chosen arcane field. Kind of like minstrels, but without the singing.

Actually, now that she thought about it. There weren't exactly a whole lot of children around. True, you did see some, but mostly those belonged to families that lived and worked here. Lin wondered if it was because the Towers refused to teach children or if it was because you didn't get hit with the magical hammer, so to speak, until you were a bit older?

'I just can't see Kaheiron refusing to help someone who clearly needed it,' she mumbled to herself as she was wandering from one lesson to another. 'I kind of wish he'd stop helping me quite so much, though. Is there no end to this learning?'

True, he didn't always do it in a way that was obvious to the person receiving the help. Actually seemed a sensible thing to do if you didn't want to get every man and his dog running after you asking for favours, Linandra thought.

Even some of the staff shared in all this. Actually, some of the staff came here from all over the world because they had heard that here they weren't outcasts and could, if needed, find help in learning to cope with whatever they thought they were suffering from.

Since they couldn't pay their way, they worked, instead. All in all, that had turned out to be a fine arrangement.

The real trouble was for outsiders, like Lin, who might grumble about all the hocus pocus, not knowing that the people she was doing so to might be just as immersed in that as the wizards in their tall, little towers.

What was it with magicians and their stupid towers anyway? Was there more magic high up in the air or something?

'Who knew—' Lin had said to herself on more than one occasion. 'I always thought that magic was just pointing your finger at something and making it go poof.'

No. Whatever was causing Kaheiron's interest in turning her into a lady, it certainly wasn't her affinity for magic. If there was one thing she lacked, it was that. If he'd been able to help her "find" some, at this point, she was fairly sure she'd have been having lessons in that too. That was exhausting just to think about.

'Thank goodness,' Lin breathed out. 'I'd hate to be stuck turning everything I touched blue or some other stupidity.'

* * *

Sometimes it was easy to forget your troubles. Sometimes you didn't even need to try. Those were the good days. And, with some time and dedication and attention to detail, you could find yourself having all sorts of good days.

Of course, it did depend on what you defined as a "good" day, but Seth figured that if he was feeling warm and happy and content, or exhilarated and tingling, those were an indication that a good day was indeed happening. What gave you those feelings? Well, all manner of things, really. There was no reason to make life more complicated than it needed to be, now was there?

He'd "escaped" from the Towers, which was a nice enough place he had to admit, but a little stuffy for his tastes. Travelling was good for the inquisitive spirit, they said. It was good for the mischievous one too, for that matter.

And if you were both inquisitive and mischievous, well, who knew what you might find?

Lifting the tall, elegantly cut glass, he sipped it experimentally. While the rim was frosted over with sugar, it seemed sweet enough to balance some of the more bitter ingredients within nicely.

'Tasty,' he said appreciatively.

'Thank you, my lord,' the keeper bowed, then retreated discreetly.

At the moment Setharrion—or Seth as he thought of himself while in this form (though he used names interchangeably, keeping a string of personas for various occasions)—was lounging on the roof terrace of The Gilded Duck.

Its owner had thought about calling it "The Golden Goose" for that was what it was to him. It laid big, fat, golden eggs into his money pouch every day via the means of a menu consisting of small exclusive portions where the price was as inflated as the portions were miniscule.

The place was neither a tavern, nor an inn, though it did serve both functions, in a way. You might say it catered to a more, shall we say, discerning clientele than your usual travellers. A clientele that valued its privacy, enough so that some of it might well arrive among the shadows and leave by the same. That wasn't saying it was one of *those* places, which generally tended to be rowdier and a whole lot more well-frequented by larger numbers of people.

The Gilded Duck was, possibly aside from its kitchens, modest in terms of noise, even eerily quiet if you were used to a livelier atmosphere. It was tastefully, if minimalisticly, decorated and had a staff that was neither seen, nor heard, unless you needed them.

It had been a most enjoyable place to discover, Seth thought. He really should thank the Archmagus for recommending it.

'Bring me some more of these, won't you,' he indicated the thin rolls on a silver platter. 'They're looking a bit lonely, don't you think?'

'Of course, my lord,' one of the staff appeared almost immediately and returned almost as quick with a new platter. This one with a small pile of the, oh-so-tasty, rolls. Normally served only a couple at a time, the Duck was happy to accommodate those with even deeper pockets than usual.

Seth had absolutely no interest in anything remotely connected to this "working" that he'd kept hearing about. It sounded fine, but it wasn't for him.

Besides, since the early days, once he'd figured out how to make the shiny metal work for him, rather than the other way around, he was happy to let them get on with things. If it turned sour, he could always go out and raid a few robbers or something, again, he figured.

Yes, it had indeed been a long time ago. It felt even longer. Seth shook a metaphorical head at his silliness back then. He'd been such a naïve young cub. The whole culture of this species was fascinating.

For instance, he long since learnt that there wasn't just one type of people inhabiting most towns but a mixture of several, not counting the animals. Whole species were further divided into their own different cultures. Some he still couldn't tell apart, others were so physiologically different that it was impossible to mistake them for something, or someone, else.

That idea had seemed so alien back when he'd taken his first few metaphorical steps into this cauldron of a society. He did still make the occasional error, but none that spoke of him as any more than a stranger in a distant land or, for that matter, from the next town over.

Admittedly, what made the difference was the small and shiny pieces of metal that were so very easy to lose: money. Apparently, if you had enough of that, you weren't thought to be strange. Someone had told him in passing back then, that if you could pay your way and then some, you couldn't possibly be strange, you had to be eccentric.

What the difference was, was beyond him.

From that you might have gathered that a lot of the townspeople in the area were a free minded lot. That wasn't necessarily true, at least, not so much amongst themselves. As someone they didn't know, as long as you paid, they were willing to overlook your little oddities (like you insisting on wearing socks on your hands for instance). If you paid them a lot, they were willing to overlook much larger ones, he'd learnt that soon enough. It had made his life easier.

The created persona of the spoiled noble with more funds than sense suited Seth well. Why hide in some straw hut when he could be having the time of his life? The lack of responsibility was a weight off his shoulder after all these centuries.

What harm was there with indulging himself for a time?

Seth preferred being, if not outright strange in their eyes, then at least a little bit different. You never knew, someone might start asking the wrong sorts of question and then where would he be? At the very worst, his mother would find out. Horrid thought, that.

That idea was a bit farfetched, but it was one that still bothered him. Those were the times when he walked through the house with half an eye over his shoulder, the tension building from his toes and up. At those times, he didn't need to *act* strange, he felt it.

Also, if you appeared a little stranger than you were, people seemed awfully keen on underestimating you. He could put that to good use, especially since, out here, his hide didn't give him away. No matter how many times he woke up like that, it still fascinated him. Not to mention, it made him feel so free.

This self-enforced anonymity wasn't so much a card he liked to play from time to time to keep in practice, as it was part of who he'd become. After centuries of being the centre of attention, it was relaxing to let someone else deal with all the worrisome details while you concentrated on something more enjoyable: like if this drink could perhaps be made even better if you added some juicy berries to it.

True, you still were the centre of attention—just one that didn't really demand very much of you—and, the best part, he could walk away from it any time he liked. As long as he remembered not to use his draconic form anywhere he was likely to be recognized, and it was unlikely that someone who'd report back to Hui'syqussedin would find out.

Seth narrowed his eyes. When had he stopped sneaking back to the dragonlands? It must have been some time ago because he could honestly not tell. Maybe he just didn't want to remember?

'I shouldn't complain,' Seth mused. 'This is the good life. I've got a good thing going here.'

Still… Maybe he should join one of the trader caravans for a journey? This place was beginning to bore him. Hadn't he explored all he could here? Shouldn't he see about seeing something else for a while? He rolled that thought over his tongue. It sounded strange even in his head.

Seth reached into an inner pocket of the elegant, but serviceable, outfit and brought out the first purchase he'd ever made. He wasn't sure why he'd kept it. It wasn't even anything valuable, much. He wasn't even sure what it was supposed to be: it was, however, tiny, glittering and very, very light.

For some time, he'd thought that money was something that just appeared, but for some reason not everyone got the same amount. Had that meant they had access to higher quality drop fields? And why did they keep switching places?

Once he'd gotten used to it, it had proven to be quite the useful little concept.

Yes, it had taken quite a bit of studying to get around to understanding the concept of "money." It had taken an even longer one to make sense of how you gained them. That was "how you gained them without knocking a bandit over the head." If nothing else, there was a limited supply of bandits. Yet, money, around here, seemed ridiculously easy for a creative dragon to lay his paws on.

He still didn't understand clothing though, not completely understand it. He knew enough to make good use of what he'd learnt, but why would people treat you differently depending on what you were wearing?

Dragons didn't bother with clothes or jewellery for that matter. They didn't normally hoard gold or silver or other treasures either. What a dragon hoarded was power and influence, and while it could be mighty profitable it was rarely tangible in the human type of sense.

It was also intricately tied into who the dragon was. How they carried themselves. How well their scales shone. The scent of their kills and if they had fine meats though they did not hunt themselves. Not that dragons ate all that much, considering their size, or that often. One thing that still threw him was how hungry he felt if he didn't eat for a ludicrously short time, like a day.

Humans, and everyone else wearing clothes really, were a lot more difficult to figure out than he'd thought. He'd approached it, as you might say, from the opposite end entirely.

By now, he had a whole set of clothes, depending on what he wanted to do and who he wanted to do it as. Seth rather enjoyed the ability to shift from role to role with just a change of a bit of flimsy material and some mannerisms.

Indeed, this current outfit had been selected for its comfort and the way people responded to him when he was wearing it. There was no possible chance that anyone would mistake him for an errant blacksmith or a delivery boy coming to call.

Seth winced. His youthful looks were, well, useful, but they also meant people didn't take him seriously a lot of the time. And that was annoying. If you were saying something that was worth listening to, should it matter how old you *looked* like even if you *didn't* have pointy ears?

Occasionally, people would look a little strangely at him, but that was to be expected he figured, especially if he was wearing one of his more risky outfits. Sometimes he *wanted* them to stare. That way, all they remembered was the clothes and they conveniently forgot about the person wearing them.

That was a neat little trick. Seth wished it worked back home.

Even now, here, he'd assembled himself an outfit of styles that normally did not meet, to say nothing about belonging to cultures oceans apart. In many places, he'd attract more than just a raised eyebrow and a comment or two about the strange young lord's taste, but, here at the Gilded Duck, he wasn't more than another lordling peculiar tastes.

Shirts were okay, though he preferred those that felt soft and silky against his skin. And they looked good. Coats were good too, if they were light. Heavy weights or winter coats were something that wasn't on any of his shopping lists, not when you could purchase some, albeit a lot more expensive than fur, magic that could keep your normal clothes warm and dry in winter. Or, for that matter, to follow where summer had migrated. Seth figured the expense was worth it.

Trousers, now there was a different matter entirely. He'd discovered quickly that he didn't like the concept of encasing his legs in tubes at all. What they did a little further up was even worse.

Shoes weren't looked at much more favourably. Sadly, while he could avoid the trousers thanks to the different styles of clothing, his feet had proven far less forgiving about walking around without something to protect them. No matter what he bought, shoes or sandals or boots, they *all* itched. They all felt wrong. But he still wore them, when he had to.

All the spells he'd tried to buy worked. It was just that, while they took away the thing he disliked about having to stick his limbs into bits of old skin (yuck), they usually took away something he needed as well. So, he put up with them.

Thankfully, if you made good use of sedan-chairs and carriages you didn't need to do much walking and could take the horrid things off while you were travelling. Very ingenious really, he thought, being able to travel without actually moving yourself.

To a dragon that was something of an alien concept.

It all left him feeling a bit exposed though, but armour, even a little, made him feel like someone was trying to clasp him in iron and he steadfastly refused to go there. He'd tried it once and didn't like it.

There were a few choice sharp edges tucked in here and there among his clothing, though. He might not care for people pointing sharp sticks at him, but he wasn't averse to pointing them at others. Still, he preferred not needing to. It was just a sort of worst case scenario. It was a more than just a bit inconvenient, not being able to use his magic when in this form.

He'd tried, but apart from what was necessary to switch him to and from his normal self, while wandering around as a human he was perfectly and utterly devoid of a connection to the arcane plane or whatever place magic actually came from. He hadn't paid much attention to those lessons. Maybe if he had, he'd have figured out if there was something he was doing wrong, or if it simply wasn't possible.

But then, if something truly horrendous happened, he could always change back. It was preferable to being killed. It'd be a shame about the clothes, though.

THE MANIC MUNCHERS

The dragonling was wrapping his tail around her neck a little too tight for Lin's taste. 'Possessive little thing, aren't you?' she said and tickled him under the chin. She was rewarded by a low thrum.

He was also, technically, a little too big to be riding on her shoulders. It was like trying to carry around Henry, the cat that had adopted Senrel, draped around your neck. After a while you really started to ache. Besides, every time he felt like stretching a wing, he ended up swatting her.

She still felt a bit sorry for the little mite. She just couldn't believe that Kaheiron had made him her responsibility, and without asking.

Sure, if he *had* asked, she might have volunteered. No one should be treated the way this fellow had been, she thought. But the point was that he hadn't asked. Lin had half a mind to just throw the dragonling away on days when this lack of asking got on her nerves even more than usual, but the tiny creature had proved to be nearly as stubborn as she was.

She'd been trying to avoid this particular little "idea" of his for some time. Kaheiron's that was, not the dragonling's.

'So, here we are,' Lin sighed. 'Wonder what this "training class" is? I bet it's really boring; everyone just sitting around and taking notes or discussing the best way to groom feathers. That sounded like something those old wizards would do alright,' she complained to the dragonling.

The dragonling chirruped at her.

'You know, I can never tell when you're being encouraging or when you're just leading me on.'

The dragonling cocked its head at her.

'Alright, alright, I'm going in. Stop looking at me like that. I'd almost think you wanted to go to this class, you silly thing.'

Lin eyed the door warily. It looked like any other door in these corridors: wooden, with cast iron decorations around the hinges and an unusually heavy-looking door handle. It fitted neatly into the arch above.

She placed her ear against the door. Nope. Couldn't hear a thing. That in itself didn't really mean much. She'd already run into one chamber that had been spelled for being soundproof, supposedly after repeated complaints that the familiar, a rowdy bird with a very penetrating voice, kept waking everyone nearby at all the wrong hours. So, why not another one?

Pressing down firmly on the handle, Lin tried to nudge the door open. It complained all the way and accompanied by a series of loud squeaks, she pushed against it, feet digging into the stone floor.

'This is ridiculous,' she muttered. Maybe she'd gone to the wrong room after all?

Then whatever had held the door back suddenly 'came unstuck. Lin fell forwards, hands still grasping the handle. The dragonling alighted from her shoulder in a hurry, showering her in complaints.

A wave of noise washed over her. Her eyes, which faced down, were seeing grass? She straightened up, eyes wide. 'What the...'

'Nooo! Shooti, don't do that! Stop it, I say. Stop it!'

The cry was heard all over the yard. Considering the noises that were coming from it already, that was no mean feat. Lin was starting to wish she'd brought some earplugs.

His slender chestnut-coloured robes flapping all over the place, the young man in question was running after a four-legged ... something, alternatingly pleading with it and scolding it. Neither appeared to be working.

What was it anyway? Linandra wondered. It wasn't anything she recognized. But then, looking around at the people and creatures that had gathered for the afternoon's class, she had to say the same about most of them.

Whatever else, mages certainly didn't go in for keeping ordinary pets.

'Is there something wrong with cats and dogs?' Lin wondered under her breath. 'I mean, everyone else likes them. Do they have, like, zero magical potential or something?'

Admittedly, there were a few that, from a distance, might have passed for either. However, when you got closer what you'd thought was an ordinary housecat or just your average pooch, it turned into anything but. And it wasn't just a question of adding on things like spikes and fangs and changing up their colour either.

'Where do they get these from?' she asked. 'Can't they just go down and take home a puppy or something? Okay, I shouldn't talk, should I?' Lin threw her winged friend an half mocking glance. 'Flying rat, you!'

The dragonling ignored the comment. He bared his teeth at another flying creature getting a little too close and let loose a loud screech.

The whole yard was full of them. Big and small. Those with two legs, four legs, even six, mingled freely with wings of every size, every type. There were small rat-like beings with large teeth. A four-legged, triple-jointed "thing," which mostly seemed to consist of mouths and legs was trying to climb up its human, who was busy trying to shoo off something with sharpened wings that refused to let go of his head. Birds and avian-look-a-likes … predators and prey, all mixed into one. There was no end to them.

A young-looking fellow with a torn robe weaved in-and-out between more sedentary creatures, trying to get back the green feathered hat that was dangling from the grinning mouth of his gambolling pet.

They only stopped when the creature ended up bumping up against Lin's leg. It sat down, cocking its head to one side. Its whiskers twitched.

'This is Pickles,' the out-of-breath owner said between mouthfuls of air.

'We've met,' Lin replied, bending down to tickle Pickles under the chin. His long back foot thumped the ground excitedly.

'D'you think he'd pass for a real rabbit?' Lin asked; black, white and brown patterns didn't really spring to mind when rabbits where concerned.

'Around here? You've got to be kidding. There's probably a green one with purple hearts all over hopping about … somewhere,' the young sorcerer scoffed.

He scooped up the rabbit, which promptly squirmed in his arms and turned into a goose. Wings flapping everywhere, it nearly knocked the young sorcerer off his feet as he dropped him.

'Hey, stop that!'

Pickles honked at him, flaring his wings, and advanced menacingly. His beak snaked out and tried to take a nibble out of the sorcerer's soft shoos.

Jumping back, the young man tried to shoo him away.

Apparently considering this some sort of victory, the goose shook itself, its feathers rippling like rain, and shifted into something lithe and nimble. Quick as lightning, it clambered up Lin's leg and clawed its way to her shoulder.

Lin nearly lost her balance as Pickles settled in on her left shoulder—the right one already being occupied. He squeaked, but slowly started purring as Lin stroked the downy fur.

The young sorcerer sighed. 'He's not really mine, you know. I'm just supposed to be looking after him. The moment I turn my back, he's gone. Don't matter what set-up I have. If I try a cage, he'll just shift into something that can pick the lock. I try locking him in, he'll burrow *through* the door. And every time something happens, they complain to me.'

'Why don't you just magic something up?' Lin asked, looking confused. That seemed to be the favoured solution around here, after all.

'Can't. Silly thing's immune to magic. Doesn't matter what form he's in. We'd never know it was him half the time if he could change his colourings too. Thank goodness for small mercies.'

'So, he always looks like this?' Lin asked. She had to squint to get a decent look at her left shoulder.

At the moment, Pickles' ears were forward, his eyes sparkling. And yes, that tell-tale black overcoat, ochre underside and little bit of white in between made him difficult to miss. It was hard to resist the little blighter when he cocked his head to one side, scrunched up his button nose and let one white ear flop forward. If there was chicken liver in it for him, he'd even live dangerously and stick his tongue out through the side of his mouth and grin wolfishly.

'You two are just as bad,' Lin scolded him gently, then turned and stroked the dragonling's snout to keep him from getting too jealous.

'His real name is Pickle Socks and yes, his master is one of the "a bit odd" ones. You want to look after him? He seems to like you?'

'Umm?'

Lin looked at the dragonling.

The dragonling looked back.

Lin looked at Pickles.

A civet looked back.

'I suppose, but,' she looked around them into the disarray, 'I think we might want to pass on this whole class thing,' Lin said, carefully retracing her steps and quickly dragging the door shut behind her, heart beating.

'Let's be really quiet about this. No telling Kaheiron we didn't go, okay?' Lin scratched the dragonling underneath the chin again. 'Or we'll all get into trouble.'

Over the coming days, Lin tried her best to deflect the topic when Kaheiron brought it up. She was sure she wasn't fooling him, but, so far, he hadn't pressed the matter. So far, as long as she kept her nose in a book and appeared to study, he seemed content to leave her alone, even when sharing his study.

Sometimes she even remembered some of the reading she was pretending to do. For several hours now, she'd been stumbling her way through a thick leather volume that had attracted her merely because she'd read the word "Dragon" on the spine. That was the only bit of the title she actually understood. She felt the same way about half the content, but the illustrations were beautiful and in colour.

From time to time, her fingers drummed on the floor as she came upon something she didn't approve of.

'Dragons CAN talk!' Linandra suddenly exploded at the tome.

A second later, the book bounced off the varnished oak desk, flailed desperately with its pages for a moment, then sagged into a heap on the floor.

Kaheiron tried to not react to the aggressiveness of the outburst. His mind had been somewhere far more enjoyable and hadn't appreciated being brought back to reality quite so harshly. Having a book nearly hitting your head, even if the person throwing it had probably not even been aware of that, could unsettle anyone.

The Archmagus wasn't the only one that had his contemplation disturbed. Nearby, the dragonling curled up tighter on the divan and stuck his head back under a wing with a grunt. He'd popped his head up to see what the fire was about. Since the universe didn't seem to be in any imminent danger of collapsing in on itself, he decided that continuing his snooze was a better use of his time.

'Look, it says so right here,' Lin stabbed an angry digit at the open book, after having retrieved it.

Kaheiron made a show of bending forwards and examining the offending text. Linandra had grown increasingly bolder compared to when she had first arrived here, he thought. He wished she wouldn't be so loud when she got annoyed, though. While a certain degree of anti-refinement could be charming about a young lady, she should use it to her advantage, not the other way around.

Ever since her reading had progressed to a point where she could begin to make sense of the texts, she suddenly seemed to want to know everything about everything. Bit of a one-eighty there, he thought. No one would have expected the so-vocally-objecting Linandra to become so attached to learning. Sometimes he wondered if it had been such a good idea to take it upon himself to teach her to read, after all. If anything, it would have kept his evenings quieter.

Too late to do anything about that now. Before he had a chance to read the full paragraphs himself, the brown volume was snatched away from his questing fingers.

'Careful there, Linandra,' Kaheiron admonished his charge. 'Remember that we are not rock-people. Don't be so brusque about everything. Calm your mind.'

'Sorry…' Lin cleared her throat noisily before starting to, somewhat clumsily, read the offending material out loud.

'So doths the dragonth who is thaid to be of the thilvertongue cansth so not be, for in allth the thime, between heaven and earth's, there hath been not a dragon, not a drake not any speicies of draco, any wich has hath the shape of the lipth or the cuveth of the longeth, to bring forth the speech of man, elf or any other tongue beknownsth to the many races of the worlth.'

Lin stumbled over the words, which just served to make her even more annoyed. It wasn't your everyday reading even if you'd had years to practice.

But with Kaheiron filling in when she struggled too much, she managed to get through the whole passage.

The Archmagus didn't need to read it. He knew that bit of text very well. It had been a thorn in his side for years.

'Why, so I do believe it does,' he acknowledged.

'That's a lie!' Lin challenged him, eyes furious.

'Is it?' the Archmagus replied, a glint of amusement in his eye.

Lin couldn't see what was so funny. 'Dragons *do* speak,' she insisted.

'It's a matter of fact that they do not.'

'I *heard* you speak,' Lin insisted, leaning forwards, her mouth making a good impression of a put-off-fish.

'Ah, but did you really?'

'I *heard* you,' the young woman repeated stubbornly.

Kaheiron resisted the urge to roll his eyes. She wasn't going to let it go, was she? Conversations like these always put him in mind of his younger days. What a terrible time he must have given his tutors back in the day. He'd always been inquisitive. He couldn't recall being quite this contentious though. Had he been? Maybe age did put things in perspective.

Still, if they had had the patience with him, he'd do well to have the same patience with others. Admittedly, sometimes that job was easier than other times. Hand to hand and eye to eye differences in opinion with other, more hot-tempered, mages he'd seen quite a few of. Especially when he first started out.

Odd really, the way they'd reduced almost down to nothing over the years. Aside from that business with Joran, the biggest battle Kaheiron had needed to break up as of late was a rather heated debate between a discussion group on the implementation of sorcery in everyday life.

Hardly the dance with danger that most laymen seemed to regard the profession to be occupied with. The Archmagus couldn't help but chuckle at the thought. Things sure had changed over the years.

'Is something funny?' Lin wondered with a touch of sarcasm.

'What? No ... no, not at all. That I have not denied, that you heard me that is,' Kaheiron stated calmly. He placed his hands on the table he had now returned to.

'What? Wait a minute. You just said yourself that dragons don't speak. Now you say they do?' Lin cocked her head to one side and gave him one of her "looks."

That was another habit of hers that he wished she could learn to stop doing. It made her look, well, like a pica bird trying to get at a honeymite. While it might look cute on the bird, on Lin it wasn't nearly as attractive.

'Those two, I believe you will find, are not mutually exclusive,' Kaheiron explained as patiently as he could.

'So, I heard you. But now you're saying you don't speak?'

'Affirmative.'

'That doesn't make any sense,' Linandra made a face.

She threw herself into a nearby chair. It shot backwards by sheer force of impact. Kaheiron winced at the sound.

Why did it have to be like this? She hated things that didn't make sense. Sadly, that seemed to be most of the world since she'd gotten involved in this hocus pocus business.

Times like these, she actually wished she'd stayed on the farm. Okay, that feeling usually dissipated very quickly. But the point was that they were there, if only for a moment, before the other memories budged them aside and knocked them over the head with a two-ton shovel just to get some sense into them.

The Archmagus grimaced. He wished she'd stop doing that, too. The furniture did come apart if you treated it too badly and he liked them. That was why he still had them, even after all these years.

'I believe you will find that it does,' he retorted. 'As this rather old-fashioned text says, neither dragons, nor any of their associated genus have the physical attributes conducive for vocalizing or mimicking the human speech parameters.'

'Huh? But they still talk.'

'Those well-versed in the arcane arts are able to create projections of sound, mimicking a voice,' the Archmagus corrected.

'Eh?'

'Magic,' he simplified. 'They use magic. Just like they can use it to create physical manifestations of both elemental forces and other matter, creating sound is merely a question of moving the right amounts of air around.'

'Oh.' Lin made a face. She still didn't think she understood half the explanation, but asking Kaheiron to clarify even further was probably useless. He'd never quite mastered the whole "speak basic" as far as she was concerned, not when trying to explain things.

With a disappointed huff, she sucked on her knuckles for a moment's thought. 'Can anyone here do it?' Lin asked.

'Among the mages you mean? I do believe so. It is not an uncommon thing for the forward-thinking practitioner of magic to utilize. I know several who like to pretend that it is their familiar that is speaking. Indeed, that little trick was the beginning of many of the rumours of talking animals. Many of those around them never realize it is a trick and actually do believe that the animal is speaking to them.'

'Oh,' escaped from Lin's lips again. She sank down, looking dejected. And here she'd thought she'd stumbled on to something really game-changing. Guess not.

'Now. Perhaps we could return to your actual studies? I believe you were supposed to be learning, not flinging my precious books across the chamber?'

Linandra sighed. 'Alright … alright … I'll be good...'

'I would settle for "quiet." There is no need to read out loud unless your audience benefits from it. You're quite capable of reading without moving your lips as well.'

'Sure, whatever you say,' Lin said.

One little bit of excitement and all the fun was being clamped down on like two tons of heated rock slamming into the ground. Looked like it was going to be a long hour left until she could get back to her own room and get some sleep.

Still on the divan, satisfied now that all the noise had died down, the dragonling went back to snoozing away happily. He didn't have to wait to get back to where they lived for that.

The next morning, they picked up right where they'd left off.

'At least lunch is our own,' Lin said to the dragonling.

He must have understood her, she thought, because he looked the happiest he had been since breakfast.

'Honestly, beastie. You eat too much,' she scolded her winged friend.

They were walking past the garden fountain, arms full of rolled up scrolls, when Lin tripped over a verge. The scrolls went everywhere, including some which landed in the water. With an indignant cheep, the dragonling alighted from her shoulder as she fell, face forwards.

'Oh, drat,' Lin exclaimed. She pushed herself back up, then caught sight of the fountain.

'Ah, no! No! No!' she dashed forwards, fishing out the soggy scrolls. 'Great. Just great,' Lin sighed, dumping the lot on the ground. 'I'm going to be in so much trouble for that.'

Not that she thought they were always all that useful. The other day she'd actually found a whole shelf full of treaties entitled "Fire: It Burns." She was sure that people with names longer than her arm—or maybe they were titles—should have known *that* already.

As if that wasn't bad enough. Half the shelf below it was taken up by several volumes transcribing some convention centuries ago where those attending had spent the entire time arguing over the truthfulness to the idea of "Water: Is It a Liquid?"

Lin glared at the dragonling, which had landed just a short distance away on the cobbles.

'And don't you dare snigger at me, do you hear?' Lin told him. 'It's probably your fault I tripped anyway.'

The dragonling drew back, a hurt expression in his whole body.

'Now, now, you shouldn't put blame where none is deserved,' one of the nearest mages told her.

The man knelt down. 'What's your name, little fellow?' He asked and reached out a hand, as if greeting the creature, but the dragonling was as interested in him as he always seemed to be in other people. That is, not at all.

'This usually brings them around,' the mage said to Lin as he patted his pockets until he pulled out something small and sticky.

To Linandra it looked like a burr gone wild. She wouldn't have cared to pick those; they'd leave several of those needle-like thorns right in her fingers, she was sure of it. Or under her nail, that was even worse. Hurt like hell they did, even after they were pulled out, even the small ones.

The mage gently waved the proffered treat right under the little dragonling's nose, but he just turned his head away, more interested in sniffing at a wing.

That was unusual, Lin thought. The dragonling didn't normally turn up his nose at a treat and a free one at that. Guess they had that in common.

A small ball of tricoloured fur shot between the mage's legs, leapt at his hand, snagged the treat, and dashed away to the other side of the courtyard.

Linandra couldn't help but feel embarrassed. She might not want to be here, but to make such a bad show of herself, that was just stomach churning. If it had been on purpose…

'What? Wait … umm … name?' Lin stuttered incomprehensively her mind just catching up with her ears. 'Err … he doesn't have any,' she admitted, finally.

'No?' the mage sounded quite shocked. 'You haven't named him? But he's your pet, surely he should have a name?'

'Well, not … exactly. Why do you keep calling it "he" anyway? Like me? Because it sounds better than "it?"'

'Because that is what he is,' the mage said while watching the dragonling trot over to investigate what Pickles had grabbed, the two of them beginning a game of tag or petball, it was hard to tell which.

'How can you tell?' Lin tried to think of anything that made her small dragon—no, wait, not *her* small dragon, just *this* small dragon—different from any other. Admittedly, she hadn't had a whole lot to compare with. Her brow knotted. How was she supposed to know?

The mage before her offered her a benign smile. 'For most, you'd be right to be confused. There are very few apparent differences between genders in the draconic fauna. But in this case, you needn't look further than the most obvious.'

'Which is?' Lin asked. She didn't think she was getting any wiser, but she sure was getting more annoyed. Couldn't this old codger get to the point already?

'His hide. Silver dragonlings, much like silver dragons, are very rare and they are, invariably, all male.'

'Oh…'

'Try to think of a good name for your new friend. I suspect you'll have a much easier time training him after that. They do respond better when given more personalised attention as well. They're quite intelligent, you know.'

Intelligent? Yes, she knew that already. Especially if it involved new and surprising ways to get to food, any food, but particularly food that wasn't his to eat. Not everyone placed protective spells on their storage jars like Kaheiron did.

'Oh … err … right … I guess. I'll have to think about it. Eh … thanks,' Lin stuttered.

The mage rose, having tried to attract the creature one last time, this time with something else. But the dragonling and Pickles were so involved in their play—which seemed to involve a great deal of dashing about and jumping on things—that they probably didn't even notice.

'Seriously, you're such an embarrassment,' Lin muttered, her cheeks reddening.

It was doubtful that either dragonling *or* shapeshifter heard her.

Linandra ended up thinking about what the mage had said all day. In the end, she'd picked up some sweets from the kitchen before retiring.

As she poked a star-shaped, oatmeal cookie closer to where her friend was slumbering, her mind was only partially on where she was putting her fingers. 'Tooth?' she said, trying out the word.

The dragonling sniffed the offering then took an experimental bite before wolfing down the rest in a shower of crumbs. He sat up on his haunches, eyes bright, and looked expectantly at her.

'And they say *I* don't have any table manners.' Lin couldn't help but laugh at her friend. Whatever else, no matter how annoyed or infuriated, to say nothing about embarrassed, he could make her, he always managed to cheer her up when she was feeling down.

She wrapped some hair around her fingers absentmindedly. 'Lightning? Do you like that? Lightning? No, apparently not.'

Sinking down further, arms crossing, she leant back on the chair, rocking it back and forth as she tried to think of a good name for her dragonling, as the mage had suggested.

'Rapid? Storm? Ceron? Blossom. Oh, I just don't know…' Lin tried to fish out another cookie, only to discover the jar was empty. Had she eaten all of them already?

No, probably not. Looking around, there were enough crumbs to make up several whole ones so, technically, she hadn't eaten all of them. Besides, the dragonling had helped. And very enthusiastically too. The crumbs where everywhere.

'Lightning, no, I passed that already. Thunder? Oh, this is hopeless,' she threw her hands up in despair. 'How about I just keep calling you Grumpy and be done with it?'

The dragonling's head jerked up. He gave off an indignant squeak.

'Ah, yes. You don't like that, do you? Could you possibly be slightly less picky? Or, better yet, help?'

'Wait? What are you doing? No. No. Not that one. Grumpy, get down off the cabinet right now. That's my—'

Her emergency jar of rolls, which she'd asked the Archmagus for (the jar, not the rolls, horrid thought), had a spell on it to keep the lid from being pried open. That didn't, however, stop it from smashing into pieces as it hit the floor or the contents from scattering across it. Some even managed to escape under the bed.

'NOOO! I'll filet you!' Linandra cried out, making a dash for the small creature.

The dragonling made a startled noise and tried to scramble up higher on the shelves.

'You DO understand what I'm saying! You little piece of … all that playing stupid … oh just you wait—'

They ended up chasing each other around in circles. The next thing Lin knew, she'd ended up with a face full of dragon, wings and all.

'Ouff … get off!' she huffed.

When Lin finally managed to convince her small charge to let go, her hair was a mess, to say nothing about her clothes.

She poked a finger through a new tear and sighed. 'You sure are getting carried away, aren't you?'

The dragonling sniffed at a strand of hair, then resolutely started to chew on it.

'Hey, stop that!' Lin cried out. She tugged her hair back, glaring at her still unnamed pet.

'Okay, okay, so I won't call you Grumpy. So, what should I call you then? It's not like you're going to tell me, are you?' She threw herself onto the narrow bed.

Now she was tired and she still didn't know what to call the little dear. Wait a minute. If he understood what she was saying … maybe?

'Hey, do you have a name already, small fry? No? Great. So, it's down to guessing games now? You know, you're awfully hard work for something so small.'

Lin flicked a crumb at him, which he deftly snatched out of the air. He looked down at her expectantly, in case there were any more.

'Sorry cookie monster, you've eaten the lot,' Lin laughed at his expression.

There was a disappointed sound from above.

Lin sighed. It looked like this was going to be a long night.

She rolled over, pulling up the covers to her ears. Maybe something would come to her in her sleep? Sleep which didn't come easy, so when Lin woke several hours later she grumbled a bit about the light.

Wait, it was the middle of the night, there shouldn't be any lights. Prying an eye open just a fraction, she discovered that the door was ajar. The flickering was coming from the lighting in the hallway.

Suddenly feeling more awake than she'd been in days, Lin discovered a sinking feeling in the pit of her stomach.

A quick scan around the room was all she needed, then she looked under the bed.

'Nope, not there either. Drat.'

The dragonling was gone.

* * *

Throwing open the door to the pantry caught the intruder unaware. He'd been so busy chewing on a piece of ham three times the size of himself he hadn't even heard the stomping feet coming closer and closer.

'Ah-ha!' Lin exclaimed. 'There you are, you little devil.'

The dragonling's head appeared from behind the ham, jaws masticating lazily. Upon seeing them, it hastily swallowed the mouthful, making a cheeping sound in her direction. It bounded forward eagerly, coming to a sliding halt on the messy floor when it discovered that Lin wasn't alone.

'My hams,' the cook cried out in despair. 'My precious hams. My preserves. The PIES! You, you little beast. Monster! What have you done?'

'Eaten 'imself silly, the thing has,' one of the people behind them said, lowering the ladle he'd been brandishing. 'ought he was one of 'em ghosties, I did.'

'I filet you! Roast you on spit! Serve you up as main course, with ginger sauce and feighfig[1] in mouth,' the cook fumed.

'You'd have a spot of trouble with that,' the third cook, a thin, gangly, young man peered over her shoulder. 'Looks like he's eaten 'em all already.'

The head cook's eyes moved over the disaster zone that was the third pantry. 'Why, so he has. Going to regret eating my figs, no mistake,' her deep voice huffed, as if she was quite happy that'd it'd serve him right.

Something else in there with them hiccupped. A pile of marrows spilled out onto what remained of the floor, revealing a tuft of black hair.

A second hiccup caused the rest of the vegetables to dislodge, showing a bundle of black and white fur. Pickles gave his best innocent performance and hiccupped again.

'Well—'s happy 's I'm too' see anyone like my foodeeh, I doh want to have the chanceee to *cook* it first,' the second cook said emphathically once he'd calmed down a bit.

'You get those manic munchers out of my kitchen, girl, or there's going to be trouble.'

'Yes, cook,' Lin replied meekly. 'I thought he was in my room, honest. I don't know where *that one* came from,' she pointed an accusing finger at the dog.

'Whaff?' Pickles said.

---

[1] A very sweet and juicy treat both fresh and dried, like a cross between a fig and a very round plum. Good for cakes and marmalade. Feighfigs do not like being picked, so not for the unexperienced gardener.

'You see he, stay there. I catch anywhere near kitchen again, I not care what Archmagus say. Muncher regret it!'

'Yes, cook. It won't happen again,' Lin said and threw her companion a disgusted glare.

Pickles made a dash for it as soon as she opened the door and Lin picked up the protesting dragonling and half carried, half dragged him back to her quarters, leaving the kitchen staff to pick up the pieces.

'Strange, the lock looks alright,' Lin mused. She ran her fingers over it. 'Let me guess, someone stopped by looking for me and the moment you saw that door opening, you were off like a shot, right?'

Shaking her head, she dumped the offending creature on the table and dropped her satchel on the bed.

'I know you don't get out as much as you'd like. But you know how much trouble you get into when I let you roam around wherever you want? Do you know how much trouble *I* get into when you do? No, of course you don't,' Lin sighed.

There was little use lecturing the adorable little thing. He just stared at you with those big soulful eyes and you just melted. Of course, he'd then proceed to dive right between your legs, make for the open door or window like a cat chasing a flame, and you'd spend hours getting your ears chewed off for whatever he got up to once you caught up with him again.

Lin was glad for the company, but, at times like that, she wondered if the trouble was seriously worth it.

The small dragon chirped at her. Rising on his hind legs he tried scratching imploringly in the air above him.

'Cheep to you too,' Lin poked her tongue out at the dragonling. 'You can't have any. You already ate half a bushel.'

Making a clearly displeased sound at this news, the dragonling lunged for the feighfig which Lin had picked up down in the pantry.

Lin jumped back. 'I said no!'

Holding the feighfig high over her head, their eyes locked. Moving slowly, circling each other in a kind of dance, the dragonling crouching low, his tail swung rhythmically from side to side.

He tried leaping for the morsel, but the weight of all the ones he'd already munched his way through kept making him overbalance. The dragonling was making unhappy and increasingly distressed cheeping noises.

'Stop cheeping at me. You've had too many already,' Lin fended off the small creature.

Making a final attempt at the prize, and unable to launch himself into the air with his usual grace, the dragonling gave up. Curling up on top of a small barrel, he stuck his nose under a wing and pointedly ignored her.

'You're going to regret eating all of those you know,' Lin said. She should know, she'd done the exact same thing … once. The ripe fruit was tasty and difficult to stop eating once you'd had your first bite, but, if you didn't, you ended up with a terrible stomach ache for several days.

'You're always getting yourself into trouble. Honestly, what would you do if I wasn't around to stop you, hmm? I don't think cheeping at anything in your state will save you. That's it! I'll call you Cheep, because you do that all the time anyway. Yes, Cheep. Hmm. I like that,' Lin said. 'Cheep it is then. Better prepare yourself for a rough few days Cheepy boy, because that's what you're in for. Maybe that'll teach you not to stuff yourself on every bit of food that comes within five metres of you.'

Cheep didn't reply. His stomach rumbled.

FAVOURED FORTUNE

Since you so conveniently appeared before me, I should thank you for saving me the trouble of summoning you,' the Archmagus said to Linandra about a week later.

He looked over his shoulder, away from the heavy bookcase he'd been scrutinising. 'Where is that flying menace of yours?' he asked.

'Around,' Lin shrugged.

'Ah…' Kaheiron coughed delicately, aiming the secretary of his mind back to the matter at hand. It looked like he still had a lot of work to do here.

'How would you like to accompany our delegation on the trip to Amorix?'

Kaheiron tried to put it as casually as possible. As just a thought thrown out there among so many others. If he did anything else, he suspected that she would refuse point blank out of sheer contrariness.

Even with such care taken, he could see an eyebrow twitch below. Alone, that didn't tell if the owner was excited at the prospect or disapproving of it.

'Really?' Linandra's voice came back at him, tinged with repressed interest.

That settled which one it was then, Kaheiron thought. Guess the young woman must be eager to get out and see something other than the Towers for a while. She was used to moving about more, he reminded himself. It wouldn't do letting her get too bored.

'Of course,' he replied. 'It's only a short journey,' and, since it wouldn't do letting her get too carried away, he followed up with, 'and it should prove conducive to your studies.'

He could almost see the small dark cloud that descended upon Lin at those words. Yes, that would do nicely.

'It's alright, I suppose,' she offered tentatively.

'It's settled then,' Kaheiron nodded, pleased at the outcome. 'Pay a visit to Madame on your way back, won't you. You know Madame, do you not?'

'What on earth for?' Lin exploded. 'Her outfits are, like, crazy! *She's* crazy.'

'Because,' the Archmagus stretched the word, 'she will need your measurements. You are most certainly not attending in any of that which currently constitutes your wardrobe. This isn't some farmer's market you are going to.'

His young charge wasn't the least bit mollified.

'Oh phooey,' Lin grumbled on her way out. 'Stupid old grouch. Madame's nuttier than a squirrel with six oaks. I'll look like an overstuffed turkey with an apple in my mouth by the time she's done. I walked right into that one, I did. Bollocks.'

'Studies, studies, studies. That's all these people ever think about. Blearrgh,' Lin muttered to herself all the way back to her room.

* * *

'You're always eating. Every time I see you, you're eating. It's not natural.'

'I'm hungry,' Seth protested, taking another bite out of the apple, then wiping the juice running down the side of his mouth with a sleeve.

'Merely because you were born starving, does not mean that you should feel entitled to spend the rest of your life "stuffing your face" as I believe the expression is around here.'

'Please, don't remind me,' Seth shuddered.

'Now, kindly descend from there. There's something I need you to do for me.'

'Really?' Seth's interest was aroused. 'I've been getting bored anyway,' the young man disentangled himself from the thick branch, landing lightly on the ground some ten feet below.

'Anything fun?'

'I think, you will find it to your liking well enough,' his visitor assured him, a smile tugging at the corners of his mouth.

* * *

In what felt like no time at all (if you asked Lin, Cheep would have disagreed resolutely, having been the one that had had to put up with several days' worth of incessant complaining), she was being jostled and fussed over like nothing she'd ever known.

'If this is what it means to be a Lady, I'm going for the other option,' Lin muttered rebelliously. Honestly, no one had been this bothered about what she should wear since her mother took her along to her very first Midsummer's Festival.

'This is ridiculous,' Lin fumed.

The knot between her eyes was already signalling annoyance at the silliness of it all. Being prodded and made to turn this way and that way on this stupid pedestal was only making it worse: she was getting seriously fed up with all of this. What did they think she was? Some sort of beast at a country fair? Best Groomed Maid of the Year?

What was wrong with her own clothes anyway? Nothing. That was what was wrong with them. Bah.

'Ouch! Watch it ... please.' She added that last as a precaution. It was never a good idea to get on the bad side of someone who's handling large, or small, needles in your vicinity.

Cheep ruffled himself up at the snapping sound of her voice, letting go of a soft hiss and his wings beating as if he was trying to take off, if his claws hadn't been firmly hooked on her shoulder.

'There, there now, Cheepy,' Lin said soothingly and stroked his back until the dragonling settled down again.

If she'd thought she'd have gotten away with storming out at this point, she would have. Lin's fists clenched tighter. Did they have to pull so hard? What was this thing anyway? It was like being clamped in iron and then having some giant come along and squeeze you for juice.

And she was being fussed over as if she was some sort of helpless maiden. One of those that did a lot of fainting in those stories she'd used to hear growing up. One of those that were always being carried off by giants, screaming. Being abducted by centaurs, screaming. Accosted by leprechauns and, yes, screaming. Did those idiot girls ever do anything useful?

She'd always thought they were beyond silly. But if this was what they were having to walk around in all day, it was no wonder they never managed to run away from anything. She felt like fainting herself right now. How did anyone breathe in this?

It was with perhaps more than just mild contempt that her family had regarded such people. What they thought of those who would choose to wait on them shouldn't even be whispered in the dark.

And now, here she was. Lin could, unfortunately, think all too well of what they would say about that.

The fact that she made a great show of not wanting to be here wouldn't be the least mitigating in their eyes. It was enough that even the possibility of her being there was, well, there. It was simply not done.

The worst part? 'You don't really dislike it that much, now do you?' that small, treacherous voice in the back of her mind asked smugly.

Linandra wished she could hit it with a flyswatter, even more so now, because it was getting uncomfortably close to the truth. Almost as uncomfortable as this stupid dress … almost.

Sure, it was flattering in a "I'm gonna swat you if you don't stop soon" way. Couldn't they just have given her an old dress in about the right size and made do with that? This manic running around they did trying to get her dress just right was driving her mad, not to mention making her slightly dizzy trying to keep an eye on them all.

Why did they need to go through all this fuss? It couldn't be that important, could it? No way. Kaheiron would never just randomly bring her along to something like that, would he? She'd be terribly out of place, she just knew it. And yet…

Oh, if only they could stop making so much noise. It wouldn't have been so bad if it was done all nice and quiet. The way they chattered to each other all the time: it couldn't all be about her, could it? Most of the time she didn't actually catch what they were saying. Just snatches of giggling and whispered conversation drifting by.

A piece of material was moving from person to person as if it was a piece of hot, burning coal. It wasn't the only thing, either. The way they kept fiddling with her hair, trying to tame it, and braid in some shiny "stuff" into it, was bothering her too.

And then there were the needles, always the needles. Bright, pointy things that were supposed to tie the materials together. Lin tensed up every time another one was brought out. She hated needles. She couldn't help it, no matter how hard she tried, not to be afraid that they were, all of a sudden, going to jump up and all stick themselves into her all at once, turning her into a human pincushion.

That was the stuff of nightmares. She'd never thought she'd actually have to live through it. This was, mind you, getting fairly close.

'Ouch!' Lin cried out, again, as a hairbrush yanked her head aside.

Maybe she should have been brushing it a bit more often? But it had been so much easier to just let it be. It was a nuisance in the morning no matter what she did, anyway.

'I do beg your pardon, my lady.'

Oh yes, and there was *that*! My lady. It was "My Lady" here, it was "My Lady" there. She was so sick of hearing it.

Lin wasn't a lady. Would never be a lady. Had no wish to become a lady. Her teeth gnashed against each other. She barely resisted the urge to pummel the dear old lady in the face.

When other little girls had dreamt of being long lost princesses, Lin's daydreaming had involved fiery steeds, gleaming armour and swords clashing in the sun.

She'd been off to rescue heroes, *being* the hero, and dashing from one marvellous adventure from another until it made her head dizzy just trying to keep track of them all.

Pretending to crush ogres in the vegetable garden (when she should have been just pulling out the weeds). Chasing kelpies up and down the little stream in the woods and then basking in the sun to dry out, alongside what could have been a tribe of fierce and dangerous basilisks (if they hadn't, in fact, been tiny leaf-lizards). Tying some rope to two pieces of wood and suddenly having a magic sword almost the same size as her that could cut through even the strongest shieldspell (had she actually been able to stop it snagging in the underbrush when she had to drag it into mock battle).

Yes, much to the distress, and fury, of her parents and other assorted members of the family, who were all of the understanding that little girls should not do things like that, Lin had had no wish to be the damsel in distress.

Maybe that was why she absolutely hated situations that she couldn't control. It was as if the very universe kept trying to shut her back into the box her parents and their parents before them had so painstakingly created.

There had been a decidedly powerful emphasis on being the rescuer, not the rescuee, in those dreams. But she'd soon learnt that girls dreaming of being adventurers weren't any more likely to have their dreams come true than did those that spent their childhood making up stories about being long lost heirs of faraway kingdoms.

And then she'd run away.

It had come as quite the shock that there was as much effort involved, and as many difficulties to surpass, trying to become someone you thought you were, but you weren't, as it did trying to be someone you're not all day.

Armour chafed. Swords were, often, ridiculously heavy. They were also sharp.

Trying to persuade some handsome knight to give up their magical blade so that *she* could use it turned out to be an exercise in pointlessness. Should any knight actually still *have* a magic sword, he certainly wasn't the handsome type, besting everyone else who also wanted it, and not the least likely to want to part with it, without you parting with a considerable amount of blood in the process.

The clothes smelled and so did the places you ended up in. And, at the end of the day, everyone still had to eat.

Guess she was lucky that domestic staff was always, well, almost always, in demand. In lieu of that, she'd actually gotten quite decent at making do in the forest.

That smelled too, now that she thought about it. It certainly wasn't where she wanted to spend a winter either.

The Towers on the other hand. Now, this place had potential. It was, Lin frowned, perfectly right to be fussed over. So why then was it annoying her so?

'Do you have to do that?' Lin snapped at the woman straightening out an errant crease in her skirt.

'Yes, milady,' the woman bobbed a curtsy and threw a desperate appeal for help in the direction of Madame.

'Now, now ... we're almost done, dear. The Archmagus was quite particular about this,' Madame twittered.

Oh yes. He would have, wouldn't he? Typical. Trying to get one up on that one was just asking for it. Even if she dared talk back to him, even poke fun at him, there needed to be just a hint of glimmer to his eyes to make her paddle her badly strung raft backwards as fast as she could from heading up that particular creek.

Lin tried to fold her arms, scowling crossly, only to find that she couldn't. The material in her sleeves were still pinned a little too tight to her sides. Fuming, she let her arms drop back down.

This was just getting to be too much. If he thought that bringing her along on this trip was such a good idea, why couldn't he just wave his hands about and make something up? There had to be better ways to get new clothing. None of this messing about with stupid needles and folding and tightening and whatnot.

She'd even asked, she really had. But no, apparently this didn't qualify for such advanced hocus pocus. Hmppf. Lazy bum.

Not that she'd actually dare call him that to his face. Most of the time she didn't even want to. She liked him, really. It was just that, right as she'd gotten comfortable in what she was doing, he had to come around and turn everything topsy-turvy ... again. It was beginning to get on her nerves. Didn't he have more important things to do than turn her life upside down, inside out and then back to front, just for the sake of it, so many times that she no longer had any clear idea of what it was, or even of what it should be?

Lin sighed. Maybe it was just one of those things, like a fashion-craze or that one week a year when everyone suddenly saw the light and that they needed to be kind and understanding to their neighbour and then promptly forgot about it again once the holidays had passed?

No, she chewed thoughtfully at the end of an errant strand of hair, that wasn't his style.

Regardless of what, did it have to involve this? The newly adorned, polished, dressed and, despite her best objections, now rather fetching, young lady muttered something *very* unladylike.

'And this colour does not suit me,' she added to her silent musings.

Around her, the activity of what might have been mistaken for a beehive in the honey season continued unabashed and unashamed. They, at least, knew what they were doing.

'I look ridiculous,' Lin growled half-heartedly.

True, she had no idea of what she actually looked like. The chamber was utterly devoid of anything even resembling a mirror. There wasn't even a polished surface of a goblet or a vase to tease her reflection out of, in here. But she certainly *felt* ridiculous.

'An outfit fit for a queen,' Madame corrected her pleasantly.

'Give me a break. I'm still not used to this "lady" stuff. Queen? Forget it. No thanks. All that walking around in crowns and clothes you can't breathe in? Yuck!'

'Yes, well, it is merely a saying, dear.'

'Are we done yet?'

'Yes … yes, quite finished.' Madame straightened out a final fold. 'Now, why don't you run along, dear. I'm sure you want to show the nice Archmagus your new dress.'

Lin couldn't imagine anything she wanted to do less, but she seized the excuse for everything it was worth and positively fled.

Or would have fled. It turned out that one thing this outfit wasn't made for, was being worn when attempting to run. Or even walk really fast. Bugger.

It would prove to be only the first of many things it wasn't designed for. It did, however, put a firm stop to anything even resembling fun, if Lin was any judge. Because, even if part of her felt like taking a whole armada of little scissors to the thing, she just couldn't bring herself to do it.

In hindsight, she should have realized that Madame, used to the odd requests, not to mention the occasionally downright weird behaviour, of some of the resident arcane population, wasn't going to balk at the actions of a mere mortal girl.

The rest of whatever preparations Kaheiron was, well, preparing, Lin didn't become privy to. It felt like there was no time at all until the morning they were meant to leave.

Lin yawned. It had been a while since she'd been up this early. Apparently, they were travelling in the Archmagus' private carriage; the small entourage that was going and Kaheiron wanted to set off at first light.

'Travelling by magic must be so much more convenient,' Lin griped quietly, while trying to wake up, get dressed and not wake up the dragonling at the same time.

That didn't work.

'No, Cheep,' Lin carefully fended off the small dragonling. 'You stay here. You hear me? Stay? S. T. A. Y!'

The little thing scratched at the door as Lin barely managed to shut it without him escaping. A low-pitched wail echoed mournfully through the stone.

'No, Cheep. I told you. You can't come,' Lin said resolutely and, feeling a right heel, turned and strode off to the waiting carriage. She felt like she was bound to get into enough trouble without his help.

A loud yowl erupted from behind the wood followed by something breaking as it hit the floor.

Linandra winced. Looked like she'd be lucky if the room was in one piece by the time she got back.

* * *

'You like it? Hur, Hur, Hur. That's alright lad, you eat up. Plenty more in the pot today,' the old woman chuckled.

Seth managed an incoherent mumble between mouthfuls.

It felt like his mouth was about to explode—out of goodness. Had he ever tasted anything like this? This wasn't just natural flavour, this was flavour with a kick, a bounce and a couple of cymbals thrown in for good measure.

Not that Seth knew what cymbals were, but if he had, he'd certainly have agreed with the allegory.

'Mmphh,' he nodded, holding out the now empty bowl. His eyes were streaming, but he just had to have more.

The only other person around the small campfire poured him another ladle of the thick stew.

'Got to have a stomach of lead you do. Not many strangers gulp down that much of ma's home cooking and not try and drown 'emselves in the stream next.'

'Are you saying there's something wrong with my food?' the old woman rounded on her companion.

'Why … no … of course not! Not at all! It's just that, well, not everyone knows how to appreciate it … properly.'

'Awhu, it does me good to see those gnashers going, yes it does.'

'Eat up boy. If it hadn'a been for ya', we wouldn't be enjoy'ing this—either of us,' the old man agreed.

'Not much to catch out here. Road too well-travelled these days. Not many inns though.'

'Really? They should know, not all journeys need a fancy house rushing past a milestone at a time.'

'Ma, no horse can run that fast, not even a really pricy one.'

'Then one of those big birdies then. They're fast. I've seen 'em. Swoosh, and their all gone,' she went back to complaining about the state of the roads and how no one looked after them properly under her breath.

'Why are you out here then?' Seth asked after having finally eaten his fill.

He'd seen the cart they had. Big, sturdy thing on four wheels it was. Just like the animals that pulled it. He just couldn't figure out why anyone would want to be moving that slow.

'They're a bit slow,' the man confessed, but ma don't hold with going fast. Slow and steady, that's what wins the race, so she says, ma.'

There was a kind of longing in the old bearded man's eyes. Maybe he wouldn't have minded going faster himself? Not that, that would have been hard.

'It'll take several more days to reach Amorix like this,' he complained.

But Seth had noted he did so very quietly and never when the lady in question was within earshot.

'Travelling,' the grey-haired and slightly rotund woman corrected him.

'Yes ma, I think he got that already,' her husband said loudly, before turning back to Seth. 'We're headed to Amorix for the Grand Festival,' he offered as a way of explaining.

Well, he certainly wasn't going to admit being familiar with the city, so

Seth feigned confusion. 'Grand Festival?' he asked.

He didn't care that much for festivals or traditional gatherings or anything even remotely similar. They still made him feel like he should be doing something important and he absolutely refused to get dragged into something like that down here too. It was bad enough having been stuck with it back home.

Parties, now parties were different. Very different. Mind you, there were some very nice treats, sweets and general yummies at festivals (especially in Amorix) that you didn't see the rest of the year, but now he'd rather send the servants to buy them rather than go himself.

Seth still thought it safest to continue to play ignorant, though.

'The Founder's Day celebrations, young man. Say, you're really not from around here, are ya?'

'No mam, I can't say that I am,' Seth admitted.

'Well, the Grand Festival, is a bit like Founder's Day, but about the biggest thing that happens on this side of the mountains,' the old man explained. 'It's held only rarely, really rarely, and ma said we'd have to be dead to miss it, didn't ya' ma?'

'That's right,' his wife chuckled toothlessly. 'Dead and in our graves. Could still be. This journey going so slow and you taking the wrong turn and bringing down all these hills on us.'

'Aough, ma, not my fault the sign had gone and broken now.'

'Hmph… You're explaining about as well as ya're driving, ya are.'

He'd always tried to avoid Amorix during the "busy" periods, and as Seth listened to the couple, the more it sounded like they'd be up to their ears in people, once they got wherever they were going. He shuddered.

Too bad he wasn't going to be able to avoid it this time. Seth winced. Just how had he managed to get talked into this?

* * *

'Andth ifs we don'th?' the largest of Joran's "guests" rumbled.

'Yezz, we don't want to play yo'ur gamezz,' another voice, harsher than the first, came from the smaller, wiry creature to his right. What it lacked in bulk, it made up in claws. Now it ran a long, thin tongue over pointed teeth. 'We don't likezz gamezz.'

A host of others joined in from the back.

Joran smiled at them with all the warmth of an ice pick. His eyes glittered, flecked with the dancing lights and random bursts of discharge.

'But you *do* want to roam these lands again. Don't you now?' Joran asked them coldly, an odd little smirk plastered over his otherwise deadpan features.

'And ifs we do?' the largest visitor looked down on the mage, green eyes narrowed.

Once, they were the ones that had ruled these caverns and the lands beyond them. That was until they'd been driven back across the hills, through the forests and into the rocks, where their deepest caves that had been the centre of their power eventually became their prison.

It was a prison without bars, without walls but not without its wardens. The guards weren't really out there, patrolling the wilds, sniffing the trails and generally moving without being seen. No, they were ones that were never far from those they imprisoned. In fact, you could say that they were insepa-rable. They were, in fact, ideas: the idea of what would happen … should they leave.

The ideas were, however, very old now. Weak. Their power was beginning to fade. Fear was giving way to curiosity, to desire.

'Old onezz. You givezz 'em to usz?'

'Oh yes, I'll give them to you. I'll give them *all* to you,' Joran grinned maliciously. 'Just do this one thing for me, one little favour, and they'll all be yours.'

This got their attention.

'And then we canth have the wizzarsth?'

'To your heart's content—should you have a heart somewhere in that speckled body of yours,' Joran agreed.

'What isz thizz favour that you speakz of?'

Joran leaned forward, away from the central spire of the softly glowing crystalline structure. Things were moving quickly now. Soon. Soon he would have enough—and then, then he'd show them. He'd show them all…

THE UNEXPECTED GUEST

'Ouch,' Lin winced for what felt like the umpteenth time (had she been able to count that high).

'Uncomfortable?'

'You're damn right I'm uncomfortable,' Lin snapped back at the Archmagus. 'This thing doesn't do anything other than go bounce, bounce, bounce at every bloody hole in the ground. Why would *anyone* want to ride in something like this?'

The shadow of a smile tugged at the corners of Kaheiron's mouth. 'And yet I believe you were quite excited when you first set eyes upon the carriage.'

'Was not!' Lin said and turned around to stare out at the scenery instead.

'It is a nice carriage,' one of the two remaining occupants conceded.

'Flying there would have been faster,' the third one countered. 'We could have been there in no time at all.'

'And among the most conspicuous arrivals of them all,' the Archmagus replied. 'This way we are merely one carriage among many. Once we reach the town that is,' he continued, after a glance out at the endless fields of grass. 'Out here, a carriage like this is somewhat more conspicuous.'

'I could disguise it,' the enchanter offered.

'Perhaps, next time,' Kaheiron replied from behind a green leather tome.

'Is it going to be like this the whole way?' Lin asked, interested against her will. It was better than staring out at the slow-moving landscape anyway. She'd seen grass before.

'You will see evidence of cultivation as we approach closer to the town.'

'Is it going to be this bumpy all the way?' Linandra asked again with feeling this time. 'Is this normal? I mean, I always thought riding in these things was *supposed* to be comfortable.'

'I do believe that other visitors have expressed the same sentiment,' Kaheiron acknowledged.

'I mean, sure, it's better than walking,' Lin pushed the curtain aside and poked her head out of the window, 'but—' her voice trailed off.

Up ahead the horses were trotting smartly on the brown road. She could feel the wind in her face. It felt like a touch of soft cotton compared to the stuffy feeling she was getting from being cooped up in the moving vehicle. She took a deep breath.

It wasn't bouncing as much when she was standing up like this either. Yes, this was much better.

The carriage wheels dropped an inch into a stony hole. Lin's head cracked against the window frame.

'Owww!'

'And that's why we don't stand,' the enchanter said.

'Sit down, Linandra, before you hurt yourself,' Kaheiron ordered.

'Is this going to take much longer?'

'Lin, we've only just left. You can still see the Towers behind us. Please be patient. We should reach the town before sundown tomorrow.'

'TOMORROW?' Lin exclaimed. Her head fell forwards, slumping into her shoulders like a retracting turtle. She was going to be stuck on this bouncing, shaking "thing" *that* long? 'Oh bollocks,' she said, with more feeling.

Several days later—far, far too many days, and inns, later for Lin's taste—the horse's hooves clattered over the stone bridge as they crossed over and into Amorix proper.

'It's so far down,' Lin breathed in. 'Is that a river … or a moat, down there?' she asked.

Every once in a while, the view was blocked by some statue lining the parapet, but she'd definitely seen something twinkling down in the shadow.

'Just sand and rocks these days. It would be more correct to say that we're up high,' the enchanter pointed out, while restacking the cards they'd been passing the time with. 'This bridge is built on the aqueduct principle, allowing us to pass from the level ground behind us directly into the main level of the city without any vertical inclination.'

'Huh?' Lin stared at him.

'Like several bridges stacked, one on top of another, to make it higher than one could have been alone. As you can see, the city itself is built upon a rock formation that is separate but still situated in very close proximity to the displacement of land. If we were to have approached it from the opposite direction, we would have had an excellent view of the sheer wall of stone and earth that is its backdrop.'

'But the ground behind us was flat?'

'Exactly.'

'Stop gawking, Linandra. I'm sure young ladies aren't supposed to lean halfway out of windows like that,' Kaheiron told his young charge while not taking his eyes out of the book he'd been reading for the whole journey.

'Were those walls? The big flat things I saw up ahead? I've never seen so many people. Do they all live here?'

'Many do. But it's usually not quite this lively. The festival has drawn both the local populace as well as visitors, and their retinues, from further afar than just the main domains surrounding us.'

Lin risked another peek, remaining behind the curtains this time, as they reached the gates to the city. They were like big blocks of stone, yellowed and darkened by age, and slabs big enough that, if you'd laid out the wall of even a large barn against them, they were still easily twice the height, four times the height … no … even more.

Their smooth surface was broken only by alcoves that were, if possible, even larger in size, and in which stood statues of figures in imposing poses. The closest to them, an impossibly slender man with a conical headdress clutched a spear... No, wait. She stared harder. They weren't statues at all. They'd been carved directly out of the stone, their backs still attached to the rock behind them from which they had been given life.

The slabs had to be that too. They must have been, there was no way any-one would have been able to move something that big, was there? They had to be carved out of the rock to look like stone blocks.

'Is the whole place made of some sort of mountain?'

'It's a bit too small to be a mountain,' Kaheiron replied, amused by her awe.

'It's a bit too big to be a rock,' Lin countered. 'Didn't think a city this size would have such fancy dressing ups.'

'I do believe that this used to be a temple island back in the old days, when there was still a sea here. It is what remains of an old volcanic plug. As you can see, the stone itself is much harder than the rock that surrounds it. If we approached from the opposite direction, on what use to be the seabed, there are several levels to climb until we reach the one that we are just entering. We still have some climbing to do ourselves before we reach our destination.'

'Which is where exactly?'

'At the top.'

'Of course. Why did I even bother asking,' Lin muttered crossly. 'Weird place to build anything on.'

* * *

'Home sweet home. I *almost* missed this place,' Seth said.

He then sneezed violently as the particles disturbed by his entry tickled his nose. 'Or maybe not...'

The sneeze bounced out into the hallway. It almost echoed between the walls, it felt that empty.

'Aaaahh ... dust ... ugh...' Seth wiped a grey sleeve across his nose. Trying not to breathe, he locked the door behind him.

'Waah... I 'ould 'have 'own,' he sniffed unhappily. 'I 'ouldn't 'have been too 'eap to pay the 'evants when not 'here ... spupid'.

Looking around, the reason for his trouble was obvious. A thick layer of dust, mixed with a bit of sand peeled off from the city, covered everything. And he'd disturbed a fair bit that had been resting peacefully on the drape that hung before the door. In hindsight, maybe he shouldn't have pushed it aside so roughly.

He took a bit more care traversing the rest of the house, leaving barely disturbed dust prints everywhere.

'Guess I should have come by a bit more often,' Seth sighed, as he rifled through a drawer. He immediately regretted that, as the deep breath drew in a large amount of even more dust.

Doubling over from the racking cough, Seth eventually managed to get himself to the other end of the room. Throwing open the arched window, he took in the warm air beyond.

'Ah … ahhh … that's better. Gods, how does anyone *do* this? Okay … okay. Just need to grab a few things. Hope the moths haven't gotten to them,' he said while looking out over the rooftops trying to gather his thoughts.

'Hmm … guess I should pick up a bit of money as well. It might come in handy. I'll need something easy to carry them in too. But yes, clothes first! Can't go anywhere without being dressed, not in this society.'

Taking more precautions this time, Seth tied a bit of cloth over his face before digging into his wardrobe or, more accurately, walking into it.

Peeling away the large sheets that had been protecting the hanging clothes carefully, as to not set off another grey storm, his eyes were immediately drawn to a brilliant spot of lemony yellow. He peered closely at the jacket which was covered in feathers. It rustled every time he moved it.

'Hmm … maybe this is a bit much?' Seth mused. There was so much to choose from, he'd be here all night if he couldn't make up his mind quickly.

'Oh yes … I need to pay a visit to the baths as well, don't I? I can't just put this on as I am,' he wrinkled his nose. 'Damn that journey. Guess I better do that in the morning *after* seeing to the staff, or I'll just get covered in dust again.'

* * *

Having tried to ignore the two guards that had been stationed outside her door since the evening before, Lin was now pacing on the carpeted floor.

She couldn't complain about her quarters. There was a rich colour to the furnishings. The walls curved gently, a constant reminder of the shape of the overall city. And the last of the sunlight, which you could just catch a glimpse of over the rooftops below—very much below—was offset by a set of lights burning in ornate green, glass-wrought cages. It gave the whole room an eerie shade, like something between life and death, she thought.

'They're big on green around here I guess,' Lin poked the glass, which gave a dull ping in return. 'Guess that's because there actually isn't any around. Just rock and dirt and sand.'

Eventually, growing tired of complaining, she allowed herself to sink onto one of the spindly chairs by the window.

She would have thrown herself onto it, but, at the last moment, she remembered what she was wearing and managed a somewhat unladylike bump instead. The crystals dangling like two small waterfalls from their filigree decorated hairpins in her hair collided, tinkling as they did so. In fact, every time she moved her head, that sound followed. It was getting more than a little distracting.

'Like putting a bell on the cat,' Lin muttered darkly. Reaching up, she touched one of them gingerly. Did they really have to stick out *this* far from her hair? It was like walking around with the horns of a couple of angels— had angels actually had slight, silver horns pointing out diagonally from their heads.

Why did she have to be stuck with those guards? What did they think she was going to do? Grab one of those oversized battle-swords that served as decoration and charge someone? That was ridiculous. Those things had to weigh more than she did.

Drumming her fingers on the nearby table, Lin tried to straighten out some of her ornate head tresses. The rest of her silky black hair had been combed out and was hanging loosely down her back, except for the two bumps into which the purply silver pins had been inserted. What an inconvenient way to dress, she fumed quietly.

'Exactly what am I supposed to do here?' Linandra demanded of the Archmagus a little later when he stopped by to visit. She tugged at one of the beads that were decorating what had been combed into her left bang. It clicked against the long piece of gold that separated it from the next purple bead.

'I feel like an idiot in this,' Lin said.

Kaheiron raised his hands imploringly, trying to ward off the not-quite-unexpected aggression. 'Easy there now. No need for violence.'

'Just tell me, okay! And why did they have to stick me in something like this?' she gestured over her dress.

'Many young women your age would, I believe, be very happy to wear such a creation,' Kaheiron said.

'Wonderful,' Lin retorted. 'They're welcome to it.'

Mostly cream, with borders in tarnished gold, it went all the way to the floor, even when she stretched to her utmost. There had been nothing for it but to dress her feet as well. As if adding on extra bits of height was a good thing. She already felt she was too tall as it was.

Eying her calmly, Kaheiron determined that diplomacy was obviously failing. Not that he was surprised there were still a fair few rough corners still to polish.

A shame because, right now, if fire hadn't been spitting from her emerald eyes and harsh words hadn't been issuing forth from between tight lips, she would have passed for practically any other young lady attending this little "get-together."

'I would say that it suits you very well,' Kaheiron said.

'You do?'

'Yes, I do.'

Lin tried to look herself over, ending up turning around in a circle. She wasn't entirely convinced Kaheiron wasn't just saying things for the sake of it.

'If you say so,' she said reluctantly. 'Not sure where this strange purple sash comes in though and what's up with these holes?' Lin asked, poking a finger against her skin, just below the shoulder.

'Those are called slits. They're quite popular among the young gentry in some circles. Of course, most people usually add a second, differentially coloured layer beneath it, to accentuate it.'

'These long sleeves are getting in the way too. Every time I try to grab something I end up dipping them into something else. I mean, my arms aren't exactly an elephant's foot you know.'

Kaheiron smiled, allowing himself to relax a little. If these were the only things Lin was complaining about, they'd already done better than he would have expected.

'Come on,' Lin growled. 'Just what am I supposed to do? I don't know anything about this hobnobbing stuff.'

'Try to relax—'

'And I ain't some freaking ornament you know!'

The Archmagus took a long, deep breath trying to gather his own wits for this full on frontal assault.

Most people gave him a very wide berth. Probably because most people objected being turned into a floating light, even for an hour or two, to say nothing about a wooden puppet, which seemed to be what they thought would happen if they angered him.

Not that he'd ever actually turned anyone into some small and furry animal, which would have, unfailingly in his mind, have ended up getting eaten, and then where would he have been? He had no idea where all these rumours came from.

But there were *some* for whom his person held no intimidation whatsoever. *Most* of the time he thought that was a *good* thing.

Lin, once she'd gotten past that first fear of him, was apparently not going to stay quiet when she was upset about something she thought he was responsible for (which, quite honestly, seemed to be a lot of the time).

'I could not imagine anyone less likely to occupy such a role,' he assured her.

Lin's eyes narrowed even further. 'Was that supposed to be an insult … or a compliment?' she asked suspiciously.

'Think of this merely as an opportunity to observe another side of life,' Kaheiron suggested.

'Couldn't you just turn me invisible or something, if you think I need to do this so badly? Do I really need to dress up in this stupid get-up for that?'

'Yes, Little One,' the Archmagus exhaled exasperatedly. 'You would be unlikely to be allowed to attend otherwise.' And I dare not even imagine what would happen if you were snuck in as part of the staff. Kaheiron shuddered at that thought.

'And don't even consider damaging your outfit as a means of escape,' he cautioned.

Judging by Lin's shift in expression, Kaheiron was glad he'd said that. He could literally see her disappointment as that loophole closed before her.

'Rats.'

'There now, Little Mouse. Today, you shall go play among the lions. Try not to bite them, they tend to bite back and they have bigger teeth than you do. And remember to pronounce your words as you practiced.'

'You mean proper for this lot?'

'Just *ordinary* proper will do for you,' Kaheiron assured her. 'And please, do refrain from actually hitting anyone. Try to be the lady your appearance says that you are.'

'Alright, alright,' Lin grumbled.

* * *

Seth exited his house via the servant's entrance. He really should have kept on a minimum staff, rather than just leaving the place empty. The dust did collect and it'd mean he didn't have to return to an empty, foodless house with no one around to aid him, should he need it. It'd also mean he wouldn't have to plan the visits in advance. Which almost never happened.

'Next time I take a vacation, I'm keeping the staff on duty,' he muttered irritably, while setting out to find someone to attend to his needs.

By the time Seth had come to the Temple City he'd been quite the affluent character. There had been no need for him to learn where most things happened or how. How the city, in fact, kept on staying a city (and not becoming, say, a pile of long forgotten stonework) and the people stayed people, via all the little bits of grease and cogwheels that kept life moving.

Now, he placed his best forbidding expression upon his countenance and set out to find someone to help him with his clothing, to find a bath (at least he knew where those were), and to arrange for a little something to eat, not to mention rehire someone to look after his house—not necessarily in that order.

Out on the street, it didn't take long for him to move from the relatively quiet area of his house to somewhere livelier. In fact, it took only one or two streets—albeit he did have to descend a level first—but there he was in luck, there were only a couple of "houses" between his own and one of the stairs that led down (or up for that matter).

Seth regarded the stone steps solemnly. They were quite steep up here.

'Good thing I don't have to climb these all that often,' he mused before entering the busy thoroughfare.

Before it had been quiet and calm (after a fashion), but the "street" that served as one of the city's aortas was anything a different world. Seth tried not to wince at the noise. People, humans or otherwise, weren't the only ones using the staircase and, while their handlers climbed the stairs quietly (outside of a certain amount of huffing and puffing), the animals did not.

'And this is exactly why I don't like walking,' Seth grumbled to himself under his breath as he tried not to breathe in the nauseating scent of a fresh deposit of dung as he passed. 'Just consider yourself lucky,' he added after a moment's reflection. 'At least you don't have to go through the lower districts.'

It didn't matter how many times he came here, the city still seemed strange to him. Sure, he had houses in several places by now, but Amorix was still head and shoulders above the other settlements. It was the kind of place you stopped in for a month or two before it started to overwhelm you.

It was even stranger than the first settlement he'd visited … almost—and that had seemed strange purely because he hadn't known what to expect here. Here, people were living in it, yes, but everywhere you looked, their lives were in little niches, tucked in beneath the feet of statues, as tall as dragons, or using smaller ones as support poles for ropes and strings.

The one area where those smaller towns definitely had an advantage though, was in the amount of people. Here, there were so many, coming in all shapes and sizes and species, and all wanting not just a piece of the city, but, quite often, the space your body was occupying too.

It didn't really matter how stern he tried to look either, Seth thought as he weaved in and out among the people. You heard about people for whom the crowd parted. Well, he seemed to have been "blessed" with the opposite: no matter where he turned, if he wasn't wearing the right clothes or had a pair of bodyguards doing the shoving for him, there always seemed to be busy people in his path.

'Maybe I should have taken the parade steps instead?' he asked himself, as he ducked into a narrow alley.

The ruckus quickly died down, dampened by the ridiculously high walls of stone and mud and brick, and Seth made much quicker progress, as long as he didn't mind jumping over the occasional hurdle.

Even on the move, the people bargained and sold (and stole too, if they had a chance) on what had been great avenues lined with plinths and columns and giant urns, beyond which even greater buildings strained for height.

They did the same in the much narrower streets further below, only louder and with more bodies and smaller animals.

Seth kicked a large, broken wicker basket out of the way and, coming upon the "bathhouse" from the wrong direction, had to finesse his way through a narrow gap.

'Blast. I thought the windows faced this direction,' Seth muttered. He could smell the faint perfumed vapours coming from the roof of the building, but, without windows or doors facing this way, there was nothing to do but to take the long way around.

The alleys, Seth had discovered, were often dead ends, but with care you could find a shortcut or two: here, ducking behind a statue; there, squeezing past the narrow gap between a dancing frieze and a wall.

In this case, the gamble hadn't paid off quite the way he'd intended.

Seth preferred to travel via the rooftops if he had to be out and about without a sedan-chair. He could pick his way across the, mostly, flat surfaces at each level with relative ease. The downside was that getting from level to level could be tricky, more often involving the scaling of a steep wall or two, as the stairs tended to be on the long side.

Walking down them, tracing your steps from the highest level down to the old seabed below, was tiring enough. Going back up again, now that was exhausting. Sure, they didn't all connect, so you had some time on level ground, but the idea was still seriously unappealing. Counting several thousand steps from top to bottom wasn't something you ran up and down every day. At least, *he* didn't.

It was a city to visit, not a city to live in: the great Temple City of Amorix.

Of course, it had been a long time since it had played the part of messenger between gods and men. Seth had no idea what had happened to change the place into what it was now. All the tomes he'd been able to find pertaining to the city's past had been seriously dry, and he didn't mean dry as in crackling pages. He might enjoy reading and learning, but those dusty old things he'd long since given up on. Half the time he couldn't understand what they said, anyway.

One thing was sure though. People had, today, made the city theirs, there wasn't any doubt of that.

Something else you didn't need to doubt was the level of service you received—if you could pay for it—and a few coins later, Seth handed over his rather dusty clothes to a waiting attendant in exchange for a light, white, robe which swivelled around his feet as he walked.

'I wonder what they used this place for?' Seth mused. 'Back in the olden days.'

As so many other things, what it had once been intended for, was not what it was being used for, and he wasn't certain he'd recognize it even if it was. Still, water was water. If you wanted a certain amount, there were certain physical structures that were required whether you were looking for a ritual pool dusted with a scattering of roses; somewhere to cavort with a harem of mermaids (which he seriously doubted anyone had ever done, seeing as they didn't exist); or just wished to clean yourself. Usually, the main difference would be in the size and shape of the pool.

Which was probably why the place was relatively untouched by the modern "improvements" that had refurbished the rest of the city.

Seth gave a small nod to a couple of nobles he recognized in the open pools, meandered under the serpentine colonnade surrounding them until he came to an ornate and very round doorway.

Beyond it lay some of the more private pools and it was with a grateful sigh of contentment that Seth, some minutes later, slipped into the shallow waters that the attendant had directed him to, and who, at Seth's request, retreated to a small bench outside of the room itself.

Looking about, Seth's eyes fell on the nubile statues, five of them, that surrounded the shallow pool, the warm waters of which were already soothing some of his aching muscles.

'I wonder what this peculiar insistence on portraying everyone in this building with as little to wear as possible comes from?' he mused.

Seth had come to understand that humanoid beings were very keen on clothes, even when they didn't need them to stay warm. So, every time he entered the former temple, he always wondered why it, in sole defiance, was equally keen on the opposite.

Even stranger was that while their bodies were quite human, their heads seemed to vary ... a lot. For instance, the one he was watching right now had the head of an antelope, antlers and all.

'Humanoids. I'll never understand them,' Seth sighed, drifting over in the water. He let his finger glide over the statue. It was life-sized, that is, assuming there were real life antelope people running around somewhere. It was quite exquisite in its detailing. Whoever had carved it had obviously taken great pride in their work.

'Wonder what old Ragnheidur would have made of this?' Seth asked of the air. 'Of course, he wouldn't have fitted in here to see it, but still...'

He'd taken the expense of a private pool, so though he could hear others, he couldn't see them. Nor could they see him.

'Much more relaxing this way, don't you think?' Seth said himself as he leaned back, dipping under the surface for just a moment.

There was an attendant standing by outside the room, which had no doors to close, but they wouldn't enter unless he called for them and Seth preferred to enjoy his baths alone.

Shaking off some of the water lodged in his hair, he took another look around. He'd never used this particular pool before. Curious really, there were not two alike.

Pretty much the same went for the statues surrounding him.

'So, we've got one antelope; two humans of different dispositions; what looks like some sort of cat, and something with more tentacles than anyone would ever ask for,' Seth shuddered involuntarily. 'Yuck. Whoever built this place, they sure had some strange tastes.'

Suppose he should be happy that they hadn't decorated the rest of the small chamber the same way. Instead, it merely consisted of a mix of cool white stone and the local sandstone, in an arcade-vs-colonnades manner, along with the alcoves he'd come to recognize as a hallmark of the city (along with its tendency to stick giant, and not-so-giant, statues wherever it thought there had been space).

The water sparkled off the highly polished ceiling and some of the walls. It was oddly soothing.

Taking a deep breath, he let himself slide back and immersed himself completely.

* * *

It felt like she'd been waiting forever. They hadn't needed to make her dress up long before lunch if all she'd be doing was being stuck in the outfit for the whole day until they were due to attend the ceremony, had they? By now, she was feeling more than just a little uncomfortable—especially since she hadn't been allowed out.

After a whole day of being cooped up in her quarters, Linandra would even have welcomed a tour of the temple-palace they were staying in. Even if it had meant listening to another lecture from Kaheiron.

What had he and the others been up to all day? There was no way that they'd take that long to dress, was there? He'd mentioned something about business but hadn't gone into detail. Actually, Lin frowned, he or the others hadn't said a word about why there were actually here, now that she thought about it.

And now he'd just popped back in to check on her? What was she? Some sort of stray dog?

'Linandra, are you listening to me?'

'What? Oh, yes, sorry. You were saying?' Lin put on her most innocent expression.

'I asked if you were ready to leave?'

'Do I have to?'

'I will take that as a yes. Excellent. I have taken the precaution to ask one of the fine gentlemen outside to escort you to the festivities. This way you don't have to worry about getting lost on the way there.'

'Wonderful,' Lin said. She didn't even try to keep the sarcasm out of her voice. She might not have known what the word meant, but she was more than well-equipped to use it.

'Wait, aren't you coming?' Lin stopped at the door. Running her eyes up and down the Archmagus' figure, he *looked* as if he was attending, if his attire was anything to judge by. She'd never seen him so "fancied up."

'I'll be along later, Little One. I have a few matters of importance to attend to. You try to enjoy yourself now,' Kaheiron said.

'Oh … right.'

Lin shook her head, causing her adornments to clink and tinkle as she left. 'You know, I don't think I've ever seen that man enjoy himself … ever. I mean, all he does is work, work, work,' she said.

The guard Kaheiron had roped into his services, who was stoically leading the way through the high vaulted corridors, didn't reply.

'You're not much for talking either, you know,' Lin complained. 'How am I supposed to have fun if everyone around me keeps doing their best not to? I mean, does he even know how to have fun?' she asked.

It felt like they'd been walking for ages before Linandra realized that the path they were taking was steadily growing in size. But even with that Lin still wasn't prepared for the sight that met her as, turning around a huge, fluted column, another room opened up before her. Though calling it a room didn't nearly do it justice.

'The Grand Hall, my lady,' the guard bowed slightly and departed as quietly as he'd arrived.

Not that Lin noticed. She just stared.

'This is … this is impossible,' she breathed.

She walked up to the balustrade in front of her, leaning over to get a better view. 'There has to be at least two levels down to the floor from here and,' her head angled upwards, 'look at the size of those. That ceiling has to be, what, a hundred metres up?'

'Not quite,' an amused voice said from over by the wall. 'Sorry, didn't mean to give you a fright,' the young man chuckled when Lin jumped at his voice. 'Well, better dash, or I'll miss all the fun downstairs,' he said.

And, just like that, with no explanations, no nothing, he just left her standing there, mouth agape. Was he laughing at her? What nerve. Slightly huffed, Lin turned back to view the chamber instead. She still couldn't believe it was even possible to build something this big.

It was huge. If you took the biggest indoor space in the Twin Towers, you could probably have been able to fit a number of them into this place and still have space left over, Lin thought.

On the other hand, it had a crude sense to it that the Towers didn't. Like if someone had tried to achieve with mere scale what someone else would have merely implied with intricate and airy designs.

'Wonder what this place was before someone tried turning it into a castle?' Lin wondered.

Trying not to crane her neck around too much, she descended down the long, flowing, staircase.

There were people everywhere: Standing by the balustrades; talking on the stairs: standing with plates in hand by the buffet: and moving with less or more purpose around the "room."

'Guess they have to,' Lin whispered to herself as her eyes scanned her surroundings. 'Seems they didn't bother about bringing chairs to this little party.'

There seemed to be all kinds, too. People that was, not furniture. The only furniture in the place appeared to be the long tables on which the various edibles of the evening were displayed.

While she heard plenty of laughter, not two alike, they all shared a distant quality, as if the owner wasn't actually the least bit amused. No surprise there, Lin thought. Lots of these folks don't look like they have a sense of humour to start with: the servants especially.

While there were smiles here and there, the biggest ones felt kind of sinister. Lin shuddered as she walked past a pair dressed in very similar costumes of white and black velvet. She thought she could feel their eyes burning into her back, but when she snuck a peek, they appeared to still be deep in conversation. Maybe she'd just imagined it?

Of course, there were plenty of genuine amusement drifting past as well. Linandra managed to avoid breaking out into a gale of laughter as she caught sight of the first uniformed guard standing at attention by the first colonnade but only by walking past very fast and straining to hold her breath.

Poor guy, she thought. If someone ever wanted to design an armour and regalia that would be fit for a chicken—albeit a rather large one—they could have stopped by for inspiration.

Still, some of the things the guests were wearing were, to Lin, equally laughable. The difference was, no one was laughing *at* them.

'And I thought *I* was going all fancy like. Coming up a bit short against these guys, that's for sure,' she mused as she tried to make her way across the floor.

Lin had seen the tables from above, but once down on the floor itself, she'd gotten a bit turned around and lost sight of them. Now she caught a glimpse again, between the bodies of the guests and servants, of the far most important part of tonight's event: food.

There were whole mountains of plates. Strangely shaped dishes struggled to break free of the diced, sliced and skewered fruit of every kind that bordered all the silverware.

The sweet, boiled brown ones that looked a bit like someone had tied a brain up in a knot where especially tasty.

'Hope these things just *look* like tiny boiled brains,' Lin popped another one in her mouth. They were far too tasty to actually *be* brains … she hoped. She'd seen the odd brain floating in a jar back at the Towers, but those had had a more "yuck" than "yummy" look to them.

Still, while the food helped, it didn't make the evening enjoyable, per se. With all the colours vibrating from stands, hanging on the walls, even lurking between the sandstone arcades, alcoves and statues (which suggested that someone had made quite a bit of effort into trying to turn this place away from its more bare and severe origin), it was beginning to give her a headache.

It probably would have been survivable, if you weren't devoid of good company, Lin decided after an hour or so.

If I have to smile and nod like a good little fool any more, I'm going to freeze into this shape for the rest of my life, Lin thought as she stabbed a fruit with a slim fork. This is not my idea of "having fun," Kaheiron. If this is what all that hobnobbing is about, well, they can keep it. Even the music is annoying: I should like to go right up there and snap those strings right off, she winced inwardly.

She would have liked to tell him just what she thought about it in person, but there still wasn't any sign of the Archmagus or the two others who'd come with them.

If I'd known I was just going to be dumped in the middle of a room full of twirling twats, I would have stayed home. How could anyone even think of this as having a good time? I mean, I don't know, but there has to be more to it than this?

Is this all that those balls were, that all those stories kept insisting on sending their would-be princesses to? Seriously? The village fair was better. And she hadn't liked that either.

Okay, so the food here was interesting—if a bit hard to figure out how to eat—but she hadn't really enjoyed getting her tongue scalded when dipping into one or two of the dishes. They'd looked innocent enough. 'They really should put up warning signs on those things,' Lin grumbled.

But where was the life? Mostly what everyone was doing was standing around talking or even just standing around. Maybe they were waiting for the right time to start talking?

Here and there, in the centre of what—for the lack of a better word—had to be called "the room," there were people swaying from side to side in rhythm. Lin assumed they were dancing.

'Seriously? That has got to be the most boring fun ever devised.'

Where was the excitement? Where was the laughter other than the occasional coquettish giggle? Where was, in other words, the party?

'Where the blast has he gone off to?' Lin muttered to herself.

She might not be able to complain very loudly, not without giving herself away, but she could still think it as loud as she wanted to, right?

Being here with company would have been bad enough, Lin decided. Getting stranded on a deserted island by someone you trusted wasn't the least bit fun. Especially when said island consisted of other people.

And the food … always coming back to the food. Sure, there was plenty of it, but was anyone really eating much of it? Not the ladies, certainly. Normally Lin wouldn't have cared, but she was hungry and she'd see the other females in here take one small plate and then proceed to take an even more delicate bite. Apparently, they weren't meant to eat much.

'Guess that accounts for some of the stares then,' she grumbled to herself, looking at her overloaded plate.

She tried not to frown. Thank goodness she wasn't wearing some of those things the women were waddling around in, or she wouldn't have been able to eat anything either. Like that big one in pink—how did she breathe in that? Either the woman had a waist like a dewwasp or she was trying to become one by emulating their behaviour.

And that one—in the voluptuous dress that spread out several times her own size—it was like watching the progress of a balloon across the floor, if said balloon had been hovering an inch above ground. The dress effectively stopped the lady in question from getting close to anything: the wired skirt a safe buffer between her and the world. If someone had actually convinced her she looked good in it, they'd have had to be a world-class liar, Lin figured.

A quick staccato on the marble floor made her step back quickly. The sound was tell-tale, even here, and regrettably familiar. It heralded the passing-by of an intimidating woman in severe black, with heels tall enough to lift her already considerable height to, well, even further heights.

Lin had already had one run in with that one and had no desire to have another. Her papa had always said that nobby people didn't have any dress-sense. Guess he'd been right about that. Suppose the old man had to have been right about *something*, among all the rest of the rubbish he'd spouted.

Thank goodness the creation they'd insisted on sticking *her* into wasn't that limiting. In comparison to some things the ladies here had decked themselves out in, she was metaphorically flying. She could still move freely, as long as she was careful and didn't step on the hem or wave the rather flighty sleeves around too much.

If she did forget, the long sleeves would stop falling elegantly over her soft olive-skinned arms and just get tangled in any random thing that happened to be around. Then her hair would change from being draped over her shoulders to just being its usual mess as she lost her balance. And then she'd be laughed at until she could make herself disappear among the rest of the guests.

'Great, Lin. Just what every girl wants. The chance to be a princess for a night. Well, if this is anything what it's like, then no thanks. I'd rather hang out with Cheep, any day.'

At least no one had asked her to dance, thank the high heavens for that. Especially not one of those creepy guys in black and white. Even just walking past them made her skin crawl. She'd heard enough of the conversation earlier to know she never wanted to be anywhere near him. Ever. And they'd been laughing about it, laughing. She shuddered again.

Lin looked around through the corner of her eyes. Where was the other one? The one that looked just like him?

Wonderful. Now she was getting skittish on top of everything else. 'Calm down girl, I'm sure Kaheiron will be here at any moment and then you can stop worrying. Just stay calm and wait. Umm … what's everyone looking at?'

Surrounded by a sudden susurration of whispered conversations, Lin felt as if she was missing out on something important. Still trying to keep an eye out, she turned around, wondering what everyone was talking about. Looking up, she realized just what had caught their attention.

'Oh, thank goodness. About time you showed up,' Lin muttered, her heart dancing somewhere between sheer relief at his arrival and annoyance at him for taking so long.

She tried to move closer, but, apparently, she wasn't the only one interested in getting a first eye's view of the Archmagus.

'Seriously, they act like they've never seen the guy before,' Lin muttered, unable to understand what all the fuss was about, while trying to weave her way through an increasingly dense throng of people.

Maybe he was one of those whose reputation travelled like an exponential mist of words, while an appearance by the man himself was a much more rare occurrence? One of those "once in a lifetime" events? Going by how everyone's eyes were burning into the backs of those in their line of sight, it was rare enough, Lin decided.

Not that she could really see much from here, but she could imagine that Kaheiron was smiling graciously enough where he was standing at the top of the balustrade. That'd explain the interests of the ladies at least. Linandra rolled her eyes. Sure, he was handsome enough, but why any woman wanted to go ga-ga over a guy was beyond her.

'What's the point anyway?' Lin grumped.

Her feelings of relief at the Archmagus' arrival occupying her mind, she was eventually caught out by the sheer mass of people, only to run straight into a human male. A man wearing black and white velvet.

Lin felt her body stiffen. Before she even had the chance to step back he pushed an ebony cane in between them, as if prying off an offending limpet. It struck her in the chest.

'Desist from touching your fingers upon my person, cretin!'

Eyes wide, Lin tried to back away hurriedly. 'I'm sorry… I didn't mean…'

The man's eyes didn't even look at her, yet she could feel the sheer loathing wash over her as if it had been a whole bucket of slimy water.

'If I want anything, *I* will make the first move. And I get—what I want.' He leaned forward until his face was only a few centimetres away from hers.

'What? Wait...'

'Yes,' the word serpented out from between his thin lips. 'That's *just* the expression.' The cane rubbed harshly under her chin. 'I don't see your escort, girl. So unfortunate. So sad. So abandoned. And it's not even midnight yet.'

Lin wished, really wished, that she wasn't alone down here. With shaking hands, she tried to push the cane away.

'Get away from me!' she said, stumbling over the words.

The cane suddenly thrust hard against her abdomen, sending her staggering backwards.

'Hold your tongue, lest I cut it out from you.'

Doubled over, Lin tried to breathe. Why was everyone around them ignoring them? Was this normal?

Legs unfit to carry her right now, she staggered backwards. It didn't carry her away, only caused her to collide with yet another person.

Great, as if I wasn't in enough trouble already. The thought came unbidden, half in anger, half in fear. What was with this place?

Now it wasn't just her first problem, the person in front. Now there was another one. Whoever they were, she could still feel them behind her.

She swallowed. Please, please, don't be the other one, Lin wished. Please don't be the other one.

'Now, now, Count Rugho. Is that any way to treat a guest?' the voice from behind her said.

It sounded light-hearted. It seemed almost, amused?

Lin felt two hands trying to steady her. She wanted to turn around, see what, who, had caught her, but the thin veil of contempt that now spread over the count's face made her freeze in place. Could this be someone even worse?

The count withdrew slightly. The cane went back to his side.

'Oh, it's you,' Rugho straightened up, voice dripping with badly disguised venom. For a moment, his whole face lit up with loathing. 'I might have known.'

Rugho regarded the latest arrival as an uninvited addition to a private party for two. But he seemed oddly reluctant to pursue the matter.

Did that mean this person was even worse? Lin tried to sneak a peek behind her.

The first thing that struck her was how young he looked. He was barely her own age—and still this scary man backed away from him?

Actually, with the dark grey tresses of his hair, you would have been forgiven for mistaking him for an old man if you'd seen him from behind, she thought. From the front, she was noticing little beyond the boyish grin and, oddly enough considering the circumstances, some mesmerizing grey eyes.

The count looked like he wanted to sneer. It hovered around his lips without ever fully breaking out.

'Favouring purple this year, are we Terrsainoh? Such extravagance. Every tailor within a hundred leagues must be crying themselves to sleep over your insistence to wear that foolish vest on top of a robe,' Rugho said, dripping with poisoned honey.

Despite wanting nothing more than to tear the man to shreds, Lin had to be forced to admit he had a point. Her would be saviour looked just a little odd. Even for this crowd.

'I'm sure even an interloper such as yourself are aware that such garments are not supposed to reach beyond your hips. Wearing them almost to your feet looks just ridiculous. And what blinding fool would wear a banded sash with such an outfit?'

If Rugho expected his barbs to strike true, he would have had better luck aiming at another target. Terrsainoh just smiled back with almost innocent amusement.

'Do you really think so?' he said. 'I thought the gold filigree was a nice accompaniment to the touch of fur up here,' the young man patted a shoulder and grinned. 'It's so white and fluffy.'

One challenge missing its mark, Rugho changed tactics and poked Lin with his cane. 'This, with you then, Terrsainoh?' he taunted. 'I should have realised. You never did have any taste.'

'My taste, as you put it, is exquisite. Don't you agree Linandra?' Terrsainoh winked at her.

Lin wasn't too fond of what was going on, but she was too stunned to find time for a reply before Count Rugho cut in.

'I shall waste no more time on one such as you,' Rugho sneered. 'One day, Terrsainoh, you will interfere at the wrong time.'

Count Rugho's feathers ruffled, his heels struck the floor heavily as he wheeled around. His cane only narrowly avoided striking either of them before he disappeared among the rest of the guests.

'Never liked that man,' Terrsainoh said as if nothing had happened. 'Horrid person. Not everyone here's like that, you know.'

Linandra no longer trying to back into a non-existent corner, with the Count's departure, her confidence returned.

'Please don't think you just saved me,' she said acidly as she pulled her hand away from her would-be rescuer. 'I didn't *need* saving.'

Terrsainoh just grinned at her. Maybe he knew she was lying? Her knees felt like jelly, even now.

'Now, now. I like to think it was *him* I just saved,' Terrsainoh chortled. 'Which would absolutely kill him, if he knew. You *did* look like you were about to throw him a straight right hook. Well, either that or faint.'

'How many times do I have to tell you—' Lin began, then, as if she just realized what she was saying, she tried to look suitably abashed. She was all too aware this was somehow not what the Archmagus had meant when he'd said "have fun."

'Ummm…' she began, wondering what you were supposed to say at a time like this.

'Not that he didn't deserve it,' the young man whispered in her ear as he pulled her into the dance. 'But perhaps it would be a good idea to avoid him. The count is said to keep a list of all people who have once insulted him or, in his eyes, done him harm. Or just one with all those people he'd like to do "interesting" things to in his spare time. I'm sure I'm on that first list several times over.'

'I'm sorry, good Sir,' Lin eventually managed to get her head at least halfway in gear, even if it wasn't quite the right one. 'But who was that … and who are you?' she asked, adding, 'you look kind of familiar, in an annoying sort of way.'

Looking taken aback for a moment, Terrsainoh laughed. 'I've got that kind of face, do I?'

'And Count Rughorn? Who's he?'

'What? Oh, yes. Don't worry about it. You don't want to know. Trust me. You *really* don't want to know. Me on the other hand, me you can call Terrsainoh, if you'd like.'

Seth felt terrible about giving her one of his aliases, but it had slipped out before he'd realized and Rugho had already played that particular card anyway. Now it was too late to change.

Lin didn't look particularly happy as it was, he realized. Was he doing something wrong? Was there something else you were supposed to do at a time like this?

'Right... Well, I should be going now...' Linandra said, edging backwards, trying to take a few quick few steps away.

This time he let her pull free. And she quickly disappeared in the throng.

Still feeling a little shaken, Lin tried to find someone she knew. That wasn't easy. There seemed to be more people following the music, now. She could see little but swirls of colour from the centre of the floor. Guess the fuss over Kaheiron had ended.

That was great, but, right now, she wouldn't mind a bit of fussing herself. Some of her defiance might be coming back, but she was still feeling a bit wobbly.

That probably accounted for why she wasn't paying as much attention to where she was going as she should have. Craning her neck, trying to track down the seemingly very elusive Archmagus, Lin wasn't paying as much attention to herself as she should have.

And, looking the wrong way, she bumped into one of the couples enjoying the display on the dancefloor. At least they had enjoyed it until the rough physical abrupt meeting with the unscheduled body in orbit that was Lin.

'Young Lady,' the old man addressed her sternly. 'That is simply not done.'

'I'm sorry, Sir...' Lin started apologetically.

'And now the music has stopped,' the female on his arm complained in a lofty voice.

'Not to worry, my dear,' the man said, 'I'm sure it will begin again shortly. And you,' his voice changed from its soothing tones, 'must clearly be a disappointment to your parents, not being wedded at your age. You have clearly learnt no restraint.'

His eyes knotted. 'I wouldn't have thought they'd allow someone with your lack of manners to attend. What did you say your name was?'

It wasn't so much embarrassment as pent up anger that coloured Lin's cheeks at that point. The trouble was she couldn't exactly contradict him without lying.

Yeah, mister. I don't exactly like you either, she thought. If thoughts were made of steel, he'd have been pierced by multiple arrowheads at that point. Just because he was elderly didn't mean he could go around saying those kinds of things to people, did it?

Before she had a chance to respond though, someone else did so in her place.

'Linandra, there you are, my blossom. You know, I really wish you wouldn't wander off like that. There is no telling what might happen.'

The voice sounded cheerful enough, like if its owner had no worries in the world. It also sounded terribly familiar.

Great... I thought I lost him. Bugger, Lin's mind followed up with a few more choice remarks. At least it wasn't that despicable count. After what she'd heard, meeting him again, it wasn't just the shivers it gave her. Still...

'Lord Essilim, how unexpected to meet you here. And here we've believed all this time that you shared nothing but loathing for attending these functions. Isn't that what you always say?' Seth continued in self-certain, smooth tones.

He sounded different then when he'd talked to the count earlier, Lin realized: loftier and dandy-like. She wasn't sure she liked it any better than the earlier version.

'Now, if you will excuse us,' Seth made a small bow to the older man. 'Come, Lin, there's someone I'd like to introduce you to.'

'You?' the old lord tried to not let his ire show. 'I might have known. Come, my dear. We shall seek out some *civilized* company.'

As the two of them departed, Lin rounded on the young man whom she'd run into earlier, starting with snatching her arm from his grasp.

'I'll have that back, thanks,' Lin snapped.

'No need to be so hostile,' Seth twinkled back.

'I don't see what's so amusing?' Introduce me to who? What are you talking about? And who are you anyway? That half-forgotten old sod couldn't wait to get away, now could he? That's *twice* now. What did you do to them to make them run away like that?'

'Well— ' the ghost of uncomfortableness raced across his features but was quickly kicked out of the bucket for shoving. 'I *do* have a bit of a reputation,' he confessed.

'As what? Incurable womanizer?'

'Ouch, that hurt.'

'Creepy stalker?'

'That too. No, wait … that was a joke,' Seth followed her as she backed up a bit. 'It's not like that. I just do all the things that they wished they could do—if they weren't so caught up in what society dictated that they and their fellows considers what they should be doing.'

'And you don't care about doing what? Not creeping out everyone around you? Silly titles?'

'Don't have one,' Seth grinned at her again. 'Title that is,' he added. 'And I'm *not* creepy.'

'Sure, you aren't. Then why d'you keep following me around?' Lin wanted to know.

'Don't need one either,' he continued. 'Got the only thing that's really important around here—money.'

Wonderful. No wonder the old bugger had disappeared so fast, Lin thought. Probably afraid that he'd catch something: like incurable stupidity.

So, that was what he was; another young idiot on the up and up who thought he could buy himself anywhere or anyone he wanted, then. Who probably thought he could get away with murder if he paid someone enough, too. Just her luck. Where the blast was Kaheiron when she needed him?

'How nice,' Lin's voice dripped with icicles.

Now, how was she going to lose him?

EVERYTHING I DO

A good night's sleep might have made Linandra feel more amiable towards the world; *if she'd had a good night's sleep* that was. She'd been tossing and turning for the entire night. Whatever she was feeling, "amiable" certainly wasn't it.

It was just like the universe to just keep piling one thing on top of another just to annoy her.

'Sweet dreams, indeed,' Lin scoffed. First, she'd had to endure riding in that horrid contraption and then she had to spend a whole evening trying to avoid making a fool of herself. The least she could expect was to get to have a look around, right?

But no. All she got were excuses. Everywhere she looked there were just excuses and varieties of 'I think you'd better stay in your room and pretend you're not there.' All because she'd ended up tripping over a hem, knocking in to the crafted refreshments as she desperately tried to regain her balance and ending up causing the whole thing to collapse, drenching the Narmonian Ambassador and his wife in the process.

The Ambassador hadn't been happy. Not happy at all. But it wasn't like she'd done it on purpose. He hadn't needed to make up all those horrid ways in which she was going to pay for it.

He probably would have gone through with them too, she thought. He looked the type. Not a nice face at all, screaming at her like that. Her father had looked like that when he thought she'd done something wrong. Now there was a memory she could do without.

She didn't like the idea of what *might* have happened—*would* have happened—if Kaheiron hadn't showed up when he did. Guess having an archmage—and especially *her* Archmagus—on your side did have advantages. He hadn't even raised his voice, but the Ambassador had acted almost as if someone had set a pair of sighthounds on him or worse. After that, there had been no end to his politeness.

Of course, she'd been in almost as much trouble from Kaheiron once they got back. Lin shook her head, trying to dislodge the memories. She didn't like getting yelled at but having people talk sternly to you without paying any attention to your complaints (or rampage) was, somehow, even worse.

There was also that nagging, little feeling that kept insisting she'd let him down, and, despite her efforts, she didn't like that. It was as if she was constantly accompanied by a talking itch that she just couldn't reach.

After a few days like that, Lin felt she was owed a little something.

Putting her back into it, Lin strained against the knot she'd made with all her might.

'Good,' she said, forcing air back into her lungs. 'That should do it. Guess sheets *have* their uses, but actual rope is even better. *So* kind of them to use thick coils of it to tie back the bed-curtains.'

Did Kaheiron really think he could just ask her to remain in her rooms with absolutely *nothing* to do? While he and the other mages just went about … doing whatever it was they were doing. That just wasn't fair.

And they weren't due to leave for another two whole days. What was she supposed to do? Just sit here and stew like some old soup or something? Bleh. No thanks. Not her.

After coming all this way, she wasn't going to go back without seeing what all the fuss was about. This was supposed to be a city. She'd never even *seen* a city before. That had to make it worth it, right?

And it wasn't as if begging was going to help. The guards at the door had looked positively *unhelpful* when she'd tried to sneak out earlier. No, if she was going to get anything done today other than just watching the walls close in, then she was going to have to take it into her own hands.

Lin straightened out, putting the final touches to her hair by pulling it up in a ponytail.

Right. She could do this.

She leaned out the narrow, glassless window.

It was a very … very long way down.

The city beyond proved as exhilarating as it did confusing. No matter where she turned her eyes, Lin found herself either looking up—and up and up—or down in equal measure.

It turned out to be more than a little bit bigger than she'd anticipated. It also contained a whole lot more people—more than she'd ever seen in one place in her entire life.

Was it then any wonder that she became so absorbed in what she was doing that she ended up paying little attention to anything else?

'I'm sure I walked down this street once before already,' Lin tried to focus on something recognizable. But aside from the feeling she'd been here before, there wasn't anything to give her a clue as to why. Although, some of narrow streets were almost identical, filled with so much that you lost the forest for the trees, so to speak.

'Wait! What was that?' Lin jolted, her eyes widening. Was that the same noise she'd heard before?

'Maybe it isn't part of city life after all,' Lin mumbled, starting to feel the space around her closing in, uncomfortably so. Her ears strained against the more normal sounds emanating from the casual lives of the people in the street. It was like a kind of popping sound with a wooden click thrown in.

It *was* the same sound. It had to be. She'd heard it several times already. And never in the same place twice. Was it a bird?

'I'd swear that thing's following me,' her eyes darted around, almost meeting themselves coming back. 'But that can't be right.'

The street looked no different than it had a moment ago, before she'd heard it. It was just an ordinary street in the market levels. There were people there: some striding ahead with a purpose; some carrying burdens (from whole baskets to single bits of fruit); and some were trying to sell as many of said burdens as possible. All of them were chattering. Indeed, the whole background sound to the market was just a droning of voices. Odd clicking hoots didn't really come into it.

None of those people seemed to hear the strange sound. Maybe it didn't mean anything to them, or it was so commonplace that they didn't even notice. So, whatever was going on, it was something they didn't need to worry about. Great. What about her? Should *she* be worrying?

Lin frowned. What *was* going on here? She'd heard it the first time; no, make that, she'd *noticed* it the first time after having stopped by a vendor from whose stall there was wafting the most delicious smell of roasted candies.

She'd looked up for a moment, but, when it didn't appear again, she'd returned to paying more attention to which of the candied delicacies she wanted to buy.

There had been this sickly pink one that seemed to be made by rolling nuts around this big, hot pan, chasing some sort of red-brown gunk around until the nut had disappeared completely. It should have been disgusting, but taking an experimental nibble on a corner revealed that it was like eating soft, gooey sugar. It also turned out to be very hot. It had made her happy, eating sugared nuts and just strolling around.

Sure, she'd been to markets before. But that had been back home. This was, you know, an adventure in its own right. Besides, it was a whole lot more colourful. It was also a whole lot bigger. The markets she'd been used to, you could almost have thrown a stone across them if you were the regional caber champion.

Here, level after level she'd moved down the streets and stairs like an errant butterfly. There had been so much to see that she hadn't been worried about finding her way back, until now.

Lin wasn't sure when it appeared next, that strange clicking sound, until she heard it just as she went past a quaint little store selling all sorts of merchandise, which all had one thing in common: they were all emblazoned by the same image. A somewhat garish, red and twisted couple of animals (which, if you looked at them from the right angle *might* have been a set of twin boars) and an odd blue doubletail snaking around them both.

'How much of this horrid stuff do they make?' she mumbled to herself. 'They can't seriously sell any of this, can they?'

It was as she put down the heavy earthenware mug she'd been handling, that she'd heard it again.

'Is it just me or did that sound louder this time?' Lin had asked herself.

It was ridiculous, but she had begun to feel a little ill at ease. Still, trying to put it out of her mind, Lin had tried to shake it off. There were all sorts of new sounds in this place. It was probably just some silly bird or something.

She'd stopped thinking that when she'd heard it yet again, a little later. And again, after that.

And every time, it seemed just a little bit closer.

Now, her heart was beginning to beat faster. Now, every time the sound came, she jumped. Lin increased her pace through the crowd.

What if someone *was* chasing her? How did they see her? How did they keep finding her?

The hounding, being chased through unfamiliar territory, it brought back memories. Dark, unpleasant memories of running, of running without ever really escaping.

Linandra's salivary glands were filling her mouth with warm stickiness. She swallowed, the tense movement making her throat constrict even further. Again, she quickened her footsteps.

But trying to appear as if something isn't bothering you and actually suc-ceeding were two very different things. By now, Lin wasn't even really trying and her progress through the streets grew more and more erratic.

It didn't help when she realized that even though she'd been able to *leave* her quarters up on high, she actually had no idea of how to return to them. The flaws of this little excursion were beginning to mount up.

Jerking involuntarily, Lin swerved to avoid a cart filled with baskets. When it suddenly stopped, she was knocked sideways.

Trying to regain her balance, she stumbled, crashed into someone's back and, when she managed to recover her senses, found herself away from the immediate hustle and bustle of the marketplace.

Lin pressed herself against the dry wall. It smeared her back with some sort of dark ochre gunk, but right now her heart was pounding so hard that she was past caring. It could join in with the rest of the effects from this little "outing." And anyway, it'd wash out. There were a whole lot of things in life that wouldn't.

Trying to steady her revolving stomach, Lin raised her eyes from the ground. Where was she?

The walls seemed higher here. Greyer, too. There weren't any windows either, not proper ones. If she looked up, there were thin slits, several stories above. She had to be near the elevation to the next level then. That meant... Oh blast. That meant this wasn't just an alley. It was an alley with only one way in—and out—and she'd just taken it.

Looked like she'd blundered a fair bit into the place too. Lin winced. This was not where she wanted to be.

Hoping that she'd just been imagining things after all, she turned around to quickly, and quietly, leave. She ended up backing further into the alley instead.

She hadn't meant to. Her feet had one of those "Matter over Mind" moments. To them, further away, regardless of the actual direction, was much more preferential than staying put. All it meant was that she moved further and further away from the life of the city.

The eyes. Those narrowed, conniving eyes burrowed into you. Lin tried to fight a shudder.

The three figures at the mouth of the alley were now assured that their prey couldn't run anywhere but towards them. They advanced slowly, Lin wanted to scream. Her mouth opened and closed but no sounds came out. Without thinking, she tried eyeing up something to grab, while not taking her eyes off the approaching men.

If she'd cornered someone she wanted something from, she'd have rushed them by now. So, what were they waiting for? Maybe they were the type that enjoyed the fear of their victims? They certainly looked it.

There wasn't much around that'd make do as a weapon, even one of dubious quality and usefulness. Besides, she'd probably not have time to grab it anyway. They would probably charge the moment her attention was distracted. Not, she admitted, that they likely considered her any kind of threat.

Lin clutched her purchases tighter.

'I get first dibs on this one,' the scar-faced one in front said.

At this, the two others hung back as he approached her confidently. Didn't look like he thought her worth taunting with words, because he didn't say anything as he did so.

As he grabbed for her, Lin swung. The satchel went almost full circle as she whirled around, building up momentum. He hadn't seen it coming. It smashed right into his face. With a loud crack, he staggered past her, hitting the wall to the right.

'You little—!'

Scarface pulled himself up, blood gushing down his face from a nose not-so-much broken as shattered. It dripped from the gums too. Teeth, apparently, didn't like getting hit on by several pounds of stone, crystal and associated metallic friends. By the looks of it, the more out-jutting parts of the figurine she'd bought had been particularly unkind. That might account for why his face now looked like it had had a date with a shredder.

'You'll regret that!' he snarled, trying to wipe away the blood from his eyes.

Picking up his dagger from the ground, the youth lunged for her without quite seeing where he was going.

'Don't damage the goods, ya fool!' his two companions shouted, almost in unison.

'Where are you? Where are you—you dirty, stinky, little rat? I'm gonna cut you. I'm gonna make you bleed,' the youth spluttered with rage.

He stabbed wildly at where he thought she was. When Lin managed to duck, he overshot his target and ended up crashing into the wall. She took the chance to try and race past the other two who didn't seem sure if they should interfere or not.

'Don't just stand there, you morons. Grab her!' Scarface snapped at his companions as he tried to right himself.

If there had been only one, she might have had a chance at this point. There wasn't. Lin didn't manage to evade them both.

If they'd been using sharp blades, it would have gone badly very fast.

'Hold still,' one of them hissed at her as he tried to lock her arms behind her back. 'And we won't hurt ya … much.'

'You're worth more … intact,' the other drawled.

'Let go of me,' Lin shouted.

She'd have been more scared if they'd pulled out their daggers like their companion. Now, she struggled against their hold.

It should have been an easy job for them. Still, they were struggling. Somehow Lin managed to push one of them away. He hit the ground, hard.

'Hold on to her ya fool.'

'*You* hold on. Got a kick like a mule this one...'

The hissing one tried to get her back under control.

Devoid of hands to hit anyone with, Lin bit him. The teeth sank in deeper than expected. He howled in pain.

'Goran? Ger you ass in gear and help me,' he shouted. 'Goran?'

The hisser looked around, wondering where his useless companion had gotten to now. A heavy thud made him jerk around.

Goran lay slumped sideways on the ground. He wasn't moving. It was unlikely that he would ever move again by the reason of having three feet of terracotta piping sticking out of his chest.

'Whoever's there? Show yourself. Or I kill the girl. You hear? I'll kill 'er.'

Her captor scraped a thin metal blade along Lin's throat. He didn't mind the quick money. He *did* mind being too dead to collect it. Looked like their blessed leader was taking his time getting back to his feet too. You wouldn't have thought someone so slight and innocent-looking could have caused such a ruckus.

'Oh, really?' a new voice inquired. 'I think not.'

The voice came from behind them, Lin realized. It didn't sound worried. If anything, it seemed bemused—as an onlooker in the theatre who suddenly found themselves on stage—but here there was no stage to be on: yet they were suddenly visible but still not part of the story.

The man hauled his hostage closer. Rather, he *tried* to haul her closer. He didn't seem to be able to grip anything as well as usual. He couldn't be frightened, could he? No, not him.

Feeling his grip lessen, Lin shook herself free, quickly bounding several metres away before tripping over the third man. Rolling over, her eyes stared, for a moment, straight at the guy that had just tried to slit her throat.

'You might want to reconsider that future,' the serene, mocking, voice suggested.

'You 'ink 'ou can just come in in here and take our, our...' Why did he feel so out of breath? 'Ours, you can't...' he coughed red. 'I can ... I...'

No air. That was the problem. If he could only get a good lungful of air. He tried breathing in which only caused his abdomen to convulse.

'W..hy ...'s there..?'

The youth fell forwards, sliding off the thin, needle-like dagger that had, not five minutes ago, belonged to his companion.

'Well, that was moderately terrible, wouldn't you say?' Seth stepped over the body.

Oh no, Lin thought. Not Terrsainoh. Not him. *Anyone* but him. Please. Don't let me have been "rescued" by *him*. Oh, I'm *never* going to hear the end of this.

'Now. I don't think these ones will give us much more grief. Do you?' Seth prodded the man he'd just killed with a toe.

'You're insane. Do you know that? Absolutely, stark-raving mad!'

'Really? That's not a very nice thing to say to someone that just saved your life ... and more,' Seth feigned injury.

'I was doing fine on my own!' Lin snapped back.

'Well, that's news to me. It sure didn't look like that where I was looking from.'

'Then maybe you need a new pair of lookers, Greyeyes.'

'Of the most ungrateful—' Seth began. His eyes suddenly grew misty. He looked down at his chest. 'Oh look, what a nasty thing to do. I paid good money for this shirt,' he said weakly. The young man's legs wobbled for a moment, then gave out underneath him.

With the blood still ringing in his ears, Seth tried to focus. Half the world seemed covered in haze. What was this strange redness he was experiencing?

He tried pushing himself back onto his feet, groaning. Had balancing on two feet always been this hard? He didn't remember. He suddenly felt like he couldn't remember anything. There was this pale misty wall between him and, well, him.

Vaguely, the sound of running drifted past.

Was that the thugs running away? What thugs? Was it just his own heart beating its last farewell? He didn't know.

Seth looked down, unseeing. There was a stickiness to his hands. Was that supposed to be there?

Strange. It didn't actually hurt. Wasn't getting stabbed supposed to hurt? This was his first experience of it, but it wasn't supposed to be painless, was it? In the stories, everyone always groaned. All he did was feel light like everything was just thinned out somehow.

The red liquid throbbed between his fingers as he stared at it, a bewildered look on his face.

He blinked, or maybe it was just his imagination.

There were sounds—people sounds—in the distance. People shouting. People running.

He didn't really hear them. They were so far away. It was all so very far away: so very, very far away.

* * *

The same thoughts were still circling like dark birds of doom, flicking from one mountaintop of thought to another, when Lin actually surfaced long enough from wallowing in misery to notice.

'You idiot!' Linandra had muttered incoherently to herself where she'd sat. 'Why did you go and do that for? Stupid! Stupid!'

She'd tried to stem the flow of the essential liquid best the she could with her hands. Tearing at the cloth and pushing it downwards as hard as she could, but it had still kept coming.

The attacker had run off with the blade, leaving only the gaping wound screaming at the world.

It hadn't even been a clean one, slim and shiny. No, it had to be spiky and dull, all serrated edges, loving to tear apart skin and flesh alike.

Why had he been so stupid? Why? What had he been doing following her in the first place?

He wasn't a fighter: anyone could see that. He wasn't used to being out here like this. Okay, so neither was she, but that wasn't the point. He certainly wasn't the "rough and tumble" type. What had he been thinking?

This was all her fault.

If she hadn't gotten bored at that stupid ball and gone looking for something more exciting... Oh why...

'Stupid. Stupid! Stupid!'

She kept repeating that to herself over and over again. Who she was berating—herself, the world, him—was anyone's guess.

Why?

People didn't just do things like that. Did they? Only in stories, that's where. "Normal" people didn't defend others. They certainly didn't jump to the defence of random strangers they'd barely even met.

At least, that's what she'd always thought. No one had ever done something like that for her. Lin turned strained and confused eyes to the figure in the centre of the room they'd been brought to.

Maybe someone like Kaheiron would come to her aid but, with the kind of power to back him up that he had, he didn't exactly have a whole lot to worry about.

This, now this was different.

Lin felt even more confused than before. It probably showed, but, for once, she didn't seem to care.

Fangs of iron, sharpened until they gleamed, squeezed her lungs even tighter. It was getting hard to breathe. The air felt so stale. The window was open, a large one over by the balcony, a door perhaps even. But it still felt like it wasn't possible to take a single breath without fighting the hot, dry air every step of the way.

'Oh god, oh god ... please don't be dead,' Lin begged between chattering teeth. '*Please* don't be dead. I'd be in so much trouble.'

He'd *looked* dead enough, already when they'd brought him here. It was all her fault. What if he *was* somehow important? What would happen to her then? What would they do?

Now, away from the alley, the people here seemed far more threatening than they'd been. Were they looking at her? She thought she could feel the accusing stares all around.

Of her once so fine clothes there was little sight. Most of it was stained or covered in things you really didn't want to know where they'd come from. What there was left of it that was. The rest of her neither looked, nor felt any better.

In her bedraggled state, they would not have let her in, if it hadn't been for the company she'd been in. As it was, the Archmagus had been in no mood to be argued with.

'I specifically told you *not* to cause undue trouble,' a stern voice suddenly scolded her.

It didn't get much of a response, just a helpless look.

'Now, now. Everything will be all right,' it continued much more soothingly when Lin looked up, eyes wide and shining. 'Now, come along. We'd better get you cleaned up.'

Lin shook her head and tried to dig herself deeper into the chair.

'There is nothing you can do here, Little One,' logic tried to reason with the distraught young woman. But she still refused to budge.

Kaheiron stepped back and, after a brief conversation with one of the healers, returned with a cold goblet, brimming with something that felt almost like ice to the touch, only it was liquid.

'Swallow,' he ordered gently.

He watched her unsteady hand grip the stem of the goblet and almost drop it. He reached out to steady it. It was a lucky thing that the healer had carried something for shock. There wasn't much call for that around here. Mostly people practiced the age-old slap around the ears to bring hysterics back down to earth.

'A palace has different requirements than most, I suppose,' he mused.

Not that he understood shock himself. Surprise, yes, he had been known to be surprised in his life. Quite a few times, actually. But once that was over, the general order was usually to look around for the bigger picture—and possibly for someone to bite for having startled you in the first place.

Still, he tried his best. With gentle hands he steered Lin, now walking as if in a big foggy cloud, back to her quarters.

At the very least, he could see to that she was made comfortable. Best to wait and hope. Things had, today, spiralled quickly out of control. They would eventually settle down. They usually did. Balance was the key; but balance took time.

Kaheiron sighed. People—no matter what their size or shape—were so difficult to manage. They rarely had the patience required to take the long view.

He checked on the windows, just in case Lin would do something foolish once she came to her senses (now, how was that for a contradiction). Right now, sleepwalking was more of a danger than guilt or fear. Kaheiron knew he should return to where he'd left off at the negotiations. But that wasn't his primary thought right now.

He'd left instructions to be notified immediately in case there was a change in either party. 'What an illustrious moment,' the Archmagus sighed. 'Hopefully a good night's rest will help everyone involved.'

And while they were sleeping in an herbal-induced stupor, it would be a good time for *him* to go hunting. The Archmagus flexed his fingers. Yes. Hunting. *No one* threatened or killed one of his people and got away with it. Not if he could help it. And there was still one miscreant left—for now.

* * *

Ears still burning from the tongue-lashing she'd received the previous day, sneaking out again had probably not been the best idea. The guards that caught her certainly hadn't thought so. But then, they'd been far more awake than she had been.

Kaheiron wasn't too impressed either, judging from his expression.

'Come on, let me go,' Lin protested at the somewhat rough handling by the guard, as she ended up before the Archmagus. They'd obviously not had any instruction to treat anyone gently, she fumed.

He didn't look happy, she thought. Kaheiron, that was. And there was something about that scowl. It had "disappointment" written all over it. It shouldn't have made her stomach tighten or her throat dry out, but it did.

'Linandra,' Kaheiron treated her to one of his most stern looks. 'I am most displeased with your actions.'

'What did *I* do? It wasn't my fault,' Lin objected reflexively. As she did, her muscles tightened again.

But it *was* my fault, she thought. She still couldn't bear to admit it out loud. Why did she feel so guilty?

'Not only did you not listen, though I carefully explained to you what not to do when attending such an important function. But to further, willingly, endanger yourself merely because you were not allowed to have everything "your way"?' Kaheiron delivered the beginning of what was probably going to be a lecture, Lin thought, with a frosty voice.

It felt like his eyes were penetrating her skull. She looked away.

'Little one—' Kaheiron sighed. He rubbed at the sore back of his nose. Raising children was a task he was particularly unsuited for. He never seemed to quite know what to say, or do, at times like these.

'Do you even realize what worry you caused?' he asked, and then, without waiting for a reply continued, 'despite everything I said to you last night, you chose to ignore my words and now, now, I find that you have, yet again— despite everything that has happened—attempted to sneak out. I believed better of you, young lady. What *do* you have to say for yourself?'

Kaheiron gave a nod to the guards. They released their hold on Lin's arms, bowed to the Archmagus, and withdrew from the chamber.

'Lin, Lin, Lin… Whatever shall I do with you?'

'I didn't exactly ask for you to *do* anything,' Lin challenged him back. It didn't snap as usual. Her heart just wasn't in it.

'No, that is true,' Kaheiron conceded calmly. Suddenly feeling a whole lot older, the Archmagus sank down on a winged chair, looking far more tired than he had just a moment ago.

'Try to understand, Linandra,' he said. 'I'm merely trying to look out for you. Once you realize that you can't scamper around the world like some unruly child and learn to accept the consequences of your actions I, for one, will breathe easier.'

'No one asked you to,' Lin said, pouting. Though her heart wasn't quite in that either.

'Are you so certain?'

Lin eyed him suspiciously. 'Well *I* can't see why anyone would.'

She sounded so indignant that Kaheiron couldn't help but break out laughing. Thick, warm tears dove down his cheeks as he tried to get himself back under control.

'And *that* is why I'm the teacher and you are not,' he winked at her between guffaws.

He straightened out his robes for something to do. 'I know that you didn't mean for anyone to get hurt, Little One,' Kaheiron said. 'That, however, unfortunately, does not change what actually happened.'

'No, sir,' Lin replied somewhat dejectedly.

As usual, she seemed to drift in and out of being respectful. Every so often though, there would be enough fire that she'd get reminded again of just who she was talking to. Strange really, most of the time she didn't even think about that. Who'd have ever believed, back home, that anyone could get used to having a dragon as company?

'Now, will you tell me why you're trying to sneak out again? I hope you weren't planning another visit to the market in case you forgot something the last time.'

Lin shook her head. No, she hadn't meant that. She tried explaining, and, somewhere between all the mumbles and restarts, Kaheiron eventually got the gist of what she was trying to say.

'I see,' Kaheiron said. He studied the young woman closely. 'And you're absolutely certain that "checking up" on this young man is the *only* thing that you are intending to do?'

He fixed her with stern eyes and asked again, 'that IS the only thing, yes?'

Lin nodded enthusiastically. Sure, she'd also like to leave the current company behind for a while. Her knees couldn't shake the feeling that, at any moment, they, along with the rest of her, would get turned into a radish ... or worse.

'Very well. But I will send someone with you, to keep an eye on you. Aside from that you are unlikely to find your way without aid; I also do not trust you to walk these halls alone. When you have finished with this little visit, you will return to your chambers, where you will stay until we leave the city.'

'But I—'

'Or you will not leave at all.'

'Oh, alright,' Lin muttered, a small spark of her normally rebellious nature returning. 'Have it your way then...'

Taking a deep breath as Linandra left the room, escort and all, Kaheiron sank further down into his seat.

Were children always this difficult? Regardless of species? Even with all these years to his name, he still couldn't understand them. Did that mean that his own youth was so far behind him?

He could still remember being young, but there were times when he felt like he'd been the responsible grown-up all his life. True, he *had* run away once. But, when you looked at it from a more distant perspective, had he really escaped from the spirit of things?

Still, Kaheiron gazed at the azure sky that dazzled the eye just beyond the window, there *were* compensations. Drumming his fingers on the armrest, he wondered if condoning the current situation was really the best course of action after all.

* * *

Lin was equally uncertain if she really wanted to go through with this. As her escort led her through a bewildering array of courtyards, walkways and even a tunnel—albeit a short one—she kept alternating between wanting to go back and the opposite.

If she'd been alone, she probably would have left. As it was, every time that feeling crept up on her, she felt too embarrassed about turning around to actually do it.

'Where in the world are we going?' she mumbled to herself as they passed alongside a very green, very big hedge.

'The Garden of Terrsainoh, my lady,' her escort bowed her through an arched opening in the hedge. 'The Archmagus has instructed me to wait for your return.'

Lin eyed the thorns warily. 'Let me guess, he doesn't get many visitors?'

She didn't really expect an answer, so she stepped inside and tried to work out where she was meant to go. It wasn't like there was a big signpost; which would have been useful, seeing as she couldn't actually see much, what with most of the vegetation being well above her head.

'There is the path,' she mused. 'I suppose it couldn't hurt to follow it … this time.'

Quite some time later and the path was long gone. Lin hadn't even noticed. Her eyes had been on everything around and above her, from the trees to the mushrooms—to say nothing about what rustled in the greenery—not on her feet or where she was going.

'Surely mushrooms don't grow *that* big? For that matter, I'm sure they're not supposed to be bright blue, either. Wonder if they're poisonous?'

Lin pushed aside some of the branches from a big feather bush blocking her way. A couple of them snapped back, tickling her over the nose with their soft downy leaves.

'Oh bother,' Lin sneezed. 'There could be a hundred people in this stupid garden and I couldn't find them if they all kept quiet. I mean, aren't gardens belonging to rich people supposed to be decorative, not a forest jungle with a mid-life crisis?'

Lin continued muttering to herself as she kept on looking for her quarry. From what she'd heard, he shouldn't, at least, be able to outrun her at the moment. Trouble was, she felt like she was doing the running for both of them.

'This is ridiculous!' she snapped at no one in particular.

Maybe she should come back another time? Why was she doing this any-way? It wasn't like she really wanted to be here, was it?

'Might as well get this over with. Then I can go back … and get yelled at … again,' Lin grumbled to herself as she moved cautiously between the var-ious plants until she found the path again. Or, at least, a path.

Someone had done their absolute utmost to bring as many different plants and flowers and trees and, yes, grasses too, as they could find here. It was, as you'd say, underfoot and overhead all at once. Only some of these grasses had clearly been swagged from a giant's lawn. Lin was sure that when you looked at grass you should be looking down.

She poked one of the thick, olive-green stems. It swayed gently, way above her head.

'Weird,' she said. 'But a least you don't talk back.'

'Do you like it?' a voice asked from behind.

Lin shot into the air as if startled by a baying pack of sighthounds. Whirl-ing around, mind and body parted company for a moment.

'Who—ah! Don't sneak up on people like that!' Lin clutched her heart, trying to force down the instinct to flee.

'Sneak?' Seth burst out laughing. A laughter which ended in a wet chugging cough. 'Agh,' he tried to hold back the spasms to his side to abate the pain. 'I really shouldn't have done that,' he wheezed.

Without thinking, Lin took a few hesitant steps forward. 'Are you alright?'

'Fine. Fine,' Seth's breathing slowly returned to normal. 'I really shouldn't do that,' he said, treating her to a mischievous grin.

It matched well with the worried, yet somehow still indignant expression Lin was giving off.

'And if anyone was doing any sneaking around here, it'd be you,' Seth said. 'I'm not really up to waltzing about at the moment, or stealing through the topiary either you know,' he gave his thigh a couple of pats and chuckled.

The whole event still bothered him a bit, and not just because it made him feel excruciatingly foolish, being downed so easily without even noticing.

He wasn't the only one feeling foolish. Lin felt much the same, standing there at the edge of the bushes. She was still having second thoughts about all of this. Suddenly, now that she was here, she worried about what to say and do.

What *did* you do at a time like this anyway?

You might want to close the space between you, a nagging little voice in her mind suggested. You're standing at the edge of an open glade you know. You look like a positive idiot when there's a whole arrangement of ornate benches right there in front of you. Oh look, there's that little water-thing that goes "pap" as well. Come on, it can't hurt just talking to him. You were all worried and agitated a moment ago. Where did all that spunk go?

Not party to her private, inner monologue, Seth watched her curiously. 'Are you okay?' he asked.

'Should you even be out here at all?' Lin burst out. 'I mean, with that wound and all? I thought you'd be bedbound or … something,' Lin said, her voice diminishing in certainty with each passing word.

'Probably,' Seth agreed. 'If I hadn't been fortunate in my acquaintances, certainly. As luck would have it, one of the healers knew more than a little about amelioration. Unfortunately for me, he wasn't able to fully heal the injuries. Some residual effect from the blade perhaps. He never did explain. Still, since I, by all rights, should be confined to a sick-bed, I have no reason to complain,' he finished off cheerily.

'Are you always this quiet?' he suddenly asked a little later when Lin didn't seem to want to say anything else.

'You seem … different,' Lin eyed him up suspiciously. 'You sound different too. You were more, well, more—'

'La-di-dah?' Seth finished for her and then chuckled as a tint of red crept into her cheeks.

'Besides, so do you,' he observed and rightly so. Maybe that's why that little wrinkle between her eyes appeared.

'I do not! Well, yes, I do … but that's besides the point. You're supposed to do that. It's, what's it called? Decorum,' Lin objected hotly.

'Exactly.'

'What?'

'You're not the only one that tries to be "proper" at such events, you know,' Seth said. 'I've found that it's useful to ... blend in.'

'Really?' Lin snorted. 'From what I saw, you were "blending out" rather than "in."'

'Is this going to be a recurring thing in this relationship?'

'What is?'

'Arguing.'

'I am not arguing with you. And we do *not* have a relationship!' Lin snapped at him.

'Interesting—' Seth said, then immediately changed the topic. 'Anyway, you never answered my question. Do you like it? My garden?'

'What?' Lin's scattered and bruised self-confidence fished around for some coherency in the madness she seemed to have gotten herself involved with. 'It's very, umm … green. Yes, very green.'

'Thanks, I hadn't noticed,' Seth replied, dryly. 'I had it all planted you know,' he continued much more brightly. 'The previous owner favoured gravel. Easy to keep and doesn't murder your water bills. Have you any idea what they charge for just one single casket of water in this place? Seriously, it's outrageous. You'd think it hardly ever rained here.'

'Casket?' Lin scrutinized the young man in front of her closely, her eyes narrowing. 'You can't put water in a casket. It'd leak out, surely?'

'I imagine that's why it's so expensive then,' Seth beamed at her. 'Maybe it's barrels I'm thinking of? Never mind. It's not important.'

'Why don't you just go outside?' Lin asked, curious against her wish. 'There's a lot more of it and it doesn't cost you anything—well, assuming you don't get waylaid by bandits or something. Then it costs a lot. You seem to have an awful luck with bandits. But, in a general sense, it's free. Most of it.'

'I *do* go outside,' Seth pretended to be affronted. 'I spend a lot of time outside. I just like being able to, you know, not being surrounded by endless walls of compressed sand dust while I'm here. That's all.'

'So, umm … how are you feeling,' Lin finally asked.

She hit herself with an internal hammer. Why couldn't she just have asked that from the start and been done with it? Then she could have avoided this whole charade. He obviously wasn't the sensible type. What type he *was* she still hadn't figured out. He seemed to flutter between various without a care in the world—or so it seemed anyway.

Could she really trust anything he said? Probably not. Then, why didn't she just leave?

'Oh, it's not so bad,' Seth replied. 'Still, don't think I'd care to do it again, if you don't mind.' He touched his chest gingerly and grimaced. 'I do hope you're intending to stay out of trouble during the remainder of your visit.'

'I didn't intend for that to happen in the first place, you know,' Lin shot back, indignantly. 'It's not like I wanted it to happen.'

Her left hand clenching, she approached the grey bench her quarry was resting on. It had a surprisingly intricate design she thought—between bouts of her cheeks flushing with heat—far too light to be stone. But it looked like stone. Marble even.

Showing off again, she thought, with a mental huff. Typical. Just like him to flaunt his money around like that. Probably made his fortune from degrading and oppressing everyone below him, if she was any judge.

'I know, I know. It still did though. I ought to know,' Seth said casually.

He didn't mean to upset her, really, he didn't. Every time he opened his mouth, the wrong thing seemed to come out. He tried to get himself together and all that happened was that he ended up saying something even more distressing, hurtful even.

She obviously still didn't trust him. Well, why would she? She didn't know him. Seth had a sudden vision of what would happen if she found out he'd been watching her and shuddered. Great, now *he* was worrying. No, best to play it safe, for now.

He reached out for the crystal pitcher standing on the spindly table next to him, knocking over several of the satin pillows. 'Oh shoot. Not again,' he groaned artfully. 'I've got to stop doing that.'

'Let me do that,' Linandra almost leapt on the unsuspecting prey, grabbing the large cushions with a vengeance.

Almost immediately, she regretted it. Looking up, she felt the heat to her cheeks. Now, why had she done that? Hadn't she just decided that she wanted nothing more to do with him?

Right. Get a hold of yourself, girl. You're behaving like a … a … a moron.

'I wish you hadn't … you know, done what you did,' she mumbled.

'Do you?' Seth watched her, eyes amused. 'I'd had hoped you'd say that you'd have preferred if I hadn't gotten hurt, doing what I did. That would have been better, don't you think? Or would you have preferred what *they* had in mind?'

'Of course not,' Lin, her nerves close to shattering, snapped.

'Then why are you acting like it?'

'I'm not!' Lin protested vehemently. 'I just wanted to see if you were alright!' She swallowed, trying to fight back tears of hurt, of embarrassment.

'I never said—'

'This was a mistake. Next time, mind your own damn business! I don't need your help,' Lin lost control and bellowed at him.

Once they'd grown hoarse from the shouting, Linandra whirled around and stomped out of there.

Seth watched her go. He grimaced. Well, that could have gone better, he thought. Maybe he shouldn't have pushed so hard?

Still, it had been difficult not to. She reacted so volatilely to being challenged, or accused. There was just something very satisfying about testing the limits of just how far he could go before she blew up at him.

He shook himself lightly. It would probably be best if he didn't indulge himself in that quite as much as he'd like to. He did want her to like him, after all.

'I know I shouldn't,' Seth said, 'but she's so fun to tease. It's like she can't see what's so obviously staring her right in the face.'

'A very forceful young lady, if I may be so bold as to say, sir.'

The voice came from a man who'd discreetly appeared from behind another set of bushes once Lin was lost from sight.

Seth ran his fingers around the edge of the glass he was offered before taking a sip. 'You may,' he acknowledged, then he made a face.

'Does this have to taste so bitter?' He eyed it suspiciously. 'One day, I will discover if medicinal concoctions are *deliberately* meant to remind you of the worst thing you've ever drunk or if those mixing them up have merely long since lost any sense of taste.'

'If the young lady is likely to become a regular visitor, should I see to alternative arrangements, sir?' the head of Seth's household staff asked. His chiten face plating gave him a natural, unflappable, expression. It also made it very difficult to tell what he actually thought.

'Do you think she likes me?' Seth asked, half his mind elsewhere.

'I really wouldn't venture to say, sir.'

'No, I imagine you wouldn't,' Seth replied thoughtfully, the tiniest hint of a smile betraying his thoughts.

The young man picked up one of the books that had been left for his perusal. Lovely leather-bound volumes in bright green and red they were. He rustled the pages a bit before flipping it open at the bookmark.

'We might have to do something about that.'

'If you say so, sir.'

'I just need to figure out how.' Seth sighed and put the book aside. 'Bring around the carriage. I'm cutting it short as it is. Time never was on my side you know.'

'Very well, sir,' the man bowed and retreated from view.

THE WALLS BETWEEN US

And a very silly boy it was, yes it was,' Lin cooed at the small dragonling, slowly waving a tiny piece of jerky right before his nose. 'Very, *very* silly. Silliest boy in the whooole kingdom.'

The meat tore from her fingers as Cheep snapped his jaws shut on it. He then fell to the ground, landing on his feet like a cat and promptly jumped up on the bed where he curled up.

'Ouch! Watch it you little terror!'

She sucked on the finger. Didn't look like he had drawn blood, just scraped the outside of a tooth against it. You could see the red welt forming already.

'What happened to your manners? You. Do. No.t Eat. My. Fingers!' Linandra admonished her companion.

It had already been a week since her return from the big city and Cheep still wasn't eating as usual. It was ridiculous, she'd decided. He'd spent the first three days after her return at the top of the cupboard. Sulking most likely, she thought. Stubborn little thing.

The dragonling was saved from the rest of the lecture by a solid set of knockings on the door.

'Wonder who that is at this hour?' Lin tied her robe a bit more firmly together before opening the door.

She wouldn't have been more surprised if it had been her parents standing there on the other side. Quite frankly, the Archmagus' dress sense looked a little out of place in the narrow corridor. He was more suited to be posing impressively against a dramatically lit sky, she thought.

'Linandra?'

'Umm … yes?' she replied. 'Something wrong? Whatever it is, I didn't do it.'

Ignoring the bait, Kaheiron held out a thin cream envelope. 'This came for you. I believe that someone is inviting you to dinner.'

'What?' Lin grabbed it from him at speed.

'Appears you made quite the impression on our young friend.'

'Well, I'm not going,' Lin turned the paper into a small crumbled ball. 'Take that! Here boy, something for you to chew on.'

She tossed the ball over her shoulder. The dragonling caught the leftover invitation by instinct, then quickly spat it out, making spluttering noises. He coughed a couple of times, then took a swing and batted it fiercely. It shot off the table, hit the far wall and rolled in under the chair.

Cheep, crouching low, hissed at it.

'Whoops. Sorry. Guess you don't like eating paper. You sure try to get your teeth into practically everything else around here. Okay, I'll get you a better treat. later.'

'I'm certain he will appreciate that somewhat more than dry, dusty parchment,' Kaheiron said, a flicker of amusement in his eyes.

Turning her attention away from the still-annoyed dragonling, Lin couldn't help but wonder… 'Why are you delivering this? By yourself? Isn't that, you know, someone else's job around here?' she asked.

Just a hint of sheepishness touched Kaheiron's features. 'I admit, I was very curious as to how you would react,' the Archmagus confessed.

'If that's your idea of having fun, you need to get out more,' Lin tried not to laugh.

'Yes, well—'

'And *you* are having far too much fun. Stop slavering, you're not a dog,' Lin told the small dragonling stalking the paper ball, closing the door as Kaheiron left.

* * *

'So, that was stunningly unsuccessful,' Seth crumbled up another bit of parchment. 'Wouldn't you say so?'

'So I would. I appear to remember advising you to exactly that.'

'Are these things *always* this difficult? I mean, I've known all sorts of women and none of them have been anywhere near as … as … frustrating to deal with,' Seth said and flopped down into the chair with abandon.

His companion coughed somewhat surreptitiously. 'Yes, well, that might have been somewhat different circumstances. As for your question. I'm afraid I cannot answer that. I have never had a mate.'

'I wish she could just make up her mind. Every time I do something nice at one end, up floats the aggression from the other. What is she? Some sort of human cork?'

'You are far from perfect in this endeavour yourself.'

'Don't remind me,' Seth grimaced. 'I suppose flowers won't work?'

'With *your* young lady?'

His companion gave him a glance that not even Seth could misunderstand. 'Good point,' he conceded. 'Hmm… So, a different approach then?'

'If I may say so, perhaps you should just try to be yourself?'

'Oh, really? I don't know about you, but most women I've met wouldn't be too keen on having a relationship with several hundred thousand bits of scales that breathe fire when threatened.'

'Perhaps you underestimate her, sir?'

'I sure hope so,' Seth sighed. 'I just don't get what I'm doing wrong...'

He tried massaging his temples, in case it'd give him some new insight. No such luck, unfortunately.

Why was he so keen on this one? It wasn't like he was want for female companionship should he desire some. It all still felt so terribly complicated to him. It was driving him mad. He'd always wanted his own independence. His own choices. No one had told him it was supposed to be this difficult.

* * *

Whatever Seth did per distance, several weeks of it, it didn't seem to be working. Eventually he gave up and decided to handle the matter personally. Some people offered the opinion that he should have done exactly that a long time ago.

And so, almost a whole month after Lin's return to the Towers, a blue carriage pulled up to the main gates.

The Towers didn't get a large number of visitors, so when they heard the sound of wheels and hooves against the gravel on the circle before the main doors, more than one head turned to see who it was. Maybe it'd be something interesting.

You could never fault "interesting" at the Towers. It was practically what the residents lived on. But not everyone was as impressed that they might have been before.

'You can't be serious?' Lin, who'd leaned out of an open window when she'd heard the carriage, just like several others, quickly dove back in when the visitor stepping out of it caught sight of her and gave her a cheery wave.

'Oh bother,' she exclaimed. 'I think he saw me.'

'Is that such a terrible thing, my dear? Friend of yours?' Mrs. Sarrrrinth purred. 'He looks quite cute … for a human.'

'He is not cute. And he is not my friend,' Lin stomped a foot on the stone floor.

'If you say so, dear. But most well-dressed, rich, young gentlemen don't wave happily to random strangers except on very special occasions.'

Linandra merely grumped something unintelligible in return.

'What was that dear?' Mrs. Sarrrrinth asked.

'I'm going to go find Cheep and then I'm going to find the deepest, cosiest hole in this whole place. And I'm going to stay there until *he's* gone. Permanently.'

'If you say so, dear. To me, it sounds a little excessive, don't you think?'

'You don't know him like I do, Mrs. Sarrrrinth,' Lin insisted.

'I thought you said you didn't know him at all?' the tabby asked with feigned innocence. She watched the flustered young woman tear off her apron and hand it to her, trying very hard not to laugh.

'Oh, bollocks with it all,' Lin exclaimed as she disappeared around a corner.

Why, of all people, did it have to be her? She wasn't sure if she felt furious, terrified or—horrid thought—flattered, but it sure wasn't helping her being civil.

'Oh, to be young again,' Sarrrrinth sighed wistfully. 'So many adventures.

Romance. Starlit walks in the moonlight. Morning gifts on your doorstep. Such times we had … such times.'

Lin would have been more than a little flustered to hear the old tabby reminiscing. At this point, she might even have been a little rude, too. That would have been the worry talking.

Now, she whirlwinded through her room.

'Here boy. Heeeere … come here. Come on out, Cheepy,' Lin called.

She bent down, checking under the bed, just in case he was hiding there. 'You're not still sulking, are you?'

She opened up the cupboard. Nope, not in there either. 'Okay, that does it. If you don't want to come, fine. I'm going without you.'

Speeding around the small room, Lin grabbed things, seemingly at random, stuffing them into her satchel.

'Right. I'm out of here,' she said.

Throwing the door open, Lin narrowly missed hitting the person on the other side.

'Whoa! Easy there,' Seth called out in alarm. 'You could have done some serious damage there.'

'Oh, just go away,' Lin pleaded. 'Just go away!'

'How am I supposed to go away? Okay. I admit it. Our first meeting wasn't to my advantage.' Seth thought for a moment and added, 'and okay, yes, our second encounter probably doesn't even qualify as a meeting, but I think I did well with that, all things considered.'

'And this third one is one too many. No wait, the *first* time was one too many. Not to mention all your other efforts,' Lin snarled back at him.

Awoken by Lin's loud voice, something rustled among the curtains, and Seth scrambled backwards as a small dragonling fluttered down, from the top of an arched window in the corridor behind him, to settle on his shoulder. Cheep rubbed his cheek against him affectionately.

'CHEEP!' Lin exclaimed. Not able to believe her eyes.

'Looks like *someone* around here likes me,' Seth said, chuckling at Lin's expression.

'You little traitor,' Lin breathed out, not having realized she'd been holding her breath. She wasn't sure if she was more amused or annoyed with Cheep's behaviour.

The dragonling seemed perfectly happy where he was, but when she reached out her hand towards him, he chirruped happily and jumped over to her shoulder instead where he proceeded to treat her to a round of affection.

'But Lin…' Seth called after her as, dragonling bobbing on her shoulder, Lin stalked off.

By now, their argument had already brought them to the long gallery, Lin was walking that fast. Her annoyed heels struck the stone floor like the march of an imperial army. If there had been more of her, it probably would have sounded more impressive, but one of her was more than enough as far as she was concerned.

One of Tse, Tes … whatever his name was, was on the other hand clearly one too many.

'Come on, Lin,' Seth pleaded. 'You don't hate me, so why are you being so difficult? You *don't* hate me, do you?' he asked, eyeing her with a mix of worry and suspicion. 'I mean, you *couldn't* hate me. You have no reason.'

'*No* reason?' Lin rounded on him. 'Did you just say "*no* reason?" I can't believe you.'

'Well … you don't. I saved your life,' Seth replied, confused.

'And that's somehow supposed to make me fawn over you like there's no tomorrow? As if you're the biggest thing to ever have happened to walk into my life. Just because you happened to save it? Which, by the way, you didn't.'

'What? No. I never said that,' Seth protested. He tried to get his head around what she was talking about. Of course, to do that, it had to make sense to her in the first place. He was beginning to wonder if it would have made sense to anyone…

'Really?'

'Of course not. Why would I think that?'

'Because—' Lin's voice faded into almost mute, unintelligible mumbles.

'Sorry. Didn't quite catch that?'

'Because that's what all girls that get rescued by dashing, young men always do in stories,' Lin finally exploded.

She grabbed her mouth in shock. What had she just said?

'Lin,' Seth tried to reason with her. 'Those are just that: stories. They have absolutely no relation to real life. None. Okay, maybe a little. Some of them. But other than that, they're just stories. Wait,' he said, his mind finally catching up with his ears. 'You think I'm dashing?'

Linandra, who by now was doing a good enough impression of a tomato to have been a contender for the paragon of vegetables herself, strode away. She pointedly kept her back to him.

'So, dashing, is it? Hmm…' Seth rubbed his soft chin. 'Gallant, I would have said myself, but I can live with dashing,' he winked at her.

'Oh, you, you … lout!'

That set off their argument again. It continued throughout the Towers. It probably would have lasted all the way past the main doors, if Lin hadn't lost track of where she was going somewhere around halfway, causing them to eventually turn left at speed and face a blind arch and a dead end.

'Whoa!' Seth bumped into Lin who'd come to an abrupt stop. 'Sorry about that.'

'Watch it!' Lin snapped at him again.

Avoiding taking the bait this time, Seth looked about. 'Where are we anyway? I don't recognize this place.'

'You've been here before?'

'A few times,' Seth admitted. 'I've known Kaheiron for many years now. It's not my favourite place to be. Too many serious, old coots spending too much time worrying about things that don't matter. Too many serious, young ones too for that matter.'

'Hey, it's important to them!' Lin flared up, feeling she had to defend her home regardless of that she thought pretty much the same.

Sure, a lot of them were grouchy. Quite a few were downright oblivious to the existence of anything outside their own little sphere. And some, especially the younger ones, weren't all that good at controlling their abilities or were busy playing pranks on each other, but she wouldn't call any one of them useless. Okay, maybe a few … but he had no right to talk about them like that.

'Okay, okay, calm down,' Seth tried to diffuse the situation. 'I didn't mean it like that.'

He reached out and tickled the dragonling under the chin. Now there was, at least, someone who was friendly. Cheep thrummed happily at the attention. And now that Lin wasn't snapping and snarling anymore, Cheep settled down too, content to be lavished attention upon.

Lin regarded him suspiciously.

'Well, you're buttering up to the new arrivals fast enough, I see,' she said, eyes narrowing. 'Usually he doesn't take to strangers, you know,' she told Seth in turn. With a great sigh, she shrugged, defeatedly. 'One outing,' she said. 'That's all you get. One. And then I will never have to see you again?'

Seth's shoulders sagged a little. He gave her his best puppy eyes impression and asked, 'Is there no other way I can convince you about this?'

* * *

Lin was true to her word, after a fashion. After all, when she'd promised him an "outing," as she put it, she hadn't, however, said anything about when.

She'd expected Seth—if that was even his real name; he seemed to listen to so many—if kept waiting long enough, to just give up and go home. He didn't. He lounged about the Towers instead.

She hadn't been particularly impressed when he'd shared that little detail with her, about his name that was. Lin had a feeling he hadn't intended to. It felt more of a slip-up than an actual share. Guess with that many names it eventually became confusing to remember them all?

Despite that, it all seemed to go well enough at first. She managed to avoid running into him for several days.

Then he started to pop up when and where she least expected him to; if she went out to pick some flowers, who would she find happily poking about the flowerbed with a trowel?

Should she take to the idea of nipping back after breakfast for an extra slice; he'd be waiting outside the kitchen when she left.

When she was asked to help out Mrs. Sarrrrinth with her rugs, who else would be there as a second pair of hands?

By the end of it, it felt like she couldn't turn a corner without him turning up on the other side. It was driving her mad ... or, at the very least, doing very little for her nerves when she got a shock every time she opened something. A few more weeks and she'd start seeing him when she broke open the tea jar when putting on the kettle, or so she felt.

So, Linandra decided that it was better to get it over with. Maybe then he'd give up and go home. Though, by now, she was harbouring serious doubt about that too.

The day in question started out calmly enough, certainly calmer than it ended.

Lin dragged herself awake at a speed that would have seen her lose the race even if all her opponents had been snails. She really didn't want to wake up. Every time she did, she had flashes of "what ifs" pounce on her like a four-hundred-pound hunting cat. By the time she was ready to go, it was already almost noon.

Seth, on the other hand, felt like bouncing on the ceiling. He just couldn't sit still. Being made to wait (even more than he had already) was bringing out his nerves. As a result, he alternated between being happily chipper and a nervous wreck. Which was which, was anyone's guess.

At the moment, he was pacing outside one of the back doors.

'You couldn't have been here a little earlier?' he complained when Lin finally showed up.

'Listen here,' she stared him down. 'I'm doing you a favour. If that's how you're gonna be, if you want, I can just as easily turn around and go back inside.'

'No, no … please, don't do that,' Seth pleaded, stumbling over his words.

'Then behave! Now, we're only going to the garden, right?' Lin asked.

Seth shrugged, and she asked him exactly the same thing when they'd traversed the entire garden and still hadn't stopped.

'Not … exactly,' Seth conceded with a worried expression. 'I found this lovely little place. It's only a little further. It's beautiful and very quiet—and private. You did say that you didn't want this to be a spectacle for the entire Towers. Not that they'd probably care…'

Lin gave him two eyefuls that made him smile nervously. He hoped he looked more confident than he felt. That wouldn't be hard.

'I did say that,' Lin conceded, still not giving an inch. 'But that didn't mean I wanted to have a picnic in the middle of nowhere. I'm warning you.

If you try *anything* funny, I'm gonna have Kaheiron bite your head off.'

Seth just beamed at her in return. It made him look positively handsome—even if his looks could still be described as boyish. Lin wasn't sure if that was a good or a bad thing. What it was, was one of those moments when she really wanted to swat him, preferably with something hard and solid.

Why on earth was she going along with this? It wasn't that he wasn't cute … or smart … or even funny, at times. Maybe the trouble was that he was all those things and he knew it.

Actually, the real trouble was that he was all those things and he was also conceited, self-absorbed and beyond help in terms of his way of life, as far as she was concerned. And she *still* liked him.

Drat, Lin thought.

Things managed to stay calm for almost a whole hour. Partly that was because Lin had been purposefully staring vacantly into nothingness, while her "companion," with his trousers rolled up and boots off, traipsed up and down the small stream, collecting rocks.

It was so ordinary, so childish, Linandra thought, the delight with which he splashed around, with water up to his ankles.

Oh, sure, he'd tried to invite her to help him, but she'd declined. Lin hadn't built rock dams across tiny streams since she was ten years old. And she hadn't wanted to come in the first place, she reminded herself.

So why then was she the one feeling disappointed. Was it because this *wasn't* what she had imagined?

Maybe it was because he, for some reason, had forgotten to actually bring anything to eat on this supposed picnic? Lin sighed. Whatever he was, "dependable" wasn't it.

Seth had looked a little disappointed when she'd refused to join the "fun." Surely he could have thought of something better than this? And she'd been so worried about coming, too. What a waste of perfectly good dread.

Eventually though, her feet too started walking in the small stream, but only because it was such a warm day and the water was nice and cool. At least, that's what she kept telling herself.

After a while, she actually started to enjoy the afternoon. Maybe this wasn't such a bad day after all?

As something caught her eye, a reflection in the water, Lin bent forwards, trying to see better. A moment later and the water from the shallow, stream splashed up, all around her, as she hit the rock-strewn bottom. The water level was almost non-existent, but that didn't stop the bubbly, little stream from happily trying to drown her.

When this friendly approach didn't work, it instead went for her clothes. A good soak was, after all, never wrong. Most people though, Lin included, preferred to choose the time and place.

Rolling over, Lin spat out the mouthful of algae she'd almost swallowed. 'You could have warned me all the stones were loose!' she complained.

'Are you alright?' Seth bounced over. 'Here, let me help.'

'I'm fine. Of course, I'm fine. Why wouldn't I be? This is just what I wanted, didn't you know!?' Lin rolled her eyes at him.

She struggled to her feet. Great. What a *wonderful* improvement to being too hot. Now every bit of clothing clung to her like a second skin: a wet, leacherous kind of skin.

Lin made for the grass just a little further up. Keeping one eye on the slippery surface and the other one on Seth, her skirt twisted around her legs. Losing her balance, she rolled back down into the water.

'Argh! Stupid stream!' Lin yelled as she tried to hit it.

Laughing, Seth reached down and pulled the struggling young woman back up. 'I tried to tell you earlier,' he said. 'You're the one that wasn't paying attention. You know, you're a bit wet,' he added.

'No kidding,' Lin replied sarcastically and tried to shake the water out of her long sleeves. 'Don't look at me like that.'

'Like what?' Seth chortled. 'At least you're not dusty anymore.'

'Oh you—' Lin whacked him with a wet sleeve. Seth tried to duck, not quite managing to avoid the flying droplets.

What a day. It had started out so bright and sunny and the world being— baring a few misgivings here and there—mostly right. Now, all of a sudden, here she was, squelching at the smallest move.

Sitting down on the grassy slope, Lin sighed. Why did these things always have to happen to her? Everyone else could go gallivanting through the forest *without* coming back home with thistles clinging to their socks; their hair in the latest fashion of "Twigs Weekly;" and a lingering aroma of something you *really* didn't want to know what it was. But her? No. Not a chance.

She shuddered at the sensation of everything clinging to her while her dress casually watered the grass beneath her feet.

'Next time, try and warn me before it happens, okay? Not right in the middle of the bleeding thing,' she said.

'I really didn't know that would happen. Honest,' Seth insisted.

'*Sure,* you didn't,' Lin replied. Like she was going to believe a single word coming out of his mouth.

Shaking his head, Seth was pretty certain Lin wasn't going to believe him no matter what he said, so he decided not to dwell further on it.

'Wait. Did you feel that?' he startled.

'Feel what?' Lin looked at her companion for the day. 'Is something wrong?'

'I don't know. It was … something,' Seth tried to reorient, but he wasn't even sure of what it had been that had stolen his attention away. 'Whatever it is, it's gone now.'

'Maybe it was just your imagination. There's a lot of sounds out here, you know.'

Seth shook his head again. This time it had a more serious tinge to it. His near-permanent, boyish grin seemed to be gone. It had been replaced with … something else. Lin wasn't sure what, but the look on his face made her examine the trees and the shadows around them.

'Are you certain that you didn't hear anything?'

'Seth,' Lin groaned. 'It's a whole world out there. It's likely to make noise.'

'No, it wasn't anything like that,' Seth protested. 'It was … wait … maybe. Oh, I don't know,' he threw his hands up in exasperation. 'It was … something.'

'There *was* this rushy kind of tingling,' Lin finally conceded. 'I probably imagined it.'

'Could you be a little more specific?'

'I don't know. Sort of like when your foot's falling asleep but the other way around and all over.'

'That's not what it felt like to me.'

'Well, it did for *me*, so there. Okay,' Lin's hands went to her hips in challenge.

She might like him. She might not be willing to admit it and he might be a bit of an idiot at times, but none of that meant she was going to let him think he'd won an argument. There were some things you just didn't do.

'Okay, okay,' Seth retreated while he still had some ground left. 'It's just not what it felt like for me, that's all. I wonder what it was?'

His normal expression beginning to drift back, a smile tugged at the corners of his mouth again. Even so, there was a trace of his serious face still in his eyes. An alertness that hadn't been there before.

'If you hadn't noticed, I'm not you,' Lin told him.

'That would be painfully obvious,' Seth agreed almost jovially.

'Oight!'

'Maybe I could help try cleaning you up? A bit of you look a little, well … messy,' Seth offered.

'No thanks,' Lin said. 'I've had quite enough of this for one day. I'm going back to the Towers.'

'But Lin—' Seth scrambled after her. 'You can't leave yet.'

'Oh, yes, I can. I'm wet. I'm hungry. And I'm going home!'

Seth tried convincing her almost all the way back, but there seemed to be no stopping her once she'd made her mind up. He'd learnt that already.

He did manage to talk her into giving him another chance though. Considering the circumstances, Seth thought that was a minor victory all on its own.

* * *

The pain was coming in spasms now. Not that he was really thinking of it as pain. Not anymore. He'd grown so used to it. The way the tingle sent shockwaves through the fatty tissues; how the currents crackled from one node to another; and they were growing … always growing. It felt goo-ooo-d.

What had started out as merely pinpricks of light, dancing under the skin, was coalescing, hardening, and breaking through the skin like rock-solid acne, only this one you couldn't scratch away.

He tried anyway, because they itched and hurt. So, he scratched and scratched with fingernails that were now resembling big, dirty claws, until the surface was just a bloody mess and the point of the crystal was peeking through like an angry red welt.

It was like teething, only all over your body.

A guttural sound emanated from the creature on the floor. It echoed through the cave. By this point, it didn't sound particularly human anymore.

That suited the rest of the "people" that were gathering just fine. Aside from those needing to enter, anyone else was barred, but they could still hear him. Sound travelled in strange ways down here, underground.

Elsewhere in the cave system, the rest of them were too preoccupied with their own preparations to worry about the moanings of some half-mad former wizard-man.

They weren't the only ones that heard him either. It attracted attention. Like that hunter, snooping around, sneaking and spying out what was happening. He'd been a bit lean, but had still made a decent-sized snack.

For weeks, months, they'd been working. Soon, they would be ready. Soon...

* * *

Time did strange things—or so they said. It could make a new life grow from the tiniest speck or it could erode down the mightiest mountain. It was all just a matter of perspective.

It could, of course, do plenty of other things too, especially if you were able to control it; then it could turn into some very dramatic sequences indeed. But to control time you needed to do more than just understand it (if indeed it was a simple "single" feature to understand). You probably had to be able to place yourself outside of it, too.

As it was, Linandra was far too busy being swept downriver on the great tide to do anything other than just watch and experience as times changed. Not that she saw it that way. As far as she was concerned, it was just a question of one day flowing into the next. And the next thing you knew, a whole set of them had flown past, just like that.

'Why can't I go?' Lin wailed. 'There's nothing wrong with today. It's a great day. We were going up to the lake and everything.'

'Linandra. While I'm pleased that you and Seth are getting along now. This is not the best time to go that far from the Towers. I would be much happier if you would stay on the grounds.'

'You can't stop me,' Lin said defiantly.

'Actually, I do believe I can,' Kaheiron replied.

Looking at the young woman, he couldn't believe he was even considering this, now of all times. Still, with Seth nearby, they should both be safe enough. Maybe he *was* being too protective?

'Very well then,' the Archmagus relented. 'Go. Enjoy your time. And be on your guard. There's been an unwholesome feeling in the air for the past few months. If you experience anything unusual, see anything strange or abnormal, I want you to come straight back here and describe it to me exactly. Do you understand?'

'Then I can go?'

'That is what I just said, is it not? Just, be mindful, Little One. While I trust Seth implicitly, I do not wish to see you hurt.'

'You worry too much,' Lin pointed out, eyes shining. Standing on tip-toe she reached up and pecked him on the cheek.

'And I want you home by nightfall,' Kaheiron called after her as she disappeared through the doors.

The last of summer still rang in the air. Nightfall was far away even if it did come a little earlier here because of the shadow of the mountains. Right now, it was the collective shadow of the trees that was the only thing that blocked out the light. A whisper of a breeze passed through them. If you lay down and closed your eyes, you could almost believe you could hear them talking.

Nonsense, of course, as anyone would tell you, well, almost anyone. There were probably a few earthier people who would try and convince you differently. There were people at the Towers that would try and convince you of almost anything, like that crazy idea that the suns were some big balls of burning gas going round-and-round themselves. Mad as a hatter that one was.

If they were right, they had sure decreased the power of the furnace. As it had started to edge towards the end of the summer, the warmth was beginning to die down, just a little.

Still, the waving leaves made a good background chorus when backed up by a few songbirds; the splashes of the occasional curious fish taking a look at the world above the water of the lake; and the random rustles that, if you were telling scary stories, would probably make you jump, only to turn out to have been caused by a rabbit or two.

It had been a very nice day indeed, as far as Lin was concerned. After all, what was there to complain about? The outskirts of the Towers' domain might be a lot less tamed than the orchard, but it was no less enjoyable. Actually, it was the undisturbed part that made it all the more tranquil. You could still reach here easily enough, but few people from the Towers ever came out here. Not without reason anyway.

Until these last few months, she'd had little reason to come here herself. If she'd wanted peace and quiet, there were places far closer to home to find them in.

'A soft breeze in the air. A warm sun in the sky. Some pleasant water in the lake to dip your feet in when it gets too hot. Nice company,' Lin sighed contently as she tucked her arms under her head. 'What more could anyone want?'

Make that *mostly* nice company, she corrected herself. She could have done without the earlier run in with those multi-footed, little terrors they called ants in these parts. And she had been sure something had been a little too interested at nibbling at her toes earlier when wading by the shore.

She'd been so sure, that she and Seth had spent at least ten minutes rushing up and down the shallow waters near the shore trying to chase it down. Against all odds, they'd eventually managed to catch it, wallowing in the shallows, barking happily at them.

Lin had managed to convince Seth to release Pickles eventually, and the little shapeshifter was now having a merry time poking his adorable nose into every rabbit hole he could find.

Even Seth seemed to be behaving himself. Not that the guy was even capable of sitting still and just relaxing for more than two heartbeats at a time. It wasn't that he always seemed to be doing something—even when he was sitting still—but often, it was that what he was doing that didn't make any sense to her.

Sometimes she suspected him on doing that on purpose. Rascal. That's what they should have named him. Between Rascal, Pickles and Cheep, she was beginning to feel clearly outnumbered.

By now, she was pretty sure that she was supposed to find it all funny. She still hadn't quite figured out what she should do about that. He was very earnest about it, that was true. It probably wasn't his fault that it also made him look like a jester who'd lost all sense of timing and direction.

Lin chuckled to herself at the thought, when a loud pop erupted from beside her making her jump in fright. A small scream escaped from her lips before she realized what was happening.

'Oh Seth! What *are* you doing?'

Lin slapped her thighs in mirth as she drank in the sight before her. He really shouldn't try so hard, she thought. He was only making it harder on himself. It wasn't long before she down in hysteric laughter after a few sparse hiccups of air.

'I can't believe you just tried to do that! You should see yourself,' she cried.

'This wasn't *quite* what I intended,' Seth admitted a little sheepishly, quickly putting the now very sticky bottle down "beside" the blanket.

'You don't say,' Lin wiped away tears of laughter as she tried to breathe.

Seth shook a newly wetted and sticky sleeve trying to get rid of the fizzy wine. He was more than liberal with sharing it, causing some of it to land on Lin.

'Don't do that,' Lin cried out, leaning back, out of the shower. She tried to sound cross, but between barely suppressed laughter and her wide grin, that just wasn't possible.

Despite everything else, and she did mean "everything," at times like these he was just like a silly boy: all awkward and, going by the tinge of crimson, more than a little embarrassed. Lin smiled. It was kind of endearing—and completely ridiculous, of course.

'Oh, sorry,' Seth apologised. Struggling out of his coat and ruffled tunic, the cloth in both released its overload of fluid as he wringed it out over the lake.

Taking the opportunity with Seth out of the way, Lin gathered herself together enough to reach out for the bottle and prevent the rest of the contents from escaping as well.

She put an eye to the bottle neck. It was hard to tell, but it did slosh about in there, so something had to be left. 'You didn't leave much,' she told him when he came back.

'I didn't know they did that.'

'Did what? Explode in your face?'

'Yes. No one has ever brought me an exploding bottle. I'm sure this one is defective. I've had this before and it's never done this when they've opened it.'

'*They* probably know what they're doing.'

'It's really nice,' Seth said as he sat back down, having draped the tunic over a couple of low branches after rinsing out the worst of the fizzing flavours. It'd smell, but he could get it cleaned later. For now, it was enough that it just dried.

'I think it's empty,' Lin said. She put the round, brown container away. 'You know, you're really no good at planning, are you? I mean, how many times have we actually managed to have a *proper* picnic together?'

'You don't need to rub it in,' Seth said as his shoulders sagged.

'Last time you nearly drowned trying to catch your clothes from escaping downriver,' Lin laughed. 'Doesn't exactly sound like the next general of the land to me.'

'Well... I—' Seth struggled to think of what to say, looking uncomfortable.

'Relax ... I'm just teasing you,' Lin smiled mischievously at him, nudging his shoulder with hers as she sat back down and patted the blanket beside her.

'Come, sit down. You might be a lousy general, but I didn't say I didn't like you.'

Seth blushed furiously. Frozen for a moment, his eyes fixed on his feet and he fiddled with the edge of the blanket beneath them. He tried to gather himself together by picking up some of the éclairs and offering them to her.

He wasn't normally like this, he admonished himself. He was sure of that. But every time he was around her, his head just began to spin, and it kept spinning until it lost its balance and toppled over.

That was usually when he did something embarrassing, not being able to catch himself in time.

'You know, I could get used to this,' Lin said, laying back on her elbows, oblivious to Seth's discomfort.

Jostled by that notion, Seth turned to her, heart hammering in his chest. 'You could? I mean, you would?'

'Sure. It's peaceful. Quiet. Even relaxing—aside from listening to you splashing about in the lake.'

'Oh,' Seth looked dejected and went back to examining his feet. 'I thought you were talking about me. Of course,' he leaned over and now a grin began tugging at the side of his face, 'I *could* help you relax. I'm quite good at … relaxing.'

'I'm sure you are,' Lin leaned her head out of the way. 'Down Boy!' she ordered, halting his approach with a hand on his chest.

'Aww, you wound me, my princess,' Seth said and dramatically rolled over on his back, playing dead.

'Oh, stop it, you're not fooling anyone,' Lin said, reached out and, without warning, tickled his side.

Seth let out a piercing shriek.

'Sorry, sorry,' Lin laughed. 'I didn't know you were that ticklish.'

'I'm not. I'm just—' Seth swallowed, she was very close to his face at this angle. A dangerous gleam crossed her eyes and he braced himself, ready for another tickling assault. Shifting by a millimetre, Lin kissed his cheek gently and smiled.

Seemingly satisfied with his complete and utter confusion, Lin rolled over onto her elbows again and watched the clouds drift by.

For a moment, Seth silently watched her and tried to will away the heat from his face.

A thought crossed his mind and the words leapt past his lips before he could catch them, 'You're beautiful, you know.'

'W-what?' Lin whipped her head around, eyes wide with disbelief, did he just..? Now she felt heat flushing *her* cheeks and, breathless, turned her eyes away.

Not that being around Seth didn't always make her feel like there was a whole horde of butterflies nested inside her body, each crying at the top of their lungs, distracting her from whatever else was there; but she wasn't used to straight up compliments, certainly not those that didn't ask her for any favours in return.

'I really—wait, what was that?'

'You heard it too?'

'Mhm,' Seth nodded. 'It came from—' he looked around, 'that direction.'

'There shouldn't be anything out here that would make *those* kinds of noises. Should there?' Lin asked, tension growing.

Seth shook his head. 'No, there shouldn't.'

'What was it?'

'I don't know. Wait here while I go check it out,' Seth told her as he got to his feet. He even made it half way across to the low-levelled set of bushes before Lin managed to stop him.

'What are you doing? We should find out what that was. We might need to get out of here quickly.'

He couldn't understand why she was refusing to let go of his arm. Lin wasn't usually this clingy. If something scared her, she'd be more inclined to look for something to hit it with than anything else; he'd learnt that the hard way. He felt like he still had the bruises … he hadn't meant to frighten her at the time. Of course, she hadn't meant to nearly give him a concussion either, so maybe it evened out.

'Lin … You know me. I would never put you in danger. I swear, on my life. I'm just going to look, I promise.'

'Not like that you're not,' Lin stated as a matter-of-fact. 'Or have you forgotten?'

'Forgotten what?'

'You're wearing nothing but your undergarments,' Lin finally blew up at him.

Seth looked down, realization dawning. 'Oh,' he said. 'Right. Yes … of course. I should probably pick up the sword too. Thanks Lin.'

He nipped back to where the clothes were drying, returning a moment later with said items in his arms.

'There, that should do it,' he said, getting ready to leave again.

'Put the clothes on *before* you go chasing the dangerous noises, you idiot!' Lin groaned.

INTO THE FRAY

Can you see anything?' Lin whispered.

Seth made some indistinct shushing sounds in her direction.

'Alright, alright. I'm being as quiet as I can be,' Linandra wriggled around a bit for more comfort and was rewarded by several scratches from the bushes they were in.

'It's too far away to make out properly,' Seth said.

'How can it be too far away to see? You heard it, didn't you?'

'It probably wasn't the same one. It was more of a feeling anyway.'

He tried not to move, just in case there really was something troublesome afoot. The uneven ground ate into their stomachs. Before them was a mass of trees and sparse patches of open ground.

'Do you see anything now?' Lin wanted to know.

There was a knot of roots somewhere quite uncomfortable. She'd swear something was crawling underneath the leaves next to her thigh. And, hidden in the prickly bushes like this, she was either tickled or scratched every time she moved.

'Try to stay still. You don't want to make a ruckus,' Seth motioned for her to settle down.

'Are you sure there is anything to see?' Lin asked suspiciously. Her voice might have been disbelieving, but it was still very, very quiet, just in case he wasn't imagining things or making them up.

Personally, she might have picked somewhere a little more romantic, she thought and slapped a bug landing on her nose. There was this tingling sensation in her stomach. Like a tiny worm was wriggling around, causing concern to multiply by the minute.

'Whatever it is, it's getting closer,' Seth said. 'I just know they're out there. I swear I can hear them.'

'Are there many?' Lin asked, repressing a shiver. It was getting late and, even in summer, the nights here weren't that warm.

'Yes.'

For Linandra, there seemed to pass an eternity until she, too, could hear something. Guess he'd been right after all. Whoever they were, they weren't bothered about keeping their movements quiet. And now that they were coming into range, Lin really wished they hadn't. The forest fled before them and she felt they really should do the same.

It didn't sound like an army on the march. Not even a mass of people could make *those* kinds of noises, could they? Lin tried to shake loose the flashing images her imagination showed her, yet those were topped by the reality coming into view.

Seth tugged insistently on her sleeve, already ripped by some unfriendly thorns. 'We should leave, now,' he whispered. 'We've stayed too long. And be quiet. If they hear us, we'll have to make a run for it. In here, they're faster than either of us.'

Into the nearest clearing thundered a stream of creatures. At least, Lin hoped they were creatures. If they were people, something truly terrible must have happened to them in the past.

Big and small. Lean and fat. Some she'd have sworn wore a full suit of armour, black with soot and gristle. Those clanked with rust at every move.

Others seemed decked in nothing but a loincloth. It was hard to tell from this far away, but even just seeing them made her insides twist into a knot.

Lin couldn't even put a name to them. She didn't need to. It was like watching a parade in the dark of everything that had ever invaded your most haunted nightmares, walking or staggering forth on two, four, even six legs.

'Go! Go!' Seth urged Lin.

He led them some distance away before he dared rise and move with less caution.

'What *were* those things?' Lin asked in a shushed voice.

'Golshaes. I've never seen this many in one place. Why would they come out like this? They *never* come out like this.'

'You know these things?' Lin wanted to know. She stumbled after him. It was beginning to grow hard to see where she was putting her feet.

'You see them moving about at nights, far from humans,' Seth murmured over his shoulder. 'Far from everything, really. They come out to hunt anything they can catch. They usually stay away from anything even resembling a settlement, though you don't want to be caught unaware in their territory once night falls. They don't usually bother me.'

'It's not night now.'

'I know. But that's not what I'm worried about. There's so many of them. If they hold their course, their path will take them directly to the Towers. We need to get back. Looks like they're taking the long way 'round. They're bigger than us, need more space to move. That'll slow them down—a little. Come on, let's go. We can take a shortcut. Hurry. Hurry!'

* * *

Back at the Towers, a flurry of activity was already crowding into the Archmagus' public chambers.

'*How* many did you say?' Kaheiron asked, an eyebrow raised in surprise.

'Twenty scores at least. Probably far more,' the enchanter before him repeated dutifully. 'It was dark. They were hard to count after the seeing spell started to fade, even without the interference.'

'We'll need more accurate information than that,' the Archmagus said. Without taking his eyes of the image shimmering in the air before him, he continued, 'Istarrian, dispatch a reconnaissance team immediately. We'll need an accurate report and it would appear our eyes are the most trusted means by which to achieve it.'

'Yes, my lord.'

'What *are* they up to?' Kaheiron began to pace. 'They never come this close or in these numbers.'

He mulled over the events of the last hour as he knew them. 'Appoint guardians to the necessary positions. And strengthen the architectural shield spells. We can't risk any of them breaching our walls.'

'Aye,' a third, already-tired looking sorcerer nodded in agreement before returning to hurriedly scratching away with his quill.

'Yes, my lord,' Istarrian said. 'Shall I send out a warning to our closest neighbours?'

Kaheiron shook his head. 'No, not yet. Prepare them, but do not dispatch them, yet. There is no need to cause undue panic. The nearest settlement is quite some distance from here and, if the reports are correct, they're headed straight for *us.*'

'As you say, my lord.'

'What do you surmise that these creatures are planning, Archmagus?' another of the assembled staff wondered.

'I do not yet know, but it is indeed troubling. They have remained quiet for generations. Why choose now to re-emerge in force? What do they hope to achieve?'

'Do you believe,' the wizard's voice lowered worriedly, 'that it could be the Sandlands that are behind this?'

Kaheiron shook his head. 'While it is true that the Sandlands and the Twin Towers have never seen eye to eye,' he cleared his desk of its burden of rolls of parchments with a flick of his fingers. 'Should they choose to oppose us directly, these are not the means by which they would do so.'

'But these clans have never before allied themselves with others. They've always considered everything other than themselves and the beings they "concoct" out of those horrid bottles of theirs to be inferior in all ways.'

'Perhaps being defeated so many times has altered their opinions,' a wizened old mage tested the thought even as he spoke it.

'I don't know. The golshaes are difficult to fathom. As long as they remained close to the mountains, I have been content to leave them be. Any campaign to eradicate them has always been seen to need more resources than such a nuisance would be worth. Why would that change now? What *has* changed now?' Kaheiron asked.

What had changed indeed? This was looking like it was going to be a lot more trouble than saving a random person in distress, the Archmagus thought.

While a single magician, sorcerer, mage—or any of the other practitioners of magic that stayed under the roofs of the Towers—was more than a match for a single golshae, even a small group, getting them all to work together against a larger foe was going to take a miracle all on its own.

'Send word out to all corners of the Towers and when everyone is inside and accounted for, seal the gates. We should still have time until their main force arrives. With some fortune on our side, we should be able to discourage them long before they reach our outer walls.'

'As you wish, my lord,' Istarrian bowed his head and, already beginning to mutter names under his breath, set off for his own office. He hadn't done such a wide announcement in years. He better loop up the main formula first, he thought. Best not to get it wrong, not at a time like this.

* * *

'You're bleeding,' Lin said, worriedly.

'You don't have to tell me,' Seth replied trying to get his breath back. He leaned heavily on the "sword" he'd struck the creature down with, wishing his head would stop spinning.

'Too close. That was too close,' he wheezed, chest heaving.

They'd thought they'd been safely out of the way of the invaders. But apparently not everyone ran with the main force. It was lucky indeed that they'd only encountered a lone scout.

'What *was* that?' Lin asked as she did her best to wrap some torn and makeshift bandages around the injury. Guess all that time at the faunatarium hadn't been wasted after all, she thought.

'That? Oh, that was a golshae, up close and personal.'

'And that?' Lin pointed towards the contraption that Seth was leaning on.

Seth tugged hard at it and it made a sickly sound as it tore from the creature's body. He frowned as he examined it more closely.

'A weapon,' he finally conceded, forced to describe the indescribable.

'How about disgusting,' Lin shuddered. 'All those edges and sharpened wires and spikes.'

'Golshaes are, by nature, not the most pleasant sort,' Seth agreed.

Still, with his own sword broken, it was the only weapon within reach. It would have to do. He only had to hope he didn't end up slicing off his own head with it when trying to wield it.

'Praise be that Cheep's still at the Towers,' Lin breathed. 'Did you see what happened to Pickles?'

Seth shook his head. 'I lost sight of him after that first encounter. Don't worry. He's probably pretending to be a rock, or something. I'm sure he's far safer than we're about to become.'

'Let's go,' he said, 'before we attract even more attention. It shouldn't be too far now.'

Linandra nodded, picking up something and hefting it experimentally. The distance between the lake and the Towers wasn't that great but, right now, it felt as distant as the moons.

* * *

Time, time wasn't on anyone's side. It merely watched, with a detached sort of amusement, as the different sides scrambled into readiness.

'Are you intending to wait them out, Archmagus?' one of the assembled wizards asked.

'If we were a well-fortified castle that strategy would have had some merit,' the Archmagus acknowledged. 'As it is, our walls are defended more by spells than by the depth of the stonework. And if the Towers had been intended to endure a siege, I'm sure it wouldn't have been designed with such an inordinate amount of windows facing outwards.'

'True. Then, what should I do with the youngest?'

'Place them in the safest location,' Kaheiron instructed. 'This is one occasion where I do wish someone had succeeded in inventing a magical portal.'

'I agree, Archmagus. But if ethereal transportation is any more than merely a legend, then it has not existed for millennia.'

'Agreed. And we don't need to worry about our enemies using them against us. That is something,' Kaheiron said.

'Our greatest defence has always lain in our people,' the magician agreed.

'Have the scouts that were sent out reported back?'

'Not yet. Too bad we don't have any far-seers here. There is some form of interference that our seeing spells is having trouble penetrating.'

'Very unfortunate, indeed. However, we must do the best we can with what we have.'

'Yes, Archmagus,' the assembled collection of spellcasters chorused.

"What we have" was in this case lots and lots of practitioners of the arcane arts. Some of them turned out to not be overly keen on being dragged from their comfortable dens to "shore up the defences." As powerful as they undoubtedly were, their inclination laid more towards academia than riding into battle.

'Young man, I simply cannot be disturbed at this time. These are *very* delicate works!' an old wizard insisted, his fluffy slippers dancing over the floor. 'It has taken me years to set this up properly. I simply can't just leave.'

'Tell that to the golshaes,' the recruiter for the offensive team told him in no uncertain tones. 'Who knows, maybe they'll listen.'

'Golshaes? I can't have golshaes in my study. Why, they'll quite ruin my experiments. I insist on that you stop them!'

'Golshaes? Did someone say golshaes?' another scraggly head poked into the corridor from a nearby door.

'Yes, Master Wizard. We're about to be attacked,' the recruiter paused for breath and was quickly interrupted.

'You're quite mistaken. Golshaes have been extinct for centuries,' the wizard huffed and slammed his door shut.

The recruiter jumped at the noise. Now he knew why no one had volunteered for rounding up the residents in this wing.

'I hope everyone else is having more luck,' he sighed.

* * *

'Can you see anything?'

'Unfortunately, yes,' Lin replied and pressed herself harder against the broken bits of masonry they were trying to hide behind.

It might have been a cottage at some point in time. Now, it was barely more than a couple of broken walls within a mixture of trees and scrawny bushes. Even so, it offered some shelter. Certainly more than they'd had if they hadn't hidden behind them.

Of course, it only worked in one direction. If another group of golshaes came up from behind, they'd be more than just highly visible, they'd be, as the saying went, "sitting ducks," ready for even the most incompetent unit of archers to pick off at their leisure.

They hadn't actually seen anything looking like an archer so far, so maybe it'd be more of a "hack and slash" approach. That wasn't much of an improvement and Seth shuddered at the thought.

'If they turn east, they'll see us,' Lin whispered worriedly in his ear.

Seth nodded. It wasn't as if that hadn't already crossed his mind. That was why his hands were all clammy and his muscles tense.

'If more arrive, they'll swarm all over us even *without* turning,' he replied and tightened the knot on the strap of cloth bound over his arm. It throbbed, so much that he'd swear he was feeling it all the way down into his feet. But it didn't seem to be bleeding anymore and that was good.

'This isn't good,' Seth continued. 'They'll be between us and the Towers soon.'

The two of them had already been through a second close encounter and had little desire to go through another. They'd been lucky that time. There had only been a couple of golshaes and they'd been smaller, slighter ones than those that made up the main units. The golshaes had also been a bit preoccupied at the time, or he'd never have been able to take them down. They weren't the *only* danger in these forests at night.

'Are you alright?' Lin asked, touching his good arm in concern.

Seth flexed his fingers, wincing. 'I think so, yes. All parts appear to still be functional.'

He picked up the "sword" from the ground that had been the prize claimed from their previous little run-in with the golshaes. Much like its previous owner, it was in a serious need of a wash. Seth doubted that even dunking it in acid would help. It'd probably dissolve.

Maybe, once upon a time, it had been a sword. Now it was merely a collection of dirty, stained metal held together by equally appalling wired strings with little sharp points poking out every so often. It was the one responsible for the cut on his arm.

'We can't stay here,' Lin insisted.

'I know. But if we move now, they'll see us.'

'Could we just wait until they pass?'

Seth risked another peek over the assembled mismatch of stone and rubble.

The sounds from the passing group were covering any whispered conversation they might have had, but they still kept their voices low. Even if the golshaes didn't care about moving through the forest quietly, there might still be ones with better hearing than the others in there.

'Do you think they know about them already?'

'At the Towers, you mean?' Seth asked. 'I don't know. I hope so.'

'They sure don't care about anyone knowing they're here. They stomp through like a herd of migrating, giant bulls,' Lin said.

'Do bulls migrate?' Seth frowned. 'Hmm, I never knew. Seems they don't feel they need to worry.'

'If they're all like the ones we've seen so far, I guess they don't. And what's that glow that surrounds some of them?'

'I don't know. But even if we make it back before them, the Towers is going to have one tough battle on their hands. I'm sorry Lin, there were more of them than I expected. I'll need to get you back. We'll wait a little longer, then we'll make a run for it,' Seth said.

A little later and they gathered themselves into small balls of energy.

'Ready? Right. One, two, three … GO!'

* * *

By now, there were many that were hurrying. But as far as Kaheiron was concerned, they weren't hurrying enough. Most of those that lived and studied at the Towers weren't inclined towards combat, and, of those that were, the majority were well past their prime.

The trouble was that golshaes were naturally immune to personally direct spells. This was not a battle that could be resolved by turning them all into beetles or butterflies. Things would have been much easier if that hadn't been so.

'I believe that one of the scouts is waiting to speak with you, Archmagus. We've already heard his report and adjusted our secondary strategies accordingly, but he insists on seeing you in person,' Istarrian said through the communication device.

'Hmm, send him up then, Istarrian, if you please,' Kaheiron ordered.

'As you wish, my lord.'

Some minutes later and Kaheiron was even less pleased about the situation than before. He hated having his own moves dictated by those of his opponent. But no matter how much experience he'd gained over the years, instinct still reared its head from time to time. You didn't corner a dragon and expect it to stay calm and quiet about it.

'Placing us in a reactive instead of a proactive role,' he complained out loud at the news. 'One should never commit all one's pieces until certain that the game can be won. Yet, it is not the wise man who plays with lives.'

Kaheiron began pacing irritably, flicking what looked like ethereal chess pieces from side to side of their equally insubstantial, yet slightly humming, board.

'Are you planning on taking charge of this matter personally then, Archmagus?' Istarrian asked, watching as Kaheiron shifted the pieces around on the hovering depiction of the Towers and its nearby geography.

'I would have preferred that it would not become necessary,' Kaheiron replied, rubbing his fingers against the top piece of his staff. Not that the ornate gold decoration could possibly shine any more, buffed and rebuffed as it had been.

'However, yes, I will. I prefer not to leave matters to chance,' Kaheiron confided in those that remained in the chambers. 'Luck is a harsh mistress.'

'She is indeed,' the sorceress closest to him agreed.

'If you are certain that you have everything in place for the defence of the Towers?' Kaheiron asked, stabbing a finger into the glowing display.

The sorceress nodded. 'There are a few matters that remain to be addressed, but we will be ready.'

'Good. And the instructions I set you?'

'All of the people you asked for have assembled in the location you specified.'

'Excellent,' Kaheiron snapped his fingers and the display vanished. 'You know what to do.'

Nodding affirmative, the sorceress in question left the chambers, thoughts already on what she needed to do next.

'If I may be so bold, Archmagus,' one of the magicians queried as Kaheiron prepared to leave. 'I can see that all those that you have chosen have not also been included among the channelers.'

'No. They'll be needing all their own powers.'

'As you say, Archmagus.'

'Pardon me for asking, these items you are collecting. If they are able to assist us, why are they not kept at the Towers?'

'Because we have a large amount of people living here who wouldn't take kindly to having their expected ethereal connections disrupted,' Kaheiron's mouth twitched in amusement. 'I thought it wisest to store them elsewhere.'

The assembled arcane users shuddered in unison. No, they wouldn't have liked *that* at all.

'No, our organization shall be our defence,' Kaheiron continued. 'From the oldest master to the youngest student, I know we will utilize everyone's strength in the defence of the Towers.'

'We have to. It's not like we can just pop out for tea and crumpets,' someone muttered.

The Archmagus carefully removed the silver-threaded, silken gloves he was wearing and put them on top of a stack of books. Next, he placed his ornate staff in a special cupboard, on the wall, where metal claws snapped out and locked it in place.

He then took off his outer robes and draped them over the back of the high chair. 'Right. Everything's been prepared. I best be off then,' he said to those still present.

And with that Kaheiron settled his belt and strode out through the doors with one solitary purpose in mind.

* * *

The old man surveyed the room. Walking in through the heavy oaken doors hadn't caused the speculations about what was going on to quiet down at all, quite the contrary.

Twice he tried to get their attention. But the loud chatter of the large gathering of mages drowned out his voice. With little time to wait patiently, the third time around, he fired off a small spell. That made them stop filling the air with worried babble. Instead, they started complaining about the lights dancing in front of their eyes and why their ears were ringing.

Eventually, Istarrian managed to quiet the hubbub in the chamber. If he had managed to single out even one word from the previous chaos, that would have been a miracle.

Considering the chaotic state of the Towers at the best of times, if you referred to the place as "the corridors of power," you had obviously never walked them. When any group got together to discuss anything—whether it was about the oranges in the orchard turning blue instead of pink when ripe, or something serious like half the roof leaking because someone had broken a container with extra picky termites—the conversation, without fail, created a ruckus.

Why would an attack by golshaes be treated any differently?

'You're meaning for us to do what?' a wizard in emerald robes erupted in shock at his words.

Istarrian waved the ethereal map into existence and pointed out a few of the most obvious changes, as the map now showed the countermeasures that they'd already taken.

'As you can see, we have established the setting of our defence,' he said solemnly. '*You* all shall be our *offence*. You will take this battle to our attackers. Several small forces should be able to strike the golshaes in several places at once. And well away from the Towers, you should be able to utilize your abilities without worrying about causing damage to your own side.'

Istarrian held up his hands at the storm of questions, protests and complaints that surged forth towards him. 'Even if you are not able to defeat all of the enemies,' he said. 'And we do not expect you to, you should be able to deplete their numbers enough that holding the Towers will not be calling upon luck in futility.'

'And die in the process?' someone at the back challenged.

'Preferably not,' Istarrian retorted. 'I am not asking you to take on a mission of no return. You need merely to delay, disorganize and, if possible, demoralize such troops as you can.'

'You're assuming that they have any morale to demoralize,' the emerald wizard countered. 'Golshaes aren't known for their intelligence, neither are the creatures they enslave to do their bidding.'

'They are strong and they are many,' Mio, a gangly young man with an unusual amount of toned muscle for a magician, informed them in a matter of fact voice.

Of all of them, he was probably one of those that had actually come properly prepared. Istarrian saw that he'd had the foresight to bring a sword and a few other odds and ends. He had also anticipated that going out into the bush with a foot-long robe with silver and satin inlays wasn't a good idea and had dressed accordingly.

Still, he did seem to have a penchant for stating the obvious.

'We have reports of several units moving towards us so there's little doubt that they're doing more than just stirring up trouble. No one has considered them a threat for generations,' Istarrian said.

'Our information has come solely from several ancient tomes,' he admitted. 'So we're not certain how much of what knowledge we have of them is accurate, today.'

One of those closest to Istarrian rubbed the crystalline end to his staff thoughtfully. 'The last serious encounter was several hundred years ago, was it not?' he asked.

'I believe so. They've been very quiet.'

'If they'd *stayed* quiet, we might not be having this problem,' someone complained.

'It doesn't appear to have taught them harsh enough a lesson,' another of the assembled agreed.

'That just means that we'll have to do it instead.'

'Overconfidence is the root of all evil!'

'Really? I thought that was hubris?'

'With their numbers, it's likely that they will have more firepower than us out there.'

'Literally.'

'Are they really the ones behind this? They *never* work together.'

'Couldn't we just create a general field spell on ground level, work in a pyroclastic element, reverse it, and just watch them evaporate?' someone suggested.

'It'd annihilate them, true,' a sorcerer dressed in blue agreed.

'And annihilate most of the forest along with it and quite possibly us too. I'm sure the Archmagus would be *most* impressed,' a scruffy-looking magician with a brown beard said, voice dripping with sarcasm.

As the din rose back up, Istarrian shook his head sadly. One powerful arcane user was something to be feared by even a mighty army. A whole group of equally potent spellcasters were more likely to be a danger to themselves than anyone else. If this kept up, they'd still be arguing while the Towers' defences were overrun. Sometimes, just sometimes, he wished that he could order around a legion of soldiers instead. They couldn't possibly be as difficult to manage. Soldiers did what their commanding officers told them, didn't they?

Another set of motions with his hands and the scenery in the air above them changed. Now, outlined in oscillating mist, was an interpretation of what the surrounding land would have looked like, had it been made of fog, light and shadow. It tingled to the touch.

'Ah, I had hoped for colour too,' Istarrian said wistfully. 'Nevertheless, it is an accurate representation, even if it is blue.'

It didn't take nearly as long to get everyone's attention this time, and he was soon explaining what was being asked of them, finishing with, 'at this stage, we do not yet know the full extent of our enemy's plan. Therefore, I ask all of you to not overextend yourselves out there. Eyes and ears open. If we can learn of the reason behind their actions, we might be able to anticipate them.'

There was a communal sigh of relief.

'Praise be. For a moment, I thought you were suggesting that we would be able to discuss this with them as rational, sentient beings,' someone quipped.

Istarrian ignored the barb. 'Mio, I'm placing you in charge. Small teams of two or three would be optimal. And keep them moving. It's best not to remain in one location for too long. And stay out of sight, too, if you can.'

'This is insane,' the emerald wizard grumbled. 'Wizards and sorcerers don't fight *in* armies. Sages, mages, magicians and enchanters—none of those make good combat footwork.'

'Indeed. If two armies clash, they'd be lucky to have a single spellcaster on each side supporting them and whatever healers they might find to bring up the rear. But this is foolish, man. You can't fight a battle with just magicians,' an enchanter said.

'Practitioners of the arcane arts,' another corrected him.

'That's what I said.'

Quelling the budding argument with steely eyes, Istarrian cleared his throat. 'I've distributed parchments with your various duties and locales to all present,' he said. 'Do read them before you leave. And please, consider your fellow practitioners out there and don't abandon them. You are not in this alone.'

Istarrian gave them their last few sets of instructions and sent them on their way. All he could do now was to hope that it would work out. Regardless of what he'd said out loud, Istarrian was inclined to agree with the young upstart.

Oh, it wasn't that they lacked the power, quite the contrary. A competent spellslinger could, in the right circumstances, be more than a match for a "regular" army division, especially if he, or she, or it, didn't have any morals or inhibitions and the enemy didn't have any long range weaponry.

The Towers had tried to foster a sense of cooperation between the various "Practitioners of the Arcane Arts" as they liked to call themselves when they were feeling officious. He, himself, had overseen that for many years and, as far as Istarrian was concerned, the various factions were as argumentative as ever.

'I'm too young to die,' the old man mumbled.

* * *

By the time Kaheiron had reached the roof, twilight had begun to fall. Soon darkness would follow. Even then, you would still be able to see far more than just your hand in front of you. The moons saw to that. Their bodies, each as different as the next, would hang in the sky like big, bright lanterns. It lent a mystical air to a night that was already full of magic and not all of it benign.

Tonight, he wasn't certain it would be enough.

He sniffed the winds. There was a hint of a chill in the air. Yes, he might not yet be able to hear those coming, but he knew they were out there, somewhere. They'd reach them just before dark. A dark that they thought would give them an advantage, surely. *They* could see well at even the lowest level of light.

Well, they weren't the only ones that could take advantage of that.

The Archmagus removed the last piece of his clothing. Taking a deep breath of the refreshing night air, he just stood there for a moment, his arms stretched out from his sides.

Then, the great black dragon, with a single beat of his wings, leaped into the sky.

* * *

Those sent out into the woods soon found themselves in a world that none of them felt they knew anymore. Not sure how long they'd been out here—the minutes felt like hours—it all blended into a blur of hiding, lurking, quick dashes and trying to run through, or away, from whatever their magic created.

The scouts had been the first ones they'd hit. But the main body of the invaders wasn't far behind, and, judging by the odd sparks in the night, the golshaes knew they weren't the only ones out here.

There was the sound of metal scraping against foliage. Rough sounds of battered wood and bodies both. Mio's ears twitched. They were coming closer.

'Not good,' the mage hiding behind a large laurel shrub, whispered. He flexed his fingers, trying to get some more life into them.

'Try to lure them behind the copse,' Mio said, breathing hard. Hah. Bet those back at the Towers hadn't counted on there being *this* many of them. Neither had he. Blast.

'*You* lure them back. I can't run another step,' the mage next to him tried not to fall over. Laboured breaths issued forth from his lungs. His heart was killing him. He was too exhausted for it to be fear. After tonight, he'd swear he didn't have anything left in him.

Magical skirmishes never lasted this long: a quick dash in, set off a few spells and an even quicker escape, that was the way of it. There wasn't a spellcaster in a thousand who had the stamina for gathering up and keeping a toe, a foot, even a whole leg, in the arcane river for any extended period of time. The longer you kept it there, the greater toll it took on your body. Eventually, it just became less laborious to deal with the matter by hand.

Of course, no one suggested you should manhandle a whole mountain to pieces one shovel load at a time, but for something like that, you'd need several people working on it together or to have a host of channelers standing by behind you as you worked. And all the channelers were back at the Towers, strengthening the defences there.

'Curses,' the young magician swore under his breath. 'What I wouldn't give for a sorcerer's staff right now.'

'What insane mandril came up with this idea? Prolonged contact with the enemy is dealt with by foot soldiers,' the second mage tried to haul his partner to his feet.

But this time, they *were* the foot soldiers, weren't they? Mio thought. To suddenly find himself catapulted into the role as there were few others available … no, it just hadn't been his first choice. Maybe next time volunteering would be the last thing on his mind.

He flexed his fingers. Good. He was finally getting some feeling back into them. Mio shook them up a bit. 'Damn. That last spell is still tingling. I'm getting numb all over.'

He still had some left in him. They all did. Best make it count for something, Mio decided. Then they'd make for the safety—what little there was —of the Towers, before the enemy stood at their gates.

Somewhere else in the forest, a second team was thinking much the same. They had seemed to have caught sight of one of the enemy's flanks. They weren't sure. It was a little difficult to tell between the darkness, the trees and the twin habit the golshaes had of not standing still and being very enthusiastic about sticking something in you and hurling you into one of the trees, if they caught you.

Also, there was a question of understanding the concept behind a "flank" in this respect, in the first place.

'What is wrong with that spell? They should have been blasted apart by now. What's that young idiot Ronald doing?' the sorcerer in charge bellowed.

He hadn't lowered his volume since the first clash, and those around him jumped every time another set of instructions, or curses (usually expelled together), issued forth.

'We're having difficulties in making the spells connect,' his second informed him.

'They're just not using enough power. If the enemy has laid their dirty hands on some shieldstones, then strike at it. Strike the shield until the power of the spells exceed the power of the stone. Keep hitting it until it cracks.'

'They're attempting that already. This shield, if it's even a shield at all, appears to drain magic. Everything they throw at it simply vanishes. It's almost as if it imbibes it, making it stronger.'

'So, is it a shield, or isn't it?' the sorcerer in charge snapped.

'We're not certain. One of the other teams say that their spells didn't actually connect with *anything*. Some twenty-five yards from the enemy group, the magic simply ceased to be. It didn't evaporate. It was as if it drained into something. Something they couldn't see. This is no mere shieldstone.'

'They need to do better than that. Get me someone close enough. Let's take a look at this from the inside. If magic doesn't work, a good wallop with a giant mace might.'

The sorcerer's second nodded unhappily. He had a feeling he knew exactly who this "someone" was going to be.

'And get me some arrows,' the sorcerer snapped. 'Some *normal* arrows. No firespelled, icespelled or crystalline ones. Just ordinary arrows. Even pointed sticks will help. I want to know if those shields stops just magical attacks or physical ones as well.'

The rest of the double-team muttered mutinously. If magic wasn't working, then what good were all those years perfecting their art? They certainly hadn't spent all that time flexing their arcane muscles only to be killed due to trying to snuff out creatures from someone's worst nightmare with a blunt axe.

Somewhere out there, in the dark, the sounds of the approaching force grew steadily louder.

Yet other teams didn't worry about avoiding detection. They were too preoccupied with trying to escape what had detected them in the first place.

'Get back everyone,' someone shouted over the noise that was the battle. 'Retreat! Retreat!'

'That's what we're *trying* to do,' another wizard struck a smaller, charging golshae beast over the head with his staff.

There were more of them than there were of the wizards. Lots more. And it didn't help that all the trees kept getting in the way of their spells either.

True, some of the spells did go *through* the trees. When they were lucky, they went through the trees and the golshaes. But you couldn't always rely on fortune to win a war, not even a tiny one.

The creatures weren't the most advanced of fighters—though neither were the mages. But they *were* tenacious and a whole lot nastier. And it was hard to concentrate on spells in the chaos that was a fight, even a minor one.

They'd used up most of their arcane strength already, and most of them were now down to using their staffs as a kind of wooden pike, all while trying to escape from the immediate area.

That didn't mean much when even the *small* golshaes carried lots of horrible, pointy things that could really hurt if they were stuck in a man or a woman. And the bigger ones weren't just better armed, they were also more brutal and far stronger.

'Stay away from them. We can't beat them like this!' someone shouted while running.

A wizard who'd slowed down, coming too close to their pursuers, was caught in a choke grip, then thrust aside with enough force to break his spine.

The rest of them continued to run for the Towers.

THE TENACITY OF DRAGONS

The wizards weren't the only ones running.

'This *isn't* going to be good,' Seth flailed at the last assailant with his captured sword.

He'd managed to kill the ones from the last time. More by sheer accident it had to be said, but he'd done it. This one, this one was in a whole different class.

It didn't help that the sword wasn't even a foot long by now. It kept breaking off, lodging parts of itself in whatever he struck.

The aggrolshae before him struck down with a thunderaxe larger than he was. Seth barely managed to roll away as the impact drove the metal several feet into the ground.

They'd run straight into it. Among the trees, in the dark, it had been standing still, no lurking, in the woods. It had been *waiting* for them. By now, the forest was so full of smells of dark and dankness, of blood and fear, that they hadn't noticed the dark mass until they were right on top of it.

Only, now, it was right on top of *them*. He couldn't keep dodging it forever. There'd soon be more of them. The noise was bound to attract attention. Time was running out and he didn't stand a chance against something nearly fifteen feet tall, like this.

It had been so close. They'd been able to see the Towers from the edge of the forest. The horde hadn't reached here. Not yet. They could hear them though, behind them. They were far too close.

'Run, Lin! Just run!' Seth shouted.

He tried to keep the aggrolshae's attention focused on him, feigning slashing attacks whenever he thought its attention wavered. Lin wouldn't stand a chance against it. He had to keep it away from her.

Ducking under another swing, he tried to concentrate on breathing. The sweat kept obscuring his vision and the dirt that the axe and creature kicked up flung themselves into his eyes.

'I can't just leave you here,' Lin cried out as the huge beast lunged for her. She stumbled over something on the ground trying to get away.

'Don't argue. Just GO!'

Seth tried to force some oxygen into his lungs. It felt like they were going to cave in on him at any moment, like they were burning.

For him, fighting was tooth against claw. Scales clashing. He wasn't used to this. He hadn't trained for it.

'I can't,' Lin wailed. 'You can't ask me to. You can't defeat it alone!'

'I can't do it *with* you here. Trust me, okay! Just go, before the rest of its friends arrive,' Seth called back, whacking the aggrolshae on the shins as it turned, making a swipe at Lin.

Lin bit back her reply, scrambling backwards, out of reach of the creature. Tears stinging her eyes, she ran, ran towards the safety of the Towers. It seemed so far away now. Just a moment ago, they'd felt like they'd made it, like they'd really found their way to shelter. Now, it didn't matter how fast she was running, what uneven ground she was tripping over, it seemed to take forever to reach them.

The ground between the forest and this side of the Towers was mostly grass. A wide, open field. They'd see her. Right? They'd open the doors. What if they didn't let her in? What if the monsters would charge right at the door, with her in the middle? Were they behind her?

Her mind rolled over and over. Every image of terror it could dream up, it threw at her. Something *was* behind her. She had to run faster. She should go back. Help her friend, somehow.

She *wouldn't* be in the way. She *wouldn't* be useless. Not at a time like this.

The blood was ringing in her ears. It was so loud. Thoughts so powerful they were drowning out all other noises. All other fears. Lin skidded to a halt and whirled around.

She screamed.

There really *had* been something behind her. The huge aggrolshae had lost interest in Seth. Instead, it was bounding towards her, its steps shaking the ground beneath it.

Lin tensed up. She tried to tell her legs to start running again. But they weren't listening. Why weren't they listening? No. No. No. This wasn't happening. MOVE!

She scrabbled around for a weapon, anything at all. One hand found something. It grabbed hold of it, tried pulling it out of the ground.

The aggrolshae got there first.

As it swung at her, she lost her balance. Stumbling backwards, Linandra felt the air bite into her as the axe passed within inches.

Releasing a bellow of frustration, the aggrolshae continued its swing, came around with its other hand, and snatched her off the ground before Lin had time to realize what was happening.

It was going to squash her. Lin could feel the adrenaline rushing through her body. The terror that came with it. Desperate, Linandra instinctively struck down with everything she had. The stick she wielded broke. It was no match for the hide and armour of the large creature.

Following through the motion, her hands continued downwards until they too smacked into the fist that held her.

The bones in her hands cracked against the bony armour. It hurt. It hurts, she thought. But it was the aggrolshae that screamed in pain and dropped her as something barrelled into it from behind.

Lin dropped to the ground with a thud. Her heart racing, she scrambled backwards, rolled over and, this time, ran for it.

The raging bellow as the aggrolshae leapt after her cut off into another yelp of pain when, with a jerk, its forward motion came to an abrupt halt. Jaws were clamped shut around the end of its tail. Skin and bone gave way beneath powerful fangs capable of slicing into ethereally enhanced scales.

Digging his claws into the ground, the dragon braced himself and heaved.

In a contest of sheer muscle power, the aggrolshae wouldn't have stood a chance. But this wasn't a tug of war and, reacting more out of instinct than anything else, it gave off a high-pitched wail and whipped around. Smaller, blunter fangs tried to bite into the silvery neck.

Aggrolshae claws rasped against the young dragon's scales. Lost in the moment, the Agrolshae had completely forgotten about the heavy axe it was dragging.

But even if neither penetrated his natural armour, the dragon shook himself, trying to get rid of the annoying pest. Giving off a thundering roar, Setharrion smashed his neck against the ground, trying to squash his opponent. The aggrolshae clambered out of the way.

The two of them became locked in an intricate and increasingly muddy dance, snapping and snarling at each other.

If Setharrion had been fully grown, it would have been another matter. But he wasn't. He *was* considerably larger than his opponent, but the aggrolshae had experience on its side. The young dragon wasn't used to doing battle with something that was capable of fighting back (bandits didn't count). His silver scales had made everyone back home go easy on him when it came to physical tussles and he was having trouble concentrating enough to call upon more ethereal powers.

Besides, now the aggrolshae had remembered its weapon. And it began taking great, big swings with it against the dragon's body. And while the blade of an axe, even one as large as this, didn't have a bite against dragonscales, the power behind each strike was harder to ignore.

Setharrion snarled. He'd have bitten the thing in half barely noticing it was there (aside from the foul taste and having needed to pick bits of armour out of his teeth for weeks afterwards) if only he'd been older.

That part of him, some curious, subconscious part that normally didn't interfere, kept insisting that if this was several centuries hence, he'd be having no trouble at all.

'Not helpful,' Setharrion grunted as the axe came to bear yet again.

He needed to get some distance between them, but the aggrolshae clung onto a shoulder and refused to let go, pounding at him like a smith with his anvil.

Cursed magic, Setharrion swore. He needed to concentrate to focus on the energy for an attack and he kept getting interrupted. Focus. Focus. There had to be something he could do other than having his snout getting beaten up.

A heartbeat later and his long tail lashed out, its end striking the beast like a whip. The aggrolshae howled and intensified its attacks. A second strike and the tip wrapped around the creature from behind. Setharrion braced himself and pulled hard.

The aggrolshae whisked through the air and crashed against some innocent beech trees, knocking over several of them in the process.

Pulling splinters the size of a man's arm out of its body as it stumbled to its feet, the aggrolshae trembled in rage. Dazed, it needed several moments to gather itself together again. With a grunt, its first effort made it walk right into a larger tree. Large enough for the aggrolshae to bounce off. It shook its helmeted head, skull ringing from ear to ear.

Those stunned moments gave the young dragon the time he needed. He began to concentrate. Energy began pooling; gathered from all around them— the trees, the air, the grass—until it grew in brightness enough to rival the four moons.

It swirled into being, an almost invisible force gathering mass as it compressed together, and, as it did, it changed rapidly alternating from a colourless state into bright blue before becoming absorbed by yellows, oranges and reds until it burned your eyes just by looking at it.

The indistinct mist danced, flames growing, their tongues licking and, tasting the air for the first time, burning hotter and brighter for every second.

Setharrion reared, gaining a further advantage in elevation. He drew back his head, then, throwing his whole body forward, he let fly a blast of fire.

The grass below blackened and dissolved into ash as the stream passed above without even touching it. It ploughed into the edge of the forest, burning straight through trees and enemies alike as if they weren't even there.

The aggrolshae disappeared in a tower of flame.

Meanwhile, having managed to reach a gate and pound on it until someone decided to take a chance and let her in, Lin had gathered the last of her energy to rush up the stairs to the second floor.

It was lined and dotted with faces. They passed by as if in a blur.

Once there, she found a window and, pressing her nose against the glass, stared out into what was beyond. It was almost impossible to see anything clearly.

Eyes wide and her heart thumping against the ribs of her chest, Linandra wiped some dirt off her face. It didn't feel real. None of it. It couldn't be real. It was just a bad dream. That's all it was. Any moment now she'd wake up, covered in sweat with sheets twisted around her ankles.

Trying to see better, she squinted. The glass kept getting in the way. There were lights and reflections of reflections.

'What is going on here?' Lin cried out to the world. 'What the hell is going on?'

Outside, by the edge of the forest, Setharrion surveyed the treeline.

The moons were giving plenty of light now, between the heavy clouds. And if they didn't, flames hopping from branch to branch as the touch of the wind brought them from one swaying tree to another along the several-hundred-foot gaping wound in the forest, did the rest.

Not even a monster could have survived that. Could they?

Was that rustling? He hoped it was just the wind. Setharrion tensed his shoulders, jaws parting slightly as, eyes narrowing, he tried to see beyond the trees. Unfortunately, one thing even a dragon couldn't do was see *through* things.

There were noises though, the clamour of armour; the echoes of weapons; and branches snapping and being trampled underfoot. The young dragon's ears flattened against his skull.

Suddenly, several loud bangs echoed out. Flashes of light, blue, grey and green erupted from somewhere in the forest. It wasn't that far away. The dragon's ears wriggled. It was getting closer too.

Before he had time to react, something burst through the border. Once free of the trees and bushes it stumbled a little as there was suddenly no vegetation to fight through. The man gave a small start, almost a squeak, as he saw the dragon, veered to the side and kept on running. A second later he was followed by several others.

Their robes torn and dirtied by the fighting—having pushed themselves to near exhaustion—one of the small groups from the Towers raced past a dragon too stunned to do anything other than just stare.

Giving a violent shake of his slender head, the silver dragon returned to watching the trees. His ears swivelled around, listening for sounds both from the woods, the sky and even the buildings far behind him.

It sounded too loud, coming from too many directions, to be more mages, he thought. Humanoid spellcasters tended to be a little lacking in the tree-trampling department. Unless he'd missed a lesson somewhere.

Setharrion backed away a bit, every muscle quivering with tense energy. His wings slowly unfurled. And a good thing that was too, for a moment later several hundred metres of treeline erupted and started spewing forth golshaes and their cohorts. Setharrion did the only sensible thing he could think of: he took to the air.

Clawing through the damp night until he was certain there was plenty of distance from any golshae mischievousness, the young dragon levelled out several hundred feet above the churning field.

Circling high above, he thought he could see even more of them moving through the forest. They were way too many for him to battle alone, even if he hadn't already been exhausted from today's events. Fatigue travelled in-discriminately between forms, as unforgiving as hunger. And there was this curious tingling sensation he couldn't quite place emanating from pockets within their ranks. It reminded him of old ruins for some reason.

He hoped that the Towers had had enough advance warning to set some-thing up to greet their unwelcome guests.

Setharrion circled away from the golshaes and descended towards the largest structure around, landing as lightly as he could on a piece of the Twin Towers' main building. For a moment, it felt like it was trying to fight him off. When it released, he dropped another foot or so. Swaying, dangerously unbalanced, he almost broke through the roof.

Righting himself, the young dragon dug a firm grip in the stonework. Then, wings flaring, he roared his defiance at the enemy.

They didn't seem like the type to be easily intimidated, but it made him feel better.

By now, the outer walls of the Towers—the few it had—were lined with wiz-ards and sorcerers, magicians and mages, and who knew what else the

Archmagus had found in the deepest recesses of the place. Any sages in residence were down with the channelers and most of the enchanters were using their abilities to keep the main defence up. A few other, more random, disciplines had only the odd person here and there and no one understood exactly what to ask of them.

Those familiars who were small enough to fit easily among the people, hovered close by their masters and mistresses, anxious beaks and talons, fangs and pincers, adding to the unease of the moment.

One of the few offensive disciplines that *weren't* represented seemed to be necromancers or keches and the reason for that was simple enough: there weren't any at the Towers. Kaheiron was known to be less than welcoming when it came to *those* arcane users. And for good reason.

Now, heads were peering out from behind nearly every window. The glass might not be terribly safe to hide behind, especially as the windows were opened, but they had confidence in the protective spells. Most of them had confidence in them anyway. There were more than one that was hiding behind the walls next to the windows instead.

None of them were keen on the sight that greeted them out there, in the darkness. Those that had made it back from the teams sent out into the woods didn't need to see them. They'd seen enough for several lifetimes. Exhausted and bruised, they were going to need to rest before daring to do any more magic.

The golshaes had proven too many for the small numbers of mages to deal any serious damage to them and most of their troops had arrived safely at the Towers.

They didn't stop there. As golshaes of every shape and kind poured out of the forest, whole sets of them immediately set about trying to destroy the outbuildings that weren't protected; hacking and pushing; tumbling rockworks, and spoiling whatever they could find.

Others fanned out, trampling over, *through* the gardens and the orchard. Mere wood didn't stand a chance.

What looked like the main body surged straight towards the Towers.

So far, they'd been unopposed. But by the time they came within striking distance from the Twin Towers, that changed.

The first wave of golshaes ran straight into a barrage: spheres of fire and ice arched high above the walls fell down on the golshaes and their allies alike, then exploded. Smaller balls of blue energy floated towards the ground , stopping short a few decimetres above the grass and then started spinning, shooting out random tendrils of power, electrocuting anyone it touched. Lava bombs punched into the ground, becoming impenetrable mounds of burning goo. And that was just the *aerial* assault.

Soon it was almost impossible to make out what was happening.

'Alright. Hold it. Hold it!' someone in charge called out.

As the first bombardment came to a halt, the mages strained to make out the result.

'Did we get them?' a small, wizened wizard with a wispy beard asked.

While the dust and smoke began to settle, the remaining golshaes marched right on. While the attack had had an effect, there were just too many. And of those protected by the shields, not a single one had taken a hit.

'They should have been decimated by that!' a sorcerer cried out. 'How many of these things are there?'

'*What* are they?'

'Why isn't it working?'

'I don't know. Try and concentrate your energies. We're not using enough power to break through them.'

The residents at the Towers attacked again, forming small and vast spells, sending them arching against their enemy like arrows of destruction. They didn't bother with aiming them. The golshaes, having already proven difficult targets, made the defenders concentrate on wide, indiscriminate attacks that would either explode, implode, or disperse into a wriggling, unpredictable selection of smaller spells on impact.

In return, a number of the golshaes gathered together and began sending smaller, concentrated balls of fuzzy energy wrapped around heavy stone boulders, smashing them against the walls of the Towers. The wizards couldn't make out *how*, but they were the same ones that were surrounded by the fields none of the Towers' magic seemed able to penetrate.

Some of those attacks arched above the roofs, then dropped like the rock they were, landing, sizzling and convulsing, with a sickly colour before exploding.

Considering the potency of the attacks, they did a minimal amount of damage, except to the strength of those that maintained the defences, who reeled under the onslaught. The defensive spells *were* holding, barely. They weren't strong enough to repel the attacks completely, and completely failed at sending those same attacks back at their casters, but they did stop the arrows and other more physical unpleasantries that were coming over to say hello.

'We can't keep this up for much longer,' one of the enchanters called out to Istarrian. 'The channelers are draining by the minute. It's these terrible bombs. Every time they hit us, they seem to somehow leech out a bit of the power in the defensive spells, more than is accounted for by the force of the explosions.'

'Yes, yes, I know!' Istarrian called back. 'I'm trying to find a way to stop them.'

'And those shieldstones. We can't seem to break through them. Whatever they are, they're not the same as ours. No ordinary stone should be able to last long against the kinds of attacks we've been bombarding them with.'

'Not a single one, certainly.'

'They must draw their power from elsewhere,' another wizard shouted over the noise of the battle. 'Find the source of that power and destroy it and those stones should be no more powerful than an ordinary spell.'

'Aye, but if we cannot … if the Archmagus does not return soon, the situation will become dire indeed.'

They all looked around for a potential source, flinching at every explosion, but all there was, was a milling mass, obscured in smoke and fire. By now, the golshaes were but a stone's throw away from the walls of the Twin Towers. Any closer and they'd be hacking away at the defences with their fists.

It was something else that caught the defenders attention, though.

'Look,' one of the mages further down the hall cried out. He raised an old and weary finger to point towards the forest.

An hour ago, the trees would have cast too many shadows for anyone to have been able to see it, but now, part of the world in flame, between the smoke and ashes, that flickering light illuminated the figure that stepped out of the forest.

The creature raised its head, sending up a braying bellow that could have been, once upon a time, laughter. Now it tore through vocal cords better suited to a carrion crawler, sending chills down the spines of all those that heard it, friend and foe alike.

Not that it had a concept of friendship, not anymore.

The golshaes closest to it drained from the vicinity, allowing it to pass unchallenged. If anything, its presence induced them to even further frenzy, as if by its mere appearance, their own powers increased.

'By all that's holy, what IS that?'

'Don't know.'

'Don't want to know.'

'Just concentrate on stopping it before it comes any closer,' Istarrian called out.

The new arrival flexed fingers with more joints than should have normally been found on a human, shivers of light passing through the shards of crystals that were jutting out of the thick, putrid skin. They pulsated, fading somewhat when passing under the tattered remains of cloth that clung to the once lanky body.

Now, standing even taller than the biggest aggrolshae on the fields, what had once been a man, gingerly touched the shieldstone it was holding in its left hand, almost caressing it.

The same crystalline structures that punctuated the creature had ravaged the stone as well. It flickered as the pulses flowed from the body and into the stone. There should have been a faint blue glow. Instead, it was a sickly pink with dirty orange swirls and patches of nothing. It looked almost alive.

Whatever it was, it turned the stomachs of those at the Towers that were watching. It repulsed them just by being there. Their knees kept insisting on wanting to sink downwards. Several of the defenders doubled over, some slumping against whatever was handy to lean on.

'What is that thing?' someone tried to breathe while throwing up.

'You wanted a source, Istarrian. I think you found it,' another said, turning his eyes away.

'By Hell's Mouth!' the vomiting sorcerer swore. 'Where's the

Archmagus. He should *be* here!'

'Has he abandoned us?'

'He would not,' another mage called back, ducking behind the wall after having set several balls of writhing flame down into the grounds.

'He didn't,' Istarrian wheezed. He was too old for this. The spirit was willing, but his body was increasingly letting him down.

'You sound so certain.'

'I AM certain,' Istarrian insisted.

'Then, where is he?' the other mage wanted to know. His legs were shaking, he was draining energy so fast just trying to stand up.

Whatever answer Istarrian was about to give was cut short by an enormous blast that felt like it rocked the very ground the Towers were built upon. It knocked over the majority of those closest to it, sending the defensive spells oscillating, wavering.

What force of the explosion that didn't travel inwards instead escaped in the opposite direction. A gaping half a crater appeared as it scooped out a large chunk of the lawn and turned it into a mixture of nothing, taking a large number of golshaes with it.

The one responsible, the newly arrived nightmare, bellowed out a thundering roar causing the world to shiver.

Setharrion barely managed to dive off the roof and take shelter behind the structures before it struck again. He landed in a tumbled heap, ears still ringing from the shock.

'Did you feel that? It sent the whole weave of enchantments in the defences quavering.'

'We can't take many more of those,' someone else cried out, as if the others didn't know that already.

Back outside, holding up its shieldstone above its head—from what little that was left of the consciousness of Joran—there came a shrieking laughter. It didn't sound like laughter, but it was eerie and crackled. He, or at this point, it, began to gather up energy for another attack.

As the crystals began their dance of light once again there came another thunderous roar echoing through the darkness. This one moved through the night, at speed, growing in intensity. It came from above.

A moment later and it passed over their heads, high above. In its wake, the sheer winds blasted them as they erupted; sizzling white and blue, energy bombs came falling from the sky. They ploughed into the golshae army, levelling anything and everything in their way.

Soon after, small stones began raining down like a gentle drizzle of hail. The golshaes first shied away from them, trying to protect themselves.

But after a few of the knuckle-sized, black stones bounced off a helmet or two, others against shoulderpads and armour, the invaders began to ignore them.

One shiny marble lodged itself between a few spikes that the owner of the leather armour had hammered into his shoulders. Most of them just bounced a few times then rolled over. When they still didn't seem to be doing anything, a few of the golshaes gave them some experimental kicks. Aside from the odd one that got kicked onto another golshae resulting in a few scuffles that were lost in the general theme of the moment, nothing happened.

The stones just lay there.

Slowly, scorched pieces of sack cloth began to follow when the rain of stones had halted. Very little of it reached the ground, most becoming the victim of attacks from both sides, mostly unintentionally.

For a time, no one, on any side, could see the other. Only the scattered lights from the remaining flickering barriers protecting those golshaes that had been close enough to a shieldcarrier even suggested anything was out there. That and the noise coming from the dying and the alive alike.

A gust nibbled at the smoky tendrils extending themselves into the air. The wind had returned. Only, this time, it came in roughly even bursts, the smoke blown away as if by the flapping of great wings.

Clearing the air little by little, the black dragon hovered over the Towers like a huge, scaly, and very angry angel.

What was left of Joran raged at the new enemy while, around him, encouraged by the appearance of their leader and able once more see, the golshaes, in turn, refocused their efforts.

Where once the red blood of man had coursed through his veins, the discharges from the crystals flecked everything, coating the arteries, organs, everything within with a layer of energy. It crackled as it fed him, supported him, enraged him. Joining the golshaes in their attack, the creature strode forwards, the attacks from the Tower, it barely even noticed.

But while their leader's appearance had encouraged the golshaes towards even more destruction, the unexpected aid of the black dragon did wonders for the spirit of the mages. Filled with a renewed sense of purpose, they rallied together.

'Their numbers do appear reduced,' one of the younger mages still on his feet informed the others. 'A little.'

'Only the hard ones to hit left then,' another quipped. 'Brilliant.'

'Less sarcasm, more energy,' Istarrian snapped, his own energy levels draining rapidly. 'No more random volleys. Make every strike count.'

'I'm too tired to aim anywhere specific,' the other mage complained. Still, he pulled himself together along with the others.

No matter what Istarrian had said, most of those present were barely standing and many of them were leaning on something for support. And so, they grasped what threads of energy they could, trying to wrighte and form them to their will.

Staffs glowed, rings shone and every familiar that could, lent its power to the next assault.

There were waves of flame. Balls of fire. Crackling sparks of lightning shot forwards and shards of ice, sharpened until they'd slice through a full-grown man in a heartbeat, sped forth. The last set of spells unleashed them all and more.

Their aim might have been erratic at this point, but the sheer amount of force in the air made it almost impossible for the golshaes to duck for cover. Some of the attacks even burrowed *through* the soil until they found something akin to flesh to bite into.

But if everyone picked the few things they had strength left to summon up, they weren't all successful.

'Stop that, you fool' someone shouted at a wizard firing off wavespells. 'You're putting out the fires.'

The golshaes kept coming, but finally their numbers began to dwindle enough to matter.

'Did you see that?' one of the defenders called out. 'That one, it almost got through that shield! Try and aim for them one at a time. They're losing power, I'm sure of it.'

Unnoticed, in the middle of the carnage, one of the small stones dropped earlier experimentally stuck out a tiny ethereal leg, then another, until it raised itself on four, spindly legs that didn't look like they'd support their weight. In another moment, they had coalesced to the same colour and consistency as the stone, only mobile and fluid. The "stone" made a tiny hop forward, then one into the air, as if happy to be free of whatever restraints had been holding it.

Feeling no resistance anywhere, the stone made another jump, a little higher this time. It was knocked sideways by the shockwave from an incoming hit. Landing heavily, the stone immediately bounced back up.

If you'd seen it, you might have imagined it waving a tiny fist in the air and shouting at whoever had hit it. They didn't, of course, but for something with no face it still managed to look agitated.

Too small for any of the golshaes to pay attention to, yet, several of the stone's companions began coming to life. Soon, a whole host of the marble-sized units were leaping and bounding and scuttling between the legs of the golshaes.

Some enterprising ones began climbing up on the creature that was making the most noise. Joran was busy trying to single-handedly demolish the Towers by any means he could—including slinging huge boulders at it as if they were paperballs. He was too lost in rage to notice, but by now the golshaes were beginning to take note.

Here and there some stones tried to climb into the nostrils of whatever was closest to them, golshae or beast of burden. Others tried burrowing under their armour. When caught, the stones were ruthlessly brushed off and stomped on. Sinking into the grass—what was left of it—they simply pushed themselves back up again.

A few, unlucky ones, were crushed between armoured fists, but most seemed impervious to harm. Dashing and darting, they skittered around, moving in and out of the barriers the shieldstones were producing. Their inertia was simply too small for their shieldstone cousins to register as something needing to be repelled, just as they didn't care about a fluttering ladybug.

As more and more came together, and as their stony bodies began an oscillation of colours, something was happening to the now flickering barriers. The shieldstones were beginning to struggle with maintaining a stable field and the barriers were growing erratic and weaker with every passing moment.

The one shield that didn't waver after a few minutes of this, was the one surrounding Joran. It only showed itself when something tried to bust through it, but beneath it, what was left of Joran howled at the new enemy. The old enemy.

Did he sense the Archmagus' presence when the great black dragon swooped overhead? Maybe. Few at the Towers had previously known of Kaheiron's little secret, and Joran had not been among them. But the metamorphosis he'd undergone had changed more than just his body, tunnelling deep into his subconscious. Either way, he changed focus from the Towers to the dragon.

It didn't hurt that the dragon was taking a personal interest in *him*. Kaheiron would have called on much greater powers and destruction would have reigned supreme, flattening the geography for miles around, had he been alone; but with the Towers and its people, and a deep fondness for the land around him, the black dragon was reluctant to do so.

Being far too big and heavy to land, even precariously, on any of the roofs below, like Setharrion had, Kaheiron instead swooped back and forth, his eyes a swirling mist of red and orange, occasionally returning to hover over the buildings like a brooding mother unwilling to leave her nest.

Looking down, Kaheiron could see that the younger dragon was beginning to recover. Good. This wasn't over yet.

But while the lesser shieldstones were being disrupted by the devices that the black dragon had dropped, and the golshaes behind them now vulnerable, there remained one that seemed unaffected: the one carried by Joran. The one that was charged—no, linked—directly to the power being created by the living crystals inside him.

The others, though, were not, and when a set of random fireballs finally broke through, there had been enough power concentrated in it to punch through a small hill. The golshaes within it were completely incinerated in the resulting explosion.

Then another went down.

And another.

The remaining attackers, wizening up to that their promised protection was no longer operational, began deserting the battlefield in droves. And when they went, their underlings followed. Soon, the only ones remaining were Joran and several of the larger, and apparently more stubborn, golshaes and aggrolshaes.

Gathering together, they charged the black dragon who had landed and was now approaching at a run. Whatever else, when a dragon of Kaheiron's size began loping, they covered a lot of ground, and fast.

For all but Joran, their attack only meant the end came so much faster, as the dragon mowed through the remaining ranks as if they weren't even there.

Kaheiron was ready for them. Smoke and dust from the battle swirling around the ground obscuring his feet and much of his legs. In the haze, his body turned into a mere dustshadow from afar.

Raw ethereal power crackled over his scales like electric discharges except these burned even more intensely. Unlike the sorcerers, magicians and others back at the Towers, the dragon wielded the magic formed from it like it was second nature, quickly dispatching what remained of his opponents until he came eye to eye with what had once been the mage, Joran.

He whipped around in time to avoid a direct hit from his still-shielded opponent. The creature let rip a furious bellow as he charged again, swinging whatever weapon he could pick up from the battlefield.

Kaheiron was a whole lot bigger than Joran had become, even now the dragon towered above the creature. But, right now, that just meant that he was a whole lot easier to hit. Every time he thought he'd managed to corner the crystal entity, it slipped away, sliding and skidding on the churned-up ground.

Where? Where did it go? There! A huge paw connected with the shield that protected Joran, flinging him into the ground. For a moment, it flickered uncertainly.

Trying to shift his attacks into something that didn't involve pinpoint precision, the dragon tried to concentrate in the midst of the chaos. He had a great deal more success with that then Setharrion had had.

'Bug! If it hadn't been for that infernal shield, I'd squash you like the ant you are,' Kaheiron snarled as something pounded on his hind foot. It came out as a great roar. His head snaked out, trying to catch the culprit before it escaped.

The crackling around his scales intensified. When Joran attacked, the two opposing ethereal forces began grinding and grating against each other.

That shield, it must have an *enormous* source of power backing it up, Kaheiron thought as he swung his body around so that Joran's run smacked right into a powerful haunch. There went his hopes for finishing this quickly.

While having returned to his true form meant he had energy reserves and stamina far beyond what any mere humanoid spellcaster could muster, eventually he, too, would tire.

The people inhabiting the Towers would, by now, be too exhausted to do much to help, Kaheiron knew that. All they could do was watch (or hide) as the battle between the two colossi raged across the burnt fields.

Trees were trampled and outbuildings crushed as the battle raged on. Sometimes, it was impossible to tell what was going on, everything lost in light and shadow, darkness and smoke.

'Can't you *DO* something about all this,' Lin gestured empathically at the partially obscured battlefield. 'Flail about a bit and make some wind or *something*! We can't see what's happening out there!'

'If you haven't noticed, young lady,' a slender mage, whose no-nonsense expression would have been more intimidating if she hadn't also looked so exhausted, said. 'Everyone is trying to gather their breath, in case *something else* comes along.'

'Also,' an older wizard said, leaning heavily against the stonework. 'We cannot possibly know if he would want us to interfere. You must have noticed, there are *dragons* out there.'

'Yes, I know that. Goodness knows how well I know that. I want to *see* it,' Lin growled.

'Mighty easy to offend a dragon. Don't want to do that now, do we?'

'Aaah! You people are hopeless,' Lin despaired. She would have thrown something at them if she'd been holding on to anything. Instead, she just tried to pierce the rolling, partially alight smoke with her eyes, leaning out of the window.

As the manbeast, eyes only for the black dragon before him, sent flying another implement of destruction, imbibed with the syrupy power of the crystals, he was knocked aside by a lash of a silvery tail.

The shield might stop the impact itself from harming him, but, like before, it didn't stop the sheer force behind it. Joran's monstrous becoming rolled into another hole: a crater from an earlier plasmic detonation.

Clamouring out of it on the far end, he found himself face to face with the new arrival. Setharrion curled his lip and hissed.

There was just enough left of the human consciousness in there to wonder where the new dragon had come from. But it was a small thought soon pushed aside by the red mist of rage that fuelled him.

The two dragons slowly circled the crater. They were like night and day, ever in motion, never quite together but still never apart. Across their bodies rippled that ethereal energy that other beings so often referred to as magic. It infused them. It danced across their scales. Horns stood like lightning rods, between which the energy discharged and grounded, growing ever stronger.

Between them, they easily encircled the hole in the ground with their bodies.

From the Towers, Lin and the various spellcasters continued to strain their eyes. Caught between the din of explosions and crackling energy, people whispered and murmured, trying to point out what they could see now that the number of combatants had dropped to single digits.

All of that magic did have one beneficial result for the onlookers outside of traumatizing their ears: it was like watching fireworks, as if some fool had forgotten to point them skyward. The general happenings were easy enough to pick out, but they all strained to see beyond that. Lin could just about make out where each dragon circled and where the hideous beast, pinned between them, tried to escape their grasp.

Still, she grumbled inwardly, you couldn't see anything properly, even with the dawn creeping up on the coming day. If anything, the daylight just meant that the crackles of magic became less obvious. The sounds, on top of the cacophony of magic, didn't help much either, as each deep snarl and booming roar from the dragons kept making their audience flinch: To say nothing about the strange, inhuman sounds coming from the creature they were battling.

Now, every time the man-beast made an attempt to escape from the crater, one of the dragons sent it back in. Always, there was one whose eyes never left it. Shifting from one to the other as silken rain, they danced and stomped. The three of them snarled and lunged and snapped at each other.

Slowly, very slowly, the crystals growing out of the creature's body were beginning to show signs of cracks. And with that, the shield was weakening.

The two dragons renewed their efforts. Until now, they'd been forced to take the attacks from Joran directly without being able to retaliate in kind, and it showed. Not even a dragon was invulnerable. They'd have some scrapes and bruises in the morning. To say nothing about a blinding headache.

Now, finally, their own attacks were beginning to have an effect. If it didn't lift their spirits, it certainly made them see the light at the end of the tunnel … and it was *on fire*.

Still not able to strike the creature physically, their frustration grew. Jaws clicked their teeth and talons quivered. If they'd been able to, Joran would have been rendered into pulp long ago. But the combined efforts *were* breaking through its defences, albeit indirectly, and the crystalline structures didn't like the stress they were being put under.

One by one the cracks grew. Then, suddenly, a smaller crystal shattered. Its structure tore into the flesh from which it was growing. For the first time in this battle, the creature shed its own blood. The black, glowing liquid dripped leisurely and singed the earth wherever it touched. The angry shriek that followed pierced through the battlefield, carrying across to the Towers and making the mages cover their ears.

The smoke and dust that had obscured the battlefield was beginning to clear. And those still with enough energy left, watched as, annoyed, Setharrion made another lunge for the shield.

He'd swear that its circumference had shrunk. He could almost get his jaws around it now. Ignoring the blistering pain as it burned, he tried driving his teeth into the thing, clawing and biting. He didn't dare do it for more than a few seconds, before Joran caught on and sent an attack his way. His mouth and insides were a lot more vulnerable than his skin.

Joran, reacting instinctively, did just that. The silver dragon yanked his snout out of the way with little time to spare.

Their attacks were growing more efficient. For every time they struck him down, more cracks appeared. For every time he used his own power, they trembled. Every time one shattered, it took another part of the creature with them. Soon, gaping wounds were covering its body and the life fluid, like viscous, luminescent, tar seeped out of them.

As each crystal broke apart, the shieldstone lost a little more of its fierce glow until it was nothing more than a dull, pale grey-purple.

Seeing that, Kaheiron rammed the shield hard. He kept on pushing, pinning Joran down with mighty, scaly paws.

The drain became too much. What little remained of the creature's protection flickered and died. The dragon's armoured forehead smashed into Joran's new body, driving it into the ground, breaking its bones through sheer muscle power.

The man-beast bellowed in rage and pain. Again and again the black dragon struck.

The shieldstone was useless now. The crystals fuelling the magic were shattering further at every impact. All that remained was a match of brawn against brawn. And while the beast that Joran had become might have squashed a human like an unwanted rat at dinner, it couldn't contend with the sheer strength of the black dragon.

With one last blow, its ribcage caved in. Heart and lungs were crushed in the impact as the protecting bone structures broke, pierced them, and then pressed down until the organs were little more than pulp.

The black dragon rose up, wings beating until his body nearly lifted from the ground. Letting loose a roar that thundered over the Twin Towers, each flap cleared the area of more of the racking smoke fouling the air until the only fire that remained was nothing but smouldering piles of ruin and carcasses.

In the carcass below him, no life remained.

Back at the Towers, the channelers fell to the ground, relief flooding them as much as the battle had drained them. All around the perimeters, those that could see what was happening were wondering what would come next. The dragons had saved them from the attackers, yes; but what if they turned around and attacked *them*? They'd never be able to fight them off, not now.

On the second floor, Istarrian pulled himself up from where he'd fallen. His body was shaking from the ordeal. His voice much the same, he still managed to steady it enough to relay the message for those that still did not know. The dragons were not to be feared. They were friends.

He'd always stood by the Archmagus' desire to keep his other form a secret; but this was one time he surely wished the man had shared it with more people.

Slowly, the main doors of the building creaked open. From behind it, those who still had enough energy to stay on their feet, and were feeling adventurous despite, everything that had happened, began to drift out.

The scenery that met them was very different from what they were used to.

Large, gaping holes had appeared in the lawn, some of which were still solidifying, the earth lining them melted into a viscous goo. Most of the ground had been scorched, turning the once green lawns and fields into grey dust with charcoal pieces along the border. The nearest trees had suffered most and now barely stood out onto the light of morning, their proud beauty ripped and torn asunder.

Half-melted icicles, some the size of a horse, were adding to the pools of water—now ashy mud—that were collecting in the depressions in the ground.

Spheres of rock so compressed, so solid, that even the medium-sized ones were beginning their gravitational journey, drawn towards the centre of the world, lay scattered across the field. Only the very smallest would remain to be collected later.

A few stray spells were still sizzling where they lay. Weapons, melted and twisted shapes of metal and bone, or just remaining puddles, littered the field.

Everywhere you looked there were the remains of golshaes of every type. Many were missing limbs. Some bodies were missing heads. Some heads were missing bodies.

They weren't just on the ground either; bits were draped over the trees, what few bushes remained and each other. More than just a few were burnt beyond recognition. Circular holes appeared on others, which, if you had raised them up, would have shown daylight on the other side, whatever caused them having passed straight through flesh and armour alike.

Twisted hunks of metal that had once been makeshift and grotesquely decorated shields, sharp and dull alike, were strewn around. One had lodged itself in a centenarian oak, driven several feet into the wood by the force of a blast that had parted it from its late master.

'Are we sure that they're all gone,' a wizard asked wearily, a tight grip on his staff, in case there were any lurking around the nearest corner after all.

'It would seem so.'

'Nasty creatures, golshaes,' the wizard said. 'Nasty. Dirty. Smelly. Especially smelly. Did I mention they're nasty?'

'Can't smell *anything* right now,' another mage told the complainer. 'Had to improvise a warding spell when that cloud came. Didn't come out quite as expected.'

A few enterprising sorcerers were beginning to poke around the nearest debris. From what drifted over of their conversations, it was hard to imagine that they'd all been under the threat of death only a few minutes ago. There were few things as powerful as unanswered questions and some people just couldn't resist the urge to ask them. Danger was, after all, a very relative term.

'Careful where you step, old boy. It's slippery just there.'

'Will predators be attracted, do you think?' a worried-looking enchanter asked. 'I would prefer not to have to fend off hungry packs of whatnots while collecting samples.'

'Only if their diet includes charcoal,' a burly-looking stablehand snorted by way of reply, his hands still gripping an extended pike with pale hands.

'Shooti! Get back here this instance!' Ronald called out as his familiar decided that the field was ripe for picking and she wasn't going to leave the first morsel to anyone else.

'Personally, I cannot believe that golshae tastes any better prior to having been carbonised,' a third mage said, surprisingly old to still be on his feet after the exhausting battle.

Istarrian would be inclined to agree. Leaning heavily on two others, he gradually made his way across to the two dragons. Not everyone was as keen to get close to the two and were giving them a fair bit of space. That was a good thing. A dragon needed a certain amount of turning radius after all.

Actually, his two supporters weren't particularly keen on the idea themselves, but the old boy was quite adamant.

He wasn't the only one approaching, though. Behind the three men came Linandra. Istarrian was merely slow, Lin's progress was jerky, even hesitant. Whatever safety the three humans offered was surely only psychological as the dragons both towered above them.

Not that she was *afraid* of Kaheiron. That just wasn't possible, even if he *was* big, scaly and whose smallest teeth were the size of her arm. That wasn't what was bothering her.

Looking up at the two of them, they might not have been each other's complete opposite, but you could have been forgiven for believing they were. Kaheiron, even in his dragon form, was a deep pitch black, with noble but craggy features, a relatively short neck and a multitude of stubby horns decorating his sloping skull.

Next to him, the silver dragon looked positively gangly, with the slightly awkward proportions of someone who still had a lot of growing to do. He seemed lithe with gentle, small features and, at the end of a long neck, an impressive curved array decorating his crest.

They both turned to face the company approaching.

'We appear to have survived the night, my lord,' Istarrian's somewhat shaky voice announced.

'I had not failed to notice this,' the dragon's deep voice came as ever without him moving his lips. 'How did we fare?'

'A few casualties, my lord. The defences succeeded in minimising most major injuries for the greater duration of the battle. Of course, we did take some heavy damage towards the end. Do you believe it is likely that they shall return?'

'Unlikely, now that they no longer possess a power source for their shields. We cannot afford to be careless, however, so we will prepare for such an event even so,' Kaheiron replied.

'As you wish,' Istarrian inclined his head.

'You did well, Istarrian.'

'Thank you, my lord.'

'Now. Go get some rest, my friend. You look tired.'

And with that, the black dragon backed up a bit. He reared up and, within a mixture of light and shadow, returned to the human form they were more accustomed to.

This meant he didn't take up nearly as much space. It also meant that he was not wearing any clothes. As a dragon that was hardly an issue, but...

Kaheiron frowned and, concentrating, managed to weave a light garment into existence along with a long, narrow sash which he used to secure the cloth around his waist.

'There. Everything seems to be in order around here,' he said, looking about. 'Such a sad state of being. It'll be quite some work returning it to order once more.'

As others began to drift closer, a few overheard the mumbled, 'I really wish that someone would devise a way to allow you to keep your clothes on,' when the Archmagus was hit near his waist by a small bullet.

'There, there now,' Kaheiron patted Lin somewhat awkwardly on the head as she hugged him, keeping hands and fingers well away from the agitated dragonling. Cheep was still fidgety and nervous after everything that had happened. 'No need for concern.'

'Just happy you're okay,' came the muffled reply from below, followed by a small jab into his chest. 'Don't scare me like that.'

'Well,' the Archmagus looked a little uncomfortable. 'It's not as if I could have asked them to make an appointment,' he said.

Linandra let go and nodded. Of course, she knew that.

'I would like as many of my stones back as possible,' the Archmagus then instructed the nearest people, 'or they're liable to begin interfering with the ethereal energies here. And try and see if you can find the shieldstones the golshaes were using as well. We might still be able to put some of them to good use.'

Several of those assembled made wry faces. They'd been making plans for those themselves. Trust the Archmagus to poke a metaphorical stick in the Wheel of Fun.

Most of the arcane practitioners that were still on their feet when the battle ended were taking the opportunity to sit down, though. What little energy they had left shouldn't be drained by needing to do something as complex as calculating the balance of a body, they thought. The ground, or a chair, or even the floor was so much more inviting. To blazers with dignity, they seemed to say. We'll worry about that later. We're too exhausted to care.

Besides, what fool would come along right now and see them anyway? Any sensible traveller should have run for miles in the opposite direction with everything that had happened in the night. Magical battles tended to be a bit on the visible side when it was dark.

And, as the chaos of the night slowly gave way to the equal, but not quite as lethal, chaos of the day, the inhabitants of the Towers began to take stock of what had happened and how best to deal with it.

Those not having been directly involved in the fight itself returned from the heart of the Towers and, alongside the least tired and least injured, began the tedious work of restoring the Towers to a more normal state.

Wearing nothing more than a thin robe, secured by the flimsy-looking belt he'd conjured up, Kaheiron began to stalk through the field, snapping orders or offering aid, whichever was needed the most. Soon, he was as muddy as the rest of them.

'He's not looking too happy, is he?' Lin said to herself as she watched the Archmagus' back. Crossing her arms, it turned into a, "neither am I," as the young woman gave the remaining dragon a withering glare.

It has been a long, and very bad, night and the day hasn't exactly started great either and he better not have any plans for making it any worse than it already was: that's the kind of glare it was.

Setharrion tried to resist the urge to sit down, hunch his shoulders and whine. He was supposed to be a dragon, not a dog.

'Is that it?' Lin asked pointedly, peering up at the slender face of her companion.

She didn't get a reply, though the dragon did look a little bit like he was checking out the nearest escape routes, even without moving his head.

'Holding back really wasn't part of the plan, was it? You owe me an explanation buster, a serious explanation, and it better be good,' Lin waved a finger under the dragon's muzzle, oblivious to how far up her companion's snout was.

The young dragon hunched his shoulders, his ears folding back and tucking up underneath his exquisite set of horns. It made him look sheepish, despite his size.

'Yes? I'm waiting,' she tapped her foot theatrically. 'And don't think that rolling over on your back and playing dead or trying to look cute is going to help you with this one!' she growled.

Setharrion whined.

* * *

A few weeks later, and from a distance, the appearance of the Towers and its surrounding landscape shad returned to something relatively normal. If you didn't know, it would have been difficult to tell that something serious had happened at all.

If you looked closer though, you'd be able to see that a lot of the vegetation was new and, if you'd been here before and had a good memory, you would have sworn that the forest now began quite some further distance away than it had previously. Same could be said for parts of the buildings proper too.

Most of the residents had returned to their normal endeavours, if anything at the Twin Towers could ever be deemed "normal."

Kaheiron had managed to recover most of his small "disruptors," but the shieldstones that the golshaes had carried had proven to be beyond corrupt. As one of the younger magicians had said. 'You get more protection out of half a kilo of pumice.'

Week followed upon week; it was easy to lose track of time with everything that was happening, and now the Archmagus found himself, once more, at the main doors to the Towers, only, this time, he didn't need to defend them.

In fact, he was dressed quite splendidly in the kind of outfit normally only used to greet guests of state. Lin thought it made him look even more majestic than usual.

Today, there was nothing more than a gentle breeze, the last breath of summer carrying, at its heart, just a touch of autumn with it. For a change, her own hair was, therefore, staying sleek and falling down her back, as it should. She'd always envied the way Kaheiron was able to make his hair behave, even when it was windy.

'This is unusual, no matter how you regard it,' Kaheiron said. His solemn words were offset by a mischievous twinkle in his eyes, not to mention the twitch to the side of his mouth.

Seth shrugged. 'Who wants to be ordinary anyway?' he said and grinned in return, earning himself an affectionate swat from the person next to him.

'You are certain that you wish to leave? Outside these walls, life will be considerably less easy,' the Archmagus prophesized.

'We'll manage,' Lin said, offering him a small but confident smile.

'You know,' Kaheiron said, rubbing his chin. 'Hui'syqussedin would not take kindly to this if she knew.'

A fleeting expression that could almost be described as terror, flitted across Seth's features. 'And that is why she will *never* know,' he said and shuddered.

'And why we can't stay,' Lin filled in. 'You two did make quite the show of yourselves before. We didn't want to take the chance that word would reach her, somehow.'

'Then I wish you well, both of you. It will be empty here without either of you. Of course,' Kaheiron added, 'there will also be considerably less trouble, I imagine. The added benefit being that my jars will be left alone. No one else here hunts through them when feeling peckish at three in the morning.'

'Don't blame Cheep. He gets hungry a lot,' Lin said. 'Besides, you've still got Pickles.'

'That *is* true,' Kaheiron agreed and gave Pickle Socks, who was circling him, tongue lolling, an eyeful.

Pickles was being a large-eared fennec today. It was very doubtful that anyone would mistake him for a real one, however cute he tried to make himself. For one thing, he was far too big. Secondly, fennecs tended towards earthy colours.

'No one's gonna fall for that, Pickles. Whoever heard of a black, white and yellow fennec?' Lin bent over and gave him an ear scratch. 'He never changes into something bigger?' she asked.

'Multivariate in form but singular in size,' Kaheiron said.

Pickles whuffed at them and wagged his tail. He was hoping another bout of serious petting might be enticed out of the people present.

The small dragonling curled around Lin's neck had raised his head at the sound of his name, then, when no treats were apparently on offer, he'd promptly gone back to sleep.

'I'm sure we can visit, if it turns out that you miss us *too* much,' Lin offered with an almost roguish grin.

Kaheiron pretended to be abhorred.

'By the way,' Seth interrupted. 'You never did tell us how those shield-stones became so powerful. Did you ever find out?'

The Archmagus shook his head. 'We don't know. Not yet. Perhaps we never will. We have only the shattered remains of the crystals from Joran's body to work with. The stones themselves turned into dust, literally, after a few weeks. I've had them all locked away, for the time being. While they do have some fascinating properties, I fear that I do not much care for the price that they extoll for their power.'

'I can imagine,' Seth said and winced at the memory of the man-beast. 'It looked rather painful to me.'

'Onwards to happier tidings, I say.' Kaheiron smiled again. 'You two best be on your way. Try not to monopolize my carriage for too long. I would like it back, preferably still functional.'

'Bleak and uncomfortable to ride in it is then,' Lin muttered quietly. 'We promise not to give it any upgrades.'

Personally, she would have preferred if they'd had one of their own. Seth had never had the displeasure of having to ride in it. He preferred to wait until the cover of darkness and then just fly to the vicinity of where he wanted to go. Well, they'd see about that. It wasn't like he couldn't afford one.

Linandra winced. She suspected he'd wise up to Kaheiron's offer to lend them his carriage the hard way.

'I'll have it sent back as soon as possible,' Seth promised. 'It shouldn't take more than a week or two, if the roads are good.'

Here, Lin again wondered if he actually knew that or if he was just making a very non-educated guess. It wasn't like he had a whole lot of experience in that area.

Neither did she, truth be told. The world was a completely different size when you were of the more "follow your feet" type. Guess it would be a new experience for the both of them.

'I still don't understand why we couldn't just fly there,' Seth grumbled.

'Oh shush,' Lin chided him, pointing at all the luggage they'd loaded on top of, and inside of, the carriage.

'I can carry that and more you know,' Seth insisted.

'Yes, I know,' Lin replied and patted him affectionately on the arm. 'You'd also be carrying *me*. And I don't much fancy the idea.'

'I hope you don't plan on buying furniture the same way?'

Lin ignored him, instead stepping up to Kaheiron and, pulling him down slightly, kissing him gently on the cheek, before allowing him to help her up into the carriage.

'I'll never get used to these dresses. How do people cope?' Lin complained good-naturedly as she smoothed out the skirt before taking her seat.

'At least you've been used to clothes your *whole* life,' Seth pointed out. He ran a finger inside the neck of his shirt. 'How do you think *I* feel?'

'You could take them off if you dislike them that much. I don't mind. Just don't catch a cold. Don't want you sniffling all the way to our new home.'

'After the hours I spent getting this right?' Seth looked horrified.

'It was only a suggestion,' Lin chortled at his expression, eyes twinkling.

An 'ahem' interrupted the conversation before it got out of hand. 'Farewell then,' Kaheiron's voice came from the window. 'Come visit sometime.'

'We will,' Lin promised.

'Look after yourself, you old fraud,' Seth nodded at the older dragon and pulled the door shut.

The carriage pulled out of the courtyard of the Twin Towers and turned down the driveway and then out onto the road. Where it would lead them— well, that was another story entirely.

*** THE END? ***

The sages say you should never laugh at a live dragon, for
thou are crunchy and good on toast.

Acknowledgements

I hope you enjoyed reading "*The Damsel and the Dragon*". I know I enjoyed writing it—even with trying to keep the characters from doing anything *too* crazy. This is a lot easier said than done, I assure you.

One of those was Pickled Socks. This little shapeshifting ball of mischief belongs to FlyingGekko and was a lot of fun to work with. He really brightens up any scene he's in and was entrusted to me through the 'name a character' tier on the Kickstarter campaign for "Academia Draconia" and I'll admit I'm in the 'nail-biting stage' of hoping I did him justice.

Thankfully, I had a lot of lovely help, and encouragement, from my editor —the ever eagle-eyed Scribecat, who deserves many, many pats on the back and a cookie, or two, or three.

Others who deserve extra praise is Nightpark, and if you're anything like me, you've been taking a break from reading just to flip back and admire the cover art she drew for this. She also did a great job on the *Seven of Stars* logo. Kaheiron would be preening himself if he could see it.

This year also saw me going from just enjoying the books of Elizabeth-Rose Best to actually having the chance to work with her. She's as talented an artist as she is a writer and in the two in-book illustrations she brought two characters to life with a smile.

They weren't the only ones either, and a big "thank you" goes out to those wonderful individuals who supported this book on its launch. You're all brilliant, I hope you know that.

Cristina Kovacs, Anders M. Ytterdahl, Wanda Aasen, Ashli T, Ashley Lachance, Juliane Völker, Elizabeth-Rose Best, KwisA Wolfy, FlyingGekko, Lark Cunningham, Aramanth Dawe, Tasha Turner, Curtis & Maryrita Steinhour, Scott Schaper, M S Payne, P Greg, Annika Kwast, KMC, Joshua Smith, A Challis, Lorin Venniro, Regina Hocke, Gordhan Rajani, Molarqy, Bob Michiels, Patrik Andersson, Peggy Turko, Tony Anjo, Andrew Glynn and Anne Cowell.

A spell in the making

A gift for those who supported this book on its launch.
I hope it brings a smile.

'You there!'

Linandra jumped at the shout ringing out into the corridor.

'Yes, yes, you,' the old wizard who'd stuck his head out through the heavy oak door nodded enthusiastically. He grinned from ear to ear. 'I did it! I finally did it!' he exclaimed.

Oh great, the old coot's gone completely barmy this time, Lin thought as he waved her into his chambers. Though this involved her actually opening the door.

At first glance, the place looked as disorganized as ever. A second, even a third one, didn't change anything. So, what was this supposedly amazing thing he'd done then?

'I did it,' the wizened old man enthused again, nearly jumping with glee. 'I perfected the cleaning spell.'

Ah, so that's why he looks so familiar, Linandra thought as, with some additional bustle, she found herself in front of a roughly-hewn bookcase filled with odds and ends. Rundelswollp never had let her clean in here. It showed.

'Now, yes, now you see,' Rundelswollp gesticulated as a small blob of air slowly compressed near the floor. Just what it was supposed to be, Lin had no idea, but even she could tell that it was odd ... and humming.

Cheep, who'd been pretending to be asleep around her shoulders, took a flying leap and landed in front of the slowly spinning ball, spitting defiance.

The dragonling began to circle the increasingly solid looking concentration of nothing, hissing every few steps.

'See?' Rundelswollp said proudly. 'Just a few more moments and it'll be ready to go.'

Not the least impressed, Cheep tried to bat at the whatsit that was now looking like a flat, fat black hole hovering a few centimetres above the floor.

Then he jumped it, claws out.

'Cheep! NO!' Lin cried out. Afraid he'd disappear into the nothing, she grabbed for him in the air. She missed.

For a brief moment dragonling and spell became locked together. After a short period of hisses, hums and a few stray bits of lightning, Cheep came out of the battle of supremacy perched on top of the black whatsit. An air of smugness surrounded him.

With an intense look of concentration, Rundelswollp removed his hands from his eyes and waved them in front of him. To Lin it looked a lot like he tried to shoo the thing away.

When nothing happened, he looked somewhat perplexed.

'I'm sure it should be moving by now,' he grumbled. 'Maybe you need to adjust for the extra weight,' he said after a consultation with his books, giving Cheep a dirty eyeful. 'Couldn't you know, mm, move him?'

'What? Me?' Linandra feigned shock. 'Do I look like I want to lose a couple of fingers?'

'Hmm, no, I suppose not.'

Apparently the adjustment wasn't hard, once he'd localized the right incantation, because soon the black bit of nothing began to trundle quite happily across the stone floor.

'It's working! It's really working!' Rundelswollp bounced with glee again.

And indeed, the spell dutifully toiled around the room, slowly leaving a trail of shininess behind it and generally bumbling into things it couldn't run over and hoover up.

Then, bored with the whole thing, Cheep decided to leap onto a table as they passed.

Free of its burden, the spell shot across the floor and smacked into the nearest pile with such force that it sent the whole thing toppling over. Books, parchments, spare quills and a large bronze pot fell every-which-way.

The black whatsit began to hoover up all the things now handily at floor level: books, parchments and quills alike.

The wizard's scream could be heard three flights down.

Lin discretely slipped away, as much to be out of the errant spell as to hide her giggles. Cheep followed suite, at greater speed, hissing retorts to the thrown books and curses following him out.

Do YOU have what it takes to face your fears?

THEN JOIN THE DRAGONCORPS
AND PROTECT THE SKIES
OF NEW RETMIA!

Academia Draconia
Seven of Stars

The school where courage matters!

Mae McKinnon

DragonQuill Publishing

Scribe Cat

Helping writers create clear, concise, and credible work!

We hope you enjoyed *The Damsel and the Dragon*!

This book was made possible with the help of an Editor.

A professional edit is an invaluable resource in preparing a manuscript for print, whether that means sewing up plot holes, tidying up runaway sentences, or catching the last few typos.

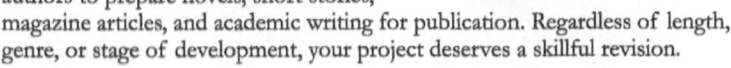

With over 10 years of experience, Ashley Lachance has worked with authors to prepare novels, short stories, magazine articles, and academic writing for publication. Regardless of length, genre, or stage of development, your project deserves a skillful revision.

Have a story or manuscript waiting for a second pair of eyes?

What are you waiting for? Don't pro-cat-stinate!

Check out ScribeCat.ca and get a free quote today!

www.ScribeCat.ca

ashley@ScribeCat.ca

@Scribe_Cat

facebook.com/ScribeCat

www.ingramcontent.com/pod-product-compliance
Lightning Source LLC
Chambersburg PA
CBHW020224260626
47156CB00002B/530